THE NEXT DOOR DUET

JENNIFER SUCEVIC

The Football Hotties Collection

The Hockey Hotties Collection

THE GIRL NEXT DOOR

MIA

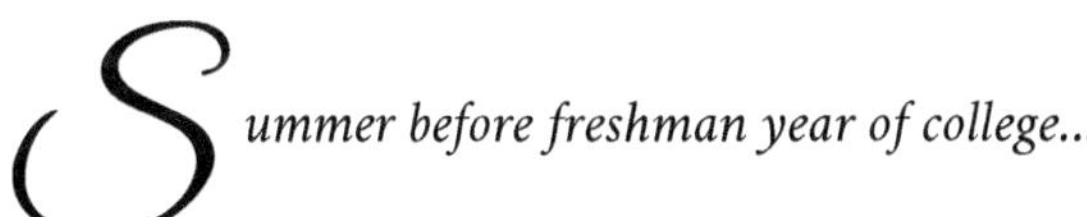

Summer before freshman year of college...

"Get your butt over here," my best friend squeals from the window where she's taken up sentinel, "you *need* to see this!"

That's a negative, Ghost Rider. I'll take a hard pass. I have zero interest in spying on a yard full of drunken classmates who are partying it up at my neighbor's house. Reluctantly, I glance up from the toes I'm painting with a pale pink polish. Coney Island Cotton Candy, to be precise.

When our gazes lock, Alyssa waves me over. She's practically vibrating with excitement. Kind of like a schnauzer.

"Everyone is over there!"

"Not true," I mutter, lacquering my baby toe with an impressively steady hand. "*We're* right here." And that's exactly where I plan to stay.

"Yeah, that's kind of the problem." She steeples her hands together before shaking them at me. "Please?" she begs. "Can't we go over there for a little bit? *Just a little?* That's all I'm asking."

That's all she's asking...ha!

I'm calling bullshit.

Alyssa knows I'd rather chew my arm off than crash one of Beck Hollingsworth's parties. I didn't mention it to her, but Beck shot me a text earlier this afternoon with all the details. If she even suspected an invitation had been issued, she would have dragged my ass across the lawn that separates our properties as soon as the first guest pulled into the drive.

No, thank you.

It's obvious from all the commotion coming from next door that the entire senior class has shown up to celebrate our newly graduated status. If we didn't live on a quiet cul-de-sac tucked away in a gated subdivision, I'd expect the police to make an unannounced visit and shut down the festivities.

Then again, no one wants to mess with Beck's father, Archibald Hollingsworth. He's a high-priced attorney with a fleet of underlings working for him. He's one of those overly tan guys with blindingly white veneers you see on television yapping about if you've been injured, you need to call them—they fight for the little guy! The dude is everywhere. Billboards. Commercials. Newspaper and magazine advertisements.

The local police have tangled with Archibald several times over the years because his son is a magnet for trouble. Let's see, there was the time (or five) when he was picked up for underage drinking. When Beck was fifteen years old, he *borrowed* his parent's brand spanking new Range Rover and did a little off-roading. And the police were involved when he super glued the locks on the high school building doors for senior prank day.

Instead of hauling Beck to the station every time he's picked up, they drop him at his front door and don't bother talking to Archibald about it. Beck is on a first-name basis with a number of guys on the force. A few showed up to his graduation party in June.

It shouldn't come as a surprise that Beck always figures out a way to circumvent the obstacles standing in his path. His parents. School. The law. It's as irritating as it is impressive. Maybe one of these days, he'll use his powers for good instead of evil.

"Come on, Mia!" Alyssa whines, all the while flashing sad puppy-dog eyes at me.

Double whammy.

My bestie knows I have a difficult time resisting puppy-dog eyes.

I wiggle my toes from the bed and grumble, "I can't go anywhere until my nails dry." I'm doing my best to prolong being anywhere near Beckett Hollingsworth. The guy drives me batshit crazy.

And that's putting it mildly.

"Great! So…five minutes?" She swings away before pressing her face against the screen as her voice turns dreamy. "I bet Colton is already there."

Ugh.

Colton Montgomery is Beck's right-hand man, so it's not a wager I'm likely to win.

Against my better advice, Alyssa has been crushing hard on Colton for more than a year. Not only is he popular, but he's a football player. Heavy emphasis on the *player* part. If Alyssa were smart, she'd find a nice guy to fall in lust with, but she has tunnel vision when it comes to the blond-haired, blue-eyed heartbreaker.

Colton has it all going on. Brains, brawn, and more than likely, a one-way ticket to the NFL after college.

The only problem is that he's aware of his own appeal.

His ego is as massive as other parts of him.

Or so I hear.

And not from Alyssa since he refuses to sleep with her. I can't decide if the situation is amusing or sad. The more Colton keeps Alyssa at a firm distance, the more determined she is to have him.

Last football season, Alyssa dragged me to every game. Even the away ones. My greatest fear was that Beck would assume my ass was there to support him. His fan club is already legendary without adding me to the ranks.

When it comes to the ladies, Beckett makes Colton look like an innocent babe. He goes through girls like most people go through underwear. Speaking of panties, the girls at our high school are always happy—hell, I'd go so far as to say thrilled—to drop theirs for him.

It's ridiculous.

He's a chronic user and abuser.

There should be a warning label slapped across his forehead.

Beware. Toxic to the female species.

But you know what?

That wouldn't stop these bubble-headed chicks from spreading their legs wide for him. I've stopped trying to figure out the appeal. All right, I'm well aware of what the attraction is. As much as I've tried to pretend I'm immune to his charms, I'm not. I just do a damn good job of burying them deep down where they never see the light of day. If I didn't, Beck would annihilate me in a heartbeat, and I have zero desire to end up a casualty on his hit list.

Given the choice, I'd rather flip through Netflix and find a movie to watch rather than be dragged over to Beck's bash.

Doesn't sitting around in pajamas and stuffing our faces with pizza sound way better than watching a bunch of our classmates get sloppy drunk, engage in way too much PDA, and puke all over the place before alcohol poisoning sets in?

I won't bother posing the question to Alyssa. There is no way she'll willingly opt for sitting home instead of stalking her crush.

Would you like to guess what Colton will be doing while I wipe the drool from Alyssa's chin?

You guessed it. He'll be flirting with every vagina he thinks he has a chance of penetrating.

Honestly, it's one of the most masochistic things Alyssa could do. I have no idea why she insists on putting herself through this kind of agony. Apparently, my job as her best friend is to support her decision to inflict untold amounts of mental anguish on to herself. I'd slap her upside the head if I thought it would knock sense into her.

My prediction for the evening goes a little something like this— Alyssa will have a few drinks, moon over Colton, before dissolving into a puddle of tears while that manwhore makes out with other girls in front of her face. Then I'll drag her home, and she'll end up knuckle-deep in a gallon of triple-chocolate ice cream.

But that's what friends are for, right?

Don't worry, I've already made my peace with it.

"Fine," I grumble with a scowl, hoping she understands the depth of my reluctance. "But let it be known that I won't be staying for more than an hour. So, you better make good use of your time, girl."

She swings around to face me, bouncing on the tips of her toes as she claps her hands together with excitement. "Yay!" As soon as she gets the affirmative, she beelines for my closet, which is half the size of my room.

I have the kind of closet most girls my age can only dream about. Shoes, purses, clothes, and jewelry. It's all there and organized.

"Cue the montage music while I find something schmexy to wear!" she squeals.

"What you have on is fine." I roll my eyes and yell, "It was good enough for me, wasn't it?"

From within the depths of my closet comes a snort.

For the next ten minutes, I'm treated to an impromptu fashion show. At the rate Alyssa is going, we won't make it to the party any time soon.

Take your time, girlfriend. I'm totally good with that.

A dozen outfit changes later, Alyssa settles on a black knit tank and white skirt that showcases her sun-kissed legs to their best advantage. Alyssa has been taking dance classes since she was three years old. She's toned with long, lean muscles.

"Damn girl, you look hot." Not that her crush will appreciate the effort. Alyssa needs to move on. I'm thinking a twelve-step program would help kick the Colton Montgomery habit.

"I would gladly live in your closet if you'd let me." She grins before doing a little twirl. "It's my happy place."

A reluctant smile quirks my lips.

My mother is a card-carrying shopaholic and has the Amex Black Card bills to prove it. She buys clothes like our house burned to the ground and nothing could be salvaged. Even with racks of space, my wardrobe is bursting at the seams. Three-quarters of the stuff has never seen the light of day. Alyssa is lucky we're roughly the same size so she can borrow whatever she wants.

Now that she's dressed and ready to mingle, her eyes narrow as she takes a hard look at me. Wordlessly, she spins around and races back inside the closet only to resurface a handful of minutes later.

"Here you go," she says, tossing two garments at the foot of my bed.

I glance at the shimmery gold tank and dark-wash jean skirt that resembles a folded-up napkin. The skirt is cute as hell, but I would strongly advise against going commando while wearing it unless you're looking to flash everyone your goodies.

Since that's not my usual style, the price tag is still dangling from the pocket. I have no idea what my mother was thinking when she picked it up.

Unsure why she's throwing clothes at me, I point to the small pile. "What's that about?"

"You need to change." She gives me a look that says—*duh* before clapping her hands together. "Chop-chop."

Changing my clothes was not part of the plan. I'm fine with going in my pajamas. It's not like I'm looking for a hookup. Or anything else, for that matter.

I shake my head and fold my arms across my chest. "No, thank you."

Her gaze rakes over me as she points to my T-shirt. "Is that a coffee stain on your boob?"

With a frown, I glance at my chest and inspect the dark spot marring the fabric of my right breast. My guess is that she's right. Caramel Macchiato, to be specific. "Possibly."

Her lips flatten. "I refuse to go anywhere with you looking like *that.*"

"Great!" I stretch out before stacking my hands behind my head. "What kind of movie night does it feel like to you? Romcom? Horror? Psychological thriller? Angsty tearjerker?" A benevolent smile curves my lips. "You can choose."

Alyssa stomps her foot on the carpeted floor. "Mia!" she wails at a decibel that could shatter eardrums. A few neighborhood dogs howl in response. *"You promised!"*

Promised?

No, I don't think so.

I scrunch my nose and tap a finger against my lips. "I don't believe I ever *promised* to do anything. *Reluctantly agreed?* Yes. *Browbeaten into capitulating?* Definitely. But *promised?* Not in this lifetime."

When she straightens to her full height, I groan, knowing exactly what's about to happen. *"Mia Evelyn Stanbury*! Do I need to remind you who was there when—"

Argh.

This is the portion of the evening where Alyssa trots out every damn thing she's ever done for me until I relent. And she'll start with Harper Hastings. The girl who bullied me relentlessly in seventh grade because Xander Rossi asked me to the movies instead of her. After months of Harper's mean-spirited attacks, Alyssa waited for the girl after school. My bestie let it be known that if Harper didn't cease and desist, she'd spread the good word that the other girl was a known bra stuffer. It must have been true, since Harper immediately backed off, and I never heard a peep from her again.

"*Yes, yes, Harper Hastings,*" I mutter, not appreciating the direction this conversation has swerved in.

Alyssa folds her arms across her chest as a smug smile twists her lips upward. "Harper Hastings is only the beginning, my friend." She arches a brow. "Need I continue?"

Silently we glare before I fold like a cheap house of cards. "Fine, I'll change." I straighten before scooping up the skirt and top and shaking them at her. "It's only because I love you and you're my best friend that I'm even willing to step foot next door."

An angelic smile spreads across her pretty face before she blows me a kiss. "Love you, too. Now kindly move your assets."

"An hour," I remind. "That's all you get."

Looking unconcerned, she waves a hand. "No worries, that's more than enough time to work my magic."

What she means to say is that it's more than enough time for Colton to ignore her, all the while hooking up with another girl. Part of me almost wishes he would sleep with Alyssa. Maybe then the rose-colored glasses would come off, and she would realize what a douche the guy is.

In one fluid motion, the stained T-shirt is stripped from my body and replaced with the gold tank. Then I slide off the comfy shorts I've been lounging in and yank on the tiny rectangle of material that doubles as a skirt.

I step in front of my floor-to-ceiling mirror that's propped against the wall and stare at my reflection before attempting to tug the skirt further down my thighs, but it's useless. There's not a spare inch of material to be found.

What the hell had my mother been thinking when she picked this up? Was she mistakenly shopping in the toddler section?

I turn around and bend over, touching my toes before peering over my shoulder and glancing in the mirror. It's just as I suspected. My thong is on full display. Actually, it doesn't even look like I'm wearing underwear since the material is wedged between the crack of my ass like dental floss.

Lovely.

Not to mention uncomfortable.

"Is there a second option to consider?" My gaze slides to Alyssa's in the mirror. "One where my ass isn't hanging out?"

"'Fraid not. I'm seriously loving the whole—is she or isn't she wearing panties guessing game you've got going on." She winks. "Play your cards right, and maybe you'll get lucky tonight."

I narrow my eyes as my lips thin. "Believe it or not, I'm perfectly content being unlucky."

"That, my dear, is only because you don't realize what you've been missing."

"Heartache, STIs, and the possibility of an unplanned pregnancy?" I flutter my lashes and smile. "You are so right."

Ignoring my comment, she tosses a pair of gold sandals at me before sliding her feet into black leather ones that strap up her legs, giving her that whole Grecian goddess vibe. She looks amazing. But then again, when doesn't she? Alyssa has long blond hair and dark blue eyes. Her skin has a natural sun-kissed glow that darkens under the summer sun.

It almost offends me that Colton refuses to fuck my friend.

What the hell is wrong with him?

"Ready to go?" she asks, checking her reflection in the mirror one last time.

I slip the sandals on before rising to my full height. "As I'll ever be."

Five minutes later, we've traversed the lawn and are walking around the side of the Hollingsworth mansion. All sixteen thousand square feet of it. Needless to say, Archibald has turned ambulance-chasing into a lucrative art form.

With every step we take, the sound of drunken laughter and the pulsing beat of music grows louder, assaulting our ears. As soon as the party comes into view, I wonder why I let Alyssa talk me into this.

It's complete chaos.

As much as Alyssa would like to convince you otherwise, I'm not a complete dud. I like to party as much as the next girl. But Beck enjoys taking his antics to the next level. He's not content to have a low-key get-together where people sit around and chill. This party is moments away from becoming one of those teen movies where all hell breaks loose, and the host wakes up naked the next morning in a dumpster five states away with a goat.

Over to the left, a few people are holding a guy upside down while he performs a keg stand.

Chants of—*chug, chug, chug* permeate the air.

It wouldn't surprise me if one of these drunken idiots is found floating face down in the pool come morning.

It begs the question of why Beck's parents would leave him alone without supervision. He might be eighteen-years-old and technically an adult, but he needs an adultier adult to keep him in check. Someone who can put the kibosh on his hijinks.

Good luck with that. His older brother, Ari, is out of the country for the summer.

Archibald and Caroline, his parents, must have realized this was inevitable. Every time they go out of town, Beck throws a huge bash. Depending on the amount of damage, he gets grounded anywhere from a few days to a couple of weeks. The threat of consequences—hell, actual consequences being enforced—are in no way a deterrent.

Believe it or not, before our parents left town for a long weekend in New York, Archie asked me to keep an eye on their son. His actual words were—*make sure no one dies.*

As if I exert that much control over Beck?

Yeah, right. Beck doesn't listen to anyone, let alone me.

Exactly what am I supposed to do?

Tattletale?

Facetime his parents so they can get a first-hand glimpse of the ensuing pandemonium?

As much pleasure as that would give me, it's not going to happen. I might be a lot of things (a rule follower and a goody-goody, if you listen to Beck) but there are lines that can't be crossed, and snitching is one of them.

This will be one more antic Beck gets away with. I suppose that's the beauty of being Beckett Hollingsworth. He doesn't give a shit about anything other than football.

The Neanderthal sport is his life.

By the time Beck was a freshman in high school, he'd already drawn the attention of Big Ten college coaches. They couldn't wait to get him on their roster. If he could have gone straight to the NFL after graduation, he would have. But that's not a possibility. Players aren't eligible to enter the draft until after their sophomore year of college. Beck's father has taken it one step further by insisting he wait until senior year because—and I quote—*no damn son of mine is going to be a college dropout.*

Beck will be proof positive that C's really do earn degrees.

As my gaze drifts over the thick crowd of glassy-eyed stares, it collides with bright green ones. A little zip of electricity sizzles its way through my veins as our gazes fasten. The muscles in my belly tense with awareness. Once I realize what's happening, I tamp down the reaction. My life has been filled with a thousand little moments like this one. Moments I like to pretend never transpired.

For all I know, it's gastritis from the sushi I picked up at the gas station last night.

Anything's possible, right?

Instead of glancing away, I hold his stare and scowl. What I've learned is that it's better to brazen out these situations than turn tail and run. Beck's perfect cupid's bow of a mouth lifts into a knowing grin before he crooks his finger.

A gurgle of laughter bubbles up in my throat.

I don't think so, buddy.

I'm not like the bubbleheads he usually toys with. I have a working brain, and I enjoy using it to make good decisions that won't come back to bite me in the ass. Unlike Beck, I have a healthy amount of self-preservation.

I press my lips into a tight line before emphatically shaking my head.

A wolfish grin spills across his face, giving him a boyishly handsome appearance. With dark tousled hair, sharp cheekbones that scream his Russian heritage, and thick eyebrows, he's a danger to females everywhere. I won't mention the chiseled body that looks like it was carved from stone. Broad shoulders and a tapered waist complete the package.

It's almost a relief when a bikini-clad girl steps between us, severing the connection. Now that his sharp gaze is no longer pinning me in place, I'm able to exhale all the air from my lungs.

Alyssa grabs my hand. "There he is," she whisper-yells excitedly over the babble of voices and music. "Oh my God, he's so freaking dreamy."

I regard the crowd of newly minted high school graduates before finding Colton.

Sure, I'll admit it. He's as hot as Beck. Instead of short dark hair, he's golden blond. It's buzzed on the sides and left long on top, so he's constantly pushing it away from bright blue eyes. He's tall and brawny. If I hadn't gone to school with him since elementary, I'd suspect he flunked a few grades. Even his muscles have muscles.

Girls are already circling around him, vying for his attention. The guy is like a rock star picking out groupies to sleep with at the end of the night.

"He's okay," I mutter, wanting to downplay his attractiveness.

"You're so full of shit, your eyes are turning brown. He's way better than *okay,* and you know it."

"Ewww." I scrunch my nose. "That's gross."

"Focus!" She snaps her fingers in front of my face.

I make one last-ditch effort to sway her. "You can do better than Colton. He knows exactly how hot he is and takes full advantage of it every chance he gets. Find someone like," I stand on my tiptoes and pick through the mass of bodies before zeroing in on the perfect guy for Alyssa, "Landon Mathews. Not only is he good-looking, he's a sweetheart."

Alyssa's expression turns thoughtful as she assesses the tall guy with inky-black hair and unusual blue-green eyes. He's standing around with a bunch of football players, laughing at something one of them said.

"He's definitely yummy," she admits.

For one glorious moment, my spirits soar. Maybe she'll drop this whole Colton Montgomery nonsense and go after someone more attainable. Landon is a great guy. He's as hot as his friends, but he's not a total asshat. Unfortunately, he doesn't get nearly the same amount of hype that Colton or Beck do since he's been labeled a good guy.

I mean, who wants to date a nice guy when you can have one who treats you like total crap?

Said no one ever.

Except…there seems to be way more truth to that statement than most females are comfortable acknowledging. Whether they realize it or not, these girls have been conditioned to crave unattainable jerks.

It's disturbing on so many levels.

"Added bonus," I continue, "he knows you're alive!"

"Um, excuse me, Colton knows I'm alive," she grumbles.

"Are you certain about that?"

She bites her lip as we glance at the guy in question who is—surprise-surprise—surrounded by a bevy of scantily clad girls competing for his interest.

Uh-oh.

Alyssa's got that look in her eye. The one that tells me not to bother trying to talk her out of her plans.

She confirms it by saying, "Wish me luck, I'm going in."

It was worth a try.

"Good luck."

One of Alyssa's best qualities is that she's not a quitter. That girl can be as tenacious and persistent as a terrier. And sometimes, just as yappy.

In this instance, it's a negative.

When she's a few steps away, I cup my fingers around my mouth and yell, "Maybe you should take off the panties so you can flash him your puss. That way he'll know you're a sure thing."

She whips around with a grin. "Excellent idea!"

My jaw drops when she shimmies out of her underwear and tosses it in my direction.

"Christ, girl! I was joking! That was sarcasm!" I glance at the wadded-up material I now clench in my hand. "What am I supposed to do with this?"

She shrugs. "Keep it as a souvenir?"

Gross.

"I don't think so." I stalk to a garbage can and pitch it. When I turn around, Alyssa is pushing her way through the crowd, moving steadily closer to Colton and his harem.

If nothing else, this should be entertaining. It takes a moment to realize that I'm alone at a party I didn't want to attend in the first place. I slip my phone from my back pocket and glance at it.

Fifty minutes and counting.

This is shaping up to be the longest hour of my life. Maybe I should head inside and grab a drink. By the number of drunken idiots

I'm surrounded by, my guess is that the booze is flowing freely. I maneuver my way through the crowd and into the kitchen before taking in the scene.

If Beck's mom saw all these people sitting their asses on her polished-to-a-high-shine marble countertop, she would probably have a conniption. She's kind of a germ-o-phobe. There's a half-naked girl stretched out on the island with a lime clenched in her teeth as one of the football players slurps tequila from her belly button.

I'm no aficionado on hygiene, but that definitely doesn't seem sanitary.

A few people greet me as I make my way to the keg and take my place in line. I'm in the middle of chatting with a girl from my French class when she turns an unflattering shade of green and bolts to the nearest bathroom with her hands slapped over her mouth. All thoughts of a refill are abandoned as she pushes her way to the back hall. I really hope she makes it in time. Caroline will be furious if she finds out someone has thrown up on her marble floors.

Once I have a frothy cup of beer in hand, I head to the patio to check on Alyssa's progress.

Am I a terrible friend for hoping she's already been shot down and has thrown in the towel for the night?

Probably, but I can deal with that.

Instead of finding a dejected Alyssa crying in the corner, I'm amazed to discover that she's clawed her way to the front of the pack. Who knows, she may actually have a shot of getting picked from the crowd.

This could be a real game-changer for her.

Guess that means I'm stuck here. I look around the patio, searching for a place to park my ass. The Hollingsworth property is about an acre in size, which is the same as ours. The space around the pool is gated with a black-iron fence and tall arborvitae that spear into the dark night sky. Toward the back of the gate is an unoccupied lounge chair with my name on it. I'll hang out there for forty minutes before dragging Alyssa's panty-less ass back to my house.

Before I can take three steps, a deep voice cuts through the raucous noise of the party.

"Well, well, well. Look who decided to make a cameo appearance tonight."

I swing around, knowing exactly who I'll find.

Beck.

As difficult as it is, I try not to notice how delicious he looks in plaid board shorts that hang low on his hips, showing off the cut lines of his abdomen before disappearing beneath the waistband. The chiseled strength of his arms and chest are enough to bring most girls to their proverbial knees.

The operative word in that sentence being *most*.

I, however, am not one of those idiotic girls.

"Coming here tonight wasn't my idea. I was dragged under duress."

"Yeah, I figured you would have better things to do than hang around with a bunch of wasted assholes."

He's got me there.

"You know me too well." When my throat grows dry, I lift the red Solo cup to my lips. Before I can take a sip, he snatches the drink from my fingers and brings it to his mouth. I watch his throat constrict as he drains the contents.

"Rude much?" My fists go to my hips. "What did you do that for?"

He shrugs. Even though it's a slight movement, his muscles ripple, and attraction bursts to life in my core. "You shouldn't be drinking."

"Excuse me?" My eyes pop wide as laughter tumbles from my mouth. "Are you being serious right now?" I wave a hand toward the drunken mob that surrounds us. It's not even eleven, and already people are passed out on loungers. "Look around, dude, everyone is shitfaced." Hopefully, there are a few designated drivers among this group, or Uber will make a hell of a lot of money tonight.

As soon as Beck smirks, I know his answer is specifically designed to piss me off.

"That might be so, but everyone knows you're a good girl. And good girls don't drink. I wouldn't want the society to revoke your membership. You've worked so damn hard for it."

My eyes narrow to slits. The attraction that had flared to life so quickly is extinguished by his teasing.

I hate when he calls me that. And he knows it, which is precisely why he continues to do it. Beck loves nothing better than to crawl under my skin. He's like a rash I can't quite get rid of, no matter how many steroids I use.

It's irritating.

"I'm not a good girl," I growl before stabbing a finger at his ridiculously hard chest. "And *you* are not my keeper. I can drink if I want to." In a haughty voice, I remind, "I'm the one who was requested to babysit *your* ass. Not the other way around."

He crowds into my personal space. Instead of retreating, I stand my ground. I refuse to let him intimidate me.

"Babysitter, you say? Hmmm…I could definitely use one of those tonight." His fingers trace a path down the center of my chest, lingering in the valley between my breasts. "Should we take this elsewhere, and you can demonstrate everything your service entails?"

His nearness does funny things to me and clouds my better judgment. Instead of pushing him away, I'm tempted to pull him closer.

My body wavers before sanity crashes down on me, and I bat his hand away. "Go to hell."

"See?" He laughs as if I've proven his point. "A good girl through and through."

"I'm not as good as you think." The words shoot out of my mouth before I can rein them back in. To be clear, they are a total lie. I *am* as good as he thinks. Probably better. I have to be.

"Is that so?" He steps closer until the tips of my breasts brush against his bare chest. "Sweetheart, I'd love nothing better than to test that theory, but we both know you'll always be Mia Stanbury, little miss perfect."

And he'll always be Beckett Hollingsworth. The guy with little-to-no impulse control who can't walk down the school hallway without finding trouble. The same one who can't be left alone in his own house for a night without inviting a hundred of his closest friends over for an impromptu party.

We are opposites in every sense of the word.

"Shut up, Beck." I've never met anyone who has the power to turn me on and piss me off at the same time. If he ever cranked up the charm, I'd be toast. He's capable of melting the panties right off a girl with one well-aimed look. I've seen it happen with my own eyes. I refuse to be one of those ridiculous females. I won't be used and tossed aside like a dirty Kleenex.

I don't realize that I've become trapped in my own thoughts until his fingers settle under my chin, lifting it so I'm forced to meet his bright gaze. "What's the matter? Truth hurt?"

"There's nothing you can say that will hurt me." If only that were true.

His face looms closer until it fills my vision, blotting out the party. My world shrinks around us until it only encompasses Beck. My breath gets clogged in my lungs and burns like a fire before spreading to the rest of my body. Any moment I'm going to self-combust.

What am I doing?

I should pull away, but I'm powerless to do anything other than stare into his eyes and fall under his spell.

"Beck, baby!" a loud female voice booms over the rowdiness of the party, "over here!"

Even when she continues to bleat like a sheep, our gazes remain locked for several long heartbeats, and I almost wonder if he'll ignore her. But she's persistent and continues to repeat his name until he severs the connection between us and swings around.

As soon as I'm released, the air rushes from my lungs, and my body sags with relief. Or maybe it's disappointment. I tamp down the emotions so I can't inspect them too closely.

What would have happened if we hadn't been interrupted?

Nothing good.

This is *exactly* why I avoid Beck at all costs. Even though we're constantly sniping at each other, there's an undercurrent of attraction that hums beneath the surface. No other guy has ever provoked these kinds of emotions in me. I want to slap him almost as much as I want to kiss him.

Sanity returns with a rush as I focus on the statuesque blonde twenty feet away. Ava Simmons is wearing a teeny tiny bikini that leaves little to the imagination. Once she has Beck's full attention, she reaches around and unties the strings that hold the tiny triangles in place. The material floats to the cement at her feet. She lets him—and everyone else in the vicinity—ogle her perky breasts before running and jumping into the pool.

People cheer, and more girls ditch their tops, following Ava into the water.

A grin slides across Beck's face as he glances at me. A challenging light enters his eyes as he jerks his dark head toward the pool. Water sloshes over the edge of the azure-colored tile as more bodies dive in.

Oh, hell no.

My heart pounds as I throw my hands up in a *what can you do* gesture. "Sorry, didn't bring a suit."

His grin turns predatory. "Doesn't look like you need one."

Yeah...not going to happen.

"As fun as that seems, I'll pass," I wave an arm toward the pool, "but don't let that stop you from mingling with your guests. Ava's waiting." Topless. From the corner of my eye, I see her breasts bobbing like inflatable safety devices.

When his focus is drawn to the people splashing around, I follow suit. It's so much easier to stare elsewhere than hold the intensity of his gaze. Even when that option includes watching a bunch of topless girls I've known since elementary school. I don't check out the guys loitering in the area, but I'm sure most are sporting wood. Honestly, if it weren't for Alyssa, I would get the hell out of here before it turns into a raging orgy.

Beck steps closer, and my gaze snaps to his. "Sure I can't persuade you to go for a swim?"

"Nope." I shake my head.

"That's too bad. This would have gone a long way to prove that you're not the good girl I've always pegged you to be."

Before I can summon up a pithy retort, he runs and dives headfirst into the water. I catch a glimpse of plaid as he disappears beneath the surface.

A mixture of relief and disappointment bubble up inside me until I'm nearly choking on them. It's the latter emotion I'm having a hard time accepting.

With a huffed-out breath, I stalk to one of the many loungers that surround the pool and settle on top of a plush cushion. I glance around for Alyssa, hoping she's given up on Colton so we can head home. It's not too late for the evening to be salvaged with pizza and a movie. Instead, I find her in the pool.

Topless.

Sucking face with Colton.

Great.

As much as I want to take off, I can't leave her here alone. God only knows what will happen if I do.

With a groan, I squeeze my eyes tight and prepare myself for a long night.

MIA

$\mathcal{L}$andon Mathews, the guy I was attempting to lure Alyssa with, settles on the lounger next to me. We had calculus together last semester and often compared notes. Even though Landon is a football player, I don't hold it against him. He's proven himself to be a good guy. And, in my experience, those are far and few in between.

"Hey, Mia." He hands me a brand-new Solo cup overflowing with beer. "You look like you could use a little pick me up."

I could use a lot more than that, but this will do.

"Thanks." Our fingers brush as I take the cup from him. Unlike when I touch Beck, no spark of attraction ignites in my blood. It's yet another reminder that you can't help who you're drawn to. Not wanting to dwell on that disturbing thought, I lift the glass to my lips and take a swig.

"I wasn't expecting to see you here," he comments.

Does everyone think I'm a killjoy?

It would seem my image needs a little rebranding.

I jerk my head toward the house next door. "We're neighbors."

"Oh yeah, that's right." He nods. "I forgot. Still...this doesn't seem like your type of scene."

I snort and glance at the pool. "Orgies generally aren't, but Alyssa wanted to see a certain someone."

He chuckles, following the direction of my stare to the water and the half-naked bodies filling it. He flicks a humor-filled gaze at me. "Looks like she found him. My guess is that you're going to be here for the long haul."

That's exactly what I was thinking. There is no damn way I'll be able to pry Alyssa out of Colton's arms. And my orgy-o-meter has reached its limit. I need Alyssa to wrap up this little make-out session so we can get the hell out of here before I'm anymore mentally scarred.

"Ugh, let's hope not." With that, I bring the cup to my lips and frown when I find it empty. I tip it further back and pat the plastic bottom, but not a drop remains.

Landon chuckles and holds out his hand. "Pass it over, and I'll get you a refill."

See what I mean? Total sweetheart.

Five minutes later, he's back with two cups of golden deliciousness. Tonight the alcohol is going down surprisingly easy. The more I drink, the more relaxed I become.

Ever since my older sister Brianna died when I was fourteen in a drunk driving accident, I've walked the straight and narrow. I've done my best to shine in school and on the tennis court, hoping it would be enough to help my parents forget their heartache for even a minute. Unlike Beck, I don't go looking for trouble. I avoid it at all costs.

So, it feels good to loosen up for a change and drop the pretense. Since my parents are away for the weekend with Beck's, I don't have to worry about them finding out that I've been drinking.

For one night, it's kind of nice.

Freeing.

Landon drops onto the lounger next to me, and we talk about our plans for the fall. I'll be attending Wesley University, which is an hour away. A lot of people from high school end up there. Landon decided not to play football and is attending Penn State.

I considered going further away, but decided against it. Part of me is afraid of what will happen if I did. Sometimes it feels like I'm the only thing holding this family together. The guy who hit Brianna didn't just steal her from us, he also stole our happiness. He sent us spinning through the universe on a different course. None of us are the same. I don't think we will be again. Instead of coming together, the three of us splintered apart. They say time heals all wounds.

It's a lie.

I chase those depressing thoughts away by draining my cup.

Alyssa was also accepted at Wesley, so we'll be rooming together next year.

Guess who else will be on campus?

My gaze cuts to Beck. There are at least three girls hanging on him. It's been this way ever since seventh grade when he shot up six inches and packed on twenty pounds of muscle.

No matter what I do, I can't seem to get away from him.

Beck was recruited by almost every college in the Big Ten Conference. I had secretly hoped he would go far away so I could finally get over this stupid infatuation, but he shot that to hell when he committed to Wesley. The most I can hope for is that we don't run into each other too often. It's a big campus with tons of people.

When I realize that I'm dwelling on Beck, I lift my glass, surprised to find it's been topped off.

My head swims, feeling pleasantly fuzzy.

Exactly how many of these have I knocked back?

I try to do a rough mental calculation that seems as complicated as calculus.

Two? Three? Four? All I know is the more I drink, the better this beer tastes.

When one of my favorite songs gets cranked up, I jump to my feet and pull Landon with me. Apparently, it's everyone's favorite song as well because the entire party throws their hands in the air and writhes to the beat. When it's over, I collapse on my lounger and giggle hysterically.

"Ready for another?" Landon rises, ready to do my bidding. He really is a nice guy. It's too bad he and Alyssa never got together. They would have been perfect for one another. Instead, she only has eyes for Colton.

Speaking of Colton, guess who else committed to Wesley?

You guessed it…Colton Montgomery.

Alyssa has sworn up and down that her decision has nothing to do with a certain blond-haired Adonis.

I hope that's the case. It would be really stupid of her to plan a future around a guy who has never bothered to give her the time of day until this party. Not that I want to be a Debbie Downer, but who knows how long his interest will last. A couple of hours, at the most.

Alyssa is a talented dancer. Her dream is to get a fine arts degree in dance and open her own studio. She was accepted at several prestigious schools and turned them all down to attend Wesley.

"No," a gruff voice cuts in before I can wrap my lips around a response, "she's already had more than enough."

I glance up, surprised to find Beck towering over my lounger. His hair is damp from his dip in the pool. My mouth turns cottony as I stare at his bare chest.

He needs to put a shirt on so I can think straight.

"Actually," I slur, taking offense to him making decisions for me, "I *will* have another." At least, I hope that's what comes out.

Beck scowls before shifting his hardened gaze to his teammate. "What the hell, dude? Why did you let her have so much? She's officially cut off."

Excuse me?

Who does this guy think he is?

Beck is the king of bad decisions. And he has the audacity to tell me—*me, for God's sake, who hasn't gotten so much as a tardy in her life*—that I can't have another drink? I'm not even driving home.

He didn't nickname me *good girl* and *little miss perfect* for nothing. I'm eighteen-years-old. If I want to cut loose for once in my life and have a few drinks, I'm more than capable of making that decision for myself. I don't need Beck swooping in and telling me what I can and can't do.

That thought alone is enough to piss me off.

"You're not the boss of me," I add belligerently with a slight curl to my lip.

Beck doesn't spare me a glance. His focus is trained on Landon. "You've been relieved of your duties. I've got it from here."

"Chill out, dude. She's fine. We're just talking. No need to bust a nut."

What's Beck's problem? Landon is right. We weren't doing anything wrong. Beck is angry, and I don't understand why. Normally my neighbor and part-time nemesis is laid-back and chill. Nothing riles him up. So, this behavior is definitely out of character.

Beck's lips flatten as the steely look in his eyes intensifies. "Take off, I'll deal with Mia."

Deal with Mia?

Since when am I someone who needs to be *dealt with*?

They glare at each other for a long, tense moment. The muscles in my belly quiver with unease as my gaze darts from one boy to the other.

What's going on here?

It feels like I'm missing a key piece of information.

The intensity dissipates when Landon takes a step in retreat before turning to me with a forced smile. "It was good talking to you, Mia. I'll see you around before I leave for Penn."

"Yeah, sure." I'm still trying to puzzle out what's going on, but my drunk brain is having a hard time reading between the lines. That's usually something I excel at since interpreting what's going on with my parents has become a survival skill.

Landon jerks his head into a tight nod before joining the crowd of rowdy partiers and disappearing from sight. I stare after him, confused by his abrupt departure.

Wait a minute—what did Beck say a few minutes ago?

"Relieved of his duties?" My gaze cuts to the six-foot guy at my side. "Did you ask Landon to *babysit* me?"

Instead of answering, he tilts his head and studies me.

When I raise my brows, he says, "That depends."

"On what?"

"If you're going to be pissed off with the answer."

Even in my inebriated state, I understand what that means.

"I don't need a babysitter," I grumble, slowly rising to my feet. I'm offended he would think otherwise. Using my arms for balance, I carefully straighten to my full height. "Let me remind you that Archie and Caroline asked me to keep an eye on *you*." I jab a finger at his chest. "Not the other way around."

When I stagger to the side, Beck leaps forward and grabs hold of my arms so I don't crash into the lounger I've been parked on.

"It's doubtful they would have done that if they could see you now."

I wave a hand and blow a raspberry with my lips. "I'm fine."

"You're hardly fine. Landon shouldn't have let you drink so much." Beck hauls me closer until his warm breath can feather across my lips, and my core clenches in response. "Have you ever been drunk?"

Nope. Usually I'm the designated driver, but that wasn't necessary tonight.

"Of course, I have. All the time."

"Is that so," he laughs, the muscles in his face relaxing. "You have a secret life I don't know about?"

It doesn't escape me that Beck is still holding me. And that I like the feel of his hands a little too much. I should push out of his arms except...I don't want to.

"That's for me to know and *you* never to find out," I singsong.

Amusement settles over his face. Now *this* is the Beck I know and try to keep my distance from.

"That's strange. I've never seen you at any of the parties and from my count, you've only had four drinks, and you're already drunk off your ass."

"I wouldn't say I'm drunk off my ass," I mumble as my head spins.

He releases my arms and gives my shoulder a little shove. I stumble back a step before righting myself.

Instead of arguing about my inebriated state, I focus on what he admitted. "How do you know how many drinks I've had?"

"I've been keeping track."

"Why? Are you keeping tabs on everyone's consumption?" There have to be at least a hundred people here. Probably more.

A sly grin simmers around the edges of his lips. "Nope. Just you, Stanbury."

His words send an arrow of warmth flooding through me, and my heartbeat picks up its tempo. Refusing to dissolve into a puddle of goo at his feet, I say, "Well, that's not creepy at all."

Unbothered by my pronouncement, he shrugs. "That's me, the creepy stalker from next door."

Neither of us mentions that every chick at this party would give their left tit for Beck to show interest in them. I'm probably the only girl who goes to great lengths to avoid his attention.

Although that doesn't seem to be doing me any good at the moment.

"I don't need a keeper," I tell him. "Certainly not you."

"That's funny. I was thinking the opposite."

I hold up my cup, needing to put some distance between us. "If you'll excuse me, I'm going to partake in another refreshment."

He nips the cup from my fingers before I can take a step away from him. "I was serious, Mia. You've had enough. You're done for the night."

Done for the night?

What is he going to do? Kick me out?

I cross my arms over my chest and shift my weight. "I'm not leaving without Alyssa." I glance around for my friend. But that's a mistake since the pool is filled with naked people who are busy getting it on.

"Alyssa's a big girl. She can take care of herself."

If only that were true.

"Come on, let's go." His fingers wrap around my wrist, and a little pop of awareness shoots through me when he pulls me to his hard body.

Oh my God! He's serious about kicking me out!

"Excuse me?" I try to push my way out of his embrace, but it's like fighting with a steel beam. He's all hard lines and powerful strength.

On the football field, he's a force to be reckoned with. "Are you actually going to throw me out of here?"

"Who said anything about tossing you out?" He laughs and shakes his head. "I'm taking you upstairs so you can sleep it off."

Well, that's a relief.

But still…

I dig my heels in, refusing to budge. "No, I can't go until I find Alyssa."

He points to a couple making out beneath the diving board. "She's right there." He pauses before adding, "She's occupied at the moment."

My gaze darts around the pool until I find my best friend. Beck is right about her being busy. Colton has her backed up against the edge of the pool. Alyssa looks like she's attempting to suction the breath right out of his lungs.

The tank top she borrowed earlier has gone missing.

My gaze skitters away. I'm not into voyeurism. Although some of these people are. There are plenty of them standing around, watching. Let's hope that no one is videoing the moment for posterity.

"It's unlikely Alyssa will leave anytime soon."

"Probably not," I mutter.

What am I supposed to do? Taking off feels wrong. But sitting around and watching people get it on feels downright pervy. I suck my bottom lip into my mouth and chew it as I contemplate my options.

"Fine," I say, "I'm going home." I take a step away from Beck, attempting to distance myself. The scent of his aftershave mingles with the chlorine in the pool. It shouldn't be an intoxicating combination.

"Sorry, Stanbury, you're staying here. The last thing I need is for you to choke on your own vomit."

Give me a break. That's not going to happen.

My fists go to my hips. "What does it matter if I sleep alone here or in my bed?"

His voice turns silky. "Who said anything about you sleeping solo?"

When my mouth tumbles open, a slow grin spreads across his face.

"Are you crazy?" I shake my head a little too vigorously, and the party spins. "Forget it! I'm not sleeping with you!"

"That's the thing, you don't have a choice in the matter. The decision has already been made."

Who does this guy think he is?

I open my mouth to blast him into next week when he says, "We can do this the hard way or the easy way. It's your choice."

What does that even mean?

Instead of answering, I jerk my arm, trying to break free. "Let go! I'm leaving, and there's nothing you can do to stop me!"

"The hard way it is."

In one swift motion, he yanks me to him, crouches down, and wraps his arms around my thighs before hoisting me over his shoulder like a sack of potatoes. I don't realize his intentions until my midsection lands against him, momentarily knocking the air from my lungs, and stunning me into silence. I blink and find the party turned upside down. It doesn't do good things for all the alcohol sloshing around in my belly.

The crowd roars and my cheeks flame as the blood rushes to my head. Cool air hits the back of my thighs and I groan, remembering my choice in underwear. When I continue to struggle, a wide palm lands across my backside.

"Ow!"

"Stop fighting me. Maybe you haven't noticed, but everyone is admiring your ass." There's a pause as he turns us around before moving toward the French doors that lead inside the house. "What the hell are you doing wearing a skirt this short?" Before I can formulate a response, he grumbles, "And with a fucking thong? I love it, but no one else should be checking out your ass."

"Here's a solution," I growl, "put me down."

"Not gonna happen."

His hand slides from one exposed cheek to the crack of my ass before he splays his fingers wide to cover as much skin as possible from the gawking crowd. I squirm at the feel of his palm resting against my naked flesh. *Especially there.* I'm not sure which option is more preferable. That people ogle my ass or that Beck continues touching me so intimately. The print of his palm feels as if it has been singed into my flesh.

When I continue to wiggle, his fingers bite into my cheeks. "Stay still." His voice turns low and grumbly. It does funny things to my insides, and a reluctant thrill spirals through me.

Beck weaves through the thick crowd. Every once in a while, he'll stop and chat as if carrying a girl over his shoulder is perfectly normal behavior. "Everyone needs to be cleared out in an hour," he says. "Got it?"

"Consider it done," a deep voice responds.

Before I'm able to get my bearings, we're on the move again. From my upside-down position, I watch the kitchen disappear as he walks through the first floor of the house. My hair swings around my face like a dark curtain, making it impossible to see. I should probably be thankful. I've never been so mortified in my life. If I'm lucky, no one will realize I'm the girl Beck has thrown over his shoulder and is carrying up to his room like a prize he won in a card game.

People clap and cheer as he climbs the staircase to the second floor. My name reverberates through the crowd like a wave. Whispers and giggles assault my ears, making the tips burn with humiliation.

"Can you put me down?" I growl, fed up with his manhandling. Thank God I won't see most of these people again. That's the only thought getting me through this moment.

Beck slaps my ass none too gently, and the sound of flesh striking flesh echoes off the cavernous walls of the hallway.

"Ow!" I yelp.

"Now that sounded like it hurt." Amusement simmers in his voice.

"What the hell was that for?" I demand. The sting of his smack resonates through my backside. No one has ever struck my ass before. Not my parents when I was younger, and certainly not anyone I've gone out with.

The audacity of this guy!

"No reason, just felt like it."

Grrrr.

I grit my teeth as he turns to the left and walks down the hallway. I played here enough times as a kid to know he's taking me to his room. Beck and Ari's bedrooms are on one side of the spacious second floor while their parents' suite is located on the other. He could probably get murdered, and his parents wouldn't hear a thing.

Not that I'm in any position to bargain, but it's worth a shot. "I'll agree to stay the night," I hiss, "if I can have my own room."

"No can do, sweetheart. You'll be bunking with me."

Aggravated by his uncompromising response, I pummel my fists against the wide expanse of his back. "You're crazy if you think I'm going to sleep with you!"

"Don't worry, you're not about to get that lucky," he chuckles. "Maybe if you beg prettily, I'll change my mind."

Ha!

As if...

I ignore the comment. We both know that won't be happening.

Ever.

I wouldn't beg Beck to spit in my mouth if I were dying of thirst in the desert, and he was my only chance for survival.

"You have four guestrooms, put me in one of those for the night. If there's a problem, you'll be the first to know."

"Wish I could, but all the rooms are taken. A few friends might crash. Better safe than sorry. Am I right?"

Damnit.

Beck isn't concerned about my wellbeing. This is another way for him to get under my skin. I'm on to his games. He's probably doing it since his parents asked me to keep an eye on him. Is that my fault? Should I be punished because *he's* an irresponsible child?

Nope. I don't think so.

I never should have allowed Alyssa to talk me into attending this party. It was a mistake. No good deed goes unpunished. This is what I get for trying to be a good friend.

Beck stops in front of a closed-door before reaching for the handle and shoving it open. It only takes two steps before we're crossing over the threshold, and he's slamming the door shut, locking me inside like a prisoner.

With him.

Once inside the spacious bedroom, he hunkers down. I breathe a sigh of relief when his hand disappears from my backside. Cool air hits my newly warmed flesh, making me even more aware of the way he had been touching me. His large hands wrap around my hips as I slide against his body until my sandaled feet are planted on the floor. Then he releases me and rises to his full height.

All the nasty names on the tip of my tongue dissolve. It's as if we're frozen in place, unsure what to do now that he's brought me here. When he inhales, I do the same. When he releases his breath, I follow suit.

What's happening?

More importantly, how do I make it stop?

How do I shake off the heavy feelings of attraction unfurling inside me?

Over the years, I've become a master at burying the emotions Beck rouses in me. With one look, they've broken free and are simmering at the surface. And that's dangerous. I don't want Beck to suspect how I truly feel about him.

Can you imagine what he would do with that kind of information?

I flinch at the thought.

Beck is careless with people's feelings. Especially the fairer sex. I've witnessed firsthand the trail of tears and broken hearts he leaves behind in his wake.

As if realizing we've become stuck in a moment, he blinks and takes a hasty step in retreat. It's enough to break the spell that has fallen over me. A million questions flood through my brain, but not a single one leaves my mouth. It's a relief when he turns away and relinquishes my gaze. I shake my head to clear it as he pulls open the third drawer of his dresser. I'm treated to an impressive view of his bareback. All those tightly honed muscles that stretch and shift with every movement.

God, but he's beautiful. Sometimes I wonder if I'll ever find another guy as sexy as I do Beck. I really hope so. The thought of being stuck on him forever is depressing.

He grabs a piece of clothing before slamming the drawer shut and swinging around to face me.

"Mia?" His voice sounds deeper, more roughed up than seconds ago. Even though I fight against it, my core clenches in response.

It takes a moment to break free of the trance that has fallen over me. I gulp, wishing there was a way to escape the situation. In two swift steps, Beck is back to invading my space. He towers over me, standing so close that the tips of my breasts brush against his shirtless chest.

"You need to stop staring at me like that," he growls.

"Like what?" I whisper, trying to play dumb.

His face hovers so closely that his warm, minty breath ghosts over my lips. All I want is to close my eyes and lean into him. To take a deep lungful of air and savor it.

How is it possible to want someone and yet hate them at the same time? It doesn't make sense.

"Like you might be interested in hanging up your good girl title."

A wave of arousal crashes over me, making my head swim.

Is that how I'm staring at him?

Like I want him to touch me in ways I've only dreamed about in the privacy of my room?

Guilty.

Here's a little secret I'm loath to admit even to myself—I find Beck ridiculously attractive. For as long as I can remember, his energy and sense of humor have fascinated me. I'm drawn to the way he doesn't give a damn. My fingers itch to tunnel through his dark wavy hair. My lips ache to settle over his. And my body trembles with the need for his large hands to coast over it.

But...

And this is a ginormous *but,* I would never—under any circumstance—admit that to him.

No matter how tempted I might be.

No matter how much he turns me on.

When Beck is this close, it's almost impossible to remind myself that he doesn't have the attention span to stick with anything other than football for the long haul. He flits from one girl to the next before moving on.

A potent blend of regret and relief rush through me when he steps away and presses something soft into my hands. I tear my gaze from his and stare at the wadded-up shirt.

He jerks his head toward the bathroom attached to his room. "Go change."

"Change?" I repeat. I must be more drunk than I suspected because for some reason, I can't get my brain to function properly.

"Yeah," his voice turns sharp, "but leave on the thong."

My eyes pop wide as his words echo throughout my head.

"As long as there's something covering you," he continues, "it won't be a problem."

What the hell have I gotten myself into?

A fresh burst of panic rolls through me as my gaze darts to the bedroom door. *If I run fast, I could probably make it out of here.*

It's not like he would physically stop me from leaving…right?

"Don't even think about it, Stanbury. You sleeping here is a done deal."

I huff out a breath, irritated that he can read my mind so easily.

Left without options that don't involve him laying his hands on me, I stalk to the bathroom and slam the door before sliding the lock into place. From the other side of the door, his amused chuckle assaults my ears. With shaking fingers, I turn on the tap until water flows into the sink before collapsing against the marble countertop.

Now that I'm alone, I try to settle everything racing madly around inside me before splashing a handful of cold water on my face. Then I strip off the tank top, skirt, and sandals. With my bra and thong still in place, I meet my reflection in the mirror. If I were smart, I would leave the bra on, but I can't sleep with wire cups. They'll dig into my skin.

Unwilling to overthink the decision, I unhook the back and allow the straps to slide down my arms before dropping the bra to the tile floor. Then I pull Beck's T-shirt over my head. I hate myself for giving in to the urge to bring the cottony fabric to my nose before inhaling a breath. My belly quivers as Beck's masculine scent wraps around me.

When I step into the room, I find Beck stretched out on the king-size bed that dominates the space. Gone are the board shorts. In their place is a pair of form-fitting black boxer-briefs that hug his impressive thighs and...

Yeah.

I quickly avert my eyes.

Sweet baby Jesus.

No high school guy should be this perfectly sculpted.

It's just plain wrong.

Beck's gaze cuts to mine, freezing me on the spot. My breath catches, and my heart stutters under the sharp intensity of his stare. Unsure how to proceed, I hover near the bathroom door. His hands are lazily stacked behind his head as they rest against the pillow. When I don't budge from the threshold, he sits up and swings his legs over the side of the bed before rising to his feet and stretching out his hand.

"Come here."

Holy shit. Is this really happening?

It feels like a dream. Maybe a nightmare. Or someplace in between.

My mind flips through the past two hours as I try to figure out how I've ended up in Beck's bed for the night. It doesn't make sense.

My motto has always been *avoid, avoid, avoid.*

This is the complete opposite.

Unconsciously, I close the distance between us. I blink to awareness when Beck's fingers tighten around mine. With a tug, I stumble forward into his embrace.

His other hand wraps around my waist. "You good?"

Even though I jerk my head into a nod, I have no idea if it's the truth. This is unchartered territory. Maybe if he would stop touching me, my mind would clear enough to think rationally. But his grip doesn't loosen. Another unwanted bolt of arousal shoots through me before settling in my lower belly.

When it seems like I'll explode from the thick tension that has gathered between us, his fingers fall away and he turns, yanking back the covers.

I stare, unsure what to do. Am I supposed to slide into his bed as if this is normal?

Just another Saturday night spent with Beck?

When I hesitate, he says, "Nothing will happen that you don't want."

That's exactly what I'm afraid of.

All I can think about are his hands on my body.

Against my better judgment, I climb onto the mattress. It's as soft as a cloud. My movements falter when he groans, his hand sliding over my bare backside. Everything in me tenses as I scamper to the far side of the bed. That little caress leaves my body vibrating.

The mattress dips as Beck settles on top of it and we both stretch out, our heads resting against the thousand-count Egyptian-covered pillows. It takes a bit of adjustment before I'm able to find a comfortable position on my side, turned away from Beck. Even though I try to ignore him, I'm ridiculously aware of his six-foot frame next to me.

A few silent moments tick by as I force myself to relax. One by one, my tense muscles lose their rigidity. I stare at the far wall before trying to close my eyes. Okay. This isn't so bad. Beck will stay on his side, and I'll remain on mine. It's a king-size bed and there's plenty of space for both of us. In fact, there's plenty of room for three or four people. I'm sure Beck has tested that theory out for himself. My guess is that he's no stranger to threesomes.

Why that thought irritates me, I have no idea. But I banish it from my head before I can inspect it too closely.

As soon as the sun peeks over the horizon tomorrow morning, I'm out of here. Or maybe I'll wait for Beck to fall asleep and sneak home. Is he really going to care at that point? It's not like he can hold me hostage in his bedroom indefinitely.

The moment I find a comfy spot and melt into the mattress, Beck wraps an arm around my ribs. I yelp as he drags me toward him until my backside is aligned with his front.

Holy hell.

I stiffen like a board as his arm drapes around my body and holds me so every part of him is pressed intimately against me.

And I do mean *every* part.

One of his hands slips beneath the hem of my T-shirt and settles against my lower abdomen. My breath becomes clogged in my throat until it feels like I'm going to pass out from lack of oxygen. The warmth of his palm singes the skin beneath it. It's all I can focus on.

"Relax," he rumbles against my ear.

Is he joking?

How am I supposed to do that?

"You know," I say, voice shaking like a leaf, "I'm fine. I could—"

"You're staying here. End of story."

I press my lips together until they feel bloodless. As much as I want to argue, I know it won't do me any good. Beck isn't going to release me until he's damn good and ready. So, I'm stuck. Pressed against him. I blow out a breath and try to do as he instructed.

The noise of the party fades as my eyelids droop. I listen for Beck's steady inhalations as my muscles gradually unlock.

I refuse to stay here.

There's no way I'll fall asleep.

He can't keep me against my will. A little longer and I can slip out of his embrace.

I stay perfectly still, listening as his breathing becomes deep and rhythmic. For some reason, it calms me from the inside out.

All I need to do is wait.

Then I can…

Drift off to sleep, wrapped up in Beck's embrace.

MIA

ndiluted sunlight slants across my face, lighting the back of my eyelids and making it impossible to stay submerged in my cocoon. With a groan, I turn away from the brilliance and promptly come in contact with something solid and unyielding.

That's strange.

I'm still drifting in that in-between place where I'm struggling to wake but can't quite break through to the surface. My fingers stroke over something warm as my brain processes what I'm touching. Tentatively, my exploration continues until my fingers graze over a flat male nipple.

What the hell?

My eyes pop open only to find a big body next to me. A muscled arm is thrown over his face, preventing me from discovering the mystery man's identity.

A choked sound escapes from my lips.

Not in a million years did I ever suspect I'd wake up next to a random dude.

I wrack my brain, trying to remember what happened last night, but it's a blur of images. It takes a moment for them to coalesce until, one by one, they flash through my head like a slow-motion picture show.

Hanging with Alyssa at my house.

Beck's party.

Sitting on a lounger and talking with Landon.

Landon.

Is that who I ended up in bed with?

For some reason, I don't think so.

The rest of the night tumbles through my fuzzy brain at an alarming pace. Landon was not only kind enough to keep me company, but also in refills.

Jeez. Exactly how much did I drink?

That must be the reason I feel like I've been hit over the head with a sledgehammer.

And then Beck, of all people, cut me off. Considering the state I'm waking up in, he should have done it sooner. Although I'll refrain from telling him that.

An image of Beck tossing me over his shoulder, carrying me through the party, and up to his room flickers through my head.

Wait a minute…were people actually *cheering?*

Oh, the horror of it all.

Unwilling to face the reality of the situation, I squeeze my eyes tightly shut and attempt to block out this whole unpleasant episode.

"Morning, sleeping beauty," comes a gruff voice chock-full of amusement.

Damn.

Damn.

Damn.

I recognize that voice all too well. It haunts my nightmares. And a few of my dreams.

He's the one I ended up in bed with?

I groan in embarrassment.

"What's wrong, Stanbury? Didn't sleep well? If anyone should be complaining, it's me. You kept me up all night with your snoring."

My eyes fly open only to find him hovering inches above me. A devilish smile spills across his face. He's loving every moment of my self-inflicted torment. As much as I don't want to notice how ridiculously hot he is, it would be impossible not to. Air rushes from my lungs as those unwelcome thoughts invade my brain.

It takes effort to focus on the conversation now playing out. "I don't snore."

"Sure you do, just like a chainsaw."

Heat slams into my cheeks. "I do not!"

He lowers his face until our mouths are almost touching. "Yeah, you do. But I didn't mind because I enjoyed holding you in my arms."

The breath leaks from my lungs.

That much I remember.

His arms were banded around me all night. And I'd slept...okay. Better than that, if I'm being honest with myself.

Arrrgh.

This is exactly why I don't drink. Bad choices are inevitably made when alcohol consumption is involved. It's much too easy to make a fool out of yourself and sleep with—

Oh, God...did we have sex?

No.

No.

No.

Frantically I search my brain, trying to remember if anything physical happened. Silence rains down on us, and my heart constricts before pounding into overdrive. I moisten my lips before pushing out the words. "Did we..."

"Don't worry, little miss perfect, your virtue is firmly intact."

There's a definite smirk in his voice.

I shift my focus to him, searching his eyes carefully.

Why would he say that?

He has no idea I'm a virgin.

I clear my throat and attempt to remain calm. Beck is the last person I want knowing my personal business. The teasing would be merciless. I'd never hear the end of it. "Why would you say that?"

"Educated guess." His eyes crinkle at the corners. "Am I wrong?"

Every muscle in my body fills with tension.

How do I answer that without giving away the truth?

A slow grin moves across his face, making him more handsome than he already is. An arrow of lust explodes in my core.

His hair is artfully disheveled. I'm tempted to reach out and run my fingers through the strands. Instead, I tighten them and resist the urge. It's so unfair. No one should look this good at the butt crack of dawn. The guy could grace the cover of a men's magazine. While I, on the other hand, probably have that whole—just-stuck-my-finger-in-an-electrical-socket look going for me.

"Your silence is answer enough."

I grit my teeth. The only other choice I have is to lie, and I'm a terrible liar.

"Plus, you let the cat out of the bag last night."

I bolt up. My eyes widen until they feel like they might roll right out of my head. *What?*

I wrack my brain again, carefully combing over our conversations. But things are still muddled.

"Liar," I accuse. There is no way I would share something so intimate with Beck. Even if I'd been completely shitfaced, I wouldn't have confessed that to him. But still, doubt lurks in the back of my brain.

"Whether I'm lying is a moot point." He chuckles, leaning closer until his warm breath can drift over my lips. "You had to think about it, which tells me you are, indeed, pure as the driven snow." He tilts his head as his eyes dance with humor. "See how easy it was to get the truth out of you?"

Grrrrr.

"You are such an asshole!" Even though I press my palms against his chest and push with every ounce of my strength, Beck doesn't budge an inch. *Get. Off. Me!*

"Being a virgin isn't something you should be embarrassed about."

Oh my God! Stop talking about it before I self-combust!

"I'm not embarrassed," I grit out.

"Then why is your face turning bright red?"

"Because I'm embarrassed, all right? There! I said it!" I snap. *"Are you happy now?"*

"Kind of."

"You're impossible!"

He shrugs. "Not really."

"It's like your mission in life is to make me feel stupid." I knew he would use this information against me, and that's exactly what he's doing. Thank God we're no longer in high school. He would probably shout it from the rooftops, and I would be the butt of everyone's jokes.

His playful manner falls away as seriousness fills his eyes. "That's the last thing I'd ever want to do."

Ha! Liar.

In one swift motion, he wraps his arms around me and rolls me over until I'm stretched out on top of him. My breath catches at the feel of his hard body beneath mine.

Holy moly.

We're so close that I'm able to see the golden flecks that dance in his irises. "I know better than anyone what it's like when people make you feel stupid," he whispers, "and I would never do that to you."

The sincere expression on his face makes this feel like the first honest moment we've ever shared. As if all the bullshit has fallen away, and I'm catching a rare glimpse of the real Beckett Hollingsworth. The notion is as disconcerting as it is dizzying.

His hands cradle my cheeks tenderly. "You're one of the most intelligent people I know, Mia. If I made you feel like you weren't for even a second, I'm sorry. That was never my intention."

A strange intimacy grows between us.

"Your virginity is nothing to be ashamed of." His voice drops lower, becoming deeper. "I like that you're still a virgin."

His words create a warmth that slowly spreads throughout my body.

Even though I'm afraid to voice the question, I'm more afraid of never discovering the answer. "Why?"

His focus drops to my mouth. In response, my tongue darts out to smudge my lips. A groan rumbles up from deep in his chest.

I gasp when his cock twitches against me. Beck remains perfectly still, his hands cupping my face. His eyes darken to a deeper shade.

"I don't know," he admits. "Maybe I want to be the first one to touch you."

My brain explodes, and the world around me ceases to exist.

"Do you want that, Mia?" He rolls his hips, and his thick erection slides against me. Sensation explodes in my core before reverberating throughout my body in the most delicious way.

A moan slips free from my lips, filling the silent room.

"Fuck," he whispers before repeating the movement.

I bite down on my lip to keep the sound trapped inside.

"Don't do that," he mutters thickly, "I want to hear you."

He thrusts against me again, stroking my heat with his length. Only this time, the head of his cock butts up against my entrance. It's gently that he prods the opening. The combined material of his boxers and my thong keep him from sliding in deeper.

My eyes roll back inside my head as waves of pleasure wash over me. He's only stroked me a few times, but already my lower lips are slick with arousal. I'm so greedy for more.

"Does that feel good?"

I whimper in response, unable to form coherent words, as he moves rhythmically against me. The friction we're creating is the most amazing sensation I've ever felt. My thong is soaked. It doesn't escape me that all Beck has to do is stretch the material to the side, and he could slide inside me.

What would it feel like to have Beck buried deep in my body? I've fantasized about it too many times to count. I've touched myself to thoughts of him, but it never felt like this.

My core tightens as he picks up his pace. I arch, needing more contact as another whimper slides from my lips.

"I want you so much," he murmurs.

I gasp as Beck rolls us over, his body stretched out on mine. His gaze burns as he yanks his boxers down so his cock can spring free before pulling my thong to the side. My eyes roll up inside my head when his thick length comes in contact with my slick flesh.

"Do you like that?"

The smooth head of his erection nudges my entrance. He holds himself rigid, only an inch penetrating my heat. But it feels so damn good. I widen my thighs, wanting more.

We've barely done anything and already there is so much pleasure rushing through my system. It's almost too much for the confines of my body. I want to drown in it and never come up for air again. No one has ever touched me like this. There have been a few boyfriends over the years, but nothing that ever progressed to this level.

"We can't keep doing this without a condom," he grits between clenched teeth. "I don't want anything to happen."

His movements still as he hovers above me with the tip of his hard length buried inside my body. The urge to thrust my hips upward and press closer pounds through me.

"Okay."

"Okay?" he repeats as if he doesn't understand.

"Get a condom," I say, arching my back, trying to get him to slide deeper. When he pulls out, I growl with frustration.

"Are you sure?"

"Yes!" In this moment, I'm certain of what I want. And what I want more than anything is Beck inside me, filling me, making me feel things I never dreamed possible.

In one swift motion, he rolls away from me and toward his nightstand. He yanks open the slender drawer and grabs something from inside.

His gaze settles on mine as he holds a thin packet in his hand. "You're absolutely sure?"

My core pulses uncomfortably with awareness. I don't think I've ever felt this achy in my life. "Positive."

He bites his lower lip as indecision flickers across his face.

"Beck, I want this." I shimmy out of my thong before tossing it to the floor.

A groan escapes from his lips when he stares at my pussy. There are no more questions as he tears the boxers from his body before ripping open the package. My focus drops to his cock.

Holy cow.

His erection is long and thick. I'm no aficionado on dick size, but he seems impressively built.

"Take off your shirt," he says, sheathing himself with latex. "I don't want anything between us."

My belly hollows out as I tug the T-shirt over my head. It joins the thong on the floor.

Unsure what to do, I lie still as his gaze lingers over my naked length. We've known each other our entire lives. It seems strange that we're about to have sex. But there's no one else I could imagine doing this with. It's always been Beck. Whether I've wanted to acknowledge those feelings or not. So, in a way, what we're doing feels right.

"Having second thoughts?"

I shake my head.

"Okay." His body loses some of its rigidity. It's almost as if he's afraid I'll change my mind. "Spread your legs."

When I widen my thighs, he carefully maneuvers himself between them, stroking his hands from my belly to my breasts.

"You're so fucking perfect."

As he palms the soft weight, I arch into his hands and press myself closer. My eyelids feather shut as he squeezes them. And then he's back to stroking over my body again. Touching every part of me. He stops at my inner thighs and attempts to pull them further apart.

When I resist, his gaze settles on mine. "I want to see you."

A protest sits perched on my lips. I've never been on display like this. As I open my mouth to voice my concerns, he lowers himself and swipes the flat of his tongue across my slit. The stroke is long and languid.

A whimper explodes from my lips as he repeats the movement. The velvety softness of his tongue circles my clit, and sensation gathers, building like a storm inside me until it becomes almost too much to bear, and I groan out my release. He strokes me the entire time, wringing every drop from my body.

After my orgasm dissipates, Beck crawls up the length of me. Heat fills his eyes as a smug smile lifts his lips. I'm too dazed to care. As far as I'm concerned, the guy has every right to be arrogant about his skills.

I'm jostled from those thoughts when he places his cock against my entrance and rocks his hips back and forth. With each thrust, he slides inside my body. I groan as pleasure spirals inside me again, but then he continues to move, and a twinge of pain overshadows everything else.

"Are you all right?" He pauses. "Should I stop?"

I shake my head. Stopping is the furthest thing from my mind. Maybe I didn't plan this, but I want to experience this moment with Beck.

"It's going to hurt," he whispers.

Beck has been so gentle. I never imagined he could be this way. It only makes me fall harder for him.

I suck in a breath and nod as I mentally prepare myself for what will come next.

He flexes his hips, and his hard length slides further inside me. I wince as pain blooms, becoming more of a burning sensation. He leans down and takes my lips with his own before carefully thrusting against me. When it feels like he can't slide any deeper, he angles himself differently and moves further inside my body.

A whimper escapes, and he swallows it down. Our tongues tangle as he holds himself perfectly still, balancing on his elbows so the full weight of his body doesn't pin me to the mattress. It takes a few moments for the sharp bite of pain to recede.

I blow out a steady breath, and he gently withdraws from my abraded body.

That can't be all there is, right?

There has to be more.

Just when I wonder if he'll pull out all the way, he slides back inside, burying himself to the hilt.

I gasp at the flash of pain as my insides stretch around his girth. It's not entirely unpleasant.

"Are you okay?" He holds himself above me. "I don't want to hurt you, Mia."

"I'm all right. Don't stop." All the previous pleasure swirling madly around inside me is long gone. My insides sting with the intrusion. His cock buried inside my body feels like a foreign entity.

He pulls out again before gliding back inside.

Once.

Twice.

By the third time, the sting has subsided, and a tiny ripple of desire sparks to life in my core.

His thrusts are gentle and rhythmic. Pleasure continues to flourish deep inside me until I'm gyrating my hips, trying to match his movements.

He closes his eyes as his breathing picks up speed, becoming more labored. His tempo becomes faster as I'm pushed to the edge again. When his body stiffens, he throws his head back and groans out his release. As his thrusts become deeper, it sets off my own reaction, and a firework of sensation explodes in my core. A flood of warmth fills me as he chants my name over and over before collapsing on top of me in a heap.

I wrap my arms around Beck and pull him closer. His harsh breathing fills my ears as I stare at the ceiling with dazed amazement.

With a huff, he lifts himself up and balances on his elbows. He stares at me with eyelids at half-mast. Pleasure swirls through his eyes. "Are you okay?"

My lips lift into a tentative smile. "I'm fine."

"Did I hurt you?"

I shrug. "It wasn't too bad."

His lips curve as he presses them to mine. "I tried to be gentle."

I give in to the nagging urge to tunnel my fingers through his mussed hair. I've never felt closer to another human being, and it feels so good.

No. Better than good.

Amazing.

There's a connection between us, one that bonds us in the most intimate way possible. It's something I've never shared with anyone else, and that makes it infinitely special. I want to soak it up and marvel at the unexpectedness of it all.

Carefully, Beck pulls out of my body and flips onto his back. The loss of his warmth and closeness is staggering. It brings unwanted questions hurtling to the surface.

Was this nothing more than a hookup?

Or did it mean something?

I open my mouth to ask when a deep voice cuts through the silence of the bedroom.

"Goddamn it, Beckett Archibald Hollingsworth!"

Every single thought swirling through my head disappears as my eyes widen. I screech at the top of my lungs and scramble under the comforter, yanking it to my chin.

What the hell?

Instead of freaking out, Beck doesn't move a muscle. More surprising than that, he looks unfazed. As if his father hasn't walked in on us. He throws a well-muscled arm over his eyes and huffs out an exasperated breath.

With his body on full display, my gaze drops to his condom-covered cock. Now that his erection has deflated, it's nowhere near the size it was earlier. If I weren't dying of mortification, I'd be tempted to investigate the situation.

"Goddamn it, Beckett Archibald Hollingsworth!"

Annoyance bleeds from every syllable.

I yelp again and glance around the room in confusion. Beck's father is nowhere to be seen, but there's no mistaking that booming voice. I've heard those very words fly out of his mouth dozens of times. That's Archie's usual reaction when Beck has done something boneheaded and gotten himself into trouble. Which he does often.

"What *is* that?" I croak.

"My phone," Beck grumbles before rolling over and swiping the thin silver rectangle from the nightstand. He taps the screen. "Hey, Dad."

Archibald's voice bursts over the line, but I can't quite make out the conversation.

Beck runs a hand through his hair. Instead of taming the locks, the movement only ruffles them more. I'm so tempted to reach out and straighten it into submission.

"Yeah, just a couple of people." A smirk curves his lips as he winks at me. "Perfectly chill."

Ha!

His dad and I snort at the same time. I might not be able to hear every word being spoken, but that sound comes across loud and clear.

Amusement flashes in Beck's eyes. "It'll be cleaned up by the time you get home. No worries."

They exchange a few more words before Beck hits the disconnect button and tosses the phone onto the nightstand.

The comforter is still pressed against my breasts. "Are you in trouble?"

"Nah." He doesn't look the least bit concerned as he collapses against the pillows. "It's all good."

My attention becomes snagged by his body. Skimming over perfect pectorals and six-pack abdominals to the muscular V and then lower to his—

"You keep looking at me like that, and you'll wind up flat on your back again."

I gasp. The arrogant smirk is back in full force.

He rolls toward me until his lips can ghost over mine. "And I would love nothing better than to bury myself in you again, but that's probably not a good idea." His hand drifts under the covers until he can cup my heat. He squeezes his fingers, and a trill of pleasure reverberates through my core. "I'm sure you're sore." There's a pause, and I realize this moment will go one of two ways. "Right?"

"Yes," I answer truthfully.

"That's what I thought." He releases me and rolls off the bed before sauntering to the bathroom.

I watch him, unable to stop myself from checking out his ass.

Lord in heaven, he is gorgeous.

As Beck crosses the threshold, he throws a glance over his shoulder. "I like the way you look naked in my bed, all flushed from sex. I could get used to it."

Thankfully, he doesn't wait for a response. Other than a pounding heart and the bubble of pleasure growing inside me, I don't have one.

And that's dangerous.

Beck is dangerous.

Now that he's no longer affecting my hormones, doubt and cynicism creep in at the edges. I'm reluctant to throw caution to the wind and believe this is anything more than sex.

Good sex.

Great sex, even.

But sex, nonetheless.

With him in the bathroom and all these heavy thoughts crashing down on me, I toss back the comforter and grab his T-shirt from the floor before slipping it over my head and down my body. I search for my thong before yanking it in place. Now that I'm clothed, I feel more in control of myself and the situation.

A few minutes later, Beck strolls out of the bathroom.

Naked.

He closes the distance between us until one hand can slide into my hair. Gently, he pulls my face closer before pressing his lips to mine.

"Thank you," he whispers against my mouth.

"For what?"

"For giving me your virginity."

Heat fills my cheeks as I glance away.

"Hey."

Reluctantly, I meet his gaze.

"It meant a lot to me." He pauses, his voice dropping. "You know this is more than sex, right?"

I shrug.

Is it?

His mouth seeks out mine again. When his tongue sweeps across the seam of my lips, I open, and he deepens the kiss. It's like being dragged to the bottom of the ocean. I lose all sense of time and space.

I'm unsure where I begin, and he ends. Beck overwhelms me in every possible way. When he pulls away, I'm dazed and more confused than ever. His breath feathers against my lips, and I want to stand here and breathe him in forever.

"Mmm," he growls, "your mouth is so fucking sweet." He presses another kiss against my swollen lips. "Just like the rest of you."

A whimper escapes from me. All the doubts crowding inside my head disappear with his nearness.

"Goddamn, I want to be inside you again." He nips my lower lip playfully. "But we can't."

My breath hitches as he turns his back on me and walks to the dresser on the other side of the room. His muscles shift with every step. It's mesmerizing. Everything about him is hard and chiseled. I know he spends a lot of time in the gym. I've heard my parents talk about his dedication to the sport and how much money his parents spend on private coaching and agility trainers.

"I need to clean up before my parents get home, or my dad will have my ass," he says.

It takes effort to blink out of the mental fog that has settled over me and focus on his words. Sheesh. I have sex one time, and now my brain is a pile of mush?

Keep it together, girl.

"I should probably get dressed." With that, I hightail it to the bathroom. I need a moment to collect myself. Maybe more than one.

Once shuttered inside the room, I lean against the door and squeeze my eyes tightly closed. Every part of me feels like it's vibrating. When my heartbeat settles, I open my eyes and search for my clothes. I find my bra, tank, and skirt neatly folded on the counter. Unlike my bathroom at home, his is devoid of tubes and bottles of products cluttering the space.

I don't remember folding up my clothing. If memory serves, I left them in a heap on the floor. The thought of Beck picking up my garments and taking the time to straighten them before setting the pile on the counter sends a shiver scampering down my spine. Why would he bother? Unwilling to linger on those thoughts, I yank Beck's comfy T-shirt off and replace it with my bra and shimmery gold tank. Then I tug the skirt up my thighs.

I glance at the mirror, assessing the damage. The reflection that greets me is just as I suspected.

Total mess. I look like I've been put through the wringer. Even though I know it won't do any good, I rake my fingers through my hair, attempting to smooth it down. After a moment, I give up.

When I leave the bathroom, Beck is dressed in khaki shorts and a black Ramones T-shirt. My pulse skitters as I take him in. I need to pull myself together and stop making such a big deal out of what occurred. People hookup all the time. I don't want to read too much into the situation.

His attention shifts to me. "What are you thinking?"

Unwilling to share my innermost thoughts, I shake my head. "Nothing."

"That's doubtful." With three long-legged strides, he swallows up the distance between us. "If I know anything about you, it's that your brain is always working."

He's right, but I'm still not sharing anything with him.

When I remain silent, he reaches out and strokes the side of my face. I'm tempted to lean into his touch, but I stop myself at the last moment. The attraction surging through me is so much more than what it once was. It's like the floodgates have been opened, and there's no closing them.

"You didn't answer the question," he comments.

And I'm not going to. Somehow, he's already burrowed his way inside my head. I need a bit of distance to wrangle these feelings back under control where they belong.

"All right, I see how it is." He flicks the tip of my nose with his finger. "Ready to head downstairs and check out the damage?"

Relief floods through me when he changes the subject instead of pressing for more. "Yeah."

The amount of regret and loss that flickers through me when he steps away is disconcerting. I've always suspected it would be like this with Beck. It's the reason I've given him a wide berth.

With his back turned to me, I press my hand against my lower abdomen as if that alone will still the butterflies that have winged their way to life inside me. Then I follow him out of the bedroom and into the long stretch of hallway.

Professional family photographs dating back to when Beck and his older brother, Ari, were toddlers dot the light gray walls. By the time we reach the curving staircase, I have a handle on myself. I pause and survey the spacious entryway and a slice of the living room.

My brows rise as I take in the party's aftermath.

Oh, boy.

"You coming?"

I blink and realize Beck is waiting at the bottom of the staircase.

"Yeah," I mutter, racing down to join him.

The foyer of the Hollingsworth mansion is elegant and stately. There is a sea of black-and-white checkered marble tile and a chandelier suspended from the ceiling that probably costs as much as a high-end car. White Doric columns break up the space between the foyer and the living room.

What seems out of place are the beer bottles and red cups crowded on the antique credenza. One cup has been tipped over. The wood where the liquid has settled is discolored and cloudy. Caroline will flip out when she discovers the damage. Every piece of furniture in this house has been carefully curated by European craftsmen.

I inspect the living room and find the mess to be just as extensive. More beer bottles and red cups litter the coffee table and floor. A wadded-up shirt, a pair of flip-flops, and a bra have been abandoned by their owners. Couch cushions are strewn about. What the hell were people doing? Building a pillow fort?

I shake my head and blow out a breath.

"Huh," Beck murmurs, rubbing his shadowed jaw, "I thought the damage would be worse."

"Really?" I glance at him. "This seems pretty bad. It will take hours to clean up."

"This is nothing," he replies dismissively.

The idea of allowing a bunch of random people from school to destroy my parent's house is unfathomable.

"Should we check out the kitchen?" he asks, interrupting those thoughts.

"Do we have a choice in the matter?"

"Nope. It's like pulling off a Band-Aid. We need to do it quickly so it's not as painful."

I groan as we step into the two-story kitchen. I've been here enough times to know that under normal circumstances, this place is spotless. It's so clean you could eat off the floor. That's no longer the case. In fact, I'd rather vomit in my mouth than eat anything off the floor.

If I'd thought the living room was trashed, this is ten times worse. Even Beck, who is usually unflappable, skids to a halt.

"Well, shit." His hand goes to the back of his neck as he surveys the damage.

"My thoughts exactly," I say with a snort.

Bottles of booze, bags of chips, empty pizza boxes, plates of half-eaten food are strewn about the room and take up every bit of counter space. Even the long expanse of island is covered with debris.

"What time are the parentals arriving home?" I ask.

He slides his hand through his hair, mussing it more than it already is. "A couple of hours."

"Alrighty then." I clap my hands together. "We better get to work." I have no idea if we'll be able to get this place cleaned up in time, but anything is better than them walking into this shitshow. We haven't even assessed the damage outside.

When Beck fails to respond, I turn to him. "Where are the garbage bags?"

"I appreciate your offer to help, but you don't have to. You're not the one who made the mess, you shouldn't have to clean it up." His lips quirk into a smile. "Don't stress. I'll take care of it."

It's a tempting offer. The idea of going home and crawling into bed for a couple of hours is enticing.

But…if I leave Beck to his own devices, there's no way he'll get done in time.

"It's fine," I murmur, mentally committing myself to three or four hours of cleanup, "I'll stay and help."

Emotion flickers in his eyes. "Are you sure you feel all right?"

Heat slams into my cheeks. Every shift of my thighs reminds me of what we were doing thirty minutes ago. "I'm fine."

He jerks his head into a nod. "Okay, thanks."

Breaking eye contact, I glance around. "I guess we should get started."

"Whatever you say, boss." Beck heads to the pantry and grabs a box of garbage bags and gloves. Without a word between us, I slip the latex over my hands and take a couple of white bags with me to the living room. Beck handles the kitchen as I tackle the other spaces. After all the bottles and random items have been disposed of, I make a sweep of the first floor. At least one good decision on his part was to lock the matching offices.

By the time I've finished straightening up, I've filled three garbage bags with remnants from the party. I've found everything from underwear to baseball caps. Satisfied with the cleanup, I return to the kitchen and find that Beck has cleared all the surfaces and has loaded the dishwasher. I grab the vacuum and run it through the first floor as Beck sweeps the hardwoods in the kitchen.

When I glance at the clock on the microwave, I'm surprised to find that almost two hours have slipped by. I survey the kitchen and two-story family room with a critical eye. "It looks pretty good in here."

Beck leans against the broom. "Teamwork makes the dream work."

"It's entirely possible your parents won't realize you invited the entire senior class over last night."

"They'll know. I'm sure Dad has already watched the security footage."

"Oh." I shoot him a frown. "Why would you have a party if you knew you'd get caught?" That makes no sense.

His lips lift into a lazy grin. "Mostly because I don't give a shit."

And there you have it. Beck's motto in life.

When I remain silent, he adds, "I'll get in trouble regardless, so might as well do exactly what I want and have a good time doing it."

That's one of the many differences between us. The idea of doing something I would get in trouble for is a foreign concept.

"I don't get you," I say.

Not the least bit offended, a slow grin spreads across his face. "It's not possible for you to make a move without carefully weighing all the consequences, is it?"

"It's called being responsible. Why are you trying to make it sound so bad?"

"Because spontaneity can be a beautiful thing." His eyes ignite with heat. "Don't you think so?"

An answering desire kindles to life inside me. "There's a difference between impulsiveness and spontaneity."

"True." He steps closer.

My breath catches when he reaches out and twirls a lock of hair around his index finger before staring at the dark strands as if fascinated by them.

"Don't you ever get tired of being so damn good?" He pauses. "Aren't you ever tempted to break out of the little box your parents have put me in?"

Nerves scuttle through me, and goose flesh rises in its wake. "No one has put me in a box. They give me the freedom to do what I want. Unlike you, I make better choices."

"You don't think I make good decisions?" His fingers continue to grip my hair as he invades my personal space.

"Look around you," I whisper, wanting to break the sexual tension building between us. "The answer is evident."

"Hmmm, you might be right." His lips lift into a wry grin before twisting with a hint of bitterness. "You've been branded the good girl, and I'll always be the bad boy. Right, Mia?"

The question arrows painfully to the heart of me. I'm not *good*, and he's not *bad*. We're just different. Both of our families have money, and we have all the trappings of wealth at our disposal, but our viewpoints and experiences are vastly unique.

Before I can collect my scattered thoughts and summon a response, a loud noise breaks the silence. Air rushes from my lungs as Beck releases my hair and peers through the French doors.

The moment his gaze flickers away, relief rushes through me, and my knees weaken. I glance at the large inflatable swan floating in the middle of the pool. A soft breeze pushes it lazily across the water. I squint and realize that a guy is sprawled on top of it. Arms and legs dangle over the rounded edges. His mouth hangs open as a snore rents the air again. He makes a few grumbling noises as he turns onto his side. The float wobbles, sending ripples throughout the calm water.

I glance at Beck. He shakes his head as if this is beyond even him. We step through the door and walk to the edge of the pool. Placing his thumb and forefinger together, he brings them to his lips. I flinch when the sharp whistle pierces the silence.

When that does nothing to rouse the jackass floating in the pool, Beck yells, "Hey! Wake the fuck up, man!"

There's not even a twitch from the guy. His total unconsciousness is almost impressive.

Beck grumbles under his breath before stalking to the pool house. He grabs a long metal pole with a net attached to the end and brings it to the edge of the water before jabbing the float.

"Time to rise and shine," he mutters.

It takes another five minutes and a handful of none-too-gentle blows for the guy to rouse from his Sleeping Beauty-like slumber. With his hair sticking up in all directions, he gradually pulls himself to an upright position before rubbing his face and staring at us with eyelids at half-mast.

He plows a hand through his mussed hair and yawns. "Hey, what's up?"

Beck hikes a brow. "It's eleven o'clock in the morning. Party's over."

The guy blinks and glances around as if only now noticing his surroundings. "Ummm...how did I get here?"

Beck shrugs. "Your guess is as good as mine."

"Sorry about that, man. Must have passed out." He scratches his head and glances at the float. "In the pool."

"No problem," Beck mutters before extending the net and towing the guy to the tiled edge.

Once he's been assisted from the blow-up swan, he takes off around the side of the house and disappears from sight.

I shift my weight and stare after him. "Any idea who that was?"

"Nope." With one side of his mouth lifted, Beck shakes his head. "Never seen him before."

We both chuckle before looking around us. The patio is more trashed than inside the house. Beer cans and red plastic cups litter the cement surrounding the pool. One of the loungers is flipped on its side. Cushions and clothes are scattered around the yard. It's enough to make me wonder what people left the party wearing because it wasn't T-shirts and shorts.

Or shoes.

How do you leave without shoes?

It's a mystery.

I shake my head and huff out a sigh of resignation. "This is only a suggestion, but maybe you should consider dialing down the parties from now on."

"I'll take it under advisement."

Beck uses the net to scoop up a couple of beer cans that bob in the water, and I pick up the cups and trash littering the cement and lawn. He runs the pool vacuum and adds a few chemicals to the water. Four trash bags later, and the backyard looks as good as the inside of the house.

I survey the area. "It appears we've accomplished the impossible."

"Yup, looks pretty damn good." He glances at me, and surprisingly, there's no smirk in sight. "Thanks for all your help. I couldn't have done it without you."

"Consider it my good deed for the year. Although, next time, you're on your own."

"Noted." The word is barely out of his mouth before he's yanking off his T-shirt and tossing it to a chaise lounge. "Interested in a quick dip?"

I glance from him to the freshly cleaned pool as the crystal-clear water sparkles in the bright sunlight. It's not even noon, and already it's eighty-five degrees. It's shaping up to be a gorgeous day. A swim in the pool after three hours of cleaning would feel oh-so-good.

But after everything that's transpired between us, is it necessarily a good idea?

Probably not.

I told myself I'd help Beck clean up and then go home where I can clear my thoughts and get a little perspective. Spending all this time alone with him is making me want things that aren't in my best interest.

Sensing the refusal perched on the tip of my tongue, Beck tilts his head before cajoling, "Come on, Stanbury. We've spent the last couple of hours cleaning, and our parents won't be home for at least another hour." He pauses before adding, "You might not realize this, but you don't have to be perfect all the time."

"I'm not trying to be," I mutter. It's difficult to admit, even to myself, but he wasn't wrong earlier when he claimed I'd been put in a little box. Except my parents aren't the ones who put me there. I did. I haven't been able to figure out another way to hold my family together. I'm afraid that if I cause trouble or make waves, it'll be the straw that breaks the camel's back, and we'll splinter even further apart. I can't allow that to happen.

"Are you sure about that?" With the sun beating down on Beck's bare chest, he looks like a god. "You're so fucking perfect that it's difficult to stomach."

His words are like a slap in my face.

I am not perfect. I'm just not careless in the decisions I make. My goal in life isn't to cause as much havoc as I can. Since when is that a crime?

When I remain locked in place, he drags his khakis down until the material is puddled at his feet. Grey boxer-briefs cling to his lean hips and thighs. Years of working out and playing football have honed his body into a work of art.

"Sometimes all I want to do is mess you up. Even if it's for a moment."

His words knock the air from my lungs, making it impossible to breathe.

A wicked grin dances across his face before he dives into the water. I track his movements as he arrows through the clear liquid, surfacing about twenty-feet from the edge of the pool. When he whips his dark hair away from his face, droplets of water scatter around him in the bright sunlight.

Staring at him makes my heart hurt.

"What's it going to be?" He treads water in the deep end near the diving board. "The water feels amazing. Don't you want to find out for yourself?"

What I should do is go home, but my feet are frozen in place.

Fooling around with Beck is stupid. And if there's one thing I don't do, it's stupid. My moment of weakness from earlier this morning is messing with my head.

Go home, my brain instructs.

I'm startled out of those thoughts when beads of water land on my bare arms and dot the gold tank I'm wearing.

Beck grins. "Come on, Stanbury. Get your ass in the water."

Before I realize what I'm doing, the top is over my head, and I'm standing in front of Beck in my bra. Heat leaps into his eyes, and my belly trembles in response. I slide the denim skirt over my hips and down my thighs. Once it lays crumpled at my feet, I step out of it and force myself to walk toward the water.

What I'm doing is so unlike me, and I can't help but feel that I'm digging a deeper hole to crawl out of. Even though I know spending more time with Beck is a bad idea, that's exactly what I want to do.

Once I reach the edge, my toes curl around the azure-colored ceramic tiles before I dive into the water. Beck is right, the pool is refreshing. The coolness slides over my heated flesh as I glide through the liquid before surfacing. I wipe the water from my face and glance around, but Beck isn't where I last saw him. I startle when hands wrap around my waist from behind and yank me backward.

"You're so fucking sexy that it kills me to look at you," he growls against my ear.

A thousand shivers scamper down my spine.

Before I can summon a response, he hoists me from the water and tosses me through the air as if I weigh nothing at all. A scream rises in my throat as I slip beneath the surface. When my toes touch the bottom, I bend my knees and push off against the tiles, fleeing in the opposite direction. I don't get far before Beck grabs me, tugging me into his arms again.

I hate to admit how much I enjoy being with him.

Don't get used to it.

For the next thirty minutes, we goof around. Every time Beck gets his hands on me, he tosses me in the air. As soon as he lets go, I slide beneath the water and try to escape. It never takes long for him to catch me again. Our hands stroke over slippery wet skin as we kiss before breaking apart and doing it all over again. There's only so much I can take before my breathing becomes labored. Even though I'm in good shape from a decade of competitive tennis, I'm exhausted. We've raced from one end of the pool to the other countless times. We can't keep our hands off each other, and I don't even want to try. For the first time in my life, I don't stop to weigh the pros and cons. I go with it.

After a while, we grab a yellow inflatable raft big enough for the both of us before hoisting ourselves on top of it. The raft wobbles as we collapse in a heap and allow the hot sun to bake our wet flesh. The sides of our bodies press together, arms and legs touching as the water lulls us into a contented state of being.

Electricity zips through me as Beck's fingers tangle with my own.

This shouldn't feel nearly as good as it does.

If I were thinking clearly, I'd hightail it home. I'd forget all about the feelings Beck rouses inside me and put some much-needed distance between us. But I'm reluctant to do that. I like the way my hand fits in his larger one and the way his body feels pressed against mine. There's a rightness that shouldn't be there, and I'm loath to do anything that will bring reality crashing down on our heads.

My breathing evens out as my body melts into the warm plastic of the raft. After a string of quiet moments, Beck rolls toward me. The float trembles with his movements. He props himself up with an elbow, and warmth fills me as his gaze rakes over my nearly naked body.

The heat of his stare lingers on my breasts, which spill from the cups of my bra. I glance down and realize that the pale pink material has turned sheer.

He leans over and captures one tightened peak between his lips. The moment he touches me, my breath becomes clogged in my throat. A moan slides from my lips as my fingers tangle in his damp hair, drawing him closer. Once he releases the stiff little peak, he pulls the material aside until my nipple is exposed. Then his lips are back, sucking the bud deep into his mouth. It's as if there is an invisible string connecting my breast to my core. Every tug of his lips sends shock waves of pleasure reverberating through me.

He scoots closer, giving the same attention to my other breast. Except this time, he pulls the material down before drawing the tightened bud into his mouth. Sensation ricochets through my body until it reaches my toes. My eyes feather shut as I arch my back, needing to close the distance between us.

His fingers caress the valley between my breasts before sliding lower to my navel. He circles the indentation a few times before one hand slips beneath the elastic band of my thong. Back and forth, his fingers arc from one hip bone to the other. My body trembles beneath his touch. Every movement drives my senses into delirium and scatters my thoughts.

"You're so fucking beautiful, Mia."

It's almost a relief when his fingers drift lower until they're able to trace the seam of my lips. An ache builds in my core and I widen my legs, wanting to give him more access. Not once do his fingers dip inside my body. They circle around my entrance, gliding over the soaked flesh before sliding upward to circle my pulsing clit. The moment he touches that throbbing bundle of nerves, a moan escapes.

His mouth fastens onto mine. I open so our tongues can tangle as his fingers feather over my flesh, forcing me to the brink. When I can't stand another moment of this sweet torture, he lifts his face from mine and presses his thumb on my clit, sending a surge of shivers through my body. His fingers continue to move until every bit of pleasure has been wrung from me, and I'm nothing more than an exhausted heap on the raft.

I crack my eyes open when Beck slips his hand free from my thong before lifting his fingers to his mouth and sucking them clean.

"So damn delicious," he murmurs, watching me the entire time.

He leans closer and captures my lips. The taste of my arousal explodes on my tongue, sending yet another ripple of pleasure through me.

Who knew something like that could be such a turn-on?

He pulls away enough to say, "Maybe I should have led with this earlier, but I'd like to take you out."

"Out?" I echo dumbly as if unable to string those words together to figure out the meaning. "Like on a date?"

Amusement dances in his eyes as his lips bow into a smile. "Exactly like a date."

My brain is telling me to walk away, but my heart is leaping for joy. I tamp down my excitement before it can become infectious.

The higher you fly, the harder you fall, I remind myself.

"You don't have to do this," I force myself to say.

The humor filling his face turns serious. "I know, but I want to."

Walk away and don't look back, girl.

You know it's the smart thing to do.

Beck Hollingsworth isn't someone you can depend on. He's proven that time and time again. He'll flake, and I'll be left holding the bag in my hands.

He lowers his face until everything around me is blotted out, and he's all I can focus on. His warm breath drifts over my lips. "Let me take you out and prove I'm serious about this. *About us.*"

Every ounce of good sense flees. "Okay."

"Good." His mouth brushes over my top lip before doing the same to my bottom. Then he sucks my lower lip into his mouth before giving it a gentle tug with his teeth and releasing it with a pop. Need bursts to life in my core. Apparently, it doesn't matter if I just came. I want him all over again.

He pulls away enough to say, "Open."

I do as he instructs, and his tongue delves inside my mouth to tangle with my own. One hand slips around my head to cradle my skull with his palm. The kiss unfolds lazily until I lose all sense of time. The only thing I'm aware of is the feel of Beck's lips coasting over mine, drawing me deeper into this caress until I'm drugged with the taste of him.

From the far recesses of my brain, a noise penetrates the thick fog that cocoons me. It's only when Beck jerks away that reality crashes down upon my head. He swears harshly under his breath as I try to find my bearings.

"It might be a good idea if your friend took off, don't you think?"

Oh, God.

Archibald.

And this time, it's not the ringer on Beck's phone.

Heat scalds my cheeks as I realize that he just witnessed me making out with his son. In my underwear. The humiliation is almost enough to swallow me whole. Why haven't I burst into flames yet? That would be preferable to brazening out this situation.

Beck rolls off the raft and into the water, leaving me exposed and vulnerable. Even though the sun strokes over my warmed flesh, a chill slithers down my spine. I sit up and band my arms around my knees to cover as much of my body as possible.

"Don't move," Beck mutters, "until I get your shirt."

"Okay." I stare at my folded legs until Archibald's loafers come into view.

"Mia?" Shock reverberates throughout Archie's voice. *"Is that you?"*

Please kill me now before this situation becomes any more excruciating.

I wince, unable to meet his eyes before lifting my hand and giving him a half-hearted wave. "Hi, Mr. Hollingsworth." Barely can I squeak out the greeting.

Beck's father stuffs his hands into the pockets of his khakis and rocks back on his heels as his narrowed gaze bounces between us. "What are you doing here?"

"We were swimming." *Amongst other things.* Even though I don't tack that on, I have the feeling he knows *exactly* what we were up to.

"I wasn't aware you two were friends." His voice becomes stilted. "I'd assumed you traveled in different circles."

"We've always been friends," Beck shoots back, glancing at me with a slight frown. "Right?"

Yesterday the answer would have been an unequivocal *no*, but I can't bring myself to say that. "Yes."

"Hmmm." Archibald's lips bow into a frown. The heaviness of his gaze is enough to make me squirm.

Once we reach the edge of the pool, Beck hauls himself out. It would be impossible not to notice the way his muscles flex and bunch as water rolls off his sun-kissed flesh. He grabs my tank from the cement and tosses it to me. I snatch it from the air and thrust my arms through the thin straps before yanking the flimsy material over my body. It doesn't cover much, but it shields my bra and thong from sight.

Sort of.

As soon as I'm covered, Beck extends his hand for me to grab hold of before hoisting me from the raft. The moment my feet touch the concrete, he releases me. I stumble before finding my balance.

I peek at Archibald and tug the back of my tank, so it covers more of my ass.

A thunderous expression settles on Archie's face as he bites out, "I'm going inside." His attention shifts to his son. "See me in the office after Mia leaves."

Beck jerks his head into a tight nod. Once his father disappears through the French doors, I force the air from my lungs, not realizing it had become trapped.

"I would seriously like to die right now," I whisper, afraid of being overheard.

"Yeah, sorry about that." He shoves a hand through his hair. "I thought we had more time."

Nausea stirs in the pit of my belly as I consider how mortifying it would have been if Beck's parents had arrived home ten minutes earlier. Archibald and Caroline are like family. How could I ever look either of them in the eyes if they saw me getting off?

Unsure where to go from here, I search Beck's expression for clues as to what he's thinking. All the lightheartedness has been sucked from the atmosphere. There's a pervasive feeling of tension that has settled over us like a heavy blanket.

Beck scoops up my skirt and tosses it to me. "You should probably head out."

He's right, but I'm reluctant to leave. If I walk away, this will end up being nothing more than a dream. And I'm scared of that happening.

"Okay." I yank the skirt up my thighs and over my hips until it settles at my waist.

Awkwardness descends. There is so much I want to say, but I have no idea how to express my thoughts. Instead of taking that leap and putting myself out there, I turn away. With every step, doubt and fear rain down on me.

"Mia?"

I swing around, unsure what I'll find.

"I meant what I said about wanting to take you out."

A burst of giddiness chases away the misgivings that creep in at the edges.

Uncertainty flickers in his eyes. "You want that too, right?"

"I do." More than I'm willing to admit because as much as I want to believe in Beck, I need him to prove me wrong.

"Talk soon?"

"Yeah."

A hint of a smile curves his lips and touches his eyes, softening the hardness filling them.

When he remains silent, I raise my hand in a wave and return home. My head spins as I relive everything that has transpired in the last twelve hours.

I'm no longer a virgin.

Beck and I are going on a date.

Alyssa will shit her pants when I tell her what happened.

It's enough to bring a gurgle of laughter to my lips.

BECK

Once Mia disappears from sight, everything inside me uncoils. Reluctantly, I glance toward the house, well aware I'm about to get my ass chewed out for the impromptu party. Although I can't bring myself to regret it. If I hadn't thrown the bash, I wouldn't have hooked up with Mia.

Fuck, I shouldn't even call it that. What happened between us is way more than a fuck and flee situation. I've had plenty of those in the past, and they've never meant a damn thing.

This feels nothing like that.

It blows me away that she allowed me to take her virginity. Even the thought of being buried deep inside her body is enough to have my cock rising to attention. Instead of giving in to the urge to follow Mia, I yank on my khakis and T-shirt.

Guess it's time to face the firing squad. Best to get it over with and move on with my day.

Silence greets me as I walk through the first floor. This place is monstrous. I have no idea why we need all this space except that Dad likes to showcase our wealth since it's a direct translation to his professional accomplishments. Over the last twenty years, he's built a successful law practice from the ground up. Now he has four partners and fifty associates. His plan is to expand and open a couple of practices in major cities across the United States.

That's where my brother comes in.

Archibald the second—or Ari as everyone calls him—will be starting his senior year of college at Wesley. If everything goes according to plan, he'll attend Stanford Law School like the old man. Ari has a four-point GPA and scored a one-seventy on the LSAT, so getting accepted shouldn't be a problem. He's one smart motherfucker. My parents couldn't be prouder.

Me, on the other hand?

Not so much.

I know Dad had hoped I would follow in his illustrious footsteps, but that's not going to happen. Unlike my older brother, I had a tougher time in school. Concentration has never been my friend. It's not that the work was too hard, just boring. My mind wanders. I get antsy. When I was in elementary school, I'd stare out the window while the teacher droned on. All I could focus on was getting outside and throwing the football around with my friends. I lived for recess.

It wasn't until second grade, after a shit-ton of calls and notes from the teacher and principal, that I was taken to a psychologist, tested, diagnosed with ADHD, and promptly put on medication. It helped to settle my ass down, but school has always been torture. I force myself to do it since it's the only way I'll make it to the NFL.

It's no secret that my father is disappointed in how I've turned out and the issues I struggle with. Has he come out and said it?

No, but there have been enough sly comments and little digs over the years to let me know how he truly feels. Maybe he thinks I'm an idiot, too stupid to pick up on what he's laying down. Just because I have trouble focusing, doesn't mean I'm a dipshit.

My father prizes intelligence over athletic ability. He might boast to anyone who will listen that his son is a talented enough football player to be scouted by the pros, but that's still second best in his book.

Ari is the heir, and I'm the spare.

I didn't ask to have ADHD. It's been a pain in my ass, but I deal with it the best I can.

What other choice is there?

The medication helps, but it's not a cure-all. Football is the only thing that holds my attention. When I have that ball in my hand, and I'm searching the field for an open receiver, my mind slows down, and I'm able to think clearly. Or maybe it speeds up, and I can see all the possibilities. It only takes a split second to process my surroundings. My brain cuts through all the guys, and I find a receiver who can complete a pass and take it down the field, eating up the yards with his cleats.

God, but I fucking love it.

It's my reason for living.

The only other thing that's come close to holding my attention is Mia. Up until this point, she's kept me at a firm distance. I don't blame her for it. Mia is gorgeous, smart, athletic, and focused on her future. She wants to be a lawyer.

We're complete opposites in every way.

I'll never be good enough for that girl.

As soon as that thought creeps into my head, I push it away.

For whatever reason, the stars have aligned, and I have the two things I want most in this world. Football and Mia. I don't want anything to fuck it up.

The moment I cross over the threshold into Dad's office, he glances from the computer screen and points to the leather armchair parked in front of his antique mahogany desk. I slip onto the chair and wait for him to read me the riot act.

Should I have invited so many people over last night?

Probably not.

My bad. Won't happen again.

When I open my mouth to apologize, he cuts me off.

"What the hell was Mia doing here?"

I raise my brows, thrown off by the question.

This is what he wants to talk about?

"We were swimming." When he glares, I shift on my seat and tack on, "It's hot out."

He snorts in disbelief. "What I walked in on was more than," he uses his fingers to make air quotes, "*swimming*." There's a pause. "*She was practically naked.*"

"She was wearing her bra and underwear," I mumble, embarrassed to be discussing the situation with my father. "She didn't bother to go home and change. Don't make a big deal out of it."

My parents have never questioned my relationships. Dad has even slapped my back a time or two and told me to make sure I wrap it up tight. The last thing I need is to get some chick pregnant at this stage of the game. And he's right.

This fall, I'll be attending Wesley. As long as I can prove myself in training camp this summer, the starting quarterback position is mine for the taking. That's unheard of for a freshman, and I damn well know it. What I need to do is work my ass off so these guys can see I'm the key to a winning season.

I've tried to convince the old man that entering the draft after my sophomore year would be better, but he's not having it. The deal is that I wait until my senior year and earn my diploma. As long as I don't get injured, there's no reason everything shouldn't pan out the way it's supposed to. The plan is to major in communications so I can lay the foundation for a broadcasting career at ESPN after I retire. Without playing ball, that communications degree won't be worth the paper it's printed on. Dad likes to remind me of that every chance he gets.

"What was she doing here in the first place?" he growls, drawing my attention back to the conversation.

"Helping me clean up after the party last night." Hell, I would much rather discuss *that* situation. Even thinking about what he walked in on has the tips of my ears burning. If it had been any other girl, I wouldn't have given a shit. I would have patted her on the ass and sent her on her merry way. But I can't do that with Mia. I should have been more careful.

"It better not be anything more than that," he snaps, shaking his head.

I straighten on the chair. There's something about his tone that rubs me the wrong way. "Why does it matter so much?"

"You know why it matters." His booming voice echoes off the wood-paneled walls before he strains forward, resting his forearms on the polished wood. "I don't want you fucking around with that girl."

"We weren't *fucking* around."

"It sure as hell looked like you were." He stabs a finger at me. "Whatever plans you might have hatched in that brain of yours, get them out right now!"

What the hell?

Are we seriously having this conversation?

"I don't understand what the problem is."

Dad leans back on his chair and stares at the ceiling before muttering under his breath, "Do I really need to spell everything out for you?"

His words feel like a backhanded smack. My jaw locks as heat floods my cheeks. "Yeah, it would be helpful if you did."

With an exasperated sigh, he glowers at me like I'm ten kinds of stupid. It only serves to piss me off more. "Mia's a nice girl. *A good girl.* The last thing I need is for you to mess with her head and hurt her."

"Why would I do that?" A pit the size of Rhode Island settles at the bottom of my gut.

A knowing smile tilts the corners of his lips. "Come on, Beck," his voice trails off as he shrugs. "You're not the most focused guy in the world. Especially where the ladies are concerned. You've spent the last couple of years screwing your way through this town, and other than me telling you to be careful, I haven't said a damn word about it."

"Mia is different," I say through stiff lips.

"Of course, she is." There's a pause. "Which is exactly why she's not for you."

Even though I shouldn't be surprised by the comment, I am. This entire conversation has blown me away.

"And why is that?" I grit between clenched teeth, forcing him to admit the truth.

The silence between us stretches until it becomes almost painful.

"Mia deserves a guy who has his head on straight, and that's not you. She needs someone like your brother." He waves a hand airily as if he hasn't just crushed my spirit. "Someone solid."

So...now I'm not solid?

My ADHD makes me a wild card? Someone unworthy?

His comments stun me into silence. For once in my life, I have no idea how to respond.

Dad must realize he's overstepped because he clears his throat and attempts to backtrack. "Look, Beckett, I love you. You know that, right?"

Laughter bubbles up in my throat.

Really?

After everything he said?

That's how we're going to wrap up this conversation?

With a—*hey, buddy...you're an idiot, but you're* our *idiot.*

My parents think I'm a fuckup who will never amount to diddly squat. And I sure as hell am not worthy of a girl like Mia.

"I'm grateful you have so much athletic talent, or I don't know what the hell you would do with your life."

Thank fuck I'm sitting for that backhanded compliment.

Unable to listen to another word of his bullshit, I pop to my feet. "Are we done here?" I stare at the space above his shoulder, not wanting to make eye contact.

Fuck that guy.

"Yeah, we're done," he sighs.

"Great." Five strides, and I'm at the door. I need to get out of here before I lose my shit.

"Beck..."

My step falters, and my shoulders stiffen, but I don't turn around. "Yeah?"

"Stay away from Mia. I don't need any problems with her parents. And that's exactly what I'll get if you go sniffing around her."

When I fail to respond, his voice sharpens. "Did you hear me?"

"Loud and clear."

And then I'm gone, disappearing through the hallway and taking the stairs two at a time before turning down the hall and slamming the door to my room. I need a joint so I can zone out and forget about the garbage my father just spewed.

For a day that started out so well, it sure turned to shit in the blink of an eye.

MIA

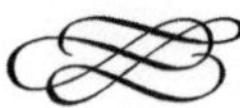

I swipe my phone from the nightstand beside the bed and read the last text from Alyssa. I fully expected her to announce that after all these years, she had her dirty little way with Colton, but that doesn't appear to be the case. Apparently, their little make-out session in the pool didn't go any further than that.

I haven't mentioned what happened with Beck. It feels too intimate to share through text message. For the time being, I want to keep the news to myself. It's been hours, and I'm still in a state of shock.

I'm no longer a virgin.

That seems crazy.

Alyssa will go off the deep end when I tell her.

As I'm replying to Alyssa's text, something pings against the bedroom window. I startle, and my head whips up. A shiver of unease slithers down my spine. I stare in that direction, ears pricked for the slightest noise, but there's nothing.

Thirty seconds later, and there's another plink against the glass.

Someone or something has to be out there.

I rise from the bed, and tiptoe my way across the carpeted floor before squinting into the darkness. When a ghostly face materializes out of nowhere, I scream at the top of my lungs and stumble back a few steps.

Large palms press against the glass as the face looms closer.

I slap a hand across my mouth as my heart threatens to explode from my chest.

What the ever-loving hell?

Slowly, the features take shape.

Wait a minute...

I rush toward the window, remove the screen, and unlatch the lock before shoving it open. *"Have you lost your freaking mind? What are you doing out there?"*

The last time Beck climbed the tree to my bedroom was the summer before sixth grade. Once middle school hit, we drifted apart. Everyone realized what a football phenom Beck was, and his popularity skyrocketed while mine stayed the same.

Not waiting for an invitation, Beck tumbles through the open window, landing on the other side before popping to his feet and slamming it shut behind him. My normally spacious room shrinks around his muscular form, making it feel tight and oppressive. As if there's barely room to breathe.

Is it strange that I was just thinking about him and now he's here?

If I'm being honest, Beck has consumed all of my thoughts today. Everything we did this morning has been playing through my head on a constant loop. Every shift of my body reminds me of the soreness between my thighs.

I've always been so good about shutting down thoughts of him.

But now?

Beck has taken up residence in my brain, and there's nothing I can do to evict him.

My gaze drops from his eyes to his lips. Arousal bursts like a firework in my core. It takes all of my self-control not to throw myself at him.

I've officially become a Beck Hollingsworth groupie.

I'm not sure how to feel about that.

"Mia," he whispers. His voice comes out sounding strangled, and it strums something deep inside.

Excitement pounds through my veins. It shouldn't surprise me that Beck is the only one capable of making me feel this way. Even when I tried to pretend the chemistry between us was a figment of my imagination, I knew the truth.

"Yeah?" My mouth turns cottony, and I'm barely able to push the word out.

"You need to stop looking at me like that."

"Like what?" Heat flames my cheeks because I know *exactly* what he's alluding to. But I can't seem to help it. I'm desperate to lay my hands on Beck. I want him inside me again, filling me to the brim.

He forces his gaze away before plowing a hand through his hair. His movements are full of agitation, and his face is set in grim lines. Only now does it occur to me that something is off with his behavior. This morning he was at ease and relaxed. That's not the case anymore. Even though we're only a few feet from one another, it feels as if there is a gaping chasm between us.

Unease dances down my spine as the excitement swirling around inside me is snuffed out. I shift my weight nervously. I want everything to feel like it did this morning, but I'm not sure how to get us back to that.

"Did you get in trouble for the party?" Maybe his parents grounded him. Archibald wasn't pleased to find us in the pool.

"No."

He shakes his head, and relief bursts inside me like an overinflated balloon. Before I realize it, the distance disappears, and I'm pushing my fingers through his dark hair. I marvel at how soft the strands are.

"What's wrong?" Cautiously I search his shuttered gaze for answers that don't seem forthcoming.

His teeth sink into his lower lip. "Nothing, but we need to talk."

Nothing good ever came from those words.

"About what?" My hands fall to my sides as if they're made of lead.

When he remains silent, I step away. It's impossible to think when we're standing so close. "What do we need to talk about?"

An uncomfortable silence stretches between us.

"Beck?" Nerves dance across my skin.

"We can't go out," he blurts.

His words are like rapid gunfire and feel just as painful.

"What?" My heart drops to the bottom of my toes.

"I'm sorry, Mia." He glances away. It's like he can't hold my stare for more than a few seconds. "As much as I want to take you out, I can't."

Disappointment blooms in my chest until I almost choke on it.

Why am I surprised?

Deep down, I knew this would happen. And still, I allowed myself to be swept away by his bullshit. I straighten to my full height and cross my arms over my chest. Refusing to beg him for answers, I press my lips together until they feel numb.

"Mia? Are you all right?"

"I'm fine." That's a lie, but I'll be damned if I give him the satisfaction of knowing how much he hurt me.

Beck plows a hand through his hair. "We both have a lot going on. I leave for training camp next week, and after that, I won't be home much. I need to focus on football. I can't allow any outside distractions to get in the way. You understand, right?"

Did he just call me a distraction?

I blink back the wetness that stings my eyes, refusing to allow the tears to fall.

"There's no need to explain. I got it loud and clear. You used me, and I was stupid enough to fall for your lies." I press a shaking hand to my chest. "My bad. Won't happen again."

His eyes flare as he shakes his head. "No, it wasn't like that..."

Laughter explodes from my lips.

Who is he trying to kid?

I fell for his smooth talk—hook, line, and sinker. In all honesty, I deserve everything I got. Lesson learned the hard way.

"You can stop with the BS, Beck." My voice hardens.

When he reaches out, attempting to stroke the curve of my cheek, I bat his hand away and retreat, needing to put as much distance between us as possible.

"Mia, please," he whispers, "you have to know that I'm sorry. It's not what I want."

The sad thing is that I almost believe him.

That he's able to break my heart all the while trying to convince me how sorry he is only proves that I'm no better than all the foolish girls who trail after him. This is exactly why Beck Hollingsworth is dangerous to the female species. Even when he's cutting your heart out, you want more.

Not bothering to respond, I stab a finger toward the window. If he thinks I'll cry and beg him to reconsider, he has another thing coming. "Get out."

When he opens his mouth, looking like he might argue, I cut him off. *"I said get out!"*

Anguish flashes in his green eyes as his shoulders collapse, and he jerks his head into a nod. He wavers for a moment before retreating to the window. Silently, he pushes it open before turning back to me. "I'm sorry for letting everything get out of hand this morning. It's my fault for hurting you."

I snort.

Beck can take his apology and shove it up his ass.

A wave of nausea crashes over me. I've never felt so used or dirty. Even though I took a shower earlier this afternoon, the need to take another and scrub every memory of him from my skin pounds through me.

I'm an idiot for believing I was anything more than a one-night fuck. Or that Beck was mature enough to have a real relationship. All he did was prove that he's exactly what I suspected he was.

An asshole who will use and abuse you before throwing you away.

Guess the joke is on me for believing I was too smart to fall for his lines.

MIA

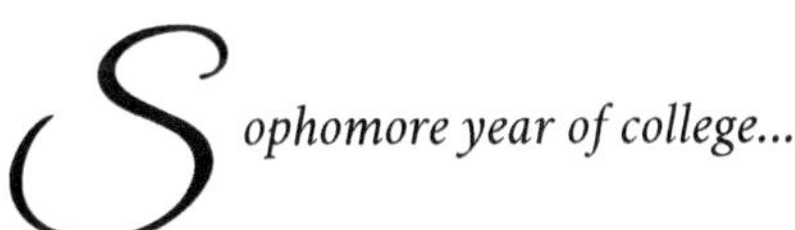

ophomore year of college...

ALYSSA GRABS my hand and drags me through the doors of the football house. For obvious reasons, it's the last place I want to be on a Saturday night. The Wesley Warriors crushed Tennessee this afternoon, and everyone is out celebrating.

"Can't we go somewhere else?" I yell, so she's able to hear me over the thumping beat of the music that reverberates off the walls. It's so loud that it feels like my brain is rattling against my skull. When she fails to respond, I add, "In case you haven't noticed, there are a ton of other parties."

We traipsed past a dozen of them to get here.

"No," she shouts, bursting my bubble. "I told Colton we would meet up at nine."

Yup, you heard that correctly.

Colton and Alyssa are officially a *thing*.

It's still relatively early in their relationship, so who knows if it will last.

Alyssa is thrilled.

And me?

Shocked speechless would be an adequate description.

But I have to give the girl props where they're deserved. She was bound and determined to bag her man, and against the odds, she made it happen.

As you can imagine, she's become something of a legend on campus, having attained the unattainable.

She's known as the Yoda of Wesley.

The jock whisperer.

Girls come from near and far to seek out her sage advice. It's amusing to watch her dole out her wisdom magnanimously like a queen.

I glance around, noticing that most of the students are football players or friends thereof. Making up half of the population are the jersey chasers. Those girls are prepared to cling to the first meaty bicep they can attach themselves to.

Without trying to be obvious, I search the surrounding vicinity for one face in particular. My muscles loosen when he remains elusive. Ever since we had sex after graduation, I've done my best to keep my distance from Beck.

The first couple of months on campus were nerve-wracking. Once I realized I wouldn't run into him around every corner, I could relax and have fun. Since our families always celebrate Thanksgiving and Christmas together, I was concerned we would finally come face-to-face, but he was conspicuously absent from the holiday parties. It's been more than a year without contact.

Other than to serve as a warning not to mess with athletes, I like to pretend it never happened. It's my dirty little secret to keep. I feel guilty about not telling Alyssa, but I don't need her pushing me toward Beck. And that's exactly what she would do. Especially now that she's with Colton.

That girl is always trying to drag me to the parties where her new boyfriend hangs out. And since Colton and Beck are roommates, I know there's a good chance Beck will be there. Until this point, I've been creative with my excuses.

Homework.

Volunteering at the tutor lab.

A meeting for the many clubs and associations I've joined on campus.

Headache.

You name it, it's in my arsenal of alibis.

Unfortunately, she wasn't buying any of them tonight. I even tried to convince her it was shark week, and she told me, in no uncertain terms, to pop a couple of Advil and woman up.

So here I am.

Thus far, Beck has been a no-show. I'm hoping my luck will hold, and it stays that way for the next couple of hours.

It takes effort and a fair amount of prodding to push our way into the kitchen where the makeshift bar is located. Every kind of conceivable booze is available, along with a few homemade varieties of moonshine.

Word to the wise—you have to be careful with those, they'll knock you flat on your ass. One-hundred-and-eighty proof Everclear is no joke.

We grab two cups of beer from the baby-face freshman football player who has been forced to man the keg before steamrolling our way through the backdoor. With so many bodies packed in the house, it's warm and stuffy.

Alyssa's head is on a constant swivel as she searches for her new beau. She's happier than I've seen her in a long time. I really hope, for her sake, everything works out with Colton. The last thing I want is for her to get hurt. He's never been one for labels or permanent situations. I'm not sure how she convinced him to pull the trigger.

"Maybe he's not here," I say hopefully.

The look she shoots me is chock-full of exasperation. "He has to be. It's his party."

Which means it's Beck's party, too.

When Alyssa grinds to a halt, I slam into her from behind. Barely do I avoid spilling my beer down the back of her shirt. I peer around her shoulder, trying to see what's going on. My gaze sweeps over the area until it lands on Alyssa's golden-haired boyfriend and the bevy of girls that surround him. There are at least six vying for his attention. I glance at my bestie to see how she's taking it. As much as Alyssa likes to pretend that she's secure in their relationship, she's not. And who can blame her?

"Why do they have to act so thirsty?" Her nose scrunches like she caught a whiff of something nasty. "It's embarrassing."

This is the downside to dating a football player—or any athlete on campus—there are always a ton of females trying to lay claim to what's yours. I have no desire to put up with that.

I lay my hand on Alyssa's arm before giving it a gentle squeeze. "You all right?"

"I'm fine." She rolls her shoulders in an attempt to lock down her jealousy before it rears its ugly head. Glancing at me, she hoists a fake smile. Alyssa would never mention it, but I know the constant groupie attention bothers her. "Colt would never cheat."

I can't tell if she's trying to convince herself of that or me. It's not like I want to be a hater, but I'll do what I have to in order to protect my friend.

"Lys—"

"Don't say it."

I press my lips together and remain silent.

What I will admit about the situation is that Colton has surprised me. I never expected him to settle down. And he's been good to her. That being said, I'll remain on high alert until he proves to me that he can be trusted with her heart. Colton has never been the poster boy for monogamy. More like the opposite.

"He's not the guy he used to be," she murmurs. "He's changed. If you spent more time with him, you would see that."

No, thank you.

When one girl reaches out and trails her fingers over the bulging muscles of Colton's arm, Alyssa clenches her teeth and pokers up like someone just rammed a two-by-four up her ass. "Looks like I need to put a few bitches in their place."

Before I can respond, she stomps away, cutting a path straight to the golden football god. She's like a heat-seeking missile. Let's hope she doesn't explode upon impact. It only takes a few minutes before those thirsty females are scattering in all directions.

A smile tilts my lips.

Alyssa is a force to be reckoned with.

Colton is damn lucky she didn't give up on him. I hope he recognizes that and acts accordingly.

And then there was one. Realizing that I've been left to my own devices, I tip my nearly full glass to my lips and take a swig. Then I pull out my phone from my pocket and fire off a quick text before stuffing it back where I found it. With a huff, I spin on my heels and promptly slam into a wall of muscle.

When I stumble back, strong fingers wrap around my upper arms to anchor me in place. I don't have to look up to realize who I've crashed into. The way his fingers burn my flesh is answer enough. A zip of adrenaline shoots through me when my gaze locks on familiar green eyes.

As soon as the attraction flares to life inside me, I stomp it out. You would think the way he dumped me after we had sex would be enough to kill any tender feelings I'd once held for him, but apparently, that's not the case.

"I didn't expect to see you here." There's a pause as he searches my eyes in the darkness. "It's been a while."

Fifteen months to be correct, but who's counting?

I step away so he has no choice but to release me from his hold before jerking my thumb over my shoulder. "Alyssa dragged me here to see Colton."

He glances toward the newly minted couple. "Yeah, they appear to be going strong. Good for them."

I almost snicker. *Really? Good for them?* Ha! "For the time being." I can't resist adding, "I'm sure it won't last."

"Wow," he murmurs, raising his hand to scratch his jaw, "that's harsh."

I shrug. I prefer to think of it as being more pragmatic than anything else.

"It's the truth."

Sadness settles over his features. "Mia, do you think we could go somewhere and—"

"Talk?" I lift the glass to my lips and drain the remainder. I need a moment to tamp down all the emotion trying to break free inside me. I'll be damned if I allow him to undo all my progress.

When I'm once again under control, I shake my head. "Sorry, that didn't work out so well last time. Let's do ourselves a favor and leave the past where it belongs. Sound good to you?"

"Yeah, sure." His broad shoulders collapse. "If that's what you want."

"It is."

An uncomfortable silence falls over us. When it turns unbearable, Beck clears his throat. "Are you still planning on going to law school?"

Is this what it's come to? Inane chitchat about our majors like a couple of strangers who met at a lame party? Someone needs to pull the plug on this conversation before it can jackhammer to a new level of painfulness.

"Yup, still pre-law."

"Ari just started at Stanford. He seems to like it."

"Yeah, I know. I spoke to him this summer about taking the LSAT. We've made plans to get together over Thanksgiving break. He's going to give me some pointers for taking the test. He also invited me to check out the campus since Stanford is on my shortlist."

Beck's eyes darken before scouring mine. "You're going to California to visit him?"

"To check out the law school," I correct. It has nothing to do with Ari and everything to do with Stanford. Ari is like the big brother I never had. We got close this summer when we interned at his father's law firm.

"That's great." His voice turns flat. "You guys are a perfect pair."

Huh?

"What does that mean?" I ask.

Wait a minute…does Beck think I'm interested in his brother?

Not that I owe him an explanation, but the words tumble out of my mouth before I can stop them. "I'm interested in Stanford, not your brother."

"You sure about that?" Bitterness twists his lips. "Ari's a great guy."

That's probably the one thing Beck and I can agree on.

"Not that it's any of your business, but Ari is nothing more than a friend." I snap my mouth closed, irritated with myself for telling him that. After more than a year of separation, it's demoralizing to realize that my attraction to Beck is as strong as it was in high school.

"Good." He steps closer, and the distance between us shrinks. "We need to talk, Mia. There are things I need to explain."

Out of nowhere, a muscular arm slides around my shoulders and tugs me close.

"Hey, babe. I've been looking everywhere for you." Arron Reinhold, the guy I've been casually seeing, kisses the side of my face. "Where have you been?"

"Right here, talking with Beck." Even though Arron has never struck me as the jealous type, I add, "We went to high school together."

"That's cool." Arron smiles at Beck before giving him a chin lift in greeting. "Great game this afternoon."

"Thanks." Beck shifts his weight as his narrowed gaze bounces between us.

Needing to escape this situation before it becomes anymore stifling, I shake my empty glass. "Looks like I could use a refill."

Arron nips the red plastic cup from my hand. "Sure thing, babe. I'll grab it for you. Be back in a minute."

I open my mouth to protest, but he's already disappearing through the crowd. Unsure what to do now that my plan has been foiled, I glance at Beck from the corner of my eye.

An amused smile tugs at the edges of his lips as his muscles relax. "He seems like a nice guy."

"He is," I grunt.

"How long have you two been together?"

"I don't know." I shrug and mutter, "A few weeks, maybe." My relationship with Arron is the last thing I want to discuss.

"So, it's not serious?" Beck picks up a stray lock of my hair and twirls it around his index finger.

"It's serious enough." I bat his hand away as my heartbeat picks up its tempo.

He steps closer. His voice lowers, and even though the music is obnoxiously loud, I hear every word, every breath that leaves his lips. The chaos surrounding us melts into nothingness.

"What if I wanted another chance?"

Air leaks from my lungs until breathing becomes a foreign concept.

Why is he doing this to me?

Because I'm with someone else?

I force my voice to stay level. I won't give away my inner turmoil. "I'd say that you were shit out of luck."

With his gaze pinned to mine, he moves closer, invading my personal space. The familiar scent of his cologne wraps around me and clouds my better judgment. When I find myself swaying toward him, I blink back to awareness and yank myself away from the precipice.

"I fucked up, Mia. What happened between us...it's not how I wanted it to go."

It doesn't matter.

None of his excuses matter.

"I can't do this with you," I whisper as panic surges through me.

"I hurt you, and I'm sorry. I never intended for it to happen."

But it did.

And now it's too late.

I don't realize I've uttered the words until he says, "It doesn't have to be."

This time, he wraps his fingers around my biceps and drags me closer.

Our faces are inches apart. "Give me a chance to make it up to you."

As I stare into his eyes, I'm reluctantly sucked into his orbit. How does he do it? How does he make me forget to take care of my heart?

"Mia?" A voice cuts into my thoughts and brings me crashing back to earth with a painful thud. "Here you go."

Beck's hands fall away. I blink, focusing my attention on Arron, who holds my newly filled cup of beer.

It takes effort to shake off the web that Beck has woven around me before hoisting my smile. My fingers tremble as I take the Solo cup. "Thanks."

Arron's narrowed gaze slides from me to Beck and then back again, where it stays pinned. His tone changes, turning gruff. "Everything all right here?"

"Yup," I say a little too quickly. "It's fine."

Arron slips an arm around my waist and tugs me close so I'm no longer standing next to Beck. Thick tension blankets the air. Beck's jaw tightens as he glares at the guy at my side. The last thing I want is for a fight to break out, although I have no idea why it would.

As if reading my thoughts, Arron clears his throat. "There's a game of beer pong going on. Any interest in taking on the winners?"

I'd be up for anything that involves getting away from Beck.

"Sure, that sounds fun." I lean into him, and the concerned expression he'd been wearing dissolves. "Let's go."

Arron drops a quick kiss on my lips before glancing at Beck. The friendliness in his eyes disappears. "Take care, Hollingsworth."

"Will do," Beck grunts.

As Arron steers me through the thick crowd, a mixture of relief and disappointment flood through me, and I can't resist stealing one last look over my shoulder. A shiver scampers down my spine when I find Beck watching me.

I glance at Arron as we weave our way through the crowd and feel...

Nothing.

Frustration blooms inside me.

I like Arron. He's a nice guy, and we have a ton in common.

Only now do I realize how hard I've been working to talk myself into this relationship. I had convinced myself that he was someone I could get serious with, but after my run-in with Beck, and the feelings that continue to simmer beneath the surface, I understand there's nothing between us but friendship.

What bothers me most is that I might never get over Beck.

I can't imagine spending the rest of my life pining after someone I can't have. And yet, that's a very real possibility.

MIA

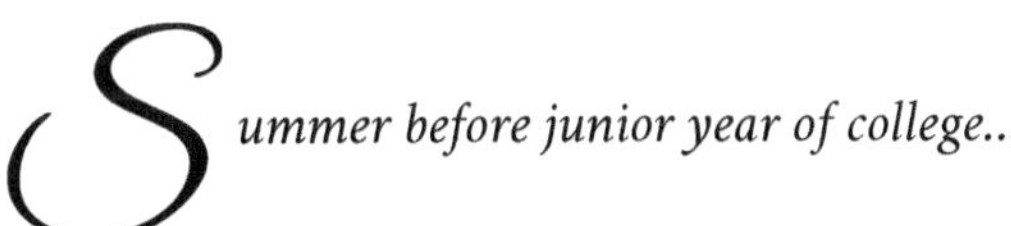

I THROW on a bikini before pulling a cover-up over my head. For the last few days, the temperatures have been soaring in the nineties. It's sweltering out, and I'm tired of being cooped up in the air conditioning. If I don't get out of this house, I'll go batshit crazy.

Since the Hollingsworth family is away on a two-week European vacation, I'm going over to take a dip. Caroline is always telling me to feel free and stop by any time I want. Since I'm usually operating in avoidance mode, I never do. But Beck has been conspicuously absent this summer, so I assume he's on vacay with his parents. Or maybe at football camp. I have no idea.

I try not to think about him.

With Dad at a business dinner and Mom playing Bunco with a group of neighborhood friends, I'm a lone, lonely, loner for the night. The house is quiet as a tomb. Sometimes it feels like it's always been like this, but that's not the case. Before Brianna died, light, happiness, and laughter had filled our home. No matter how much I want to

"

change it, there doesn't seem to be anything I can do. Mom and Dad drift through their lives on autopilot. Dad works at least eighty hours a week, and Mom fills her time with retail therapy.

I didn't realize how lonely of an existence it had become until I went away to college and lived in the dorms. It took a while to get used to the constant commotion. Now, when I return home for breaks, I'm reminded of the loss all over again.

I shove those depressing thoughts from my head and grab a towel from the bathroom before heading next door. The moment I step outside, the hot air hits me like a wave. Even at nine o'clock at night, it feels like a sauna with the temperatures hovering in the upper eighties.

Unable to wait, I hasten my step. It's not until I walk through the black-iron gate that surrounds the Hollingsworth pool that my step falters, and I realize the critical error that has been made.

Beck isn't at school or on vacation with his parents.

He's here.

Swimming.

Silently I watch as he pushes off the far end of the pool, arrowing gracefully through the water. My mouth dries as I track his movements. I hate the attraction that leaps to life inside me whenever I catch sight of him. It's like a living, breathing entity. I've tried so hard to stomp it out, to deny its existence, but it refuses to be eradicated.

Luckily, Beck hasn't caught sight of me. There's still time to backtrack before he's ever the wiser. Beck surfaces at the midway point of the pool before rising to his feet. As he straightens, he shakes the water from his dark hair. It scatters around him, and the muscles in my belly contract as a burst of arousal explodes in my core.

Every time.

It's like this every damn time I see him.

I hate it.

Even more, I hate that he's the only one capable of making me feel this way.

His eyelids lift as his attention fastens on me. It's like he knew I was watching him.

Which is impossible…

But that's exactly how it feels.

A slow smirk curves his lips. It's like a punch to my gut.

"I was wondering if I'd ever see you again." There's a pause. "Seems like you've been avoiding me."

He doesn't realize how right he is.

Or maybe he does.

The way his gaze rakes over my body is like a physical caress. One that leaves me restless and fidgeting beneath the heaviness of it. Even though I'm wearing a cover-up that reaches mid-thigh, Beck has the rare ability to make me feel like I'm standing before him naked. It's disconcerting and serves as a reminder as to how dangerous this guy can be.

Toxic, really.

I won't try to fool myself into believing that Beck isn't my Kryptonite. I spent years trying to do that. There's no point.

"You're looking good, Mia."

His deep tone sends a fresh wave of nerves cascading over my bare flesh.

When I fail to respond, he continues. "How's your summer going?"

"It's good." My gaze stays locked on him. It's like I can't look away.

Why does he have to be so damn hot?

Twenty-one-year-old Beck blows eighteen-year-old Beck clear out of the water. It's like they're not even the same guy. Everything about him is bigger, broader, more finely sculpted. It's doubtful I could wrap both hands around one bicep.

"Have you been playing a lot of tennis?"

I'm definitely starting to salivate.

Did he ask me a question?

It takes a moment for my mind to play mental catch-up. I clear my throat as my eyes skitter away. "A bit."

When he chuckles, my attention returns to him. The sound strums something inside me.

His teeth flash in the darkness. "Dad tells me you've been interning at the office."

My head bobs in relief at the innocuous conversation. "Yup, I've been working full-time."

"I'm sure that's been keeping you out of trouble."

I snort as my muscles lose their rigidity. "I've never been known for my antics like some people."

A slow-moving grin overtakes his face. An answering ribbon of attraction curls in the pit of my belly. Nope. Not even gonna go there. This seems like the perfect time to take off.

I point to the gate. "I'm going to—"

"Leave?" He pops a brow. "So soon? Didn't you come here to swim?"

I shake my head.

"Really? Aren't you wearing a suit?" There's a pause. "And isn't that a towel in your hand?"

I glance at the fluffy material I'm holding and frown.

Damnit. Caught red-handed.

"That's all right." I swat my hand and take a tentative step toward freedom. "You're obviously enjoying some alone time, and I wouldn't want to disturb that."

Beck stretches his arms out in front of him. His muscles ripple with the arcing movement as his fingertips skim the surface of the water. "There's enough room for both of us, don't you think?"

Unfortunately, the pool is big enough for the Olympic swim team. So, yeah…there is.

He knows I don't want to be alone with him. Can't he let me slink away without calling me out on it?

"No worries," I wave a hand, "another time."

"Damn girl," he laughs, eyes crinkling at the corners, "do I frighten you that much?"

Abso-fucking-lutely.

"Don't be ridiculous!" I bristle and straighten to my full height. "Why would you say that?"

Challenge sparks to life in his eyes. "Because you avoid me like I've got a contagious disease."

"For all I know, you do."

"Nope. Totally clean." He gives me a wink. "I always wrap it up tight."

Ugh. "Gross."

"So prove it."

"Excuse me?"

"Prove that you're not afraid to be alone with me," he continues.

I force out a laugh even though my mouth has turned cottony. "I don't have to prove anything to you."

"You're right." He nods. "Then prove it to yourself."

I gnaw my lower lip. If I'm not careful, it'll be a bloody mess in a matter of minutes. I glance at the gate, tempted to walk away without another word.

"Come on, Stanbury," Beck cajoles, his voice turning silky. Too many panties to count have fallen around ankles from just such a tone. "You came here to swim, so do it. I wasn't planning to stay much longer. Then you'll have the pool to yourself. Isn't that why you came over? To cool off?"

Yes, it is. But Beck wasn't part of the deal.

I stare wistfully at the water from the cement patio. It looks so inviting. It's crystal clear and sparkling. Already beads of sweat are rolling down my back, and I just stepped outside. I've been looking forward to this all day.

It's not like I owe Beck an explanation.

And I certainly don't have anything to prove to him.

But...

Maybe he's right about needing to prove it to myself. If I can swim with him and nothing happens, then I can stop going to such great lengths to avoid him. Avoiding Beck at home and on campus is exhausting. It takes a ton of energy to constantly be on guard.

By his own admittance, he isn't planning to stick around for very long. There's no reason we can't swim together for ten or fifteen minutes without me ending up wrapped around him and sucking face.

So what am I concerned about?

"Fine." The word slips from my mouth before I can stop it.

When his lips bow up at the corners, I have to tamp down the nerves that flutter around in my belly like a million butterflies.

Why do I feel like I've fallen into a well-laid trap?

Like a deer in headlights, I stand frozen, waiting for Beck to get back to swimming laps, but he doesn't move. Instead, he continues to watch me. I lower my gaze, needing to break eye contact. Even though I'm not looking at him, the heat of his stare crawls over my covered body.

It takes a moment to gather my courage and shed the cover-up shielding me from view. With his attention focused solely on me, it feels like I'm putting on a striptease which couldn't be further from the truth. Nerves skitter along my spine as my fingers grasp the hem. With a shaky breath, I yank it over my head in one fluid motion before tossing it to the plush lounger. It takes eight steps to reach the edge of the pool and dive headfirst into the water.

As soon as I'm submerged in the cool liquid, all the anxiety swirling through me vanishes. This feels just as amazing as I imagined it would. It's a refreshing slice of heaven. My body hums with pleasure. If I had allowed Beck to chase me away, I wouldn't be enjoying this now.

All I have to do is keep my distance.

How difficult can that be?

As I resurface, Beck's attention stays focused on me. A satisfied expression fills his face. No matter how much I try to pretend otherwise, I'm ridiculously aware of him on every level.

Every shift of muscle.

Every flick of his green eyes.

I'm all too cognizant of the attraction that buzzes between us.

Pretending to ignore him, I swim a few laps. As far as I'm concerned, he's not there.

That's what I tell myself, anyway.

"How's Arron doing?"

I glance at him with confusion. "Who?"

"I guess that answers the question, now doesn't it?" One side of his mouth hitches in amusement. "The last time we ran into each other, you were with some guy named Arron."

Oh, right.

"Yeah," I mutter. "We're not together." Two weeks after that party, I told Arron that I thought we were better off as friends. He didn't agree, and I haven't spoken to him since.

"That's too bad." He doesn't sound the least bit sorry. "What about now? Is there someone special in your life?"

These questions are becoming much too personal.

"I thought we were going to swim," I blurt, unease weaving its way through my voice.

"We can't swim and talk at the same time?"

Actually, I would very much prefer we didn't. It's difficult to ignore him when he won't stop yapping at me.

"I'm trying to figure out what kind of competition I'm up against," he says.

"Excuse me?" I whip around, disconcerted to find him a few feet away. When the hell did he get so close?

Ignoring my question, he asks one of his own. "Do you remember the last time we were in the pool together?"

All too well.

I've done my best to forget about that morning, but it's been singed into my memory. Even thinking about the way he touched me under the blazing sun sends a thick shaft of desire spiraling through me.

I press my lips together and shake my head.

"Liar," he accuses.

"No, I'm not."

"Well, I remember how good it felt when I—"

"Beck!" I snap. "You know what? This isn't working. Maybe I should go home."

He raises his hands in a gesture of surrender. "All right, all right. Sheesh. I was just making conversation."

"Well, don't."

"Fine. We'll talk about something else."

"We don't have to talk at all," I shoot back.

"Oh, come on, where's the fun in that?" Humor simmers in his voice. "We have so much catching up to do."

I scrunch my face. "Do we?"

"Sure." There's a pause. "So, where's your sidekick?"

The further I propel myself away from him, the more tension seeps from my body. "Alyssa left for England last week. She's spending the year there."

"Huh." Surprise fills his eyes. "Colton never mentioned it."

There's a reason for that.

Colton and Alyssa called it quits after six months. Alyssa never came out and specifically said it, but I suspect Colton broke up with her because he wasn't ready to be tied down to one specific girl. Alyssa might not realize it yet, but she's better off without him. I hate that he broke her heart, but hopefully, the year away will do her some good, and she'll get her groove back. I'm not used to seeing my bestie down in the dumps. She moped around for a while and then applied for the study abroad program. Alyssa has been my best friend since middle school. This will be my first time flying solo without her. The plan is for me to visit during Christmas break, but that's five months away.

"How's she doing?" he asks.

As I tread water, my muscles loosen. "She's fine." I don't want Beck to report back to Colton that she's not living her best life.

I don't bother reciprocating the question. Colton is the one who pulled the plug on their relationship. I'm sure he's doing just fine— drowning in groupie pussy.

After a few moments of silence, he asks, "Are you interested in playing a game?"

I shoot him a cautious look. "What do you have in mind?"

His arms cut through the water as he swims closer. "How about truth or dare?"

Truth or dare?

The tension that had sprung to life inside me dies a quick death. "Seriously?"

Isn't that a kid's game?

I've played a few times with Alyssa and a couple of friends. Truth mainly consists of revealing deep-dark secrets about your latest crush. Dares might be twerking in front of a passing car or calling the above-mentioned boy.

It's juvenile stuff.

Why would Beck be interested in playing that?

What's next?

A rousing game of Marco Polo?

When I don't offer a response, he arches a brow. "Are you down with it?"

A kernel of unease blooms in the pit of my belly, which is ridiculous. What's the worst that can happen?

It's probably best not to answer that.

Sidestepping the question, I shoot back with, "Isn't it time for you to leave?"

His mouth curves into a full-blown smile. The effect is devastating. It does funny things to my belly. "If I didn't know better, I'd think you were trying to get rid of me."

That's *exactly* what I'm attempting to do.

Instead of admitting the truth, I shrug and tamp down my growing discomfort. "Wouldn't want you to be late for whatever plans you have tonight."

He swims so close, I'm able to pick out the tiny flecks of gold that dance in his green eyes.

"For you, I've got all the time in the world."

The way his gaze pins me in place makes me realize that engaging in this game is a mistake, but it feels too late to back out now. The moment I saw him in the pool, I should have quietly retreated instead of allowing myself to get baited into joining him for a swim.

"You can start," he says casually, as if there aren't any ulterior motives at play.

And maybe there aren't.

Maybe I'm paranoid.

It's a game, I remind myself.

No biggie.

The sooner I get this over with, the quicker he'll get bored and take off. I need to stay focused on that.

"Truth or dare?" Tiny ripples lap at my shoulders as a warm breeze wafts over my exposed skin.

"Truth."

I search my brain for an interesting question, but nothing comes to mind. "What's your favorite thing to do?"

He pretends to yawn, looking completely bored. "That's easy."

If he says sex, I'm out of here.

"Football."

Everything inside me relaxes. That answer isn't exactly a shocker. Ever since Beck could walk, he's been tossing around a football with his brother. He started out with flag football before moving on to Pop Warner youth leagues. By the time he hit middle school, Beck was a star on the football field with a cannon for an arm. In ninth grade, he skipped playing freshman or JV and went straight to varsity as the first-string quarterback. In college, he's broken state records in total career passing yards, passing touchdowns, and total pass completions.

I blink back to the present when he asks, "Is that it?"

I jerk my head into a nod.

"All right, guess it's my turn," he says lazily, eyes turning flinty. "Truth or dare?"

That's a no-brainer. If I choose a dare, Beck will come up with something to humiliate me with. I know how his mind works, and I refuse to fall for any of his sly trickery.

"Truth."

I expect a surface-level question like the one I asked, but that's not what I get.

"How many guys have you slept with?"

My heart stutters before beating into overdrive. *"What?"*

He enunciates the words as if I'm hard of hearing. *"How. Many. Guys. Have. You. Slept. With?"*

"I'm not going to answer that!" I sputter. "It's none of your damn business!"

"You have to." He shrugs as if this isn't a stupid game he talked me into playing. "I've already answered your question, now it's your turn to answer mine. Fair is fair."

Heat floods my face. "I didn't ask something so personal."

"You could have asked me anything you wanted, and I would have answered truthfully. But you didn't, and that was your choice."

I scowl, hoping he'll laugh and tell me to forget it.

"Tick tock, Mia. Answer the question." His voice drops. "Are you worried I'll tell people all your secrets?" He shakes his head. "I won't. Anything you share stays between us."

That's not the point. I don't give a rip if he cries it from the rooftops. What I don't want him to find out is that—

"Answer the question," he prods. "It's not that difficult."

I press my lips together.

"Mia—"

"One!" I groan as humiliation floods through me. *You're the only person I've slept with. Okay? Just you.*

Ugh!

His eyes darken to a deeper shade of green as he treads water. "What happened with Arron?"

I glance away and jerk my shoulders, unwilling to reveal the real reason our relationship fizzled out. "I don't know. Got busy with school."

He cocks his head. "And there's been no one else since?"

"You asked your one question," I snap, face flaming with embarrassment. "You won't get anything more from me."

"Fair enough, your turn."

Wait a minute…that's it? He's actually going to drop the topic of my limited sexual experience?

I'm as shocked as I am relieved.

"Can we end this stupid game?" I ask with a glare.

He shakes his head. "Not yet, we just started."

I huff out an exasperated breath and grunt out the question. "Truth or dare?"

"Dare."

I glance around the yard. "All right, I dare you to do a backward flip off the diving board."

Added bonus—it'll get him away from me, so I have some much-needed breathing room to collect my scattered thoughts.

Beck is a lot to take in.

He glances at the blue springboard before flicking his attention to me. "That's your dare? You want me to flip off the board?"

"Yup, that's it." Goosebumps prickle along my arms as I grow uneasy under the steady intensity of his stare. "After this, I'm going home." Where I can avoid Beck for the rest of my life. Clearly, this idea has backfired. I'm no closer to getting over him than I was in high school.

"You can quit after your next turn," he informs me with a smirk.

Grrrrr.

"Fine." I stab a finger at the board. "Do your flip so we can get this stupid game over with."

"You got it, sweetheart." His powerful arms cut through the water as he swims toward the side of the pool. When he reaches the ceramic tile edge, Beck hoists himself out of the water. His muscles ripple, and my mouth dries.

No one should be this devastatingly handsome.

It defies the laws of nature.

For now, I'll silently enjoy the show and pretend heat isn't pulsing to life in my core. Rivulets of water run down his back before continuing to his naked ass.

What the—

"Where are your shorts?" I croak.

He throws a devilish look over his shoulder before a wide grin breaks out across his face. Mischief dances in his eyes. When his feet land on the concrete, he straightens to his full height.

Oh.

My.

God!

He's naked!

Full-on naked!

It's not like I haven't seen the goods before, but that was two years ago. I've tried so damn hard to eradicate the image from my brain.

"In the house." He tosses out the comment nonchalantly, as if it's no big deal I've been swimming around naked with him for the last half an hour.

How did I not realize it sooner?

Maybe because I was trying to avoid looking at him altogether?

My tongue darts out to moisten my lips. They feel as dry as the Sahara.

"Don't be shy, Stanbury, take a good look." There is so much heat filling his voice that it could burn me alive. "I don't mind at all."

It takes effort to avert my focus. "Just do the dare."

I need to get this over with before something happens between us. Something I'll inevitably regret.

"Don't rush me, woman." He raises his hands, palms out. "I'm moving." There's not a bashful bone in this guy's body as he saunters to the diving board before climbing up the stairs.

Once on the board, he pauses as his hands grip the metal railing before strutting to the end that juts out over the water. Beck softens his knees before taking a few preliminary bounces. His cock flops around, and I can't help but laugh. The sound breaks the sexual tension brewing dangerously between us.

A smile cricks the corners of his mouth. "Is there something funny?"

I press my lips together and shake my head. "Nope, not at all."

"All right, if you say so." He bounces, and his dick continues to slap against his lower belly and balls.

I don't think I've ever seen something so ridiculous. I'm all but dying now. My shoulders shake at the image he makes standing on the board in all his glory. Even when he's making a complete jackass out of himself, he's still gorgeous. All six foot three inches of him.

"You ready to be blown away by my mad skills?" he asks, bouncing away gleefully.

I clear the laughter from my voice and remind, "It's a backward flip."

"Oh, yeah." He points at me. "I almost forgot."

"Maybe this isn't such a good idea," I say. "Seems like you could do irreparable damage to some rather sensitive pieces."

An unconcerned expression settles on his face as he shrugs. "It's sweet that you're concerned about my tender bits and pieces."

Hardly.

"A dare's a dare, right?"

"Yeah, I guess." Here's my chance to end this stupid game. "If you want to quit, I'd be fine with that."

A knowing glint enters his eyes as he smiles. "Sorry, sweetheart, you're not getting out of this that easily. I'll have to keep my legs together when I land and hope for the best."

He turns around until I have a perfect view of his ass. I hate to admit it, but Beck has one hell of a gorgeous backside. The urge to squeeze those perfectly shaped cheeks rushes through me, and I have to tamp down the impulse that stirs inside.

With his back to me, he stands at the edge of the board until his heels can hang off the end. He holds his arms straight out in front of him and takes a few initial bounces before bringing them down to his thighs. Beck squats and launches himself off the board. I hold my breath as he tucks into a ball, legs rotating over his head before landing in the water.

I hate to admit that I'm impressed. The guy gets a ten for perfect form.

Once he breaks through to the surface, I ask, "Did your giblets make it out all right?"

"Yup. Kept my legs firmly pressed together." He gives me a wink along with a sly grin. "Just like you've been doing for the last two years."

All of my good humor evaporates as I narrow my eyes.

Now that I know Beck isn't wearing board shorts, I keep at least ten feet of distance between us at all times. When he swims closer, I back away. But still, it feels like I'm being stalked in the pool. And I can't migrate to the shallow end unless I want to get an eyeful of him.

Not that he would mind.

He tilts his head as a smirk simmers on his lips. "You afraid I'm going to give you cooties?"

I shrug and keep a tight rein on my nerves. They're vibrating like crazy. "Anything's possible."

"Ready to take your turn?"

What I'm ready for is to get this over with. If I play my cards right, I'll be out of here in three minutes. Five, tops. And then I'll be able to breathe easier.

I jerk my head into a tight nod.

"Truth or dare?"

Ha!

I'm not falling for that again.

"Dare."

"A dare, huh?" he drawls before pursing his lips. A thoughtful look enters his eyes. "All right, I got one." There's a pause as my anxiety ratchets up a few hundred notches. "Your dare is to kiss me."

My arms and legs freeze, and my body sinks to the bottom of the pool. Right before my head can slip beneath the surface, I kick my feet and propel myself upward.

"*What?*" My voice comes out sounding high-pitched and shrill.

"And you have to wrap your legs around my waist while doing it."

No way!

"But—but...you're *naked*." My voice escalates until it's barely a squeak.

"So?" He raises a brow. "It's nothing you haven't felt or seen before."

"We're not going to talk about *that*," I bite out harshly.

"Why not?"

"Because..." My voice trails off as I search for a way to escape the situation, but there isn't one. I'm stuck. Goddamn it. Why did I agree to play this stupid game in the first place? It might have sounded innocent in the beginning, but it's turned out to be anything but.

When I remain stoically silent, he says in a challenging voice, "You're not going to puss out on me, are you, Stanbury?"

I blink back to the present.

To the naked guy treading water in front of me.

"No."

Surprise flickers across his face. Trust me, he's not the only one shocked by my surrender. I'm feeling a little stunned myself.

Beck might be the only guy I've had sex with, but he's not the only one I've fooled around with. The sad truth is that every time I get close to sealing the deal, all of my Beck-filled memories rush to the surface and ruin everything. Even though I don't want to, I end up comparing the guy I'm with to my hot, next-door neighbor. And they always come up lacking.

It's frustrating. I've tried to convince myself that what I experienced with Beck wasn't nearly as good as what I've built it up to be.

But not even *I* believe that.

Maybe this is my chance to prove that Beck isn't as amazing as I remember. One mediocre kiss with too much saliva is all it would take to move on and stop dwelling on him.

Beck grins before he raises his hand and curls one finger in a *come here* gesture.

Am I really going to do this?

I suck in a shaky breath before carefully exhaling it from my lungs and forcing myself to close the distance between us. When I'm only a foot away, I pause, unsure how to proceed. Tension and excitement spiral through me. My hands flutter tentatively to his shoulders before my nails bite into his flesh.

His eyes darken with desire.

What am I supposed to do now?

My movements falter, and I stare pleadingly, willing him to take control of the situation. This is more difficult than I imagined it would be.

"Come on, Stanbury," he murmurs, "you've come this far. Don't stop now."

I press closer until our bodies can brush against one another beneath the water.

Inside, I'm freaking out.

This isn't a big deal.

You're wearing bikini bottoms.

Any other girl would be wrapped around him like a python, devouring him whole.

All you have to do is pretend you're one of those girls.

Averting my gaze, I widen my thighs before wrapping them around his waist.

"Eyes on me," he says gruffly.

My attention snaps to him as I swallow down my nervousness. There's a fire burning in his bright green eyes. It kindles an answering flame deep in my core.

My ankles hook around his waist, bringing me flush against his taut abdominals. Like the rest of him, they're rock solid. I'm tempted to explore the grooved musculature with my fingers, but don't dare. He stares at my mouth as his tongue darts out to lick at his lower lip.

A punch of arousal slams me in the gut.

All right, maybe it hits a little lower.

With a pent-up breath, I wait for Beck to make the next move. Instead, he remains still, eyes focused patiently on me. Seconds tick by, and it becomes obvious that he isn't going to take control of the situation. A fresh wave of anxiety crashes over me. This is my dare, and Beck is going to force me to follow through with it.

Okay. I can do this.

Unsure how to proceed, I tilt my head, bringing my face closer until his breath can drift across my lips before mingling with my own. The intimacy is dizzying. It's like I've been drugged. We stay frozen, breathing each other in and out before I work up the courage to press my lips against his.

Everything about Beck is hard and chiseled. Except for his lips. I forgot how soft—almost plush in their plumpness—they are.

A strange sense of boldness surges through me, and I angle my head, stroking over his top lip before repeating the caress with the bottom. Beck doesn't move a muscle. He gives me the freedom to explore him at my own pace.

A sigh of pleasure leaves my mouth before floating in the air between us. His hands wrap around my backside. Both of his wide palms settle on my cheeks before tugging me closer, pressing me against his body. I tangle my arms around his neck until there is no space between us. My nipples pebble at the feel of his unyielding strength. Heat builds like an impending storm in my core.

He groans when my tongue slips inside his mouth. His grip tightens on me, fingers sinking into flesh. In the beginning, I was desperate for him to take over, but not anymore. There's something empowering about the way Beck allows me to control the situation. We both know that if he wanted, he could have me out of the water and flipped onto my back, panting beneath him.

Instead, he allows the kiss to unfold leisurely.

At my speed.

There is no pressure, only pleasure. So much that I'm almost drunk with it.

Our tongues tangle, sliding against each other. The exquisiteness of the movement is more erotic than I could have dreamed possible. My fingers slide into his hair to hold him in place. Barely am I aware that I'm grinding my pussy against his stomach.

It feels like my body is spinning out of control.

When I pull away, he grumbles, "Not yet."

Relief pounds through me.

Maybe I dragged my feet about following through with this dare, but now that my lips are on his, I want to take full advantage of the situation. If I'd thought kissing him would prove that I'd over-embellished his skills, I was woefully mistaken.

I reposition my head before my mouth settles on his. When he opens, my tongue slips inside, and I lose myself in the feel of him. The way our tongues tangle, becoming one, weaves a dream-filled cocoon around us. The outside world disappears. A moan slips free as I continue to move against him.

The friction feels so damn good. Need gathers in my core. It pulses through my body like that of a steady drumbeat as I remember what it felt like to have Beck's thick erection sliding inside me.

I need so much more than this.

The words are on the tip of my tongue when a sound penetrates the Beck-induced haze that has fallen over me. A whimper of protest erupts from my throat when he pulls away. It takes a moment to regain my bearings.

Why did we stop?

I'm on the verge of exploding. Any moment, I'm going to come right out of my skin. It's the best and worst feeling in the world. I want his mouth back on mine, dragging me under so I don't have to think about the repercussions of my actions.

"Dude, I thought we had plans."

Those six words are like a bucket of cold water being dumped over my head. The fog evaporates, and I'm once again clearheaded as I blink up at Colton. A shit-eating grin lights up his face.

Oh.

My.

God.

Please tell me this isn't happening.

"Hello there, Mia," he chortles. "Can't say I expected to find you here."

Colton knows *exactly* how I feel about Beck. When he and Alyssa were together, he tried numerous times to cajole me into joining the three of them, and I always shot him down. After a while, it became a running joke between us. He would ask, and I would refuse.

The biggest kick in the ass is that I only have myself to blame for my current predicament. All I want to do is slink home with my tail tucked between my legs, but that's not possible since I'm pinned against Beck's body. And he doesn't seem to be in a hurry to let me go.

"Colton," I mutter. Any moment I'm going to burst into flames. To be found like this is beyond humiliating.

He stuffs his hands in the pockets of his shorts and rocks back on his heels. "So, what have you crazy kids been up to?"

Ugh. He is so loving this.

"Wait in the car," Beck snaps, "I'll be out in ten."

Heat fills my cheeks, making them feel like they're on fire. I'm sure they resemble overripe tomatoes by now. It only adds to my upset.

At myself.

For allowing the situation to get out of hand.

What is it about this guy that makes me lose my head?

"You gonna come out with us, Mia?" Before I can respond, Colton continues. "I doubt the chicks we're supposed to hookup with tonight will appreciate that, but oh, well." He shrugs. "Sucks for them."

Chicks we're supposed to hookup with...

I press my palms against the steely strength of Beck's chest and try to push out of his embrace, but I don't get far.

Why am I such an idiot? How many times do I need to get burned by this guy before I finally learn my lesson?

"Dude," Beck snaps, "get the fuck out of here before I beat your ass."

Colton holds up his hands in a gesture of surrender as if he doesn't understand why Beck is pissed off. "Whatever. Don't get your panties in a bunch." As he slips through the iron gate, he calls over his shoulder, "You got ten. Wrap this shit up, and let's go."

Once Colton disappears around the side of the house and we're alone, I slam my fists into Beck's chest. "Let go of me!"

"Mia—"

"No!" I shake my head, unwilling to hear him out. No more excuses. "Just let me go."

"Give me a chance to explain!"

With his arms locked around my body, it's impossible to move.

"Don't bother. It was just a stupid game." Even though I try to keep the hurt and anger locked deep inside, it all comes flooding out in a rush. "You better get moving. You've got *chicks* waiting for you."

I hate the jealousy that drips from my words.

"They're just a couple of random girls we're supposed to meet up with tonight, that's it."

I can't hear anything through the pain that has all but swallowed me whole. "I don't care. Let me go." I feel like such a fool.

"Mia," his voice becomes so low that it sounds as if it's been dredged from the bottom of the ocean, "please."

"Let go!" I pound on his chest with my fists. If only it were possible to do damage. Instead of hurting him, I'm inflicting pain onto myself.

When he refuses, I snake a hand between our bodies until I'm able to wrap my fingers around his balls. His eyes flare as mine narrow. Once I have his undivided attention, I give them a good squeeze.

A hiss of breath escapes from his lips.

As soon as he releases me, I bolt toward the tiled edge and hoist myself from the pool. I glance over my shoulder and find Beck where I left him. He's hunched over with his hands cupping his dick and balls.

"Was that necessary?" he groans.

"Yup." Even though he's in pain, I can't bring myself to regret the damage I've caused. He deserves every bit of agony.

I grab my towel and cover-up, hightailing it from Beck's yard before he can recover.

As I'm about to push through the gate, he calls out, "This isn't over, Mia."

I swing around. "That's where you're wrong because nothing was ever started."

With that last parting shot, I walk away, leaving him to hold his balls.

Hopefully, he'll be too sore to use them tonight.

We'll just consider that a little gift to the chicks he's meeting up with.

BECK

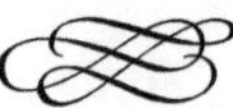

For years, I've fantasized about Mia touching my junk. Although, in my mind, it was more of a caress. Maybe there would be a little licking and sucking thrown in for good measure. In no way did I expect her to try popping them.

Fuck me.

My poor balls throb with a strange mixture of need spiked pain. Surprisingly, that last maneuver wasn't enough to kill the desire rampaging through my system. Although it took the edge off. All I have to do is think about Mia's curvy body pressed against mine, and I'm once again rising to the occasion.

My tongue swipes across my lower lip, and a taste that is distinctly Mia explodes in my mouth. I don't want to dwell on how different the outcome would have been if Colton hadn't interrupted us.

Stupid motherfucker.

The moment he realized I had my hands full of the only girl I've ever wanted, he should have turned around and walked away. Fuck the chicks we're meeting up with. Instead, he took joy in pissing her off, and now I'm back to square one. She wouldn't even give me a chance to explain.

Does she really think I have any interest in other girls?

Hell, no. It's always been Mia.

Colton is the one trying to drown himself in pussy, not me. He might not be willing to admit that he fucked up when he cut Alyssa loose, but deep down, he knows he made a mistake. I have no idea why Colton thinks nailing as much ass as he can get his hands on is the solution. The only thing it's going to do is up his chances of contracting an STI.

Right now, I'm all but wishing it on him.

With a sigh, I swim to the side of the pool and hoist myself out. I scoop up my towel, running it over my hair and body before heading inside the house. As I jog up the staircase to the second floor, I force down my growing erection. I'm not sure what's worse. A case of blue balls or bruised ones.

Seems like I was dealt both.

Every time I take a step forward with Mia, something inevitably happens, and I get shoved back four or five steps. It's like playing a game of Chutes and Ladders. Those damn chutes will get you every time.

I jump in the shower and lather up under the warm fall of water. What I should have done was turn it ice cold. My fingers stroke over my cock, and I realize that I'm going to have to rub one out. Otherwise, I'll be stuck in this perpetual state of need, and I'm not willing to put up with that. I close my eyes and remember how good it felt to have Mia's body wrapped in my arms. The way our mouths fused together as she gyrated against me has my dick turning hard as a rock.

So.

Fucking.

Hot.

My fist tightens as I pick up speed. Seven strokes later, I throw my head back and groan out my release as water pours over my body. It feels nothing like when I came inside her, but it'll have to do.

Mia would freak out if she knew that she was my go-to spank bank material. I'm tempted to shoot her a text and let her know, but it would only aggravate her more, and I'm not about to do that. I irritate her enough without even trying.

My phone chimes with an incoming text. I glance at it, knowing that Colton has grown impatient. But that's too damn bad. He can cool his ass in the car after the way he jacked up my night. I would have rather spent it with Mia than sitting around with a couple of girls, watching Colton make moves in his quest to get laid.

Although, let's be honest, he doesn't have to try very hard. Colton is the pied piper of pussy. He can get his dick sucked anytime he wants. There are always girls waiting for his text. They don't care if it's a one-time deal. As long as there's no expectation of something more, he'll keep them around.

Not bothering to respond, I toss the phone on the bed and grab a T-shirt and a pair of jogger shorts. I thrust my fingers through my hair and head out the door. Colton glances up from his phone as I slide onto the front seat of his convertible Beemer.

"Took you long enough," he grumbles. "I was about to take off without you."

"Too bad you didn't do that when you realized I was busy."

"Give me a fucking break," he snorts. "We both know Mia can't stand your damn ass. What were you gonna do? Screw her in the pool? You might not realize it, but I did you a solid. That girl would have hated you even more than she already does."

Fuck. He's right.

If we'd taken it any further, she would have been more pissed off than she already is.

When I don't respond, a grin slides across his face as he cups his hand to his ear. "I'm sorry, what's that?" He pauses for a moment. *"You're welcome, Colton? Thanks for saving me from myself?"*

"I wouldn't go that far," I mutter, slouching on the seat and staring straight ahead.

"Please. I couldn't get Mia to come out with us if there was even a slight chance you would show up." He cocks his head. "Doesn't that tell you something?"

Of course, it does, but I'm not ready to throw in the towel just yet.

Colton has turned into a real surly bastard since the breakup with Alyssa. One of these days, he's going to get a fist in the face.

"Just drive," I snap, unwilling to continue the conversation.

"You know I'm right," he singsongs before starting up the engine and squealing from the driveway. "I hate to be the one to break it to you, but it's never gonna happen with that girl. You need to move the fuck on."

I slouch further onto the buttery-soft leather. He's not telling me anything I don't already know, but that doesn't mean I want to hear it. Especially from him.

"Maybe," I bite out, "you should do yourself a favor and take your own advice for a change."

His jaw tightens as he stares at the ribbon of road in front of him. "Don't think I'm not trying," he mumbles. "Every damn night, I'm trying to get over that girl."

"You fuck so much," I snort, "I'm surprised your dick hasn't shriveled up and fallen off. Remind me to buy you some balm for your birthday."

A hint of a smile lifts his lips, but it doesn't quite reach his eyes. "Don't I know it, brother."

Silence falls over us as Colton turns the Beemer onto the main stretch of road.

He clears his throat and continues to stare straight ahead. "Did Mia mention Lys at all?"

I glance at him and consider sharing the intel I've gathered. Maybe it'll help him realize that she's really gone, and he needs to take his own advice and move on. Colton would never admit it, but he blew up that relationship because he was too chickenshit to have one.

"Guess she's studying abroad in London for the year."

His lips tug down at the corners. "No shit?"

"Yup."

"Huh."

He says nothing more, and I don't bother asking questions. That's the beauty of our relationship. We don't need to sit around, whining about our feelings and crying over the girls who got away.

At the end of the day, what the hell would it change?

Not a damn thing.

MIA

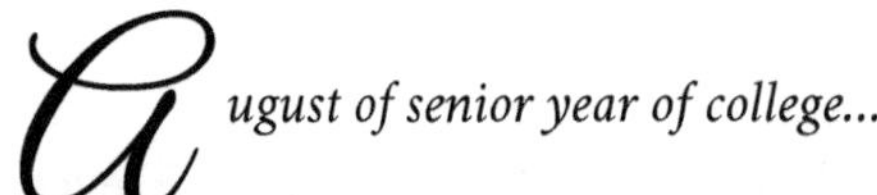

ugust of senior year of college...

I PULL my Jeep over to the curb and hit the hazards before jumping out. A burst of hot air hits me as I search the thick crowd of people flowing in and out of the airport.

The moment I see her blond head, I shout at the top of my lungs, "Alyssa!" There is so much noise and people that it takes a few minutes for her to notice me. "Over here!" I wave my arms like a crazy person to grab her attention.

A bright smile lights up her face as she drags a pile of suitcases behind her. Alyssa doesn't understand what the concept of traveling light entails. Actually, for her, this *is* traveling light.

I race toward her, maneuvering around weary passengers. As soon as she's within striking distance, I throw my arms around her, pulling her close and squeezing her tight. For a solid minute, we jump up and down with excitement.

"It's so freaking good to see you!" Unable to contain my giddiness, I hop from one foot to the other.

"It's good to be seen," she laughs, embracing me again. "I missed your face!"

"I missed yours more!" Tears of joy prick my eyes. My parents bought me a plane ticket for my birthday last year, and I flew over to visit during Christmas break. We had an amazing time. I met all her new friends, and we visited museums and Buckingham Palace. We drank pints at the local pub and flirted with cute footballers.

Who knew that soccer players were so sexy?

My trip to England gave me a whole new appreciation for the sport.

I pull away, holding her at arm's length, before giving her a quick once-over. "You look fantastic!" Alyssa has always been tall and muscular from years of dance, but she looks sleeker. In the shorts and T-shirt she's wearing, her muscles appear both longer and leaner.

She grins and does a little twirl on the sidewalk. "Thanks, babe. You're not looking so shabby yourself."

A shrill whistle rents the air, and we both turn toward the cop loitering near a squad car. He points a finger at us. "Breakup the love fest, ladies, and move it along before I write you a ticket."

I give him an apologetic wave before grabbing the largest suitcase and dragging it toward the Jeep. "Holy hell," I grunt, "what do you have in here? A dead body?"

"Surprise!" she laughs, "I brought you one of those cute footballers we met."

"Ha! I wish." Those accents alone were enough to dampen my panties.

Gathering my strength, I hoist the bag into my Jeep. It takes another ten minutes to jam all of her suitcases into the trunk and backseat. It's like an impromptu game of Tetris. By the time we slide onto the front seats, I'm a sweaty mess, and officer friendly is glaring at us.

"Too bad he had a massive stick wedged up his ass, he was kind of cute." Alyssa blows him a kiss as we roll past and merge into traffic.

Once we hit the freeway and are barreling toward campus, I reach over and squeeze her hand. "I know I said it before, but I'm really glad you're back." Junior year wasn't the same without her. "I was kind of afraid you might become an ex-pat."

With a soft sigh, Alyssa leans her head against the cushion. "I had an amazing time in London, and I did consider extending my visa," she rolls her head toward me, "but I wasn't about to leave you here all by yourself. It's senior year, baby! We have to spend it together!"

I flash her a grin, relieved that my bestie is home where she belongs.

Alyssa and I chatter about everything that happened during our time apart. She tells me about all the cool people she met and her dance classes. Once a month, she took amazing weekend trips and traveled all over Europe. The more she chatters, the more envious I become, wishing I'd done something like that, too. It sounds like an incredible experience.

"How did you leave things with Jack?"

Jack is the British guy Alyssa started dating a few months ago. When I visited over Christmas break, they had been just friends. He was definitely smoking hot. And that accent…

Yeah.

Alyssa huffs out a weary breath and closes her eyes. "It wasn't serious. We both knew I'd be leaving in August, so we kept it light."

"Smart. No broken heart to deal with on top of jetlag."

"Definitely not," she snorts. "I refuse to be in that kind of situation again."

The *situation* she's referring to is Colton Montgomery.

Neither of us say anything more on the topic.

I nibble my lower lip as we swing into the apartment parking lot.

Freshman and sophomore year, Alyssa and I shared a dorm room. Wesley has a strict policy about first-and-second-year students living on campus. Junior year, I rented a house with a bunch of girls I met in the dorms. It worked out well and was fun. Although there were always people coming and going, and that got old after a while.

When Alyssa confirmed that she would return for senior year, I found us a two-bedroom apartment a few blocks from campus. It's on the third floor and has a tiny balcony. The building is centrally located, so we can easily walk to a few restaurants and a small grocery store. I moved my stuff in on the first of August and have been living there for a couple of weeks. Alyssa's parents brought over her bedroom set, and we were able to piece together enough furniture to fill the apartment.

Alyssa beams as we pull into a parking space near the front entrance of the building. "I love this place! I'm so pumped you could get us an apartment here!"

"Yeah, it's super convenient. We can walk to campus and the parties…" my voice trails off. There's only one tiny problem, and I'm kind of afraid of how she'll react when she finds out.

So, I put it off.

And then off some more.

And now I've run out of time. I have to come clean before it's too late.

"Um," I clear my throat and turn off the engine, "there's something I need—"

Before I can force out the sentence, Alyssa jumps out of the Jeep and walks around to the back. Reluctantly, I follow, knowing I need to get this over with. Maybe it would be better if I wait until we're inside the apartment. Once she sees how awesome it looks, she'll fall in love with it. Then, hopefully, what I have to tell her won't be such a big deal.

We grab the smaller suitcases and set them on the sidewalk before pulling out the behemoth that feels like it weighs at least two hundred pounds.

Seriously, what's in here?

As we drag her luggage to the lobby door, it swings open, and two guys stroll out.

Alyssa grinds to a halt and grabs my arm. Her nails bite into my flesh. "What the hell is *he* doing here?"

Crap.

I glance at Colton and Beck, who return our stare with interest. "Right. I, ah, meant to tell you about that."

Her eyes narrow to slits as she frowns. "About what?"

"They also live here."

"I really hope you're joking," she says flatly, clearly displeased by the news.

It would be so much easier if I were. By the steam coming out of Alyssa's ears, she's more pissed off than I imagined she would be.

"Sorry, Lys. When I signed the rental agreement, I had no idea they lived here or that we're neighbors."

"*What?*" she growls.

I wince. Maybe I should have held off on the whole *neighbor's* part.

"Hey, Lys," Colton murmurs, swallowing up the distance between them. If he knew what was good for him, he'd give his ex a wide berth. Alyssa looks like a rabid dog who could attack at any moment.

Instead of biting his head off the way I expect, she pointedly ignores him. "Did you hear that?" With wide eyes, she makes a big production about glancing around as if looking for something. "It almost sounds like a ghost from boyfriends' past."

This isn't good.

After more than a year and countless relationships, I had assumed Alyssa moved on, but her reaction is proving that's not the case. During the year she was away, she gave me a play-by-play on the boy situation in London. She definitely got a taste of what England had to offer in the guy department. Every time I spoke with her, she was talking about someone new.

And then there was Jack.

Not once did she mention Colton. And since she wasn't asking questions or digging for information, I avoided the topic of her ex as well. I knew she wouldn't be pleased about this, but I didn't expect her to go off the deep end.

Big mistake on my part.

Beck glances at me, and I shrug in response.

Not dissuaded by Alyssa's cold demeanor, Colton tries again. "It's really good to see you, Lys." When she continues to avoid eye contact, he pulls her in for a hug.

She bares her teeth and growls before fighting her way out of his arms.

Alyssa dismisses him by turning her attention to Beck. "Hello, Beckett. It's lovely to see you." She flashes a mega-watt smile at him. "Did Mia happen to mention the welcome home party I'm having this Saturday at Bang Bang? If you're free, definitely stop by."

Beck's lips quirk upward. "Nope, she didn't mention it." I hear the humor simmering in his voice. He knows there is no damn way I would invite him to a party.

I wince when Alyssa gives me a bit of side-eye.

"Hmm. That's strange. She must have *forgotten* to mention the party to you the same way she *forgot* to mention that a certain someone who shall remain nameless is my new neighbor."

I narrow my eyes.

You know what? I was feeling like a shitty friend for not telling her about our living situation, but now?

Not so much.

"Hey, what about me?" Colton interrupts, "Don't I get an invite?" When her glare intensifies, he adds, "How about for old times' sake?"

Alyssa tilts her head and glances around again. "It's so strange the way I keep hearing something."

"Really, Lys?" Colton's voice drops. "You're acting like a child."

Oh, boy.

I sigh.

If Colton wanted her attention, he's got it now.

With a scowl, Alyssa spins toward him. Two steps bring her close enough to drill her finger into his chest. Anger vibrates off her in heavy waves. *"I'm the child?* That's rich! You dumped my ass because you couldn't keep your dick in your pants! Don't you *dare* turn this around on me!" Her voice escalates. People passing by stop and stare. "You and I are *not* friends. We will *never* be friends! I was an idiot for thinking you were anything other than a *manwhore!*"

Even though I'm pissed that Alyssa invited Beck to her welcome home party, I wrap my arm around her shoulders and drag her away from Colton before the situation can spiral any further out of control.

Tears prick her eyes as she blinks back the moisture and glances around, only now realizing that she's drawn an audience. A dull red color floods her cheeks. My guess is that the jetlag has caught up with her.

Not one to shrink away, she meets the inquisitive looks from the surrounding people with a scowl. "Move it along! Show's over, there's nothing to see here."

Maybe I should talk to the building manager and see if there's a way to break our rental agreement. If this episode has proven anything, it's that Alyssa isn't over Colton as much as she led me to believe. And living in this close of contact with her ex won't end well for any of us.

I drop onto the bench after a two-hour practice under the blazing sun. I'm fucking exhausted and want to jump in the shower and wash away all the sweat and turf sticking to me. As I peel off my jersey and throw it in my locker, Colton does the same.

We've been playing football together since we were kids. We know each other's quirks and tells. Half of the time, he knows which play I'm going to run before I do. I never have to seek him out on the field, he's always where I expect him to be. As far as football is concerned, we have some kind of weird mental connection.

Which is exactly why the last couple of practices have been so concerning. No matter what I threw out there today, he wasn't where he was supposed to be. It's not uncommon to have an off day. We all have them. You have to stay focused and work through it. But this has turned into more of a slump and that, we can't have.

Not with the season right around the corner.

I've got plans this year. And they include bringing home a conference championship. Breaking a few more NCAA football records before I leave wouldn't be so bad either. But I can't do any of that without my wide receiver being dialed in.

And he's not. I don't know where his head is, but it's not where it should be.

Colton doesn't bother making eye contact. He's too busy shoving his shit into his locker. His agitation is palpable. He knows there's a problem.

It's been eating at him for a while.

The locker room turns quiet as Coach stalks through with his Wesley Warriors ball cap pulled low over his eyes and a clipboard clenched in his hand. "Montgomery," he barks, "get your ass in my office as soon as you're dressed."

Colton jerks his head into a nod but keeps his lips pressed together.

Coach Taylor glares at the group of half-naked guys and snaps out a few more names. When he's done, he slams the door to his office with so much force that it rattles on its hinges.

Devon Baker, a three-hundred-pound lineman, calls out, "Better bring some lube with you, Montgomery. Doesn't look like he's in the mood to give it to you gently."

Colton glares before giving Baker the finger. There is, unfortunately, truth to the statement.

Our first game against Tennessee is in two weeks. I need Colton to pull his head out of his ass and play like I know he can. I've got enough of my own bullshit going on without worrying about him.

Whatever this is, he needs to get it figured out fast and stop bringing it on to the field. "So—"

"Don't even say it, man." He falls silent, ripping off the rest of his padding as if it's choking the life out of him.

"Say what?" I ask, doing the same.

"That I'm off my game." He gives me a bit of side-eye. "That it's been off for a few weeks."

I shrug and backtrack. Coach is already going to rip him a new one, so maybe, for the time being, I'll keep my trap shut, and we'll see what happens. "Wasn't going to mention it."

"Good." His brows pinch together as he shoots an anxious look toward Coach's office. "For once in his life, Baker is right. I'd better grab some lube. Coach is going to ream my ass."

Nik Taylor is one of the toughest coaches you'll find in Division I football. He runs his program like a tight ship. If he's giving one-hundred percent to his team, he expects his players to do the same. If you're not willing to bleed for the guys standing shoulder to shoulder with you on the field, there's no place for you on this roster. He's the reason both Colton and I committed to Wesley. Practice may be grueling, but we're better players for it. Ever since Coach Taylor took over the program, the Warriors have won their conference along with five national championships. I'm looking to keep the momentum going, not shit the bed during my farewell season.

"Please," I snort, wanting to put him at ease, "Baker is a bonehead. Don't listen to a word he says."

Colton shrugs as concern flickers in his eyes. He's never been one to expose his true feelings. This is the first time I've seen his mask of indifference slip from place.

"Look, man, we all have off days. Don't stress about it."

"Easier said than done," he mumbles.

We fall silent, stripping out of our gear before hitting the showers. Now that Coach is cloistered in his office, the locker room turns rowdy. Everyone has caught their second wind. Guys are talking about the parties happening off-campus. The team has been at Wesley practicing twice a day since the beginning of July. We've spent hundreds of hours going over plays, practicing, working out, and watching game film. With school starting up next week, this will be our final hoorah. Everyone wants to cut loose and party their asses off before we have to buckle down for the season.

I hit the shower, wash up, and grab a towel before heading to my locker. I find Colton on the bench, staring pensively at his hands. I'm not sure if he's deliberately hanging back, waiting for the team to clear out, so they don't hear Coach rip him a new one, or if something else is bothering him.

"Come on, get a move on it," I prod. "I want to get out of here."

"Go on without me." He glances toward the office. "I have the feeling this will take a while."

I pull on a pair of athletic shorts before shoving my feet into slides. "Does this have anything to do with Alyssa?"

"Fuck if I know," Colton sighs, dragging a hand over his face.

I'm surprised when he doesn't shut down that line of questioning. The Colton I grew up with would never let a girl mess with his mojo on the field. But then again, Alyssa is the only girl he's ever dated. In all honesty, it shocked the hell out of me when they got together. Who would have suspected Colton could be monogamous?

Or that he wanted to be.

Just when I was getting used to them as a couple, he cut her loose. The call of the wild turned out to be too much temptation to resist. I had assumed Colton would move on without a problem. But maybe I was wrong about that. I'm not saying I have all the pieces to the puzzle figured out, but here's what I know—he's been messed up for a while now, and it's gotten worse since we ran into Alyssa.

Unsure if I should continue, I say, "You could talk to her."

"Yeah, I tried that." He snorts and flicks his attention to me. "That girl could give Coach a run for his money in the ass reaming department."

One side of my mouth hitches.

"You heard her. She wants nothing to do with me. In fact, she'd rather I not breathe the same air as her." He shakes his head and chuckles under his breath. "If Lys had her way, she'd rather I didn't breathe at all."

He's right.

"Can you blame her?" The way he dumped her was harsh. From what I heard, it involved a text message.

Any trace of humor that had sparked to life in his eyes vanishes as he goes back to staring at his clasped hands. "Nope, not at all."

As I yank my T-shirt over my head, Colton asks, "Are you going to Alyssa's party?"

I shrug and try to play off the question. Not because I haven't given the invitation any consideration. You bet your damn ass I have, but I don't want to rub it in his face. There are some couples who can part ways and remain friends.

Alyssa and Colton are not one of those couples.

When he remains silent, I say, "You could always crash the party."

"Somehow, I don't think that would go over well."

"Have you considered giving her a gift she really wants?" When he raises a brow, I smirk. "Like your balls on a silver platter?"

He wads up his sweaty practice jersey and throws it at my face. I bat it away before it can make contact.

"You're a dick," he laughs.

I grin, relieved the tension has been broken. "Tell me something I don't know."

"Welcome home, bitch," I shout, attempting to be heard over the pulsing beat of techno music as we clink our shots of Fireball together and toss them back. The cinnamon-flavored liquor burns a fiery trail down my throat, killing any bacteria in its path.

"Holy shit, that's terrible!" I sputter, coughing as tears gather in my eyes. "No more shots. I'm tapping out."

She laughs and orders another round.

Alyssa is in her element, chatting with friends who have shown up to celebrate her return to Wesley. For the festivities, she bought a short sparkly silver dress that clings to every curve. Her hair has been curled and left loose so it can float around her bare shoulders. The girl looks seriously hot. And I'm not the only one who thinks so either. There's been a ton of guys sniffing around, and she's been flirting with all of them.

Not that I've been keeping track, but my guess is that she's downed at least half a dozen shots. More impressive than that, she's standing upright and doesn't look the least bit affected. Apparently, dancing wasn't the only thing she worked on in England.

My head is already swimming, and I haven't consumed nearly as much. A few mixers and three shots.

When a song with a great beat comes on, Alyssa squeals and grabs my hand, dragging me to the dance floor. "I freaking love this one!"

We shove our way through the crush of bodies before carving out a tiny space. Our hands go in the air as we lose ourselves in the music. It's not difficult. All I have to do is close my eyes, and everything that has been nagging at me melts away into nothingness. The mounting stress of applying to law school and trying to figure out the next chapter of my life floats away on the beat.

One song bleeds into the next, and we continue to shake our asses, shouting the lyrics in each other's faces. At one point, I grab Alyssa's hand and twirl her around. A smile lights up her face as she laughs hysterically.

Friends come and go as the music continues.

As the DJ plays another song, Alyssa leans in and shouts, "I need to use the bathroom."

"Want me to come with you?"

"Nah." With a shake of her head, she waves me off. "I'll be back in a sec, stay here so I can find you."

In the blink of an eye, she's swallowed up by the crowd, and I'm surrounded by a writhing mass of bodies. The club is dark with strobe lights that flicker. It's difficult to tell what limbs belong to who. Music reverberates off the walls before seeping into my bones. Even though I'm alone, it's all too easy to lose myself in the rhythm.

Alcohol pounds through my system, making me feel alive and free. I want this feeling to last forever. Or, at the very least, until the end of the night.

Male hands wrap around my hips and tug me close. I turn my head and find a guy I recognize from a few of my classes. He's always seemed nice enough.

"Hey, beautiful, want to get out of here?" he slurs.

"No, thanks." I shake my head, hoping Alyssa returns quickly.

"Aww, come on," he growls against my ear, tugging me uncomfortably close. "You're so damn sexy."

"Thanks, but I'm not interested." Why can't these guys take no for an answer? Is it really that difficult of a concept to comprehend?

As I attempt to knock his hands away, they disappear on their own, and a deep voice I recognize all too well says, "You heard her the first time. She's not interested, so do us both a favor and back off."

I spin around, surprised to find Beck standing beside me.

The guy jerks his chin in my direction. "Is she with you?"

"All you need to be concerned about is that she's not with *you.*"

The guy's lips flatten as he glares. From the look on his face, it's obvious that he's thinking about starting something with Beck. Which is surprising. Most people take one look at the muscular QB and back away. This idiot must be drunker than I suspected.

The last thing I want is Alyssa's welcome home celebration ending with a brawl.

In an attempt to avoid conflict, I press my body against Beck's. His arm snakes around my shoulders, and he hauls me so close that my breast flattens against the steely strength of his chest. Tingles of awareness shoot through me as my nipple pebbles. When I try to put some distance between us, he pulls me closer.

There's no way he doesn't feel my arousal.

"Whatever," the guy grumbles before disappearing through the crowd.

Now that it's just the two of us, Beck repositions me until I'm crushed against his front. I inhale a breath, and the scent of his woodsy cologne wraps around me.

"I don't like other guys touching you," he growls in my ear before nipping the delicate flesh with his teeth.

His possessiveness sends a sharp thrill through me. As much as I don't want to like what he's saying, I do.

Way too much.

With a groan, my arms slip around his neck to tug him closer.

"You're fucking killing me in that dress, you know that, right?"

Alyssa made sure I was appropriately attired in club-wear. The black dress I'm wearing is short and probably a size too small. It showcases all of my curves. Normally, I don't have the girls on display, but they're out tonight.

"I didn't wear it for you." That's a big fat lie. I knew there was a chance he would show up after Alyssa issued an invitation. Maybe I wanted him to see what he couldn't have.

Considering that I'm wrapped up in his arms, it would seem like that plan backfired spectacularly.

His fingers bite through the material and into my backside. "Is there another guy I should be concerned about? Someone I need to rip apart with my bare hands for touching you when you look like this?" His voice deepens. "Because I will if I have to."

The muscles in my belly clench at the jealousy filling his voice.

"There's no one else," I admit. It would be easy to pretend that he has reasons to be envious, but there's no point, and I've never been one for games.

His body loosens, and his jaw unlocks. "Good to know."

When he steps away, his warmth disappears, and a sense of loss fills me. Before I can figure out where he's going, he grabs my hand and spins me around until his front is aligned with my back. His fingers brush over my sides before wrapping around my ribcage. It's been so long since his hands have been on me, and I've missed his touch more than I've wanted to admit.

With a groan, my head lolls back until it can rest against the solidness of his chest. Beck lowers his face to my neck so that his warm breath can feather against my skin. My arms loop around his neck as he holds me close.

Why does this have to feel so right?

It would be so much easier if it didn't.

One song blurs into the next, and the throng of people dancing fades until it's just the two of us. Beck holds me so close that I'm not sure where he ends, and I begin. The feel of him wrapped around me is intoxicating. His fingers rest under the swells of my breasts, singeing me through the slinky fabric of my dress. I writhe against him, wanting to feel his hands on me.

"I can't take any more of this," he growls before spinning me around to face him. "I need to touch you."

Not waiting for a response, he grabs my hand and tows me through the crowd.

"Where are we going?" I stumble in my heels, trying to keep pace with him.

"I don't know. Some place where we can be alone."

A thrill of anticipation spirals through me before settling in my core. As turned on as I am, there's a tiny voice in the back of my head that questions whether we should be doing this.

"Are you sure this is a good idea?" I ask.

"It's the best damn idea I've ever had," he throws over his shoulder.

As we move past the long stretch of bar, I catch a glimpse of Alyssa through the crowd. Instead of smiling and laughing like she's been doing all night, her brows are beetled together, and there's a scowl twisting her lips.

"Alyssa," I murmur, pointing to her as Beck hustles me along.

"Leave them alone. They need to get their shit hashed out."

Huh?

That's when I realize she isn't alone. Colton is with her.

No wonder Alyssa looks so pissed off. Before I can decide what to do, the bar area disappears, and we're turning down a narrow hallway and past a set of bathrooms. When we come to a door, Beck reaches out and turns the handle. I think we're both surprised when it swings open. And I'm even more alarmed when he tugs me inside and locks us in the dark space.

BECK

Without hitting the lights, it's impossible to tell if we're in a storage closet or an office. Either way, I don't care. I need to get my hands on this girl before I explode.

In my jeans.

"Beck—"

I tug her close and seal my lips over hers. When her palms flatten against my chest, I half-expect her to push me away. Instead, her fingers dig into my shirt. My tongue sweeps over her mouth. When her lips remain sealed, I nip at her lower one. She yelps, and I plunge my tongue inside.

The sound of her whimper reverberates inside my brain.

It's the best fucking sound in the world.

One I want to hear more of.

It doesn't take long for Mia to melt. Her hands slide up my chest before wrapping around my neck and drawing me closer. I'm starving for the taste of her. For years we've been dancing around each other, and I can't take any more of it.

Whether she realizes it or not, things are going to change.

My hands drop from her waist to the roundness of her ass. I widen my fingers before squeezing the softness and pulling her flush so she can feel the thickness of my erection. I'm so fucking hard for her. No one has ever driven me this crazy.

After I've plundered the sweetness of her mouth, my lips blaze a hot trail to her chin. A groan escapes from her when I nibble at the curve of her jawline.

"We shouldn't be doing this," she whispers.

Is she serious?

I can't think of anything else I'd rather be doing. And I'll be damned if I leave this room without getting my fill of her. She may want to deny it, but she melts every time I put my hands on her.

The black dress she's wearing is dangerous. She looks hot as hell. The moment I spotted her on the dance floor, I knew the night would end with her wrapped up in my arms and my hands all over her body.

My fingers trail from the curve of her ass to the hem that barely skims her thighs before I give it a slight tug. "Nice dress."

"It's Alyssa's."

"I figured, but you look amazing in it."

"Thanks," she sighs, bearing more of her neck to me.

Does Mia even realize what she's doing?

It's all the invitation I need to continue. My lips roam over the delicate flesh of her neck before drifting to her collarbone and kissing the smooth skin of her exposed breasts.

Fuck…I want to rip this dress off her body. Images of her stretched out in my bed flash through my head like a slow-motion picture show.

One hand slides beneath her dress, shoving the slinky material over the curve of her bare ass. As my hand explores the supple skin, I realize she's wearing a thong, and it makes the erection I'm sporting even more painful. My finger traces the slender length of fabric from the elastic around her waist to her slit. Even through the thong, I can tell she's completely soaked.

"Beck," she moans.

"I need to touch you, Mia." I pause as my heart races. "Do you want that, too?"

A deafening silence crashes around us, and I wonder if she'll deny me. If that happens, I'll have no other choice but to step away.

"Yes."

The breath rushes from my lungs in a painful burst as she gives me the green light to proceed. When I stroke my fingers over the damp material, she arches her body.

"Please," she murmurs.

My fingers slip beneath the thong to stroke over bare flesh. I caress her silky lower lips, never once dipping them inside. Restlessly she shifts against me. A whimper of protest escapes when I ease my hand away from her.

"Shh." I press my mouth to hers before swallowing her displeasure. I hook my fingers in the band around her waist before dragging it down her hips and thighs until the tiny scrap of material puddles around her ankles. Now that my eyes have adjusted to the darkness, I realize there's a desk shoved in the corner of the small space. I drop to my haunches and snatch the thong from the floor before shoving the lacy scrap in my pocket. As I straighten, I wrap my arms around her so that my hands splay wide on her naked backside before lifting her from the floor. Her legs band around my waist until her core is pressed against me.

Mia groans, her hips gyrating with need.

Fuck...All I want is to feel her naked flesh against mine.

It only takes three steps to swing around and set her on the desk. Once her ass hits the metal top, I drop to my knees. Anticipation floods through me as I push her thighs wide and bury my face against her heat.

There have been too many times I've fantasized about this moment not to take full advantage of it.

I need to feel her.

Taste her as she explodes on my tongue.

Hot licks of arousal rampage through me.

Even in the darkness, her gaze pins mine in place. She is completely at my mercy. There haven't been many times when I could say that. Carefully, I rub the pad of my thumb across her slit, caressing the soft lips of her pussy. With lazy strokes, I circle her heated entrance. Mia bows her body, widening her legs until she is fully exposed to my touch.

I glance up, wanting to see the pleasure unfold across her features. My fingers tease her, coming close to sinking inside before skittering away. She shifts impatiently as her frustration grows. Every couple of strokes, I slide my thumb over her opening before swiping it across her clit. Her body tightens as a breathy moan falls from her lips. It's sweet music to my ears.

"Beck," she whimpers, "please."

"What do you want, baby?"

"More."

"More what?" I know exactly what she's asking for. I'm as eager for it as she is.

Unable to resist tormenting her, I press my finger deep inside her tight sheath before dragging it out again.

"God, yes," she breathes.

When her muscles clench around me, I nearly come in my pants.

So fucking hot.

If I keep this up, I won't last long. But I'm going to have to because this moment isn't about me, it's about the girl I've been chasing all my life. I won't lie, it's a foreign concept to put someone else's pleasure above my own. With other women, it was always about my gratification. I made sure they enjoyed themselves, but I was there for me.

This couldn't be more different.

Mia is different.

All I want to do is give her pleasure. I want to see the satisfaction unfold on her delicate features. I want to feel her muscles contract around me. I want to taste her excitement.

I want it all.

My fingers glide through her arousal before circling the tiny bundle of pulsing nerves. The way her hips move against my hand tells me she's close.

Her growing excitement only increases my own.

Needing to taste her, I lean in and swipe my tongue across the lips of her pussy. The honeyed taste of her explodes on my tongue.

"Beck," she moans, "that feels *so* good."

Damn right, it does.

"I know, baby," I murmur against her heated flesh. "I want you to enjoy this."

"I don't think I've ever enjoyed anything more." Her voice slurs as if she's drunk with pleasure.

My lips quirk as I nibble at her sweetness. I could stay buried against her soaked skin for hours.

Days.

Fucking years.

The word *forever* flickers through my head. I'm not ready to go there quite yet, but I'm not too far from it either. In the back of my mind, it's always been Mia. No other girl has ever come close to making me feel what she does.

Somehow, I need to make her mine.

And this, it's a start.

I hope.

When Mia spreads her thighs impossibly wide, I run the flat of my tongue over her core before circling her clit and spearing it deep inside. When she groans, I do it all over again. We fall into a rhythm as I continue thrusting into her softness.

When her body tightens, and she lifts herself from the desk, I know she's on the verge of splintering apart. I don't change the tempo of my movements. I keep everything the same until she grows frenzied. Until her harsh breathing is the only sound that fills the tiny room.

"Let go," I whisper.

That's all it takes to send her crashing over the edge. She groans out her orgasm, spasming around my tongue. I don't let up as she rides the wave, grinding herself against me.

When her muscles finally loosen, she slumps onto the desk with a contented sigh. Her legs stay splayed open as I withdraw my tongue from her sheath and lick her shuddering softness with long, languid laps.

She's so fucking creamy.

I want to devour it all.

With a satisfied sigh, she stretches out against the metal surface. Her head hangs off the edge. I give her swollen pussy one last kiss before straightening to my full height. The picture she makes sprawled out with her dress bunched around her waist and her body limp from the intensity of her orgasm is enough to send me hurtling over the edge.

Even though it's dark, I burn the image into my brain. She's so perfect, it's almost painful. The only thing that could make this moment better is if she were mine.

I step closer, lowering my body to hers until my lips can settle against her mouth. The head of my throbbing cock lines up to her entrance. When I thrust my hips, she makes a small mewling noise deep in her throat.

I pull back enough to whisper, "I'm giving you fair warning. Your days of running from me are numbered."

Her movements still.

"Do you understand what I'm saying?"

She remains silent as her teeth sink into her lip.

Instead of pushing for an answer, I nip at the plump flesh and tug it from her teeth, sucking the fullness into my mouth before releasing it.

"Are you going to make me chase you?"

"Beck, I—"

I smack a kiss against her lips. That's all I needed to know.

"Challenge accepted."

I shovel a spoonful of Honey Nut Cheerios into my mouth as the door to Alyssa's bedroom swings open, and she stumbles out. The sleek, sophisticated girl I picked up from the airport the other day is nowhere in sight. The transformation is almost impressive.

Alyssa's blond hair is sticking up from every angle. It wouldn't surprise me if birds have nested in the disarrayed strands. Eyeliner and mascara are smudged under her eyes, giving her a raccoonish appearance.

The girl is one hot mess, which hopefully means she had an amazing time at her party last night. I wasn't expecting Alyssa to show her face until at least noon. I left the club around two o'clock and promptly passed out on my bed. I have no idea when Alyssa made it back to the apartment.

"Hey," my spoon pauses midair, "how are you feeling?" By the looks of her, I'm pretty sure I know the answer to that question.

"Stop shouting." She winces before grabbing the sides of her head. "Please, I beg of you."

"That good, hmm?" The way she was tossing back shots last night was enough to make me nauseous. I didn't consume nearly the amount she did, and I was feeling it. How else do you explain my lapse in judgment?

Alyssa should probably thank her lucky stars she didn't die of alcohol poisoning.

"Let me guess, you're looking for a little hair of the dog that bit you?" I can't resist teasing her. "I'm sure we have a bottle of tequila around here somewhere. Want me to get it?"

"God, no." Her skin turns an unnatural greenish hue at the mention of alcohol. "I'm never drinking again."

I snicker. Alyssa has never been a big drinker, but she likes to have a good time. I give it a week or two before she's back on the horse again.

Once her color returns, she points to the kitchen. "I need massive amounts of Tylenol and Gatorade."

She staggers into the other room before returning with a humongous bottle of the orange sports drink. Her fingers fumble as she attempts to twist off the cap.

"Why did you let me drink so much," she groans, successfully prying off the top and chugging a quarter of it. Then she presses her fingers against her mouth before releasing a loud belch.

"If memory serves, I told you several times to slow down, but you weren't in the mood to listen. At one point, you called me a buzzkill." When she remains silent, I ask, "Exactly how many shots did you have?"

"I lost count after eight." She shakes her head and waves a hand. "Please, I can't even think about that. It'll make me sick. Never mind, I'm already sick." She points to her room. "I'm going back to bed. Wake me up tomorrow. Or maybe the day after that. Hopefully, I'll have bounced back by then."

Alyssa walks a couple of steps before swinging around to face me. With her free hand, she grabs her head as if she's trying to hold it in place. "Wait a minute." She raises a hand and massages her temple. "Were you busting a move on the dance floor with Beck, or was that a tequila-induced dream?"

I wince at the memory and glance away guiltily before shoving another spoonful of cereal into my mouth. I was really hoping she wouldn't remember that part of the evening.

If only it had stayed as innocent as dancing. My face heats as I recall the way Beck set me on the desk and spread me wide, licking me until I orgasmed.

When I fail to respond, she takes another step and jabs a finger at me. Her eyes lose some of their haziness. "Yeah," she mutters, "you two were *definitely* dancing. His hands were all over you. And you, *ya little hussy*, were totally enjoying it."

Oh, God...

This isn't a topic I want to delve straight into at nine o'clock on a Sunday morning. In fact, I don't want to think about it ever again. For reasons I can't explain, I am ridiculously attracted to Beck. Even though he is all kinds of wrong for me, my feelings have yet to dissipate. Every time I catch sight of him, my heartbeat skitters, and the muscles in my belly contract.

He's the last person I want to feel this way about.

His words from last night ring unwantedly in my head.

Your days of running from me are numbered.

Was he serious?

I'm not even sure what that means. Hopefully, nothing.

Alyssa waves her hand in front of my face. "Hello? Earth to Mia. Come in, Mia."

I snap out of those disconcerting thoughts. "Sorry," I mumble.

"Please tell me I wasn't hallucinating. Because if that's the case, I really *am* going to lay off the booze."

"No," I admit, "we danced together." I'm reluctant to give her further details. The last thing I need is Alyssa rooting for a relationship that is doomed to fail before it even starts.

Last night was a bad decision on my part. We need to leave it at that.

You know what this situation calls for?

A change in topic.

I raise my brow and turn the tables. "Is there anything *you* would like to tell me about?"

"Huh?" Her face scrunches.

"I saw you at the bar with Colton."

She blinks away the confusion as her expression hardens. "Can you believe that guy had the audacity to show his face after I purposefully went out of my way *not* to invite him?"

"Umm, maybe?" I pause. "Any interesting conversations?"

She moves to the armchair before slumping onto it and squeezing her eyes shut. "He wants to be friends," she mutters. "Don't worry, I was extremely clear about where he can shove his friendship."

I bet she was.

My lips lift into a smile. Once you've landed on Alyssa's shit list, there's no way off it. Poor Colton. He should walk away while he still can.

"Maybe that was the closure you needed to move on. Feel any better about getting it out of your system?"

Even though her eyelids remain closed, her lips tug down at the corners. "Surprisingly, no."

"I'm proud of you for giving him a piece of your mind. That took balls," I tell her.

She snorts. "As far as I'm concerned, he can shove those up his ass as well."

"Sounds like his ass is a crowded place."

Alyssa cracks open her eyelids and stares at me for a moment before we both burst out laughing. "Yeah, it does."

BECK

I glance at my phone and maneuver my way through the crowd of students traveling across campus like cattle. These people need to move their asses, or I'm going to be late. Class starts in less than five minutes, and walking in like I don't give a shit isn't the first impression I'm looking to make.

Once I reach Mitchell Hall, where the English classes are held, I take the stairs two at a time. Less than a minute later, I'm sliding onto a chair. With a huff, I pull out my computer and wait for Dr. Hayes to get class underway.

Devon Baker plunks his ass down next to me.

Great.

Like I need this distraction. Devon runs his mouth like he's getting paid by the minute. English isn't exactly what one would call a high-octane class. It will take every ounce of my focus to concentrate for a full fifty minutes.

With a grin, he fist bumps me. "Dude, I didn't know you were in this class."

"Last-minute change to the schedule." My advisor emailed me last week and dropped the bomb that Composition is a requirement for graduation.

So here I am.

And I'm not a happy camper about it either.

The thought of writing a bunch of papers makes me want to blow my brains out. And no, I'm not being overdramatic. I suck at writing. There's a reason I pushed this course off for years until I was able to forget about it. Unfortunately, my procrastination has now bitten me in the ass. When I grumbled about it to Coach, he told me he'd reach out to the professor and make sure she kept him in the loop as far as grades were concerned.

Talk about a double whammy.

Like I need that guy riding my ass all semester with a crop.

Needless to say, senior year isn't exactly off to a great start.

"I'm so freaking stoked about getting Hayes for this course," he says.

Seriously?

Those have to be the last words I expected to hear coming out of Devon's mouth.

He's one of those athletes who cobbled together a bunch of bullshit classes and slapped a major on it. He better hope his ass makes it to the NFL because I have no idea what else he'll do.

Before Devon can continue yapping, Dr. Hayes takes her position at the front of the classroom. I glance around and realize the lecture hall is packed to the gills. Since this is a required course, there's a mix of students. The freshmen are the easiest to pick out. They look all fresh-faced and eager to learn. The older ones, like me, look bored and want to get this over with.

"Hello everyone, and welcome to Composition!" This woman is a little too bright-eyed and bushy-tailed for a nine o'clock on a Monday morning. She needs to take it down a notch. Or maybe several. "My name is Rebecca Hayes, but you may call me Dr. Hayes."

A few people chuckle as she continues talking. I fidget as boredom sets in before sneaking a peek at my phone and wincing.

Three minutes.

Only one-hundred-and-eighty seconds have ticked by so far. How am I going to make it through this class for a full semester?

I force my attention to the professor as she delves into the requirements and expectations. A small part of me dies when she mentions a fifteen-page paper due at the end of the semester.

Fuck my life.

She might as well expect me to write a full-on book.

"Damn, but she's hot," Devon whispers, his eyes laser-focused on Dr. Hayes. "I've got a boner with her name written on it."

I scrunch my nose and glare. "Seriously, dude? I didn't need to know that. From now on, keep all dick comments to yourself."

"What can I say? It's the truth." He glances around the lecture hall. "Trust me, I'm not the only one with a chubby. Why do you think this class is so jammed packed?"

"Because it's a requirement." Duh.

"Did you check out her legs?" He doesn't wait for an answer. "Doesn't she make you hot for teacher?"

He snickers when I roll my eyes.

"She's fine."

Note to self—find a new place to sit.

I can't have Devon chirping in my ear all semester, or I'll end up failing the class.

"Bro, she's way better than that," he murmurs, salivating all over himself.

This guy is killing me. It takes effort to harness all of my concentration and tune out his noise. I don't understand why he's flipping out over this woman. Sure, she's pretty with blond hair cut in a sleek bob and deep brown eyes that sparkle with intelligence as they sweep over the lecture hall.

Most professors aren't exactly style icons. The word *dowdy* comes to mind. Although there's nothing frumpy about this woman. The black pencil skirt and white blouse she's wearing hug her generous curves. The first two buttons of her shirt have been left open, displaying a hint of cleavage.

All right, fine. I get it. She's a hot professor. But there's no way my mind can go there when I'm concerned about the workload she'll be piling on. Had I remembered this course was a requirement, I would have taken it last spring when I wasn't in season.

Now I'm fucked.

This class will bury me alive.

I clear that depressing thought from my head and zone back in as she says, "I'd like to introduce my teaching assistant." She points and smiles to someone sitting in the front row. My gaze follows her line of sight until a girl rises from her seat and turns to face the lecture hall.

A little zip of surprise sizzles through me when I realize it's Mia.

"Damn, she's hot, too." Devon rubs his hands together with anticipation. "This is going to be an awesome class."

I shoot him a scowl. "Shut the fuck up, Baker."

"All I'm saying is that she's hot." He holds up his hands and shakes his head as if he can't understand my irritation. "It's a compliment. Chicks love compliments."

I huff out a breath. "You really don't understand anything about women, do you? One of these days, some nice girl is going to kick your ass." My annoyance drains at that thought. "I only hope I'm around to see it happen."

"Please," he snorts, "the ladies love me. I have to fight them off with a stick."

Devon isn't wrong. The entire football team, even the benchwarmers, have their fair share of jersey chasers. It's a perk of being an athlete at Wesley. Most of these guys enjoy taking full advantage of it. It's easy for the attention to go straight to your head.

Both of them.

Once again, I focus on Mia.

Maybe this class won't be so bad after all.

Not that I wasn't expecting it, because it seems to be her modus operandi, but Mia has gone into avoidance mode. I'd hoped that we could level up our relationship after what occurred at Bang Bang, but that hasn't happened.

Which is fine.

She wants to be chased?

I'm game.

MIA

"I'll see everyone on Wednesday," Dr. Hayes announces, dismissing class for the day. Before the last word leaves her mouth, people scatter like rats trying to abandon a sinking ship.

I look around, careful to avoid eye contact with Beck. He's one of the few students who hasn't shoved their shit into their bag and taken off. I'd hoped that by ignoring him, he would get the hint and not wait around. It's not like we have anything to discuss.

We made out a week ago.

End of story.

Other than glancing at him when Dr. Hayes introduced me as the TA, I've kept my back firmly turned to him. Although that doesn't mean I haven't felt his gaze burning holes through me. It was all I could do not to squirm on my chair and peek over my shoulder.

Somehow, I resisted the urge.

Barely.

It's shitty luck that I've ended up TA'ing for Beck's class. What are the odds?

I've tried so hard not to think about the way he touched me at the club, but it's always simmering in the back of my mind. I'm ashamed to admit how many self-love sessions I've had regarding that incident.

I just need to get through the school year, and then we can go our separate ways. I won't have to worry about running into him around every corner. When my heart clenches at the idea of never seeing Beck again, I sweep the feeling aside and ignore it.

I give Beck a bit of side-eye only to find him taking his sweet damn time packing up his stuff.

Ugh.

Can't the guy do me a solid and move it along?

A nervous sweat breaks out across my brow as I try to delay the inevitable.

"Mia," Dr. Hayes says, "do you have a moment?"

And just like that, a lifeline is thrown.

Thank you, Dr. Hayes!

With a rush of breath, I haul the strap of my bag onto my shoulder before racing to the podium.

First semester of freshman year, I ended up in Dr. Hayes' Composition class. I've always enjoyed reading, but she helped me fall in love with the written word. Dr. H gave me the confidence I needed to let my creativity flow. After that semester, I registered for every course she offered at the university.

From beneath the thick fringe of my lashes, I watch as Beck and his friend—who I'm guessing is also a football player, because he's got that whole doesn't-have-a-neck thing going on—pack up their belongings before moving to the center aisle and heading toward the exit.

A relieved breath escapes from my lips when the door closes behind them. I was looking forward to working with Dr. Hayes this semester, now I'm dreading it.

The pretty blond professor snaps her briefcase shut before glancing at me. "Thanks again for taking this position at the last minute."

The graduate student who was originally scheduled to assist her ended up taking the semester off, so she asked me to fill in. There's really not much to the position. All I have to do is copy handouts and grade papers. If there are students who need extra attention, I'll meet with them.

"It's not a problem," I tell her. "I'm happy to do it."

At least an hour ago, I was.

Now? Not so much.

"How's the law school application process going?" she asks. "Did you finish them up?"

I shake my head. It's another thing on my to-do list. "Not yet. I'll be working on them over the weekend."

"If you want me to proofread anything, just text me. I'm more than happy to help." She smiles. "I can't believe you'll be graduating this spring! It doesn't seem like all that long ago you were in my freshman comp class."

My lips lift at the memory. "Tell me about it. The last couple of years have flown by."

"I'm so proud of you, Mia. You've done well at Wesley, and I have no doubt that you'll get accepted at every school you apply to." She reaches out and squeezes my shoulder. "You're going to do great things, I just know it."

Her words of praise leave a thick lump of emotion sitting in the middle of my throat. "Thank you, I appreciate you saying that."

"It's the truth. You've worked hard, and now it's paying off."

"I hope so." There's a fear in the back of my mind that I won't get accepted into law school, and I'll have to figure out a plan B.

"Everything will work out." She gives me a little wink. "We need more strong women in the world showing the boys how it's done."

I laugh and glance away. "I don't know about that." I've never considered myself a strong woman.

"With a great education, your options are limitless. Never sell yourself short."

"Thanks, Dr. H." Her words of encouragement mean a lot to me. She's someone I've always looked up to as a role model.

"You know better than that," she says with a mock frown. "When we're alone, you can call me Rebecca."

I nod.

"All right, we should get out of here. Unfortunately, I have an English department meeting to get to." She rolls her eyes. "Hopefully, there's still coffee left upstairs. Lord knows I'm going to need it."

I chuckle as she picks up her briefcase, and we head up the carpeted stairs to the exit.

After we push through the doors and into the corridor, Dr. Hayes says goodbye before turning toward the elevators that will take her to the fifth floor where the English offices are located. With one final wave, I pull out my phone and glance at the screen, noticing a few messages have popped up during class. As I take a step, a deep voice cuts through the quietness of the hallway.

"Hey, stranger."

I yelp in surprise and nearly bobble my phone when I find Beck leaning casually against the brick wall.

Turns out I wasn't nearly as successful in evading him as I'd originally thought.

Damn.

My gaze rakes over him, taking in every detail. I'm powerless to stop my physical reaction to him. My heartbeat picks up its tempo, and a million butterflies wing their way to life inside the confines of my belly.

I grab the strap of my bag and hug it closer as if that will protect me from him. "What are you doing here?"

"Just wanted to talk." He stares at me as if trying to sift through all of my private thoughts. "Seems like you're avoiding me again."

Doesn't he realize that I'm always trying to avoid him?

"Sorry, that's not the case. It's been busy. Speaking of busy," I take a hasty step away and point toward my salvation which comes in the form of an exit, "I really need to go."

The corners of his lips tilt upward as he lazily pushes away from the wall and saunters toward me. "Calm down, Stanbury. All I'm after is some conversation." There's a pause. "For now."

That's exactly what I'm afraid of.

"What do you want to discuss?" Before he can open his mouth, I blurt, "If it has anything to do with Composition, you should probably speak directly with Dr. Hayes. In fact, if you hurry, you can catch her at her office." I don't bother telling him that he won't find her there.

His lips tremble as if he's amused by my verbal diarrhea. "Sorry to burst your bubble, but you're the one I want to talk with."

"Oh." My shoulders fall.

"You kill me, Stanbury." A chuckle escapes from his lips. "Most girls can't get enough of me. And yet, you can't get away fast enough." He tilts his head. "I can't be the only one who sees the irony in that, can I?"

I shrug. "I guess you could always make it easier on yourself and find one of them instead."

He moves closer until his body towers over mine. "You're right, it would be a hell of a lot easier, but those girls don't interest me. You're the one I'm after."

His candor has me drawing in a breath.

"Wait a minute." His eyes dance with humor. "Have I actually managed to surprise you into silence? Can't say I thought that would ever happen."

It takes effort to shake myself out of the stupor I've fallen into. "Beck—"

"Go out with me, Mia." He pauses for a beat. "Give me another chance."

Is he joking?

No way.

Even though part of me wants to give in, my better judgment prevails, and I shake my head. "No, that's not a good idea."

"And why is that?"

"Because," I gulp down my rising nerves before forcing out the rest, "it's just not."

He presses closer until I have to crane my neck to hold his steady gaze. His voice drops. "I'm sorry for hurting you, Mia. Give me an opportunity to prove I'm not the same guy."

A chance like that would require me to put my heart on the line, and I'm unwilling to do that.

Not even for Beck.

Or maybe I should say, *especially for Beck*. He's the one guy who has the potential to cause untold amounts of pain.

"No." My breath catches at the back of my throat when he reaches out and traces the pad of his thumb against my lower lip. It takes everything inside me not to close my eyes and sink into his touch. Instead of doing that, I force myself to retreat, creating a sea of distance between us. My Beck-induced haze subsides, allowing me to think clearly again.

"It's better if we remain friends," I tell him.

His brows lift. "Are we friends?"

Maybe.

Sort of.

When I keep my lips pressed together, he grins. "I guess that's a good enough place to start." He slings his arm around my shoulder and hauls me close. "What do you say we have lunch together?" He gives me a wink. "As friends, of course."

"Um—"

No. Absolutely not. Every time I'm around this guy, I turn to putty in his hands.

"Excellent. I know the perfect place. You like subs, right?"

Not waiting for an answer, he steers me toward the doors that lead outside.

I groan.

What have I gotten myself into?

Better question—how do I get out?

BECK

Grinders R Us is the best coffeehouse on campus. It's where everyone stops to grab their daily dose of caffeine. Sometimes more than once. As I walk past the small brick building, a familiar profile catches my attention, and my footsteps falter.

There's been no movement on the Mia front. It's been a week since I asked her for a second chance and talked her into having lunch with me.

All right, maybe *forced* would be a better word for it.

No matter what I do, I can't seem to make headway with this girl. I've dropped by her apartment unannounced.

She's not there.

Or so Alyssa tells me.

I've tried hanging around after class, but she's cagey. Sometimes she heads up to Dr. Hayes' office.

I'm getting desperate.

Getting?

Ha!

You trucked by desperate a couple of years ago.

It takes a moment to snap out of my thoughts and to realize that

153

I'm pressed up against the picture window, fogging up the glass like a serial stalker who's left his van running fifty feet away.

As I take a quick step from the coffee shop, her gaze flits to the window and locks on mine. The smile curving her lips falters.

Busted.

Not knowing what else to do, I lift my hand in a tentative wave. That's when I notice she's not alone. There's a guy parked across from her.

Jealousy rushes through my veins as I straighten to my full height. Before I can get a game plan together, I'm yanking open the door and flying through it. Mia's dark eyes widen when she sees me barreling toward her.

If I honestly thought she didn't feel *something*, I'd cut bait and move on. But the girl melts every time I lay my hands on her. And if that's not hot, I don't know what is. Am I really supposed to walk away from that kind of attraction?

I don't think so.

When I'm close enough, I catch the tail end of their conversation.

"I was thinking if you're free this Friday, we might…"

His words trail off when he realizes that Mia's attention has become snagged by something else. Or maybe I should say—*someone else*.

The guy sitting across from her glances at me. I see the moment recognition sets in. His whole face lights up like he won big bucks on a scratch-off. "Hollingsworth, my man! How are you doing?"

"I'm good." His overly friendly demeanor has me searching his face, wondering if I know him. Although, I'm pretty sure I don't. Let's face it, this campus revolves around football. People recognize me everywhere I go. "How about you?"

He grins, vibrating like a puppy with excitement. "I'm awesome!"

Now that pleasantries are out of the way, I stare at Mia. "Hey."

"Beck," she murmurs as heat stings her cheeks.

Her attention never deviates from me. Which is exactly where I like it. The guy she's with doesn't seem to notice. What an idiot.

Before I can say anything else, he gushes, "That was a fantastic game last weekend. You killed North Carolina. There's no way you guys won't take home a championship this year!"

"That's the plan." Normally, I can talk all day long about football. Everything from the last game we played, who landed on the injury list, stats, to the upcoming draft. You name it, I can shoot the shit about it.

But right now?

Football is the last thing on my mind. It's not even a thought in my head.

"Hey, you want a coffee or something?" Her date jumps up from his seat like a Jack-in-the-box.

When Mia opens her mouth—most likely to protest—I cut her off.

"Thanks, I'd love one." I dig around in my pocket for a couple of bucks.

He throws up a hand and shakes his head. "No way, Hollingsworth, it's on me!" And then he's gone.

I have to say, getting rid of him was easier than expected. Once he takes his place at the back of the line, I settle on his seat.

Mia's eyes flash with irritation. "What do you think you're doing?"

I point to the chair as if it's obvious. "Sitting."

"I mean, here." She pauses before adding, "With me."

"I'm keeping you company while your boyfriend fetches me a coffee."

"He's not my boyfriend," she mutters, looking away.

A wide smile spreads across my face. "Good to know."

"It wouldn't matter if he was, because you and I aren't getting together."

"Never say never."

"I'm saying it, Beck." She enunciates the word. "*Never*. It's a firm *never* from me."

I shrug and push onward, undeterred by her negativity. "Stranger things have happened."

"Not that strange." She huffs out an exasperated breath. "Let's get back to the original question. Is there a reason you stopped by?"

"Actually," an idea pops into my head, and I run with it, "there is. I thought we could drive home together next weekend."

Confusion flickers across her face. "What's next weekend?"

"It's my parent's twenty-fifth anniversary party, remember?"

She winces. "It must have slipped my mind. Between school and applications, it's been busy."

"You're still going, right?" Everything in me stills as I wait for her answer.

"Yeah, I promised my parents I would."

Excellent. It works out well because next weekend is a bye week for the team, so we don't have a game. I'm looking forward to getting off campus and taking a breather. Even if my parents are throwing a massive shindig, at least Mia will be there. And maybe I'll have a chance to put my hands on her and seduce her over to the dark side.

"What do you say? Want to share a ride and reduce our carbon footprint at the same time?"

She bites her lip and diligently avoids eye contact. "That's probably not a good idea."

"Why not? You don't want to leave the earth a better place for the next generation?"

The corners of her mouth hitch into a faint smile before she presses her lips together, and it disappears.

"Wait a minute," I point to her face, "was that a smile?"

She shakes her head. "Nope."

"Yes, it was," I say with exaggeration. "I saw your lips twitch."

"It was a muscle spasm. Nothing more."

"I don't think so."

She shrugs.

I settle against the chair. This little exchange is going better than I expected. "How about we agree to disagree?"

"Fine." She clears her throat. "I'm all about eliminating our carbon footprint. It's riding with you that I'm dubious of."

"And why is that? Are you afraid you might succumb to my devastating charms?" I give her a wink. "Don't worry, I'll do my best to fight you off."

She rolls her eyes. But they're still simmering with humor, which is a good sign. It's sure as hell better than her usual reaction. So, I'll take it.

I lower my voice. "FYI—if it helps, I'll let you touch me as much as you want."

"Beck…" she murmurs, dropping her gaze to the coffee cup in front of her.

Unable to help myself, I place my fingers under her chin and lift it, so she has no other choice but to look at me. "What?"

"We talked about this."

"Did we?" I wait a beat. "And what did we decide?"

"That we're better off as friends."

"Yeah, about that," with my fingers still gripping her chin, I lean in and press closer to the table, "I've given it some thought and decided to nix that idea."

Her mouth opens.

"Here's your coffee!"

The spell is broken when an oversized container of java is placed in front of me. "Hope you like cream and sugar."

Damn, that line moved quicker than I thought it would. Mia jerks out of my grasp, and I reluctantly settle on the chair as my hand drops to the table.

"Great, thanks."

"My pleasure, Hollingsworth!"

When he takes a chair from a nearby table, dragging it next to Mia, I rise to my feet and grab my drink. "I should probably get moving, but thanks again."

"Anytime." His voice turns a little wistful. "Sure you can't stay for a while?"

"Sorry." I jerk my thumb toward the door. "I've got class."

His face falls. "Maybe another time."

I glance at Mia and wonder what the hell she sees in this clown. This guy's interest should be focused on her, not me. What a dumbass.

"Think about my offer and get back to me," I tell her.

"That's not necessary, I'll drive myself," she says quickly.

I shrug as if it's no big deal. "You know where to find me if you change your mind."

"I won't."

Yeah, that's exactly what I'm afraid of.

BECK

"Is there anyone who hasn't outlined their paper yet?" Dr. Hayes asks at the end of class. Her dark gaze slides over the sea of students before coming to rest on mine.

Between my football schedule and cracking the books, I've been buried. I've jotted down a few ideas, but it hasn't progressed any further than that. I'll admit to dragging my feet on this. Have I mentioned how much I hate writing papers?

With the fiery passion of a thousand burning suns.

I really need to pull the trigger and get some words on paper. It's already mid-September. The semester is flying by, and football will only ramp up in intensity the deeper we get into the season. Most of the professors at Wesley are pretty cool when it comes to allowing me to hand in assignments a few days late or rescheduling a test if it conflicts with an away game.

And why shouldn't they be?

Everyone knows that the football program brings in the big bucks. And big money means that these professors can fund their research projects. It's a mutually beneficial relationship. No one wants to bite the hand that feeds them.

Devon elbows me in the ribs. "Dude, professor hottie is totally checking you out."

"Huh?" I try not to pay too much attention to what comes out of Devon's mouth. It's ninety-percent bullshit. Both on and off the field.

"Dr. H, dumbass. She's been checking you out the entire hour."

Sometimes I wonder if Devon has taken one too many hits to the head. Concussion testing has clearly failed him.

"You are seriously one lucky bastard," he continues when I fail to show the appropriate amount of enthusiasm. "Dr. H is the scholarly version of Jessica Simpson. And we all know how I feel about her."

Unfortunately, we do. I was hanging out at his house last year and walked in on him spanking the monkey to thoughts of her. It was a permanently scarring experience. I can never un-hear those groans again. Even thinking about the incident makes me shudder.

As soon as Dr. Hayes dismisses us for the day, I pack up my computer and immediately beeline toward Mia. My plan is to leave after practice on Friday evening, and I want to make sure she hasn't changed her mind about hitching a ride.

I know there's not a snowball's chance in hell of that happening, but I gotta ask, right?

Plus, it's another opportunity to talk to her. And I'll take whatever opening I can find.

"Beck," Dr. Hayes calls out, "would you mind sticking around for a quick chat?"

Damn.

The look of relief that floods Mia's face as she scampers from the room hits me where it counts. Right in the old ego.

"Sure, no problem." I swing around and head back to the front of the room.

Dr. Hayes flips through a few papers before glancing at me as the lecture hall empties. I never really noticed it, but Devon is right. She does bear a strong resemblance to Jessica Simpson with her blond hair, deep brown eyes, and curvy body. I shake that thought from my mind and focus on what's being said. The sooner I can get this over with, the quicker I can get out of here.

Maybe I can catch up to Mia.

Not that she'll wait around.

"I wanted to check-in and talk about the progress you're making on your paper," she says.

Well, shit.

I shift my weight and come clean. There's no point in lying. "I haven't started writing it yet, but I've narrowed down the topics."

She raises a brow. "All right, I suppose that's a start."

I flash her a grin, and my muscles loosen. "I've been meaning to get moving on it." Actually, I was hoping Mia could give me some direction. That's part of her TA job, right?

"Let's start with your top two choices and see if we can get you on the right path."

"Sure." I grab my notebook from my backpack before flipping through the pages. "The first topic has to do with the long-term effects of concussions on football players." I glance up to see how that subject has resonated. When she nods, I continue. "And the second is compensating athletes at the college level."

With a thoughtful look, she tilts her head. Her bangs slide over her eyes, and she lifts her fingers, tucking a thick lock of hair behind her ear. "Hmmm, those are both interesting choices."

Relief flows through me that she's on-board with the themes I'm considering. "I'm not sure which one would work better."

"There's a lot of research available regarding concussions and helmet testing. So, my advice would be to go with that one."

"Yeah," I admit with a nod, "I was thinking the same thing."

Great.

When I shove my notebook into my backpack, Dr. Hayes lays her hand on my forearm. Surprised by the contact, my movements falter. I glance at her fingers before staring at her in question.

"Don't run away yet." Her lips curve into a smile. "I spoke with Coach Taylor last week. He mentioned how important it is for you to keep your grades up, so you don't get benched." She steps closer. "I told him I would work closely with you to make sure that doesn't happen."

"Thanks. I appreciate it."

Her gaze stays pinned to mine. "I have to admit that I'm always impressed with the athletes we have on campus. It's not easy to balance academics along with athletic responsibilities. That's a lot of stress and pressure to deal with."

A strange prickle of unease blooms in the pit of my belly, but I quickly brush it away. Under normal circumstances, when a woman touches me and stares at me like I'm a juicy steak, I'd assume she was flirting, but that can't be. Dr. H is my professor.

"It's nothing I can't handle."

I'm oddly aware of her fingers draped across my forearm. It's like they're burning a hole through my flesh. When I remain silent, she flashes another smile and leans toward me. The way she angles her body gives me a straight shot down her blouse. I have to be a good ten inches taller than her. Even though I'm not trying to peek down the front of her shirt, it's hard not to notice the generous swells of her breasts.

"Just know my door is always open if you need help with English or any other subject. I'd be more than happy to help you."

Umm...

"Thanks." I pause, wishing she would remove her hand. "If anything comes up, I'll let you know."

"Please do." The way she continues staring only heightens my unease. "I've worked with several athletes over the years, and it's always been a rewarding experience for both of us. I wouldn't have a problem reaching out to your other professors and asking for extended deadlines on your behalf. Most are accommodating, especially if they know a student is working closely with a colleague."

This has to be the strangest convo I've ever had with a teacher.

Not to mention, most uncomfortable.

I can't decide if she's talking strictly about academics or not.

Either way, this conversation has left a strange pit sitting in my gut. I'm probably reading something into the situation that isn't there. Dr. Hayes is a beautiful woman. My guess is that she doesn't need to troll her classes to get laid. She's probably got guys lined up around the block.

I'm definitely making a mountain out of a molehill.

When she lifts her hand, the unease dissolves and leaves me feeling like an idiot.

"Why don't we plan on getting together later next week, and we'll discuss your progress. That way, I'll know you're on track." Her lips lift. "How does that sound?"

"Sure, that works."

"My goal is to give you the necessary tools you need to be successful. Not only at this university but in life."

"I appreciate your help." I'm a dipshit for questioning if there were ulterior motives at play. Dr. Hayes is just being friendly. She obviously goes above and beyond for her students.

"If you have any questions, my contact information is on the syllabus."

"Yup." I hitch my backpack higher onto my shoulder before taking a step in retreat.

"Here, just a minute." She grabs a small pad of paper and a pen before scribbling something down. Then she tears the page off and holds it out to me. "That's my cell number. Usually, it's only available to my grad students, so please don't give it out."

I take the paper and look at her name and number. "Thanks."

"It's the quickest way to get ahold of me."

I glance at her before stuffing the scrap into the front pocket of my jeans.

"If you have any questions, shoot me a text. Even if it's to talk or unload. All right?"

"Yeah," I mutter, feeling weird again, "thanks."

She picks up her sleek black briefcase. "Well, I need to get to my office. I'm meeting with a group of graduate students to work on their thesis."

"Okay." I inch away from her. The more distance I put between us, the better I feel. I lift my hand into a wave. "I'll see you on Friday."

She winks. "If not sooner."

I jerk my head into a nod.

And then I'm gone, taking the carpeted stairs two at a time before pushing out through the lecture hall doors into the empty corridor. Once I'm there, I expel the breath from my lungs, not realizing I'd been holding it.

Am I nuts, or was that woman coming on to me?

My guess is that I'm losing it. There is no way Dr. Hayes was flirting.

It's all in my head.

It has to be.

MIA

$\mathcal{I}$ park the Jeep in the circular drive and grab my duffle bag before heading up the wide stone steps in front of the house. The door is unlocked, which means someone has to be home. Once inside the two-story foyer, I call out, "Hello?" I pause and wait for a response. When silence greets me, I raise my voice and bellow, *"Mom? Dad? Are you home?"*

"In the kitchen, honey," Mom yells back. "I hope you're hungry."

Is that a joke?

I'm always hungry.

Especially for a homecooked meal.

I set my bag next to the front door before heading through the hallway that leads to the kitchen. Mom is at the oversized marble island chopping vegetables. A smile lights up her face when she sees me. I give her a quick kiss and hug before beelining to the fridge and pulling out a bottle of water. Happy to be home for a few days, I settle on the stool across from her.

"How was the drive?" she asks.

"It was fine." I pause for a beat before adding, "Although my Jeep made a few weird noises when I started it up. But it went away and didn't give me any other problems."

"Hmm." Her brows beetle together. "Make sure to mention it to your father when he gets home."

"When will that be?" I untwist the cap and lift the bottle to my lips, taking a long swig.

"Tomorrow morning." Even though the smile remains intact, it doesn't quite reach her eyes. "He's been out of town the last few days."

"Where did he go this time?" It feels like my father spends more time on business trips than he does at home. The man needs to take it easy. Whenever I mention it, he tells me that he loves his job and has no intention of slowing down anytime soon.

"New York, maybe." Mom lifts her shoulders. "That man is always on the go. At this point, all of the cities blur together."

"One of these days, he's going to have a heart attack." It's something I think about all the time. I don't want to lose anyone else. "He needs to stop working so hard and enjoy his life."

"You're preaching to the choir, honey. I keep telling him the same thing," she murmurs, focusing on the carrots and celery she's chopping, "but you know how he is."

Yes, I do. He's a workaholic, and I'm not sure if that will ever change.

"Your father's birthday is coming up soon," she says, "and I've been thinking about booking a cruise for us."

I perk up. "That's a great idea!"

She glances at me and quirks her lips into a tentative smile. The sadness that is always present in her eyes vanishes. "It's been years since we took a vacation." Looking thoughtful, she pauses before shaking her head. "It must have been before…" Pain flashes in her eyes, and she quickly glances at the vegetables on the cutting board.

"I know, Mom," I say softly. "Don't ask him, just book it."

She worries her lower lip. "You really think I should do it?"

"Definitely. That way, he'll be forced to take the time off."

"True," she sighs. "I'll give it some thought."

I rise to my feet. "Do you need any help with dinner?"

"Nope, it's all under control." She looks at the clock on the stove. "It should be ready in an hour."

"Okay. I'm going up to take a bath and relax a little." I love my apartment at school, but I miss my jetted tub.

"Take your time, honey. We can eat whenever you're ready." She dumps the veggies into a sauté pan. "Maybe we can rent a movie and hang out tonight. Or did you make other plans?"

"I'm all yours." A low-key evening with Mom is exactly what I need.

She smiles, and the last wisps of sadness disappear from her eyes. "I wasn't sure if you'd want to get together with a few friends and go out."

"No one is around, they're all at school."

"I'm sure Beck is back." She gives me a look chock-full of speculation. "I wondered if you two would drive home together."

"He asked," I admit reluctantly, "but I said no."

"How come?" She uses an oversized wooden spoon to push around the vegetables in the pan. "Beck is such a lovely boy."

First of all, he is *definitely* not a boy.

And second—

"No one on the face of this planet has ever referred to Beckett Hollingsworth as *lovely*."

She throws a look over her shoulder as her lips tremble upward. "Oh, I don't know about that. He's pretty darn lovely to look at, don't you think?"

My mouth drops open. "Oh my God! Did you seriously just say that?"

"I did," she chuckles. For the first time in forever, there's a light-heartedness to her. It's nice to see.

"You know," she continues before I can recover, "I've always thought he had feelings for you."

"Mom," I groan, embarrassment licking at my cheeks, "he does not. Trust me on this. Beck has more girls sniffing around him than he knows what to do with." Which is exactly why I keep shutting down his advances.

Fool me once, shame on you.

Fool me twice, and I deserve everything I get.

Ignoring me, she muses, "Remember how protective he was when you two were kids? That boy always sat next to you on the bus." A distant look enters her eyes as if she's tumbled back in time. "I always felt better knowing he was looking out for you."

Of course, I remember. It's probably where my infatuation with Beck stems from.

"He really is a sweet boy. Maybe a little misunderstood. I wish his father wouldn't be so hard on him."

I scrunch my nose. "You think Archie is hard on Beck?"

"Yes, I do. He treats Ari like the heir to the kingdom. I'm sure it was difficult for Beck to grow up in his older brother's shadow. Everything came so easily to Ari. School, athletics, popularity. He never had to work for any of it. And Beck," she shrugs, "he's different. Sometimes it seems like no matter how hard that poor boy tries, he will never please Archie." She glances at me. "When Brianna was alive, you both had your own interests. We tried to cultivate them without making you girls feel like you were in competition with each other."

That's true.

Brianna was a gifted artist. She loved to draw and paint. Even though she did well in school, math was always a struggle. Academics came easier to me. And picking up a tennis racket felt like second nature. My parents attended art shows and tennis tournaments. They never made us feel like one was more favored or important than the other. We each had our own talents, and when one of us did well, they always applauded it.

Now that I think about it, I guess what Mom is saying isn't wrong. Archie *does* treat his older son like the heir apparent. He's always crowing about Ari's latest accomplishments. And Beck is an afterthought.

A kernel of pity blooms inside my chest.

Does it bother Beck that Archie lavishes so much attention on his brother?

How could it not?

"Anyway," Mom says, drawing me back to our conversation. "Beck seems to be doing well for himself."

"Yes, he is." I fall silent as Mom's words swirl through my mind. It takes effort to push all thoughts of Beck away, but that's nothing new. "Okay, I'm going to head upstairs for a bath. I'll be down in a bit."

"Sounds good, honey." I take a few steps toward the hallway when she says, "Oh, I forgot to mention that I picked up a dress for you to wear tomorrow. You're going to love it."

"Thanks, Mom."

"Let me know what you think. It's draped over the chaise in your room."

"Will do," I call over my shoulder before jogging up the stairs.

Fifteen minutes later, I'm soaking in a frothy tub of bubbles. With my head resting against the porcelain edge, I close my eyes and let the tension leak from my body. I hate to admit it, but I can't stop thinking about what happened at the club. The way Beck set me on the desk and…

Yeah.

What is it about him that makes me lose total control?

Even thinking about the way he buried his face between my legs sends a tidal wave of arousal crashing over me. The pleasure he's capable of is like nothing I've ever experienced before. Is it any wonder I find him so damn addictive?

An uncomfortable ache throbs to life between my thighs as I shift in the warm water.

Don't do it.

Don't you dare touch yourself and think about him.

With my eyes closed, my fingertips trail across my breasts before carefully circling around the puckered tips. Hot licks of need spike through me. It's one thing to have Beck bring me to my knees and quite another to touch myself while conjuring up an image of him. If I were smart, I would ignore the heat swirling through my core, but I can't.

I'm too turned on.

My hand disappears beneath the sudsy surface until its able to stroke over the lips of my pussy. When my fingertips brush over my clit, I groan and spread my legs wider. One image of Beck with his face pressed against my core and his tongue dancing across my silky flesh is all it takes to push me over the edge. My muscles spasm as I moan out my orgasm. My fingers keep moving, stroking over my clit until I've wrung every shudder from my body.

The moment my mind clears, I groan. Only this time, it has nothing to do with pleasure.

What the hell is wrong with me?

Frustrated with myself for this infatuation that refuses to die, I suck in a breath and sink beneath the surface until my entire body is submerged.

Beck is a weakness I can't afford. I keep waiting for him to lose interest and move on, but that has yet to happen. What I know is this —if I'm not careful, he could break down every last one of my defenses, and I'm afraid it's only a matter of time before that happens.

MIA

I stare in the gilded mirror propped against the far wall of my room before twisting and turning, trying to assess myself from every angle. When I saw the gorgeous gray garment Mom had mentioned last night, I'd thought it was a dress. But it's actually two separate pieces. The top is beaded and sleeveless with a high neck. The skirt is a tulle concoction that flutters around my knees.

There is no way I would have picked out something like this for myself. And yet, it fits me perfectly and transforms me into a fairy princess. Once dressed, I move to the vanity and apply a bit of silvery eyeshadow that glitters and shiny lip gloss before twisting my hair into a sleek bun at the top of my head.

By the time I grab the small silver sequin clutch that has a stash of makeup along with my phone, Mom and Dad are waiting downstairs in the entryway.

Archibald and Caroline's anniversary party begins promptly at six o'clock and is being held at their estate. I peeked out the living room window a few hours ago, and there was a small fleet of trucks parked in front of the Hollingsworth mansion. Caroline is known for throwing elegant and sophisticated parties.

Mom is wearing a chic black shift dress that accentuates her trim figure. Diamonds drip from her ears and decorate her neck. Dad looks handsome in a black suit with a crisp white button-down and purple tie.

"I knew that dress would fit perfectly," Mom greets in a smug tone as I walk down the staircase. "You look stunning."

"You're an absolute vision, honey," Dad pipes up before pocketing his phone. He's worse than a teenager with his electronics. You would think the stock market depended upon Daniel Stanbury knowing every little hiccup.

I fluff the tulle with my hands as I arrive at the bottom step. "Thanks, Mom. It's a beautiful dress."

"Remember," she admonishes, "you make it beautiful, not the other way around." She gives me a little wink before tugging me close and dropping a kiss on the top of my head.

I glance at Dad, happy we're all together for a change. Mom and I had a great time last night curled up on the couch watching movies and eating popcorn. We laughed and talked about everything. Except Beck. After my little self-love session, I was relieved she didn't mention him again.

Dad walked through the door two hours ago, arriving home late. When I asked how the trip went, he shrugged and said as well as could be expected. Mom's face fell when he mentioned leaving again at the end of the week.

How will their marriage get better if he's never around to work on it?

I'm tempted to pull him aside and tell him that, but I'm not sure it's my place. They're the ones who need to fix their marriage, not me.

"We should probably head over," Dad says.

Mom grabs the small silver-wrapped gift sitting on the table near the door.

I glance at the pretty box in her hand. "What are you giving them?" I have no idea what you buy for the couple who has everything.

"A five-hundred-dollar spa gift certificate." She flashes me a smile. "I was thinking they could indulge in a couples massage."

Mom is so good at these things. "I bet they'll love that." I know I would.

"Yeah," she says a bit wistfully, "who couldn't use a bit of pampering from time to time?"

Note to self—tell my father to buy her that for Christmas.

As Dad reaches for the brushed nickel door handle, his phone buzzes with an incoming call. He quickly nips it from his pocket. One look at the screen has his brows knitting together.

"For goodness' sake, Daniel, you just returned home." Mom's voice bristles with impatience. "Can't we enjoy one evening without work interruptions?"

Not that I blame her for being irritated, but her remarks leave me flinching with unease.

"Sorry," Dad mutters, not bothering to take his gaze off his cell. "I need to take this call." He glances up with a contrite smile. "It shouldn't take more than ten minutes, then I'm all yours." He presses the phone to his ear and opens the front door, quickly ushering us outside. He mouths, "You two go, and I'll be over as soon as I wrap up this last piece of business."

Mom's lips flatten into a tight line. It's clear that she's fed up with his behavior. "You have ten minutes before I send Archie over to drag you to the party."

Relief washes over his features as he gives her a quick peck on the cheek. Once we cross over the threshold, the door closes behind us.

I glance at Mom to see if she's all right. "You need to book that cruise ASAP," I say quietly. "Getting him away for a week is the only way he'll take a break."

"Yeah," she mutters, sounding unconvinced, "I'll call the travel agent on Monday and see what we can do."

As we step off the brick pathway onto the lawn that connects the two properties, the heels of our shoes sink into the grass. At eight-thousand square feet, I always thought our house was massive, but the Hollingsworth mansion is double that. It's palatial. Mrs. Graham, the housekeeper, should hand out a baggie of breadcrumbs to visitors so they don't get lost.

As we arrive, there's a line of cars pulling into the circular drive before guests hand over the keys to guys dressed in white button-down shirts and black slacks. The valets take the vehicles and park them along the end of the street. Once we reach the front door, it opens before we can raise a fist to knock, and we're immediately ushered inside by Mrs. Graham. A waiter in a crisp-looking tux is stationed strategically near the front entrance with a silver tray of crystal flutes filled with champagne.

We grab a glass of the golden bubbly liquid before walking through the massive entryway toward the kitchen. Guests mingle in every corner. Mom and I greet a few people before making our way outside to the patio. A large white tent has been erected in the backyard. Since it's early fall, and the temperature is seasonable, the flaps have been tied back. Tables with stunning pink and white flower arrangements dot the interior. Crystal chandeliers hang from the ceiling of the tent. Sleek white seating areas are grouped together. All the decor is done in shades of pink with silver accents. It's all very elegant.

On the far side of the tent is a parquet dance floor. A stringed quartet plays classical music. Mom mentioned that later tonight there will be a DJ and dancing.

Even though there must be at least a hundred people present, my attention is immediately snagged by Beck, who looks handsome in a suit and tie, as he loiters at the bar with one of his cousins.

His fingers are wrapped around a thick crystal tumbler filled with amber liquid on the rocks. My breath becomes wedged at the back of my throat as his gaze drifts over the crowd before settling on mine. When heat leaps to life in his eyes, all I can think about is the way I touched myself last night in the tub.

I shove the memory from my mind before a blush can rise to my cheeks. A hum of unwanted attraction sizzles through my blood. My hand flutters to my lower belly to settle the horde of butterflies trying to wing their way to life.

No matter how patient I've been, these feelings never seem to dissipate. If anything, they've only grown stronger. I'm wondering if my attraction to Beck will ever fade.

It's almost a relief when Archibald and Caroline join us. When Archie asks where Dad is, Mom rolls her eyes and tells him about the business call. Even though I try to focus on their conversation, my interest is drawn to Beck. I'm hyperaware of his every move. The way his focus stays trained on me sends a surge of shivers careening down my spine.

It's only when Mom elbows me gently in the side that I snap to awareness. Her lips twist into a smile as she nods toward Beck's father. "Archie was asking how classes are going this semester."

Heat fills my face as I refocus my attention. "Sorry." I shake my head and lie through my teeth. "I was admiring the decor."

"You might have been admiring something else," Mom says under her breath before taking a sip of champagne.

Her mumbled comment sends another wave of heat flooding through me. It takes effort to keep the smile plastered across my face as I return the elbow. I do my best to ignore her as her shoulders shake with silent laughter.

Archibald and Caroline take a moment to glance around at their hard work.

"It was all my lovely wife. She spent the last couple of months planning this party, and it turned out beautifully."

Beck's mother beams at the compliment.

"Everything is gorgeous," I tell her, relieved that no one other than my mother noticed the reason for my distraction. If this is how the rest of the evening will go, I'm in trouble. I bring the flute to my lips and swallow down the bubbly liquid.

Caroline glances around the festivities with a satisfied expression. "I think we all know this is a dry run for when I finally have a wedding to plan."

That simple comment sends the champagne down the wrong pipe, and I sputter. Tears sting my eyes as a wide palm lands on the spot between my shoulder blades.

"Your parents can't take you anywhere, can they?"

Still coughing, I whirl around to find Ari, Beck's handsome older brother. A wide grin curves his lips. Before I'm able to react, he pulls me into his arms for a hug.

"Long time no see, squirt," he whispers in my ear.

Throughout college and the first year of law school, Ari came home during the summers and interned at his father's practice. This year, he received a prestigious clerking position with a law firm near Stanford. I haven't seen him since last Christmas.

"Good to see you, too," I laugh, squeezing him tight. "I missed you this summer. The office wasn't the same without you."

"I'm almost afraid to ask who your standing lunch date was." Before I can answer, he says, "Please tell me it wasn't Mark from accounting."

I burst out laughing as the knot in my belly loosens. "What do I look like, a glutton for punishment?" Mark is a nice guy, but that doesn't mean I want to spend my entire lunch break learning about the nitty-gritty world of payable and receivable accounts. The lunches where he tagged along with us only solidified the notion that I made the right decision not to pursue a career in accounting.

Caroline shoots my mother a sly smile. "They make an adorable couple. Don't they, Julia? Maybe there'll be a wedding in the near future, after all."

A gurgle of surprise rises in my throat as Ari tugs me even closer. "Looks like there's some plotting and scheming underfoot."

Unsure how to respond, I press my lips together and remain silent.

From the corner of my eye, I watch as Beck joins our group. His lips are drawn down at the edges, and I fidget beneath the heat of his stare.

Unsure how to extract myself from this uncomfortable situation, I lift the flute to my lips and guzzle down the champagne before wiggling the stem. "If you'll excuse me, I need a refill."

"Someone's thirsty," Ari chuckles. "Would you like me to get you another?"

I slip easily from his hold. "No, thanks." And then I'm off, sliding through the crowd with a relieved breath.

When I was a kid, I used to think Beck was Ari's mini-me. They both have the same dark wavy hair, bright green eyes, and athletic build. Now that they are older, the differences are more perceptible. The breadth of Beck's shoulders is a little broader, his chest is a smidge wider, his arms bigger and more muscular.

There is such a strong family resemblance that it would seem natural to be attracted to both. But I'm not. When Ari had pressed me close, I'd felt nothing. My pulse didn't skitter. The muscles in my belly didn't contract. My core didn't flood with arousal.

It's a disconcerting realization.

Needing a breath of fresh air, I hand my flute to a passing waiter. Instead of grabbing another drink, I rush from the tent. As much as I want to avoid Beck for the rest of the evening, I realize my time is running out. He won't allow me to elude him indefinitely. One thing I realize about my neighbor is that when he wants something, the guy goes after it with a single-minded determination.

And what he wants, is me.

MIA

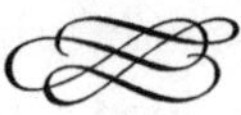

So far this evening, I've been able to evade Beck's evil clutches.

Barely.

He's spent all of his time stalking me through the party like I'm prey. It's exhausting to get embroiled in conversations as I keep a cautious eye out for him. The guest count has swelled, and a lot of them are family or close friends, so Beck has been dragged into countless exchanges.

His frustration is palpable.

It's kind of amusing.

If my luck continues to hold until the end of the night, I'll be able to slip away without him laying his hands on me.

By now, the party is in full swing. The quartet has been replaced by a DJ, and everyone is on the dance floor busting a move. Even Archie and Caroline are out there enjoying themselves. I search the crowd until my focus settles on Mom and Dad.

Shocker—Dad has his phone in his hand and is staring down at it. His thumbs are moving over the screen like crazy. Mom stands a few feet away with a hollow look in her eyes as she lifts the champagne to her mouth and finishes the glass.

Pursing my lips, I shake my head.

What is wrong with him?

Why can't Dad take a few hours away from work like he promised? I'm tempted to march over and grab the phone from his hands. Maybe then he would smarten up and pay attention to his wife.

As I take a step toward them, my feet grind to a halt when Beck sidles up to my mother with a fresh glass of champagne.

Like she needs that.

They converse before her gaze sweeps over the surrounding area. I quickly duck behind a potted plant, watching as she shrugs and shakes her head.

Damn. That was close.

"Who are we hiding from?" a voice whispers in my ear.

I yelp and jump in surprise. Thank goodness I'm not holding a drink. It would be all over the front of me.

I spin around and glare at Ari before smacking his arm. "What are you doing sneaking up on me like that? You nearly gave me a heart attack."

He crouches next to me and uses one hand to part the floppy leaves before staring through them. "You didn't tell me who we're hiding from. Is it Mark from accounting?"

"Oh God," I groan, "is he here?"

"Yup. I had an incredibly tedious conversation about the gross profits of the firm and what overhead could be cut if we're looking to improve it. Here are my thoughts on the matter—his position should be the first to go."

His comment brings a smile to my lips.

"Don't worry, if you're avoiding Mark, God's gift to the accounting world, he's," his words drop off before he says with a shitload of humor dancing in his voice, "*oh, I see who has you cowering in the corner.*"

"I am not cowering!" When I poker up to my full height, the top of my head knocks into Ari's chin, and he staggers back a step before grabbing his jaw.

"Ow! Damn girl, that hurt!"

I cover my mouth with both hands and suck in a sharp breath. "I'm so sorry! I didn't mean to do that!"

He swipes his tongue across his teeth and winces. "I think you might have chipped a tooth."

"No!" I groan, embarrassed to have caused such damage.

He straightens and drops his hands. "Just kidding."

My shoulders collapse in relief as I shake my head and glare. "You're such a jerk."

Instead of responding to my comment, he says, "Uh-oh, looks like you've been made."

I glance at the spot across the tent where Beck and my mother have been conversing. Ari is right. As we speak, Beck is bulldozing his way through the crowd with a determined look on his face. A few people reach out, trying to detain him, but he's either not paying attention or deliberately ignoring them.

"I've got to go!" I squeak, taking a step toward the flaps of the tent. If I'm quick enough, I can disappear and make myself scarce.

Before I'm able to escape, Ari reaches out and grabs hold of my hand. "Oh no, you don't. How about we add some gasoline to the fire?"

"Huh?" I blink.

What the hell does that mean?

"Come on, let's dance."

I throw a cautious look over my shoulder at Beck as his brother drags me through a crowd of people. As we make our way to the dance floor, the music changes from an upbeat, fast-paced song to a slow one. Ari carves out a small space for the two of us before wrapping his arms around me and tugging me close. His cologne wafts around me, but it doesn't make my senses go haywire.

From the corner of my eye, I watch Beck settle at the edge of the dance floor with a scowl as he shoves his hands in the pockets of his suit pants.

Is Ari trying to make his brother jealous?

I glance at him. "Why are you doing this?"

A grin flashes across his face before he lowers his mouth to my ear.

"What do you mean? I'm trying to help you out," he says innocently. "Seems like you want my brother to get the hint that you're not interested."

A rush of nerves scamper across my skin as I peek at Beck, only to realize he's disappeared from where he had taken up sentinel.

When I remain silent, Ari says with a chuckle, "Or am I wrong about that? Either way, the ball's in your court, squirt. I guess it's up to you to make the next move."

I nibble at my lower lip. This is what I wanted, right? For Beck to move on and leave me alone.

Except…

Relief isn't rushing through me the way it should be. And the sense of loss I feel is enough to swallow me whole.

I groan, knowing exactly what I have to do.

BECK

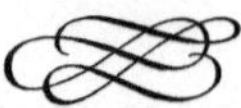

Tonight has officially ended up in the shitter. I'd been looking forward to spending time with Mia away from campus, but that hasn't happened. It doesn't take a genius to realize that she's been avoiding me all evening.

For fuck's sake, she was hiding behind a potted palm.

No girl has ever gone to such great lengths in their quest to evade me.

It's official. My ego has been completely annihilated.

And then there's Ari, that rat bastard. Every time they were together, his arm was tucked around her waist. I'm this close to wrapping my hands around his neck and squeezing the damn life out of him.

Exactly when did he become so interested in Mia?

I can compete with a lot of guys, but not my brother.

Out of the two of us, Ari is the better man. There isn't anything he hasn't tried and succeeded at. High school, football, college, law school. Nothing fazes the guy. He comes, conquers, and then leaves.

If I didn't love him so damn much, I'd be annoyed.

My father can't sing his praises loud enough. At least the old man has one son who will do him proud in life. We all know it won't be me.

Unable to stomach the sight of them dancing, I swing away and cut through the crowd before beelining for the exit. On my way out, I snag a bottle of beer from the waiter. The area surrounding the tent is packed with guests. I glance at the house, wondering if it's possible to seek refuge in there, but it's ablaze with lights. Through the windows, I see more people milling around and chatting. They're everywhere. Escape doesn't seem possible.

If one more person asks about football or the draft, I'm going to throw myself in the pool. I'm talked out. I want to be alone and brood.

"Hey, Beck!" my uncle shouts from twenty feet away, "we haven't had a chance to catch up. How's the season going?"

I shake my head and cup my hand around my ear. "Sorry, can't hear you."

He waves his arm and says loudly, "Get over here, kid!"

I point to the house. "I need to check on something for Mom. I'll catch you later."

When he turns away, I breathe a sigh of relief and head in the opposite direction, ducking behind the tent to the far end of the property. Lights have been strategically placed throughout the yard and pool area. The further I venture from the tent, the more engulfed by darkness I become.

With a bottle of beer clutched in my hand, I collapse onto one of the chairs arranged around the brick firepit and stretch my legs out in front of me. I twist off the cap and bring the bottle to my lips before taking a swig. It's cold and refreshing, but does nothing to ease the growing ache in my chest.

The thought of Mia and Ari together makes me sick to my stomach. I've been focused on her for so long. Sometimes it seems like forever. How am I supposed to forget about her and move on? Is that even possible?

I guess I'm going to find out. If there's one lesson I've learned, it's that you can't force someone to like you.

It's a bitter pill to swallow.

The noise of the party fades as I slouch on the chair and stare at the bright pinpricks of light that dot the clear night sky. Maybe I'll hide out here for the rest of the evening. It's not like anyone will miss me.

"Is this chair taken?"

I jerk out of my misery only to find Mia staring at me.

Even though my heart constricts, I shrug and wave a hand. "Be my guest."

Carefully, she tucks her skirt beneath her before settling on the white Adirondack chair next to mine.

"Where's Ari?" I wince at the bitterness that shoots out of my mouth.

Jeez.

Jealous much?

I might have known this girl my entire life, but she still has the strange ability to twist me up into little knots. It's the most ridiculous thing, and yet, all I want to do is be around her. She's a brightly shining sun I find myself gravitating to.

Her eyes flicker to mine before darting away as her fingers twist nervously in her lap. "He's in the tent dancing with your grandmother."

"That sounds about right. Now that Nana has a brand-new hip, she's back to shaking her booty like it's the seventies."

A tiny smile tips the corners of her lips. "I have to admit, she's got some enviable moves. Everyone has formed a circle around her while she out-twerks your brother." Mia pauses before adding, "My guess is that she's had a few drinks."

"Probably more than a few," I chuckle. "Nana Betty loves her gin and tonics with a twist of lime. I used to make them for her all the time when I was a kid."

"I remember."

We fall into silence as Mia stares at her fingers.

Why is she here? She's done everything humanly possible to avoid me this evening. And now, the moment I stop chasing her, she seeks me out? It makes no damn sense.

No matter how old I am, I will never understand girls.

They're like the Bermuda Triangle.

Or a Rubik's Cube.

Totally unsolvable.

When I can't stand another moment of silence, I ask, "Why are you here? Shouldn't you be partying it up?"

With Ari.

The guy she's obviously interested in.

My lips twist with resentment as I pick at the bottle label with my thumbnail. There's no doubt about it, I am in full-on sad bastard mode. She should leave before I jackhammer to an all-new low and embarrass myself any further.

From the corner of my eye, I watch her fingers become more erratic. If I didn't know better, I'd suspect my presence made her nervous. But that's wishful thinking on my part.

"I wanted to talk to you."

Me?

Really?

"Oh?" I can't imagine why. Is this where Mia drops the bomb that she's filing a restraining order against me? Nothing would surprise me at this point. "What about? Seems like you've been working really hard to avoid me all night." Not to mention, the last couple of years. It might have taken me a while, but I finally got the memo.

Message received loud and clear.

Even though it's dark, a blush hits her cheeks.

"You're right," she admits. "That's exactly what I've been doing."

Woah.

What's going on here?

An actual acknowledgment?

I sit up a little straighter on my chair. "Are you going to tell me why?"

The sounds of the party fill the air between us, and I wonder if she'll answer the question.

"I don't want to be hurt again."

Fuck.

She's talking about what happened between us after our senior year of high school. I took her virginity and told her that I wanted more. Then my dad got in my head, and I backed out.

"I'm sorry, Mia. I never meant to hurt you." I shake my head. "When I asked you out, I was serious." I glance away and admit, "But I chickened out. Most of the time, I don't think I'm anywhere near good enough for you."

"Why would you say that?" she murmurs, voice filled with disbelief.

A bitter chuckle escapes from my lips. "How could I not? You're amazing at everything, and I'm," I shrug, "me."

"*Beck,*" she whispers.

I grow restless under the heaviness of her gaze. As much as I don't want to have this conversation, it needs to be said. "It's the truth. You could do so much better than a guy like me." I've struggled with ADHD my whole life. The disappointment my father feels has chipped away at my self-esteem over the years. Maybe that's not the image I project to the world, but it's how I feel deep down inside.

A strangled groan leaves my lips as I realize how much I've revealed. Now she'll think I'm a pathetic loser. All I'm doing is making Ari look better. It's the story of my life.

I drag a hand over my face and focus on the trees that creep at the edge of the property. Embarrassment bubbles up inside me like a geyser.

What the fuck was I thinking?

Maybe if I ignore her long enough, she'll leave. Nothing about this evening has worked out the way I thought it would. I'm ready for it to be over. Mia has spent years avoiding me. It shouldn't be too difficult to do the same until graduation.

From the corner of my eye, I watch as she rises to her feet.

Thank fuck.

A dozen bottles of beer, and maybe I'll forget this conversation ever took place. I'm not one to get blackout drunk, but right now, it's the best plan I can come up with.

Instead of returning to the party, she closes the distance between us. It's only when she lowers herself to my lap, that I stare at her in surprise. My hands settle on her waist so she won't tumble off my thighs as her arms slide around my neck.

"Do you remember what you asked me two weeks ago outside Dr. Hayes' classroom?"

She's so damn close that her warm breath drifts across my lips. Barely am I able to concentrate on the question she poses.

"Beck?" Humor tinges her voice.

I blink and wrack my brain. Two weeks ago? Outside Hayes' classroom?

Oh…right.

Mia had used her stealthy avoidance tactics to thwart me, but I'd loitered around and waited for her.

"You asked for a second chance," she reminds softly.

Yup, that's right. And she shot me down before I could blink.

"I remember," I mutter, wondering where she's going with this.

She presses closer. The light floral scent she's wearing wraps around me. I suck in a deep breath as need pulses through my body.

"Ask me again," she whispers.

A little zip of electricity sizzles through my veins. I search her eyes, trying to sift through her thoughts in the darkness. Is this some kind of joke? Are all of my parent's guests planning on jumping out and laughing hysterically when I ask this girl out again only for her to reject me?

Nerves settle in the pit of my belly. "Will you give me another chance?"

Her mouth brushes over mine. Back and forth, she caresses my lips until I'm close to losing it.

"Yes."

With a frown, I drag myself away. "You're not fucking with me, are you?"

The corners of her lips quirk. "No, I'm not."

"You sure?"

"Yes," she laughs, "I'm sure."

"All right then." Every muscle in my body loosens. "Carry on with what you were doing."

Instead of waiting for her to come to me, I press my mouth against hers. As soon as she opens, my tongue slips inside. Mia's arms tighten around my neck. That's all it takes to get lost in the taste of her.

"It's nice to see you two have finally worked out your issues," a smug voice says from behind us. "I was beginning to lose hope."

Son of a bitch.

I pull away from Mia enough to twist around and glare at my brother. "Get out of here before I kick your ass." Even though Mia is perched on my lap, I press her protectively against my chest.

"Don't worry, I'm going." He chuckles before throwing his hands up in the air. "I don't even get a thank you for pushing you two crazy kids together?"

I snort as Ari disappears as silently as he arrived on the scene.

For a moment, I stare at Mia. "So, what now?"

She purses her lips and pretends to ponder the question. "You kiss me."

"I can do that," I murmur, not needing to be told twice.

MIA

"Okay," Dad peeks around the hood of my Jeep, "try starting it again."

I turn the key, but nothing happens. Not even the clicking sound that means the engine is trying to turn over. Dad grumbles before straightening to his full height. I open the door and hop out, coming around to the front.

With our heads bent together, we stare at the engine.

"Any ideas?" I ask, already knowing the answer. Neither one of us understands a damn thing about cars, except how to drive them.

Dad scratches the side of his head, looking perplexed. Ask him anything about the stock market or assets and equity management, and he can give you a dissertation that would bore you to tears.

Ask him about cars, and he's as silent as a church mouse.

"Nope," he says cheerfully, "I got nothing." He puffs out his lips as he continues staring. "I guess the next step is to call the garage and have it towed."

My shoulders collapse. This Jeep is my baby, and I hate being without it. It was a gift for my sixteenth birthday. Hands down, best present I've ever received. I don't want anything to be seriously wrong with it. Someday I'll need to buy a new car, but I hope it's not anytime soon.

"Give me a minute to grab my keys, and I'll drive you to school."

As Dad jogs up the stairs to the front door, Beck pulls his shiny black Ford F-150 into the driveway and parks alongside my lifeless Jeep.

The tinted window disappears to reveal Beck in the driver's seat. His gaze bounces from the Jeep, with its hood popped open, to me and then Dad, who has stopped on the porch. "You need a jump, Mr. Stanbury? I've got cables in the back."

"No, I don't think it's the battery, the damn thing won't even turn over. I'll call for a tow, and then take Mia to school. Even if we get it started, I wouldn't feel comfortable letting her drive it. The mechanic will have to check it out first."

Beck nods as if that makes perfect sense. "I'm heading to Wesley. Mia is welcomed to hitch a ride. There's no reason for you to spend two hours in the car."

Dad runs a hand through his silvered hair. Uncertainty flickers across his features as he shifts his weight and considers the offer. "You sure you don't mind?"

Beck shakes his head before shooting me a smirk. "Nah, we live in the same building. It's not a problem at all."

Dad turns to me with a hopeful expression on his face. "Are you good with that, honey?"

"Sure, it'll save you the trip." Even though I'm trying to play it cool, nerves tingle at the bottom of my gut.

As soon as the first word slips from my mouth, Beck is throwing open the door and jumping out of the truck. "Are your bags in the backseat?"

I nod as he opens the passenger side door and grabs my duffle bag before walking around to the back of his vehicle.

Once he slams the door, he turns to me. "Ready to go?"

I blink in surprise. "Um, yeah."

Dad closes the distance between us and draws me in for a hug. "I'll text you tomorrow and let you know what's going on with the Jeep, and then we'll figure out how to get it to you."

"Let me know when it's ready, Mr. Stanbury. I can drive Mia home."

"Thanks." Dad reaches out to shake Beck's hand. "I appreciate all your help."

"Sure thing." Beck sends a wink my way. "That's what neighbors are for, right?"

"Yeah." Dad stares at us as if realizing something is different about our interaction and isn't sure what to make of it. "All right, drive safe."

With our goodbyes out of the way, Beck walks around to the passenger side and holds the door open.

I raise my brows. "My goodness, quite the gentleman."

His lips quirk with humor. "This is me attempting to sweep you off your feet with impeccable manners." He presses a quick kiss against my lips. "Is it working?"

I shoot a cautious look at my dad to see if he noticed the affectionate gesture. Thankfully, he's already on the phone with the tow company. Beck grins, seeming to know what I was thinking before securing me inside the truck.

I might be willing to give Beck a shot, but that doesn't mean I'm anywhere near ready to share that news with my parents.

With a smile on his face, Beck settles next to me. My mind spins as he turns the key and starts the engine before pulling the truck into gear.

"Wave to your dad, sweet pea. He looks concerned about your welfare."

I force my hand to rise as we pull out of the circular drive.

Beck is right. Dad is standing with his hands planted on his hips, frowning as the truck drives away. I have no idea what his reaction would be if he knew I was getting serious with our neighbor.

Although my guess is that he wouldn't be pleased.

As a child, Beck was hell on wheels. Constantly challenging authority and pushing the limits until someone snapped. His youth is dotted with rash indiscretions. That behavior continued well into high school.

Has he settled down over the years?

Grown and matured into the kind of guy I can trust with my heart?

That remains to be seen. It would be impossible to ignore all of my reservations, but I'm cautiously optimistic.

Last night, while dancing with Ari, I realized that I've been running from Beck because he scares me. My feelings for him scare me. They've never wavered, only intensified, and that scares me more than anything. Those thoughts swirl through my mind as the highway stretches out in front of us, and the city grows more distant in the rearview mirror.

Beck glances at me before reaching out and snagging my fingers with his larger ones, giving them a gentle squeeze before dragging them to rest on his thigh. "I won't hurt you again, Mia. I promise."

I glance at him, surprised he's able to read me so easily.

Does that scare me even more?

You bet your damn ass it does.

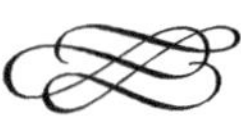

I rap my knuckles against Dr. Hayes' office door.

"Come in," is the muffled response from the other side.

As I push open the door and poke my head in, she glances up from her desk and smiles. Papers are spread out all around her. "Thanks for stopping by. I wanted to check-in with you regarding the progress you've been making." She pauses for a beat. "Please tell me that you've been working on the paper."

I crack a smile. "Yeah, I have."

"Good. I was worried after our last conversation. It seemed like you were dragging your heels about delving in."

"You're right, I was," I admit. "It's a little overwhelming."

She wags a finger at me. "You athletes are all alike."

I really hope not. School might not come easy, but that doesn't mean I don't work at it.

As I get ready to slide onto the chair parked across from her desk, Dr. Hayes rises to her feet and points to the small couch against the far side of the office. "Would you mind if we sit over there?" She arches, thrusting the fullness of her breasts against her silky white tank. My gaze skitters away, landing on the navy sweater draped across her chair. "My back has really been bothering me." She closes the distance between us. "That's what grading papers for several hours a day will get you."

"I bet." I hustle over to the couch, which is more of a glorified loveseat. There's no way two people will fit comfortably on it, especially when one of them weighs in at two-hundred-and-twenty pounds.

I drop onto a cushion and keep my attention focused straight ahead. Her thigh brushes against mine as she settles next to me. All of those uncomfortable feelings she stirred in me the last time we spoke come rushing to the surface.

It's not like there has been anything blatant about her behavior. But still…

I don't like the way it makes me feel. I shift restlessly, wishing there was more room between us. It feels like she's practically sitting on my lap. It's awkward.

"How has your week been going?" she asks, unaware of the thoughts circling through my head.

I glance at her from the corner of my eye. "Good."

"You're a man of few words, Beck Hollingsworth," she chuckles. "The strong silent type."

That would be because you make me uneasy.

Even though I don't say it out loud, the words are perched on the tip of my tongue. Any moment I'll blurt them out.

Dr. Hayes flips through her notebook until she lands on a page with my name scribbled on top of it, along with a few notes. She shifts her body until she's able to face me. Our thighs are no longer touching, but our knees are pushed together. I remain still, so we don't brush up against one another any more than we have to.

I glance at her face, trying to get a read on her thoughts. Her expression is open and friendly, that of a concerned professor. There's nothing about her demeanor that would lead me to believe she's aware of the discomfort she's causing.

"Let's talk about the sources you've come up with and where you are in the process of drafting your outline."

I blow out a steady breath, and the tension filling my muscles dissipates.

"There are a lot of studies out there regarding concussions and contact sports, so finding research material hasn't been an issue. I've already gathered six different sources." The more I talk about what I've found, the more comfortable I become. "One problem I'm running into is that there's so much information, I'm having a difficult time narrowing down my focus and organizing it."

"Sometimes having too much information can be as problematic as not finding enough." Her lips lift. "Think about your thesis statement and try to stick with information that supports the main points you're trying to convey." She gestures toward my backpack. "If you have your outline, I'd love to take a look and give you some direction."

"Sure, let me grab my computer."

"Great." She relaxes against the couch and crosses one leg over the other. Her skirt rises a few inches up her thigh.

I pull out my laptop from my backpack and fire it up. Once the document pops up on the screen, she scoots toward me. The soft curve of her breast brushes against my bicep.

I clear my throat and stare pointedly at the screen. "Would it be easier for you to read if I give you the computer?"

"Nope," she presses closer, "this is fine."

Silently, she scans the document. Every once in a while, she'll point to a word or section. When she does, something hard and pointed drags across the bare skin of my arm. I'm really hoping it's not her nipple, but what else could it be?

When she glances at me, I'm startled to realize how close her face looms. A couple of inches at best.

"Have you started writing your first draft?" Her attention falls to my lips.

"Umm, yeah," I mutter.

She continues staring. "Do you want to pull it up?"

"Sure." I refocus on the computer. Every time I hit a key, my arm rubs against her boob. Finally, I get the document pulled up and jerk the screen toward her. I want to get this over with and get the hell out of here.

Dr. Hayes makes a humming noise deep in her throat as she reads over the draft. "This is great. You're definitely on the right track."

"Awesome." I snap the laptop closed with more force than necessary and shove it in my backpack.

Hallelujah, we're done. I can leave.

As I'm about to spring to my feet, she places a hand on my thigh. My gaze drops to her fingers in surprise.

"Let's plan on meeting up again next week. I know how easy it is to get off-track, and I want to make sure you're continuing to make steady progress."

"Oh." Well, damn. That's not what I wanted to hear.

"I see such potential, Beck. I'd love the opportunity to tease it out of you. I really believe you could benefit from a little one-on-one instruction."

"I don't know if I can work that into my schedule," I mumble, unsure what to say. One-on-one instruction is the last thing I want from her. My gut is telling me it's not English she wants to tease out of me.

Dr. Hayes squeezes my thigh before lifting her hand away. The moment I'm free of her touch, I pop to my feet.

"Beck?"

It's only after I freeze that I realize I've stopped directly in front of her face. Her eyes are level with my junk, and it seems like she's staring straight at it before she glances up.

"If you need anything, you can always text me."

No, thank you.

Instead, I force myself to say, "I'll be sure to do that."

And then I flee from her office like the hounds of hell are nipping at my heels.

MIA

As I crest the second-floor landing of the library, my gaze sweeps over the tables strategically placed near the anthropology and sociology section, but I don't immediately notice Beck.

I'm about to pull out my phone when a high-pitched giggle draws my attention to a girl lounging on top of a study table. I'm not able to see who she's talking to, but my guess is that it's a guy. I know flirty behavior when I see it.

Dismissing her, I glance away and continue searching for Beck. Maybe we were supposed to meet on a different floor or section. When another laugh erupts, I glance at her again. She shifts, and I catch a glimpse of dark wavy hair.

I don't need to see any more to know she's talking to Beck. I step to the side, and his handsome features come into view. The strawberry-blond-haired girl perched on the table leans over, giving him what I assume is an unobstructed view of her cleavage.

Jealousy bubbles up inside me like a geyser before I quickly stomp it out. I'm not one of these girls who want to spend every spare moment of her time fending off other females. I also don't want a guy who will flirt with every vagina he comes across.

This is precisely why I was reluctant to give Beck another chance.

It hasn't even been a week since I agreed to go out with him, and already he's chasing after other chicks?

No, sir. That won't be happening on my watch. We can snuff this out as quickly as it sprang to life. Thank God he showed his true colors before I could become any further invested. I'm not even going to confront him. He can screw himself.

I'm out of here.

As I take a hasty step in retreat, ready to stomp down the stairs, Beck glances over and catches sight of me. A wide smile lights up his face as he waves me over like he wasn't caught red-handed with another girl.

Does he really think I'm going to be all right with this behavior?

Hell, no. He messed with the wrong chick. I'm not one of his bubble-headed groupies who will put up with anything for the chance to be with him. I hitch my backpack up higher on my shoulder before stalking toward him.

Not once does Beck's attention deviate from me. As I reach the table, I open my mouth to blast him into next week.

He beats me to the punch. "Hey, babe. Missed you."

His fingers tangle around mine before he tugs me closer. Thrown off by the affectionate greeting, I trip over my own feet and stumble toward him. He slides one hand into my hair before bringing my face to his and kissing me. It's nothing more than a fleeting caress, but it's enough to stir something deep inside me.

What the hell is going on here?

Confusion swirls through me as I glance at the girl on the table. She grins and continues swinging her long legs.

Shouldn't she be upset that Beck is making out with someone in front of her?

None of this makes sense.

Only then does it occur to me that maybe—*just maybe*—I got the scenario wrong.

Beck keeps a tight grip on my fingers as if unwilling to let me go. "Callie was keeping me company while I was taking a break."

I clear my throat and force out an introduction. "Hi, I'm Mia. It's nice to meet you."

Can you imagine if I hadn't kept my jealousy under wraps and lost it? Even the thought is enough to embarrass me.

Callie flashes a full-wattage smile that nearly blinds me with its intensity. I'm tempted to smack this girl for being so damn perfect with her bouncy hair and amazing body.

"I'm Callie." She swivels toward me. "Beck has been telling me all about you."

"Really?" As if I needed any more evidence that I jumped to the wrong conclusion.

"Yeah," she enthuses. "There are going to be a ton of disappointed girls on campus when they learn Beck is officially off the market."

Officially off the market?

Is that what's happened?

I give Beck a bit of side-eye to get his take on the matter. He grins as if amused by my reaction.

"I should probably take off." Callie hops gracefully from the table. Her perfect breasts jiggle enticingly with the movement. I sneak a peek at Beck to see if he's watching. I mean, how can he not be? Her breasts are big and bouncy. I'm almost entranced by them, and I'm not into girls.

Instead, his gaze stays trained on me. A little hum of awareness zips through my veins. It's almost as if Callie and her gravity-defying boobs aren't on his radar.

"I've got a ton of homework to finish up. I'll see you in class, Beck." She turns to me and waves. "Nice to meet you!"

Beck gives her a chin lift as I return the sentiment.

Once she's gone, I mutter, "Callie seems nice."

"Yup, she's cool. She cheered freshman year and then quit." He shrugs. "It was too much of a time commitment."

Cheerleader. I could definitely see that. She's peppy.

When I attempt to pull my hand free so we can get to work, he tugs, and I tumble onto his lap. His hands band around my waist to hold me in place.

He cocks his head as a smile simmers around the edges of his lips. "You thought I was flirting with her, didn't you?"

"Nope." I shake my head. "Never crossed my mind." There is no damn way I will admit that to him. Even if it is the truth.

His grin widens until I'm tempted to smack him. "I'm serious about being with *you* and only *you*. I don't have any interest in other girls."

I glance away. Whatever this is between us is moving at lightning speed. Am I ready for that?

"Mia," he whispers, recapturing my attention. "You don't have anything to worry about."

There is so much sincerity overflowing from his green eyes that it's impossible not to believe him. "Okay."

"I've waited a long time for this. I'm not going to fuck it up."

How can I possibly resist a guy who says something like that to me?

Even though we're in the library, I press closer and lower my lips to his. It's all too easy to lose myself in the taste and feel of him.

After a handful of moments, he groans and pulls away. "If you keep that up, we won't get much work done."

It might be worth it.

"Stop looking at me like that," he whispers. "You have no idea what it does to me."

I inhale a shaky breath. He's wrong about that because it does the same to me.

Studying.

Right.

We need to get to it. I'm supposed to be helping him with his paper. When I attempt to rise from his lap, his hands stay wrapped around my waist.

"One more kiss," he growls.

A smile curves my lips as they settle over his. This time, I try not to get lost in the feel of him, but it's not easy. When I pull away, our faces stay close, his breath becoming mine.

"I was thinking, if your Jeep is ready by the weekend, we could take off Saturday after the game." He pauses. "And I could take you out."

My breath catches at the idea. "On a date?"

He presses another kiss against me. "Yup, we're talking dinner and the whole shebang."

His smile is contagious. "Now you've piqued my interest."

"Good. It goes a little something like this—I'll pick you up and take you to a nice restaurant, and then afterward, we'll find a secluded spot to make out for a while. We can pretend we're back in high school again."

I laugh, loving the sound of that.

"Maybe we should practice the making out part to be sure we get it right." I add shyly, "We can head back to my place after we're done working. Alyssa won't be home for a while."

"Nope," he says firmly. "All messing around will have to wait until after the date. We're going to do this right."

My heart melts into a puddle of goo.

What's this guy doing to me?

A grin flashes across his face. "What?"

I shake my head and trace his lips with my index finger. "You're not the guy I thought you were."

"I'll take that as a compliment."

When my finger dips inside his mouth, he bites down gently, and I gasp before pulling it out.

"Nothing is going to mess this up," he murmurs.

A little bubble of happiness bursts in my heart. I really hope he means everything he's saying. Because this Beck, the one he's slowly revealing to me, is someone I could fall for. Even though the idea of putting my heart in his hands is a frightening one, I'm no longer sure I have a choice in the matter.

"We should probably hit the books." I need to focus on something other than the emotions crashing around inside me.

With one last kiss, I slide from his lap and settle on the chair across from him. Beck emails me a copy of his outline along with the rough draft for comp class. It takes about twenty minutes to look it over, add suggestions with the editing tool before sending it back to him. Then he gets to work, sifting through his research and working on his paper.

Before I realize it, two hours have slipped by.

"How did your meeting with Dr. H go?" I ask before stretching my muscles.

"Fine, I guess." Something indecipherable flickers in his eyes, and I'm not sure what to make of it. "She said everything looked good."

"From what you've shown me, you're on the right track. Once you finish up with the rough draft, the process should move faster." I pause before adding, "Consider yourself lucky that you didn't get Dr. Templeton for this class. He's so boring and long-winded. Dr. Hayes is amazing. Don't you love her?"

He glances away, and his smile fades. "Yeah, she's okay."

Just okay?

Everyone on campus adores Dr. H. Beck is the first person I've run across who hasn't sung her praises. She goes above and beyond for her students. She's always trying out new teaching methods to keep her class fresh and interesting.

I tilt my head and try to puzzle out why there's been such an abrupt shift in his demeanor. It's like a mask has fallen over his features.

"Did something happen?" I ask. Although, I can't imagine what that could be.

"I don't know." He shrugs and fidgets with his pen. "I'm not sure."

"What do you mean?"

Beck shoves away from the table and folds his arms across his chest. I try not to get distracted by the movement. God bless, but he has amazing biceps.

I'm pulled out of my perusal when he says, "She's nice. Friendly." There's a pause, and his voice drops. "Maybe a little *too* friendly if you catch my drift."

Huh?

I shake my head. *"Too friendly?"* No one has ever complained about Dr. H being *too* friendly. In fact, that's what makes her such a great teacher. Every month, she hosts a book club meeting for students at her house. There are appetizers, drinks, and intellectual conversation where everyone is free to express their opinions.

Seriously, who does that?

There's not another professor on campus who is more beloved than her.

So, I'm uncertain what Beck is driving at.

"I don't know," he mutters, clearly frustrated by his inability to express his thoughts. "Maybe it's all in my head. Forget I said anything about it."

If there's a problem, I want to know what it is. I reach out and lay my fingers over Beck's before giving them a squeeze. "No, tell me."

He huffs out an exasperated breath before pressing closer to the table. "I've met with her twice now, and each time, it feels like she's coming on to me."

What?

No way!

It takes everything I have inside not to burst out laughing. It's the look on his face that forces me to keep the sound buried deep inside.

He's serious.

He believes this is happening.

"Okay," I say carefully, wanting to get to the bottom of this. "What has she done to make you feel so uncomfortable?"

He withdraws his fingers from mine and grows restless before glaring at something in the distance. "I don't know." He jerks his shoulders. "It's the way she stares and talks to me. She keeps touching me." He bites his lower lip. "When I was in her office, she sat way too close on the couch. Her boob was pressed against my arm. It was weird." A dull red color settles in his cheeks.

"Anything else?" I prompt, waiting for something that is more of a smoking gun.

"She gave me her cell number and told me to text anytime."

"I've had her number for years," I tell him.

When he presses his lips together and doesn't say anything more, I continue, wanting to put him at ease. "I've always found Dr. H to be super friendly and affectionate. I've been in her office a lot of times, and we always sit on the couch when we talk. We've grabbed coffee together. Maybe she shouldn't be so physically demonstrative," I shrug, "but that's just who she is. Most students don't have a problem with it."

I'm not sure if I'm making the situation better or worse.

"So…you think I'm overreacting?" he asks.

Definitely.

But I don't have the heart to tell him that. Instead, I say, "I think you've misinterpreted her actions. If she realized her behavior made you uncomfortable, she'd be upset." I search his eyes, hoping I've laid his concerns to rest.

"I don't know," he mutters. "Maybe you're right."

My lips lift at the corners. "Trust me, I am. She's being friendly. Nothing more."

His face clears as he nods. "All right. You know her better than I do."

When he stretches, flexing his arms, my mouth turns cottony, and all thoughts of Dr. Hayes are instantly forgotten.

He grins as if he knows exactly how he affects me. "You ready to get out of here?"

"Yup." I pause for a beat. "Are you sure I can't convince you to give me a sneak peek of what the *make-out* portion of the evening will entail?"

Heat flares to life in his eyes. "Sweetheart, if I gave you a preview, you wouldn't want me to stop."

A thrill of anticipation shoots through me because he's right. Since we've gotten together, we've held off on sex. We're taking this relationship slow. That being said, I'm all but dying to get my hands on him.

And vice versa.

The wait is killing me.

But it's worth it.

Beck is worth it.

Nerves prickle at the bottom of my gut as I park my truck in Mia's circular driveway and cut the engine. This is the same nauseous feeling I get in the tunnel, waiting to run onto the field before a game. Like I'm going to puke. I have no idea why taking Mia out on a date feels like such a big deal, but it does. All I know is that I want everything to be perfect.

I grab the flowers from the front seat and take the wide stone steps two at a time before ringing the bell. The sound echoes inside the cavernous entryway. I run a hand over my button-down shirt and khakis one last time.

Wait a minute—are the khakis and dress-shirt overkill? Maybe I should have kept it casual. I'm not looking to spook her.

Damnit.

It's too late to do anything about it now.

Why did I think this was a good idea?

After a few agonizing moments that feel like an eternity, the door swings open, and Mia stands on the other side of the threshold. That's all it takes for the doubts filling my head to disappear.

Neither of us say a word as her lips lift into a hesitant smile.

This.

This is exactly why I wanted to take her out.

My gaze rakes over her from head to toe. She's wearing a black sweater that hugs her breasts and a short, dark-wash jean skirt paired with black tights. Her hair hangs in loose waves that frame her face and tumble around her shoulders.

My mouth waters. It takes every ounce of self-control not to reach out and yank her into my arms.

"Hi," she says, breaking the silence.

"You look beautiful." It's the only thought running through my head.

"Thanks." She ducks her chin as color blooms in her cheeks.

Sometimes I don't think Mia has any idea how gorgeous she is.

She points to my hand. "Are those for me?"

I glance at the flowers before shaking my head. How the hell could I forget about them? It took at least twenty minutes to pick out the perfect bouquet at the florist.

I thrust them toward her. "Yeah, sorry."

She takes the colorful blooms before burying her face in them. "They're beautiful. Thank you. No one has ever brought me flowers before."

It makes me doubly glad that I made the effort.

She nods toward the kitchen. "Let me put them in a vase, and then we can leave."

I shove my hands in my pockets as she silently pads down the hall. I hear the faucet run, and then she's back, carrying a crystal vase in her hands before setting it on the table in the entryway.

She slips her feet into black heels that make her legs look even longer.

How the hell am I supposed to keep my hands to myself all night?

I clear my throat and those thoughts from my mind as I rock back on my heels and glance around. "Are your parents home?"

Mia shakes her head before grabbing her purse. "Nope. Mom went to visit her sister, and Dad left on Thursday for another trip."

That's probably for the best. I have no idea how Dan would feel about me dating his daughter. He likes me well enough as the son of his friend and neighbor, but am I good enough for Mia?

Probably not.

But like she said, we're taking this relationship slow. I won't worry about jumping over that hurdle until I clear this one.

"All set?" I ask.

"Yup." She closes the door behind her as we head to the truck. When she reaches for the handle, I brush her hand aside and open it. Once she's safely secured inside, I close the door and jog around to the driver's side before sliding onto the seat and starting up the engine. A few moments later, I'm pulling from her drive and heading out of the subdivision. I wave to the guard in the gatehouse before we hit the main road.

"You never mentioned where we were going." Her fingers tangle together in her lap.

It's difficult to believe she could be nervous. I reach out and grab her fingers, wrapping my hand around them.

"I made reservations at Marco's. It's an Italian restaurant on the other side of town." I glance at her. "Have you ever been there?"

"It's one of my dad's favorites. We used to go there all the time when I was a kid." Her eyes grow distant. "I can't remember the last time we had dinner there."

"They have the best eggplant parmigiana."

"The spaghetti and meatballs are good, too," she adds with a smile.

I nod in agreement. Marco's is one of those restaurants where you can't go wrong no matter what you order. It makes me doubly glad I picked that place to take her. Other than group dates when I attended prom and homecoming, I've never taken a girl out on a date before.

I pull the truck into the crowded parking lot and cut the engine. We exit the vehicle before heading inside to the hostess station. The ambiance is upscale, and the lighting is dim. The dining room is cavernous with high ceilings that give it a spacious feel.

It's the perfect place for a first date.

If I play my cards right, it'll be one of many.

I'm almost tempted to pat myself on the back for a job well done, but I'll save that until after I drop her off. Although, so far, we're off to a good start.

The hostess grabs two menus and seats us at a white cloth-covered table in the main dining room near the stone fireplace. I make sure to pull out Mia's chair before taking a seat across from her. A waitress stops by and fills our water glasses as we peruse the menu.

"Any idea what you're going to order?" I ask.

A thoughtful expression flickers across her face as she shakes her head. "There are so many options to choose from. It all looks amazing." She glances at me. "Maybe the lasagna."

"Yeah, that sounds good," I agree, "but I'm going for the eggplant."

As she continues to study the menu, I glance around the dimly-lit room before my attention gets snagged by a couple tucked into the corner. I blink and refocus my eyes to make sure they're not playing tricks on me. When the man shifts, I get an unobstructed view of him. My heart kicks up its tempo as he leans across the table and locks lips with the woman seated on the other side.

There's no mistaking the guy.

It's Dan, Mia's father.

What's most disturbing is that the woman he's with is not his wife. She looks nothing like Julia. There's no way to even confuse the two.

What the hell?

Didn't Mia say that her father was out of town for business? If that's the case, what is he doing here with another woman?

I drag a hand over my face, knowing this is going to blow my whole night apart.

"Instead of lasagna," Mia murmurs, still staring at the menu, "I'm going to try the lobster stuffed ravioli."

Fuck.

Fuck.

Fuck.

When I fail to respond, she glances at me. "What do you think?"

"Oh, ah…" Even though I have no idea what to do, I realize staying is not an option. At some point, Mia will notice her dad, and I can't allow that to happen.

"You know what? We should go somewhere else." When her eyes widen, I add hastily, "Some place better."

"You want to leave?"

I wince at the shock lacing her voice. "I want our first date to be special, and this isn't going to cut it."

She lays the menu down in front of her. "I can't tell if you're being serious or not."

"Dead serious," I say nervously. "Let's go."

As Mia opens her mouth to pelt me with questions, our server arrives at the table with a smile plastered across her face.

"Hello, my name is Kimber, and I'll be your waitress for the evening. Have you ever been to Marco's? If not, welcome!" Her gaze bounces between us. "The chef has created several specials this evening—"

"We won't be staying," I interrupt.

Mia's eyes bulge, looking like they might fall out of her head. Kimber, our perky waitress, stares at me with an equal amount of surprise.

"Beck, I don't—"

"Sorry for the inconvenience." I bolt to my feet like a lunatic. This whole evening has burst into a fiery ball of flames. I'm not sure if I'll be able to recover from this catastrophe. But what other choice is there?

I can't allow Mia to catch sight of her father.

"Ready to go?" She stares at me in bewilderment as I extend my hand.

"Ummm…"

"Great, let's get out of here!"

Mia glances at our waitress as if she might be able to explain my odd behavior. When I don't retract my hand, she tentatively lays her fingers in mine and carefully rises from the chair. Not wanting her to see Dan, I scoot my body to the side and block her view.

It's all I can do to hustle her ass out of here as fast as humanly possible. If I haven't destroyed my chances with her, maybe we can find a different restaurant and start this date over again. We can pretend this never happened. Although, that's probably wishful thinking on my part.

Thirty steps, and we'll be in the clear.

I swipe my hand across my brow and realize I'm sweating. This has turned into a real shitshow. I tighten my grip around her fingers and drag her from the table. She makes a squeak of protest before stumbling to keep pace with me. Once we reach the entryway where the hostess station is located, the pressure in my chest loosens, and I can once again breathe.

That was a close one, but I did it. I hustled her out of there before any damage could be done.

Mia tugs on my hand. "We can't leave!"

Why the hell not?

"I forgot my purse at the table." She points toward the main dining room.

Goddamn it.

I'm tempted to leave it behind and chalk it up as a casualty of the evening.

"Wait here," I growl with more force than necessary, "and I'll grab it."

Her brows slam together as her mouth pops open in protest.

"Please," I plead, "just wait here." I stalk away before she can argue. As I arrive at the table, I glance at Dan from the corner of my eye. He's still staring at the woman across from him as if he doesn't give a damn that they're in a public place where anyone could see him cheating on his wife.

With a scowl, I shake my head.

If his daughter wasn't with me, I'd march over there and ask him what the hell he's doing. Instead, I swipe Mia's black purse from the table and spin on my heels before grinding to a halt.

Mia stands frozen at the entrance of the dining room. With wide eyes, she stares past me. Her mouth hangs open as shock fills her face.

Fuck.

That, unfortunately, seems to be the word of the evening.

I look over my shoulder, but Dan is oblivious to the fact that his daughter is at the same restaurant as his side piece. Her father's atten-tion is focused on the blonde sitting across from him. Their hands are clasped, and the besotted expression on his face speaks volumes. There's no way to misconstrue what's playing out.

I close the distance between us until I can slide an arm around Mia's waist. "Come on," I say gently, "let's get out of here."

She stays rooted in place. Her focus never deviates from the couple on the other side of the room.

"Mia?" I lower my voice, trying to reach her. "We need to go."

"You knew about this?" Hurt seeps into her voice.

The accusation arrows to my heart before exploding upon impact. I shake my head. "No, I noticed them after we sat down."

"That's why you wanted to leave." She nods as if a puzzle piece has fallen into place, and my odd behavior now makes sense. Her shoul-ders sag beneath the weight of this knowledge.

"Yeah." There's no longer a reason to hide the truth.

A sheen of wetness coats her eyes as I steer her toward the exit.

"Come on."

"Should I say something?" She sucks her bottom lip into her mouth as she contemplates the question.

What the hell is the protocol for a situation like this?

Damned if I know.

"No, let's get out of here. You can think about it and then decide what to do."

As I secure her inside the cabin of the truck, a sigh escapes from my lips. It's a relief to be out of the restaurant. The more distance I put between her father and us, the better off she'll be.

I glance at Mia only to find her staring pensively out the wind-shield. Pain radiates from her in heavy waves. Unsure how to comfort her, I reach out and snag her fingers before squeezing them.

Even though I suspect the answer, I still ask, "Are you hungry? We could go someplace else to eat."

She shakes her head. "No, just take me home."

Once I pull into her drive, I put the truck in park and angle my body toward hers. If I could take away her pain, I would do it in a heartbeat.

Silently she reaches for the handle.

As she pops it open, I ask, "Do you want me to come in?" I tack on before she can get the wrong idea, "To talk?"

She shakes her head. "Thanks, but no. Right now, I want to be alone, so I can figure out what to do."

"You don't have to do anything," I tell her. "Whatever is going on is between your mom and dad. It has nothing to do with you."

"I know." With a heavy sigh, she steps out of the vehicle. "I'm sorry about tonight, Beck. I appreciate the effort you put into planning our date."

I force a smile to my lips, wishing there was something I could do or say to make the situation better. When I remain silent, she jerks her head into a nod.

"Bye," she says before slamming the door.

I watch as she walks up the stone stairs and lets herself into the house. Her gaze fastens on to mine, and I raise my hand to wave before she disappears inside.

This date has turned out to be an epic fail. Not in a million years did I ever expect our night to end like this.

Unable to sleep, I stare sightlessly at the ceiling. No matter how much I try to block out what I saw at Marco's, I can't. The image of my dad having an intimate dinner with a strange woman refuses to be buried.

Even though I know what I saw and how I felt in the moment, part of me wonders if it's possible I could have misconstrued the relationship. Was it a dinner between friends? Or colleagues?

From across the restaurant, I could see the besotted look in Dad's eyes as he stared at the blonde across from him. How long has it been since he looked at Mom that way?

I sift through my memories, going back years, but can't come up with a definitive answer. If Dad ever looked at Mom like that, it was before Brianna died.

Beck's words ring unwantedly throughout my head.

This has nothing to do with you.

He's right, it doesn't. This is between my dad and mom, but still... seeing him with another woman feels like a betrayal to our family.

How could he do this?

After everything Mom has been through, how could he inflict more damage?

I turn onto my side and curl up in a tight ball under the covers as a wave of nausea crashes over me. This isn't the kind of secret I can keep from Mom. She has a right to know what's going on. The thought of telling her makes me sick to my stomach.

I glance at the clock on the nightstand. It's after midnight, and I'm no closer to finding sleep than I was two hours ago. Maybe I should go downstairs and make a cup of tea.

As I throw off the covers, there's a tap against the windowpane. I pause as my heart thumps a painful beat against my ribcage before squinting into the darkness. The breath rushes from my lungs as Beck's features materialize on the other side of the glass. I hurry across the room and unlatch the lock, shoving open the window.

"What are you doing here?" Relief and happiness swirl inside me at the sight of him.

He stares at me from the thick tree branch he's perched on. "I wanted to make sure you were all right. What happened earlier was brutal."

"You could have texted or come to the front door."

"It's been a while since I climbed your tree." He shrugs as a smile lifts his lips. "Kind of seemed like a grand romantic gesture. Don't you think?"

I shake my head and unsnap the screen from the window before pulling it off and leaning the metal frame against the wall. "You're crazy."

"Only for you." Beck balances his weight on the branch before levering himself through the window. He lands gracefully on the floor before popping to his full height and dusting himself off. I quickly slam the window closed and clip the screen back into place.

"Are you doing okay?" He closes the distance between us until he can tug me into his arms. "I was worried."

Unable to help myself, I melt against him before burying my face in his chest. I have no idea why his presence is so comforting, but it is. "I'm all right. Still in shock, I guess."

He wraps his arms around me, pressing me closer before dropping a kiss on the top of my head. "Have you made any decisions?"

I huff out a breath and mumble, "I called him."

"Really?" Beck pulls away. "What happened?"

"It went straight to voicemail."

"Oh." He draws me to him again before tucking me beneath his chin. I hate to admit how perfectly we fit together.

"Dad texted five minutes later. He said he was in the middle of a business dinner and would call in the morning."

"Un-fucking-believable," Beck mutters.

Anger floods through me before pooling in my voice. "I was so tempted to text back and ask how dinner with his whore was."

"Shit, Mia…" he whispers against my hair before squeezing me tighter.

A fresh wave of tears stings my eyes. "Can you imagine the look on his face if I had done that?"

"I'm so sorry, baby. I wish I had hustled you out of there before you caught sight of them."

I burrow my face against Beck before inhaling a big breath of him. The woodsy scent of his cologne settles something deep inside me. "You have nothing to be sorry about. *He* does."

A humorless chuckle falls from my lips when I remember sitting down to dinner at Marco's. "I'd thought you had changed your mind about us going out. All of a sudden, you were acting weird and trying to drag me from the table."

"Nothing could be further from the truth. I'd been looking forward to dinner since I asked you out. I'm sorry our night got ruined."

"Yeah," I say softly, lifting my head from his chest. "Me, too." Maybe I haven't wanted to admit it to myself, but I'd been looking forward to this date. Probably more than I should have. I'm trying to be cautious and smart and take things slow, but Beck is making that difficult to do.

He lowers his face until his lips can graze mine. The moment we make contact, all the noise rioting in my brain goes silent. Beck angles his head as his mouth roves gently over mine. When my lips part, his tongue slips inside to dance with my own.

My palms glide over his chest until they're able to lock around his neck and pull him closer. Somehow this kiss mutes all the pain vibrating deep inside me, and for that, I'm grateful. I don't want to think anymore.

I just want to feel.

And *this* feels amazing.

I pull away enough to whisper, "Stay the night with me?"

"Is that what you want?"

"Yes." After everything that's happened tonight, it's what I need.

"Then I'll stay."

BECK

$\mathcal{B}$efore Mia can untangle herself from me, I scoop her into my arms. She squeaks in surprise as I carry her to the bathroom before depositing her onto the long stretch of marble countertop. Silently she watches as I close the plug on the white porcelain tub and run the water.

Once it's at the right temperature, I swing around to face her. "A bath will help you relax."

She bites her lip. "Are you going to join me?"

"Nope." I shake my head. "This is for you."

When the tub is almost filled, and steam is rising from it, I position myself between her legs. I gather up the material of her pink tank top and carefully pull it over her head before dropping it to the floor. She sits before me in tiny white shorts with pink hearts stamped across them.

I reach out and cup the soft weight of her breasts, squeezing the fullness. Her nipples pebble against my palms before I release them and trail my fingers down her ribcage until I reach the elastic band of her shorts. I hook my thumbs beneath the material before dragging them down to reveal even more sun-kissed flesh. She lifts her backside so I can slide the thin cotton over her hips and down her thighs. The shorts get added to the small pile on the floor.

She makes such a pretty picture sitting naked in front of the mirror. This girl doesn't understand the power she holds over me. She could have had me on my knees years ago.

I lean forward, kissing one breast before nipping at the hardened tip. Then I give the same treatment to the other. The whimper that falls from her lips has my cock stiffening with need. I have to remind myself that what I'm doing isn't for me, it's for her.

I lick a hot trail down the middle of her ribcage to her bellybutton before sinking lower. My hands slide to her inner thighs, opening them gently until my mouth can settle on her pussy. When I swipe my tongue over her opening, Mia groans and arches her back. My hands slide from her thighs over her hips until I can cradle her backside with my palms. I bury my face against her heat, laving her sweetness with my tongue.

The goal is to make her forget about everything she saw tonight. Even if it's only for a few moments. I want the pleasure to overtake the pain.

When she's dancing on the edge, I pull back, not wanting her to spiral out of control. With one last kiss against her lower lips, I rise to my feet. Mia's head is tipped back, and her eyes are closed.

"Do you like that?" I press a kiss against her mouth before scooping her up and cradling her against my chest.

"Mmm." Her eyelids flutter open as she lifts her lips to mine for another kiss.

The moment my mouth settles on hers, our tongues mingle. She purrs before slipping her arms around my neck and tugging me closer.

I'm breathing hard and close to coming in my boxer-briefs when I pull away. "You should enjoy your bath before it gets cold."

The dazed look filling her eyes is like a punch to my gut.

I lower her into the tub until she's settled against the sloped porcelain. A sigh of contentment slips free as her body sinks into the steaming water.

"Do you want it hotter?"

"No." Her eyelids feather closed. "It's perfect."

My gaze roams over her naked body.

When we were kids, she was all long limbs, knobby knees, and elbows. It was around seventh grade when Mia's body changed. Her breasts and hips filled out. Every time I saw that short white tennis skirt against her tanned thighs, I would sport wood. Or I'd catch a glimpse of her in the hallway at school. The way her shirts stretched across the soft curve of her breasts left my mouth watering.

Even thinking about it now makes me groan.

I really need to get out of here and stop staring at her until I can get a better handle on myself. As I head for the door, her eyes crack open.

"Where are you going?" she asks sleepily. She's in full relaxation mode, and that's exactly where I want her.

"I'll be back in a minute. Just enjoy yourself."

I disappear from the bathroom before she can ask further questions. Once in the hallway, I cross over the catwalk and move down the staircase before heading to the kitchen. I grab a mug from the cabinet and fill it with filtered water from the fridge before setting it in the microwave. While the water is heating, I search the cabinets for tea. As I come across a box of chamomile, the microwave buzzes.

Perfect timing.

I grab the mug and seep the bag in the hot water.

When I return to the bathroom, steam has permeated the air, and Mia is lying against the rim of the tub with her eyes closed. I settle next to her with the mug in my hands.

Her dark eyelashes flutter. When she sees me, her lips lift into a satisfied smile.

"I brought you something."

She sits up and takes the mug from my fingers. "You made tea?" Surprise dances in her eyes.

I shrug. "It wasn't a big deal."

She glances at the drink before releasing a sigh. "You're making this awfully difficult."

Not understanding the comment, my brows draw together. All I'm trying to do is make her feel better. Maybe I'm doing a piss-poor job of it. "What do you mean?"

"I'm trying to hold myself back." Her gaze flicks to mine. "I don't want to get too excited about this." There's a pause before she adds, *"About you."*

Not that I blame her for it, but I hate that she feels the need to protect herself from me. It makes me wonder if I'll ever be able to earn her trust.

"I'm not that guy anymore." I reach out and trail my fingers along the curve of her jaw. "I'm trying to prove that to you."

She sinks into my touch. "You're doing a good job of it."

"Guess I need to keep it up." That's all I can do.

Mia brings the mug to her lips and takes a sip before setting it on the edge of the tub. "Thank you."

"You're welcome." I pause before adding, "Whatever you need from me, all you have to do is ask, and it's yours."

Her body sinks beneath the surface of the water. When she's fully submerged, she widens her legs until she's completely exposed. My gaze drops to her spread thighs before skimming up her body to settle on her face.

"Tell me what you need, Mia." My voice turns rough with pent-up arousal.

She remains silent as I trail my fingers through the water. Carefully, I circle one breast until the nipple tightens before doing the same to the other. A sigh of pleasure escapes from her.

"Is this what you wanted?"

She shakes her head.

My fingers drift lower, swirling around the indentation of her belly button before moving downward and feathering over her lower lips. She widens her legs as I circle my thumb around her clit. Her body grows restless beneath my touch.

"Feel good, baby?"

"God, yes."

Not once do I dip my fingers inside her tight sheath. I continue tormenting her, driving her closer to orgasm. She bites her lower lip to stifle a whimper.

"Need more?"

"Please."

I slip one finger inside her body. As I pull away, her inner muscles tighten, and a whimper of protest falls from her mouth. I circle her clit a few more times before sinking deep inside her. She finds a rhythm and gyrates against my hand. Her body tightens as her muscles convulse around me. The pleasure that falls from her lips has my cock throbbing with need. I don't think I've ever wanted anyone more than this girl.

Once her orgasm dissipates, I lean over and take her mouth with my own.

"I love watching you fall apart," I whisper against her lips.

Her eyes flare as color flags her cheeks.

"You know what I love even more?" I ask.

The dazed expression clears as she shakes her head.

"When you orgasmed on my tongue at the club. Your pussy got so fucking wet. I wanted to lap it all up."

When her mouth falls open, I grin before plunging my tongue deep inside her sweetness. How will I ever get enough of her? It doesn't seem possible. As much as I'd like to sink inside her body, that won't be happening. This is about Mia's pleasure, not my own.

This is the first relationship I've been involved in. Everything before this was a string of meaningless encounters. There was never a reason to hold back or take things slow.

But Mia is different.

She's the first girl who has ever mattered. What we have, what we're attempting to build together, is more than physical. I don't want her to think it's based on sex.

"Why don't you finish your tea before it gets cold, and then I'll help you out."

She lifts the mug to her lips and takes another sip. "I'm done."

I grab a plush navy towel from the rack before holding it out so she can step into it. She rises gracefully to her feet as water sluices down her body.

How is it possible that she's this perfect?

As she stands before me, I drag the towel over her damp skin, starting first with her shoulders. Once they're dried, I stroke up and down her arms. I move behind her, swiping at the long line of her spine before dropping to my haunches and running the towel over her rounded cheeks.

I press a kiss against each perfect globe before sweeping the plush material over her legs. When no moisture remains, I place my hands on her hips and turn her, so she's facing me. It's gently that I stroke the area between her thighs. She groans as the cloth slides back and forth with enough pressure to create friction.

Her hands grip my shoulders as her eyelids feather shut and her head lolls back. By the time I'm done, her pussy is more wet than before I started. I remove the towel and lean closer, pressing a kiss against her clit. My tongue swirls around the tiny bundle of nerves. Then I dry her belly and ribs before circling the plush material over her breasts. Her nipples tighten as I swipe over them. When I'm finished, I pop to my feet, sucking one hard bud into my mouth before lavishing the same attention on the other.

"I think we're done here."

"That's unfortunate." Her cheeks are stained with color, and her eyes are heavy-lidded.

I chuckle before scooping her up into my arms and carrying her into the other room. Gently, I place her in the middle of the queen-size bed. Her gaze stays locked on mine as her thighs fall open.

Fuck, but she's beautiful.

Pink.

Soft.

Inviting.

Those are the only words that rush through my brain.

I kick off my shoes and yank the back of my T-shirt, pulling it over my head before tossing it to the floor. The athletic shorts and boxers are the next to go as I shove them down my thighs until the material is puddled around my feet.

I crawl onto the bed and up her body. Her legs wrap around my waist, cradling my thick erection against her softness. All it would take is one thrust of my hips, and I could sink deep inside her body. Instead, I keep a tight leash on my control. She moans and rubs her slick heat against my hard length.

"Don't you want to be inside me?" she murmurs.

"More than anything," I breathe, "but tonight, I'm going to hold you in my arms."

Questions circle through her dark depths. *"Really?"*

"Yup."

"Naked?"

"Damn right."

"I'm glad you're staying," she whispers, tugging me closer.

"Me, too." The only thing that matters is that Mia is here in my arms.

That she's mine.

Or, at the very least, on her way to being mine.

And maybe I'm on my way to being hers.

MIA

My sleep is deep and filled with dreams. Most, I can't hang on to. The one I find myself immersed in before waking is filled with Beck.

The sexy neighbor I've crushed on forever.

The guy I've avoided for the past seven years out of self-preservation.

Dreams and memories intertwine until they become one. I can't remember if he touched me last night or if it was all part of a delicious fantasy. Once I'm able to shake the last dregs of sleep, I stretch my limbs as the memories from last night crash down on me.

Beck climbing through the window.

Running a bath and stripping me bare.

Making me a cup of tea.

Orgasming.

Drying me off and carrying me to bed.

And then falling asleep in his arms.

I roll to my side only to find the space next to me vacant. Not only is the bed empty, but the sheets are also cold to the touch, which means Beck snuck out a while ago. Disappointment surges through me, threatening to swallow me whole. I flop onto my back and stare at the ceiling before tugging the sheet over my naked breasts.

Doubt creeps in at the edges and makes me question everything. Most of all, myself. More than anything, I want to believe in Beck. I want to believe that the pretty words he's strung together mean something. That his feelings are real.

Like mine are.

Not wanting to dwell on those troubling thoughts, I throw off the covers. As I'm searching for pajamas, Beck walks through the door carrying two plates. I'm slammed with the realization that he didn't pull a disappearing act.

The guy made breakfast.

Giddiness bubbles up in my chest like a geyser.

As soon as Beck sees me, a wide smile tips the corners of his lips. "Morning, sunshine. Sleep well?"

I rake a hand through my hair, knowing it's in disarray. "Yeah, I did." Probably because his arms were banded around me through most of the night.

He gives me a sexy little wink. "Me, too."

Naked, I crawl back onto the bed and tuck the sheet under my arms before reaching for a plate. "Hope you don't mind I made breakfast."

Is that a joke?

I stare at the dish in surprise. Chocolate chip pancakes with whipped cream and maple syrup. There're also three slices of bacon and a hash brown patty. This is exactly what my perfect breakfast consists of.

Is it a coincidence?

Questions dance in my eyes.

His lips lift as he points to the plate. "All of your favorites."

It takes effort to clear my throat along with the emotion that has become wedged in there. "I noticed." I shake my head, trying to get a handle on the situation. "How did you know?"

"Remember when our families used to go out for brunch together?"

Of course, I do. Picking out a dress for our Sunday morning get-togethers was agonizing. I usually ended up changing my outfit a bazillion times. Even though I swore up and down that I wasn't dressing with Beck in mind, that's exactly what I was doing.

"That was a long time ago," I murmur, mind cartwheeling.

"You ordered the same thing every time." His eyes darken to a deeper shade of green. "And you'd make these cute little noises deep in your throat when you ate the pancakes."

Heat slams into my cheeks because he's not wrong. I *love* chocolate chip pancakes, especially when drenched in whipped cream and syrup.

Yummy.

"I always looked forward to brunch with your family." His grin turns wicked. "Watching you devour your pancakes gave me major wood."

It's official—my face is on fire.

I can't believe he felt that way.

"Don't look so shocked." He taps the tip of my nose with his index finger and smirks. "It's always been you, Mia."

I never realized. Girls have been chasing after Beck since seventh grade. How was I even on his radar?

"I forgot something in the kitchen." He sets his plate on the night-stand. "Be right back."

Before I can open my mouth, Beck disappears through the doorway and into the hall.

Now that he's gone, I suck in a deep breath and try to wrangle all of my emotions back under control. But it's not easy. Every time I think I have a grasp on Beck, he does something that blows me out of the water.

He's not the guy I thought he was.

How could I have been so wrong about him?

I focus on my plate and use the side of my fork to cut through the fluffy pancakes. Chocolate oozes from where I slice through the stack. Beck saunters into the room with two glasses of orange juice.

My fork stalls midway to my mouth as I stare.

What's this guy trying to do to me?

He stumbles to a halt. "Is something wrong?"

Beckett Hollingsworth made me pancakes.

And a hash brown.

And bacon.

And brought me orange juice.

How could anything possibly be wrong?

It's all too right.

I shake my head and shove the forkful of warm fluffiness into my mouth before I say something I might regret. A soft moan escapes as my eyelids flutter shut. The pancakes practically melt in my mouth. Once I swallow them down, I open my eyes. "They're delicious. Thank you."

He stares intently at my lips before giving his head a little shake. "No problem," he mutters, grabbing his plate and settling on the bed next to me.

It's almost impressive the way Beck wolfs down his breakfast. I forgot what a big appetite he has.

I laugh and point to his clean plate. "Hungry much?" I've barely made a dent in my food, and he's already done.

He grins before patting his flat belly. "Starving."

"I could tell."

When I'm finished, Beck runs the plates down to the kitchen. Less than two minutes later, he's back and sliding into bed. He tugs me into his arms, and I nestle against his chest. When he runs his fingers through my hair, I close my eyes, enjoying the comforting touch.

"Have you come to any decisions about your dad?"

Ugh.

Until this point, I've been successful in shoving those unwanted thoughts to the back of my brain where I don't have to dwell on them. But I can't avoid the issue forever.

"Not really." Once we slid between the sheets last night and Beck wrapped his arms around me, I fell into a deep sleep. "If you were me, what would you do?"

He blows out a steady breath as his face grows serious. "I don't know," he admits. "We have different relationships with our fathers." His voice softens. "And your family has been through a lot more than mine."

Thoughts of my sister swirl through my head. Nothing has been the same since Brianna died. Most of the time, it seems like my parents are going through the motions of living their lives.

Although, the man I saw last night looked nothing like the Dad I know. He looked happier than I've seen him in a long time. Ten years younger, at least. Instead of having his face buried in his phone, he was actually paying attention to the person sitting across from him.

"Is it possible your mom is aware of the relationship?"

That thought never occurred to me.

"I don't know." It's difficult to imagine that my mother would knowingly sit home alone while my father screwed around on her.

"Maybe you need to give it more thought before you make any rash decisions. Like I said last night, what happens in their marriage is between them."

"Yeah," I mumble, feeling more confused than ever, "I guess."

Beck reaches out and tangles our fingers together. The moment our skin comes in contact, electricity zips through me. All at once, I'm aware of my naked state. And that he's only wearing boxers. A punch of arousal hits me in the core. Before I can change my mind, I toss the covers aside and crawl on top of him. Beck's eyes widen as I straddle his waist.

"Did I thank you properly for breakfast?"

"Umm…" When he gulps, it's enough to make my confidence soar. "Yes?"

My fingers slide through his hair as my lips hover over his. "You deserve another thank you."

His hands go to my naked back as I press him against the mattress.

"Mia," he groans.

I arch a brow, enjoying the strange power I seem to hold over him. It's a heady sensation. There's nothing but the thin cotton of his boxers separating my heat from his thick erection. All I want to do is grind myself against him.

Instead, I scoot lower, kissing his chest and stroking my fingers over the hard slabs of his muscles. I've dreamt about doing this for years. My tongue swipes over his nipples, sucking first one and then the other into my mouth.

A sigh escapes from Beck as he tunnels his fingers through my hair.

I slide lower, kissing my way to his rock-hard abs before arriving at the elastic band of his boxer-briefs. I slip my fingers beneath the material, sweeping them back and forth against his warm flesh. I've caught glimpses of his cock, but never this up close and personal. I tug at the boxers until his boner springs free.

His dick should come with a warning label—*object larger than it appears.*

I glance at him and smirk. "Impressive."

Beck releases a strained chuckle. "Thanks. I take great pride in it."

I refocus my attention on him before stroking my fingers over his erection. "You should." Wanting him naked, I slide the boxers down his hips and over his thighs before tossing them to the floor.

His cock is hot to the touch and feels like silk-covered steel. I'm enamored by the feel of him. With soft strokes, I pet him, running my fingers down the length before carefully palming his balls. Beck groans as I worship his body. Moisture beads at the slit of his erection, and I lean down, swiping my tongue over it. There's just a hint of saltiness.

He releases a deep guttural sound that vibrates in my ears and restlessly shifts his hips.

When I repeat the gesture, he growls, "Damn, baby, that feels good."

Surprisingly, I'm enjoying this as much as the chocolate chip pancakes. I can't get enough of him. Luckily for us, we have hours to explore one another before heading back to school later this afternoon.

As I lean down, ready to take him in my mouth, there's a noise from within the house. I poker up and twist around toward the open bedroom door. "Did you hear that?"

Before Beck can answer, a voice calls from downstairs—

"Mia? Are you up yet?"

Dad.

Oh, God.

Beck meets my wild-eyed stare with a version of his own. *"Dad?"* I squeak, heart pounding harshly against my chest.

"Of course," he laughs, his voice getting closer as he climbs the staircase. "Who else would it be?"

I leap from the bed and stumble, all but crashing against the door to slam it shut. Beck rolls off the edge and jumps to his feet. He grabs his boxers before staggering sideways as he yanks them up his legs.

"Get in the closet!" I whisper-yell, grabbing my robe from the chaise and tugging it on so I'm no longer naked.

I can't believe this is happening.

What the hell is he doing here?

There's a rap of knuckles against my bedroom door.

I run my fingers through the tangled length of my hair before forcing myself to walk to the door and pull it open. I paste a smile on my face when I find Dad on the other side.

"I thought you were out of town until tomorrow." The lie leaves a bitter taste in my mouth, but it's the best I can come up with under the circumstances. Resentment and anger swallow the nerves that had been rushing through my body only moments ago.

"Change of plans," he says with a shrug. "The conference ended early, so I thought we could grab breakfast before you leave for school. Sound good?"

Images from the restaurant last night roll through my head. A million questions sit poised on the tip of my tongue. It's all I can do to keep them trapped inside.

Unable to look him in the eyes without exploding, I glance away. "Um, yeah. Give me a few minutes to get ready."

"Great, I'll meet you downstairs."

I watch him retreat before turning toward the staircase. When he disappears from sight, I close the door and lean against it before squeezing my eyes tight.

How am I supposed to sit across from him and act like everything is normal? As if he hasn't blown my world apart?

"Hey, are you all right?"

I open my eyes and find Beck standing in front of me. He cups my cheeks before tilting my face toward his.

"Not at all," I whisper.

"Then don't say anything. Give it some time."

"I'm not sure I can do that." I glance away before shrugging. It feels like the weight of the world is resting on my shoulders. "I guess we'll see how it goes."

His thumb strokes over my bottom lip.

"Do you want me to come with?" He searches my eyes. "Because I will."

Warmth spreads through my chest that he would even consider putting himself in that uncomfortable situation. Even though the offer is tempting, I shake my head.

"Are you sure?" His lips lower before brushing across mine. The movement is sexy and comforting all at the same time.

"It'll be better if I go by myself."

"If that's what you want." He presses a kiss to my mouth before murmuring, "Let me know when you return from breakfast, and we'll head back to school."

"You don't need to wait."

"I'm not leaving without you." He smacks one last kiss against my forehead before his hands fall away from my face. "You better get dressed."

Dread settles at the bottom of my belly as I grab panties and a bra from the dresser and pull them on before heading to the walk-in closet and picking out jeans and a sweater. Not bothering with my hair, I grab an elastic band and pull it into a simple ponytail.

As I walk toward the door, I glance at Beck as he lounges on my bed. "You'll sneak out after we take off?"

"Yup."

"All right." I have to force myself to leave the room. "I'll see you soon."

"I'll be waiting."

As I descend the staircase, I spot Dad sitting on the antique bench in the entryway. His face, as usual, is buried in his phone. My feet grind to a halt as I'm slammed with a thought.

Is he texting the woman I saw him with last night?

All the calls and texts he's received before shuttering himself away in his office for hours on end whirl through my head. Work was always the excuse he gave for the countless trips he took.

Was it all a lie?

The realization makes me nauseous.

I don't want to view my father as anything other than the man I've loved with all my heart since I was a little girl. But how can I do that with everything I know and suspect?

When Dad glances up and catches me studying him, he stuffs his phone in his pocket and rises to his feet. Carefully I search his face for any trace of guilt, but there is none to be found. Somehow that makes the situation worse.

"You slept late," he says with a smile, eyes crinkling at the corners.

I shrug. "Just tired, I guess."

"I'm glad you got a chance to rest up." There's a pause. "Did you take the Jeep out and make sure it was running all right?"

"No, not yet." The Jeep is the last of my concerns.

"Okay, I'll grab the keys from the kitchen, and we can get moving." He's already walking through the hall when he asks, "Any place, in particular, you want to go?"

Even though I have no idea if Marco's is open for Sunday brunch, I'm tempted to throw the suggestion out there. Instead, I say, "How about The Honeybun?"

"Sure, I could go for that." After a moment, he returns to the hallway with a furrowed brow. "Did you already eat? There are pans and dishes on the counter."

Oh.

My mind cartwheels, grasping for an explanation that will make sense. It would be all too easy to lie and say I made myself breakfast for dinner last night. But I'm loath to do that. Lying has never come easily to me. Especially when it involves my parents.

"Yes," I force the words from my mouth, "I ate earlier."

"Oh." His head is turned as he stares at the sink. I know what's coming next. I can almost see the wheels spinning in his head.

"Is someone here with you?" he asks hesitantly.

I blow out a steady breath and straighten my shoulders. "Beck is upstairs."

It's almost comical the way his brows shoot up across his forehead and into his hairline. If this were any other conversation, his reaction would make me laugh.

"Beck?" Shock weaves its way through his words. *"Hollingsworth?"* He waves his hand toward our neighbor's house. *"From next door?"*

I wince as his voice continues to escalate.

"Please tell me that he stayed in a guestroom."

Again, I could lie. It would be the quickest way to end this uncomfortable conversation. Dad probably wouldn't believe me, but it's doubtful he would push the issue. We would pretend that I didn't have sex with Beck and move on with our lives. But there's no reason for me to do that. I'm twenty-one years old. Who I sleep with is none of his business.

"No. He stayed with me." Those five words are like a lead weight that sits uncomfortably between us.

"I don't understand any of this," he mutters, plowing a hand through his hair. "Are you two seeing each other?"

"Yes, we are."

Confusion swirls through his eyes. "How long has this been going on for?"

"It's a relatively new development."

He blows out a steady breath as his broad shoulders collapse. "I have no idea what to say about all this."

"You don't need to say anything."

"Is your mother aware of what's going on?"

I shake my head. "No, we haven't told anyone yet."

Tentatively, he steps toward me. "As much as I like Beck," there's a pause, and I steel myself for what will come next, "he's not the right guy for you."

I echo with disbelief, *"He's not the right guy for me?"*

His frown deepens into a scowl. "Come on, you know *exactly* what I mean. Beck doesn't have a serious bone in his body. His life is football. Other than that, he parties and sleeps around. I don't understand why you would be interested in someone like that."

My mouth falls open. "Dad! That's not true!"

He closes the distance between us. "That kid has always been a troublemaker. I used to feel bad for Archie and Caroline, always having to clean up his messes."

"That was in high school," I grit out. "He's changed. People are capable of it."

"Has he really changed that much?" Dad snorts and rolls his eyes. "Because I find that difficult to believe."

"Yeah, he has. Maybe you need to look at the person he is today instead of judging him for the one he used to be."

"Oh, please," he mutters. "Archie says he still gets into trouble."

I shift my weight and glare, frustrated with this conversation. "Have you ever considered the possibility that Archie is as biased as you are?"

He presses his lips together before jerking his shoulders into a shrug. An uncomfortable silence settles around us before a puff of breath escapes from him. "The last thing I want to see is you get hurt. Beck isn't the type of guy to be faithful."

Ha!

That's rich.

How can he look me in the eyes and say that?

Dad pokers up to his full height. "What's that supposed to mean?"

I flinch and realize the words have unintentionally slipped from my mouth.

"Mia?"

My heartbeat hammers in my ears until the sound is all I'm cognizant of. He stares as if he no longer recognizes me. What he doesn't realize is that the feeling is mutual. "I saw you last night, Dad."

He doesn't so much as blink. Not even a flicker of guilt enters his dark eyes. His lack of response is almost enough to make me question what I saw.

When he remains silent, I repeat myself, louder this time. "I was at Marco's last night and saw you having dinner with a blond woman."

Dad laughs, but the sound is forced. "You're mistaken, I was in Cincinnati."

He's lying. I know what I saw. He was at the restaurant. His dishonesty this morning is almost as hurtful and disappointing as catching him with another woman was last night. He'd rather create doubts in my mind than own up to his own shady actions. I never expected this kind of behavior from him.

It only hardens everything inside me.

"Stop lying. Beck is the one who spotted you, Dad. He didn't want me to see, so he tried to hustle me out of the restaurant. But I saw you anyway." I fold my arms tightly across my chest. "Would you like me to call him down here?"

His jaw tightens as anger flashes in his eyes. "That won't be necessary."

My voice drops as I shake my head. "You were never out of town, were you?"

"No."

Even though I was expecting the answer, it still hits me like a sucker punch.

As painful as this line of questioning is, I push on. "Who is she?"

The anger dissipates from his eyes as sadness creeps in. "Does it really matter?"

Of course, it matters.

"You've been cheating on Mom." My eyes pop wide with disbelief. "So yeah, it kind of matters."

"She's a colleague," he begrudgingly admits.

Un-fucking-believable.

"How long has this been going on for?"

"A while," he mutters, looking away.

What does that mean?

A few weeks?
A few months?
A few years?
Longer?

It makes me sick to my stomach, and I find myself unable to continue. My belly churns, and for a moment, I wonder if I'll throw up. My arms drop to my sides as if they weigh a thousand pounds. "How could you do this to Mom?"

"I never meant for it to happen." His shoulders slump. "I—"

"That doesn't matter!" I cry with frustration. "You've been sneaking around and having an affair with another woman! Not only have you lied to Mom, but you've also been lying to me!"

"My personal relationships have nothing to do with you." He plows a hand through his hair. "You don't understand what it's been like since Brianna died."

"Really?" How can he say that? "I know *exactly* what it's been like! You're not the only one who lost her! Mom lost a daughter, and I lost my only sister! We *all* lost her, Dad, it wasn't just you!" Tears sting my eyes as anger boils in my blood. "How dare you use Brianna as an excuse for your infidelity!"

Heat slams into his cheeks as he winces. For the first time since his affair has been dragged into the light, he looks ashamed. "I'm not using her as an excuse," he mumbles.

"That's *exactly* what you're doing." I'm so disgusted by this conversation that I don't even want to look at him.

"Losing her was more than any of us could endure, and we all dealt with our grief differently."

"Did you ever consider," I shoot back, "that we should have dealt with it together instead of splintering apart the way we did?"

"Her death was so painful." His eyes grow distant. "Sometimes, it felt as if the grief was more than I could deal with."

I know, but still…

"What about Mom? Does she have any idea what's going on?" Maybe Beck is right, and she's aware of Dad's infidelity. If that turns out to be the case, I'm not sure how I'll be able to look at either of them the same way again.

He shakes his head. "She doesn't know."

"You have to tell her, Dad. You have to make everything right. This can't continue."

Emotion flickers in his eyes before his gaze darts away.

A sliver of dread snakes down my spine as an uncomfortable silence stretches to the breaking point. "You *are* going to end this, right?" Panic and disbelief weave their way through my voice.

He drags a hand over his face. "The situation is more complicated than you can understand."

"You know what I understand?" Before he can respond, I continue, voice rising with every word. "That you made vows to Mom, and when Brianna was taken from us, you took the easy way out and had an affair. *That's* what I understand."

The sound he makes when he swallows is audible. "I need to think about what's best for everyone."

What the hell does that mean?

A strangled laugh slides from my lips. "You know what would be best for me? If my family stayed intact." My voice fills with anger. "I think Mom would agree with that, don't you?"

When he presses his lips together and remains silent, I'm struck with a heartbreaking realization. It's as painful as a two-by-four slamming into the back of my head.

"You have no intention of ending this affair, do you?" The words might be arranged in the form of a question, but it's not.

We both know the answer without him having to verbalize it.

"It's complicated," he repeats weakly, as if that makes it better.

"No," I snap, losing my patience, "it's not. You have a wife. A woman you've been married to for over twenty-five years. Explain what's complicated about it?"

The acidic taste of bile rises in my throat.

His reluctance to end this relationship makes me realize that it's not a casual affair. Even though I had purposefully dropped the issue a few minutes ago, I now feel the need to press for an answer. "How long has this been going on?"

"A while."

"A year?" I spit.

He stares mutely.

My voice escalates. *"A few years?"*

His stubborn silence sends a wave of nausea and anger crashing through me.

"This is your chance to do the right thing," I grit out. My hands tighten into useless fists that hang at my sides. Disappointment and exasperation churn in my gut. I don't think I've ever felt this disgusted with anyone in my life. Let alone, one of my parents.

How is this issue not cut and dry?

Not once has he shown an ounce of remorse or offered to end his affair. And that's frightening. This woman—whoever she is—means something to him.

Possibly more than we do.

Unable to stomach the sight of my father, I swing around and force myself up the staircase. Putting one foot in front of the other feels like a Herculean effort. When I'm halfway up, I pause and glance down at him. He hasn't budged from the foyer. "If you don't tell her, I will."

Spitting out those words feels like the equivalent to dropping a bomb.

It's appalling that I have to threaten him.

He jerks his head into a tight nod but offers nothing more.

As I stare at my dad, I realize he's not the man I thought he was.

How could he be?

The father I've revered since childhood would never hurt the people he loves the way this one has.

This man is nothing more than a stranger.

MIA

"I can't believe you didn't tell me what was going on!" Alyssa shoves me in the shoulder, and the force sends me careening into a random guy on the walking path.

My hands grasp his chest for purchase as he holds my upper arms to steady me. Heat fills my cheeks. "I am *so* sorry!"

The guy grins, making no attempt to release me. "It's not a problem."

Alyssa grabs my arm and yanks me free. "Sorry, bud, she's taken."

He shrugs. "That's too bad."

Alyssa snorts before dragging me down the path.

"I'm going to kill you," I mutter through clenched teeth.

"No, you're not." She doesn't sound the least bit concerned by the threat. "You love me too much to do that."

"Hmmm," I scrunch my face and contemplate the statement, *"do I?"*

"Yup." She links her arm through mine as we continue walking. "Anyway, back to the original convo we were having before you rather clumsily threw yourself at that guy."

When I glare, she grins and keeps yapping. "I can't believe you kept this from me!"

"It wasn't like that," I try to explain. "It just happened."

"Please, girl. The Mia and Beck saga has been years in the making. It didn't just," she makes air quotes with her fingers, "'happen'. This courtship has been moving at glacial speeds."

She might be right. All I know is that I don't want to discuss the Beck situation until it picks up traction.

Giving Alyssa a little taste of her own medicine, I shoot back with, "It's not like you've been entirely forthcoming about Colton."

It's almost comical the way her face goes blank. "That's because there's nothing to tell."

I narrow my eyes and search hers for the truth. "Are you sure about that?"

"Positive." It's airily that she announces, "Colton Montgomery is part of my past, not my future."

I have my suspicions as far as Alyssa's ex is concerned, but that's all they are at this point. *Suspicions.* As I open my mouth to delve deeper, my phone rings.

The music from my ringtone has my belly doing a painful flip. Every time my cell makes the slightest noise, dread nearly swallows me whole, and I hold my breath until I'm on the verge of passing out.

I dig through my bag in search of my phone. After a few moments of rooting around, my fingers lock around the slim cell. Nerves prickle along my flesh as I glance at the screen.

Mom.

Alyssa jostles me in the shoulder. "Aren't you going to answer that?"

"Yeah." I force out the air that has become trapped in my lungs before sliding my thumb across the green button. "Hey, Mom."

Silence greets me from the other end. I'm about to repeat her name when she clears the thick emotion from her throat. That's all it takes for me to realize she's spoken to Dad. In some ways, it's a relief that I won't have to break the news to her.

"Mom? Are you all right?"

Alyssa waves a hand in front of my face. When I glance at her, she mouths, "What's going on?"

"I'll tell you later," I whisper. "Sorry."

Eyes filling with concern, she nods and points to the fine arts building on the horizon. "I need to go."

I wave as she takes off. Even though my one o'clock class starts in less than five minutes, I head toward a bench situated under a tree before settling on it. There's no way I can push off this conversation until later.

When the line remains silent, I say, "Mom, talk to me."

She sniffles. "Have you spoken to your father?"

I don't want to lie, but I don't necessarily want to admit the truth either. It seems like it would only make matters worse.

"No," I wince and force the fib from my lips, "not recently."

Tears clog her voice, and it makes me furious all over again that Dad has inflicted so much pain. Mom doesn't deserve this. If there's any kind of silver lining to be found in this situation, it's that they can start fresh and repair the damage to their marriage. Maybe even be stronger for it.

"He left." A sob breaks free from her. "He packed his bags last night and walked out."

Shock crashes over me like a wave as I stare sightlessly at the students bustling across campus.

When I remain silent, she says, "Mia? Did you hear me?"

It takes effort to shake myself from the mental fog that has descended. "Yes, I heard."

She cries quietly on the other end of the phone, and my heart breaks all over again. There's nothing I can say or do to comfort her. Rage rushes through every part of my body.

"I can't believe this is happening," she whispers.

"I'm so sorry." It takes effort to keep my voice level and not curse his name. "Did he say why he was leaving?"

The sound of her tears falls faster. "He's in love with someone else." Disbelief and confusion drip from every word. "He said that our marriage has been over for a while."

It's as if the air has been knocked from my lungs, and I can't breathe. I can only sit on the bench gasping as people walk by laughing and chattering, oblivious that my world has imploded,

Is he really walking away from us?

It seems impossible.

"Do you want me to come home?" I ask. "I could leave after my next class and stay the night."

She sucks in a shuddering breath before blowing it out. "I appreciate the offer, sweetie, but you need to stay there. It's important that you focus on your classes."

I snort out a laugh, knowing there's no way I'll be able to do that.

"Are you going to talk to him? What about seeing a counselor?" I pause before adding in a hopeful tone, "Maybe he'll change his mind."

"I have no idea what I'm going to do." Bitterness gathers in her voice. "But if he doesn't want to be married to me, then I damn well don't want him back."

I rub my temple and consider the next step. "It might be a good idea to talk with a lawyer and get some legal advice."

"Oh." A heavy silence falls over us. "Yeah…maybe I'll do that."

At a loss for words, I say, "I'm sorry, Mom."

"Me, too, sweetie. Your dad was right about one thing. Nothing has been the same since Brianna died." Grief and sadness fill her voice. "Maybe I shouldn't be surprised by this, but I am."

It's true that nothing has been the same for our family. We pretended to pick up the pieces of our lives and move forward, but that was a façade. Instead of dealing with the pain of her loss, we buried it. Dad delved into work and started an affair while Mom drank too much and shopped.

And me?

I set out to be the perfect child so they wouldn't miss the one they lost. I tried to shine as if that would be enough to overshadow her death.

In hindsight, it sounds stupid.

How could that possibly fill the void Brianna left behind?

My sister died seven years ago, and sometimes it feels like the wounds are as fresh and painful as when it happened. We've all been tiptoeing around our grief instead of facing it head-on.

"Call if you need anything, Mom. I can come home anytime."

"I'll be fine, don't worry about me."

We disconnect, and I stay seated on the bench, staring at the phone in my hand.

"Mia?"

I glance up only to find Beck staring at me. His brows are drawn together as if he can't figure out what I'm doing. "Aren't you supposed to be in class?"

"Yeah."

He settles beside me before searching my face. "What's going on?"

"Mom called." Tears fill my eyes. "Dad packed his bags and left."

Beck stares in surprise before wrapping his arm around my shoulders and tugging me close. "I'm so sorry." He presses his lips to the top of my head. "Are you all right?"

I shrug, still feeling dazed. After my conversation with Dad Sunday morning, maybe I should have expected this outcome, but I really thought he would do the right thing. How could he choose her over us?

How could he do that?

"Is your mom okay?"

"No. She's been blindsided. I offered to come home, but she didn't want me to."

"If it'll make you feel better, I can call my mom and have her check on Julia."

It's not a bad idea, but I'm not sure if Mom wants anyone—let alone our neighbors and friends—to know what's going on.

As I consider the offer, I bite my lip and shake my head. "No, not right now. I'll call her when I get home later."

He nods and squeezes me tight. "Let me know if there's anything I can do to help."

"Thank you." When I lift my face, he brushes his mouth against mine.

"You know I would do anything for you, right?" he murmurs between kisses.

The corners of my lips tremble upward. A few months ago, I could have never imagined trusting Beck enough to lean on him for emotional support. And yet, here we are. In a few short weeks, he's become one of the most important people in my life.

The irony isn't lost on me that the one man I thought I'd always be able to depend on has flaked, and the one I would have never dared open my heart to is proving himself to be someone I could fall in love with.

BECK

A small knot of tension sits at the bottom of my belly as I rap my knuckles against Dr. Hayes' partially open office door. She glances up from her computer screen and smiles before waving me in.

"Thanks for stopping by." She pulls off her glasses and sets them on the desk next to her coffee cup. "I read over your latest draft and have a few suggestions." She leans back in her chair. "I thought it would be easier for us to discuss them in person rather than emailing back and forth.

"Sure, no problem."

"Great. Want to get started?"

I nod.

As I take a step toward the desk, she waves to the tiny loveseat. "Let's sit on the couch, it'll be more comfortable."

Comfortable for who?

Certainly not me.

My step falters as I clear my throat and search for an excuse. I'm trying to keep as much distance between us as possible. "My computer is kind of heavy. It might be better to set it on the desk while we work." I'm grasping at straws. My computer weighs a pound or two at the most.

Her lips twitch with amusement. "The coffee table will be just fine."

Damn.

Mia's words swirl through my head.

She's friendly.

She isn't coming on to you.

She's one of the most beloved professors on campus.

You've misinterpreted her intentions.

Dr. Hayes rises from her desk and slides past me while I stand rooted in place. When her body brushes against mine, my anxiety levels spike.

It's all in my head.

I'm being too sensitive.

Once she's settled, I glance longingly at the office door before forcing myself to close the distance between us. My lips flatten when I realize she's positioned herself smack dab in the middle, not leaving much room on either side.

When I hesitate, she pats the cushion beside her, and I have no other choice but to sit down. I squash my six-foot frame as close to the armrest as possible and keep my attention focused straight ahead as I set the computer on the coffee table and fire it up.

Any distance I had purposely left is eaten up when she scoots closer.

With our thighs pressed together, she pulls out her notes and glances at the computer screen before pointing out where more clarification is needed. For the next thirty minutes, we meticulously move through the body of the paper. Mia has been helping me to edit when she has time, so it's not a total mess. As we work side-by-side, my muscles loosen. Other than our bodies pressed close, she hasn't done anything else to make me feel uncomfortable.

It's a relief to realize that Mia was right. I'm an idiot for thinking this woman was coming on to me.

Dr. Hayes wraps up her critique by saying, "Keep working, and we'll meet up again next week to check your progress. If you follow the suggestions I've made, there's no reason you can't get an A on this paper, and frankly, in this class."

An A?

Pigs flying out of my ass seem more likely than that. I've never received an A on a paper in my life. Sometimes it was all I could do to eke out a B.

"Why is that so funny? I'm being serious." She points to the computer. "This is shaping up to be a great paper. One I look forward to reading."

Now *that* makes me laugh.

I shrug and shake my head. "Writing has never come easy to me." Even though I was dreading this meeting, it's obvious there was never anything to be concerned about. "I appreciate you spending so much time with me."

"Helping students realize their full potential is one of the most rewarding aspects of my job." She shifts, and our knees touch. "It's one reason I'm so passionate about my work." Her hand flutters to mine before covering it.

My gaze drops to our clasped fingers. "Well, um, thank you, Dr. Hayes."

"When we're alone, you can call me Rebecca."

"Right." This meeting has taken a turn for the awkward. I don't care if she's touchy-feely or not. I don't like it. Now that the paper has been wrapped up, all I want to do is escape.

When I attempt to retract my fingers, her grip tightens, halting my movements.

"Beck—"

I glance up and realize her face is much closer than before.

"I had hoped you would take advantage of my offer to work one-on-one with you. Kind of like a mentor." She tucks an errant lock of hair behind her ear. "There is so much I could teach you, if you would let me."

Relief rushes from my lungs when she lifts her hand from mine.

Instead of pulling away, it settles on my thigh, where it rests danger-ously close to my balls.

Friendliness is one thing.

This is something altogether different.

"Um—"

Before I can say anything more, she's on her knees between my legs. Her other hand drops to my thigh before she slides both toward my junk.

Hunger flashes in her eyes before settling on my lap. "I've been very patient about waiting for you to get the hint. So, I've decided to take matters into my own hands." As those words leave her lips, her fingers wrap around my cock.

Holy shit!

"Dr. Hayes," I choke out as a strange paralysis takes over. I can't move. My muscles feel locked in place.

"Rebecca," she corrects, tongue darting out to smudge her lips. "Call me Rebecca."

"I'm not—"

There's a knock on the office door. My head jerks up as it opens in slow motion.

"Dr. H—"

Oh, fuck.

Mia.

I would recognize her voice anywhere.

"Now's not a good time!" the professor shouts, but it's too late.

As Mia falters over the threshold, her wide gaze locks on mine before sliding to the woman between my outstretched legs. I quickly knock her hands away, hoping the situation doesn't look as damning as I imagine it does.

"I, um, sorry," Mia mumbles before taking a hasty step in retreat. Hurt and shock swirl through her dark depths before she quickly slams the door closed.

The thick wood reverberates on its hinges as silence settles around us.

"Well, that's not good." Dr. Hayes rises gracefully to her feet before running a hand over her pencil skirt. "Luckily, Mia is my teaching assistant, so it shouldn't be too difficult to smooth this over." Instead of looking embarrassed, a smile curves her lips before a chuckle escapes. "Did you see the look on her face? I think we shocked the poor girl."

We?

I don't think so.

I sure as hell wasn't a willing participant in this.

Not bothering to answer, I bolt to my feet and snap my computer shut before shoving it in my backpack.

"Next time, we need to make sure the door is locked." She gives me a little wink before sliding behind her desk and sinking to her chair.

There won't be a next time.

"I need to go," I mutter. All I can think about is finding Mia and explaining what happened.

With my backpack slung over my shoulder, I leave the office and jog through the hallway to the elevators. Bypassing them, I take the stairwell, sprinting down five flights before reaching the ground floor. I push through the metal door into the lobby but don't see Mia's dark head anywhere.

A few guys from the football team are shooting the shit outside Mitchell Hall. When they call me over, I wave them off and run past. My heart skips a beat when I see her striding about twenty yards ahead of me. I hasten my pace, pushing through the people on the path. A few grumble before glancing at me. When they realize who I am, they shut their mouths.

"Mia!" I call out when I'm close enough, "wait up!"

She doesn't glance over her shoulder, but I know she heard me because she picks up her pace, as if trying to escape. There's no way in hell I can allow that to happen. When I'm within striking distance, I reach out and wrap my fingers around her upper arm to stop her. The moment I make contact, she whips around and bares her teeth.

"Don't you dare touch me!" she hisses. Anger vibrates from every cell of her body. I don't think I've ever seen her so enraged.

"Mia, give me a chance to explain!"

When she attempts to jerk her arm from my hold, my grip tightens.

"If you don't let go," she growls, "I'll scream."

Fuck.

No matter how much I want to tell my side of the story, I can't force her to listen. Reluctantly, I release her arm. I'm almost taken aback by the fury and disgust swirling through her eyes.

"It's not what it looked like." My heart slams harshly against my ribcage until it feels like it might explode.

A humorless laugh falls from her mouth. "*Really?* Because it looked like Dr. Hayes was moments away from giving you a blowie."

I wince as her voice increases in decibel with each syllable. A few students walking past, turn and stare with curiosity.

"She asked me to stop by her office so we could go over my paper." My tongue darts out to moisten my lips. "Everything was fine, and then she was on her knees."

"And you didn't push her away?" Her brows jerk up with disbelief.

"It all happened so fast." I plow a hand through my hair.

"You sat there and let her touch you," she accuses.

"No!" I shake my head. "I—"

"*What?*"

"I don't know," I whisper, wishing she would calm down and give me a chance to explain. My thoughts are all jumbled together, and I'm not making sense. It looks like I have something to hide when nothing could be further from the truth. "I tried to tell you that she was hitting on me."

"Yes," she snorts, "it really looked like she was forcing herself on you."

"Maybe it didn't look that way, but that's exactly what happened!"

She searches my eyes for a long moment before shaking her head. "I don't believe you."

My shoulders collapse in defeat. I'm not sure what more I can say to make her understand the situation. When Mia retreats, it feels like there is a yawning chasm sitting between us. Reaching her no longer feels possible.

I take a hesitant step in her direction, only wanting to bridge the growing distance between us. "Mia, I said that I would never hurt you, and I meant it."

"I'm such an idiot for believing in you." Tears well in her eyes. "You're no better than my father."

Her words are like poisonous darts that pierce my flesh. All I've tried to do is prove that I'm not the guy I used to be, and I've failed.

"You know that's not true," I murmur through the pain that blooms in my heart.

What could I have done differently?

I wasn't lying when I said it all happened so fast. For a moment, it had felt like I was paralyzed, powerless to stop Dr. Hayes from touching me. For a guy my size, it's ridiculous that I couldn't stop a tiny woman from laying her hands on me.

Shame and guilt bubble up inside, nearly swallowing me whole.

"I can't do this with you," she says, interrupting the thoughts that churn in my head, "I need to go."

When I reach out, she backs further away as if she can't stand the thought of me touching her.

"Please, don't leave like this." It feels like Mia is slipping through my fingers and there's not a damned thing I can do about it. "Can we talk later?"

She shakes her head and straightens her shoulders. "No, you've hurt me for the last time."

Before I can say anything else, she spins away and heads for the walking path that cuts through campus. Instead of going after her, I remain rooted in place. Chasing Mia will only push her further away.

I plow a hand through my hair, knowing there might not be a way to fix this.

It's altogether possible that I just lost the only girl who ever mattered to me.

MIA

$\mathcal{I}$ hop out of my Jeep and smooth down my skirt before hurrying into El Toro, a popular Mexican restaurant in town. Under normal circumstances, this is one of my favorite places to eat. The chicken enchiladas are to die for.

But today?

I don't really have much of an appetite.

Mom drove down so we could have lunch together. It's been a couple of days since Dad dropped his bomb, and I've been checking in to make sure she's doing all right.

So far, so good.

As I arrive at the hostess stand, I see Mom has already been seated at the back of the restaurant near the window. There's a huge margarita sitting in front of her. When the hostess leads me to the table, I give Mom a quick hug before settling on the chair across from her.

"Hi, sweetie," she says. Her gaze drifts over my floral-colored blouse and red skirt. "You look nice."

"Thanks. You do, too." I'm relieved to see that she hasn't fallen apart. I was worried she would be dressed in sweats. Not that I would blame her. Instead, she's looking fashionable in a black knee-length skirt and a pale pink blouse. Diamond earrings drip from her ears, and a matching tennis bracelet is wrapped around her wrist. Her black Chanel Jumbo Flap Bag sits on the table next to the window.

Mom picks up her glass and takes a healthy sip before setting it down. "This is quite good," she marvels. "Would you like one?"

Day drinking?

I shake my head. "No, I have a class in two hours." Not that people don't show up after having a few drinks, but still. It's never been my thing.

"Tell me what's going on in your life." She pauses before adding, "Sometimes it feels like all we do is talk about your father. I'm tired of it."

For a moment, I consider spilling the beans about Beck, but then I realize she didn't know we were seeing each other in the first place, so what would be the point?

"There's nothing new to report." It's probably for the best I never got around to telling her. Our relationship lasted a hot minute before it crashed and burned spectacularly.

I should have trusted my instincts instead of believing Beck was capable of change. It's disheartening to realize that my dad was right.

Mom purses her lips and searches my eyes. "Hmm, now why don't I believe you?"

I'm saved from further questions when our waitress arrives on the scene. Since I already know what I want to order, I don't bother perusing the menu. It's what I get every time I'm here. Chicken enchiladas with beans and rice.

Yum.

Their mole sauce is freaking delicious. I could eat it by the spoonful. All right…so maybe I've done that once or twice.

Mom orders a chicken burrito and finishes her margarita before requesting another. I'm a little surprised by how quickly she sucked the sugary drink down.

After Brianna died, Mom was no stranger to having a few glasses of wine in the evening. During particularly rough patches, she'd polish off a bottle on her own. Numbing the pain with alcohol was one way she coped with her grief. I don't want her using it as a crutch to deal with the implosion of her marriage.

Once again, it makes me furious with Dad for yanking the rug out from under her feet.

The waitress leaves, and I nudge Mom's glass of water toward her.

When I can't stand another moment of the simmering tension, I say, "I know you don't want to talk about everything that's going on, but are you doing okay?"

She hoists a fake smile. "Of course, honey. I already told you there's nothing to be concerned about. It'll all get sorted out."

"I can't help but worry." I reach across the table and lay my hand over hers. "I want to help you through this, but I'm not sure how."

"I'm sorry." She stares at our clasped hands, and tears fill her eyes. "You should be worrying about senior year, not me."

"You have nothing to apologize for," I say, startled by her outburst of emotion. "You didn't do anything wrong." My voice grows steely. "Dad is the one who left without attempting to work through your issues." It's as if he struck a match, threw it in a puddle of gasoline, and then walked away when it turned into a raging inferno. It still blows me away that he could do this.

"It's my fault." When a tear slides down her cheek, she quickly swipes it away. "After your sister died, I checked out. I've spent the last couple of days going over everything in my head and what bothers me most is that I wasn't a better mother to you."

Her words leave me feeling as if there's a vise constricting my chest so tightly it's impossible to suck in full breaths.

"Don't say that, Mom. You did the best you could."

"It's the truth." She releases a sigh and stares out the picture window we're parked in front of. It's a gorgeous day. The sun is shining brightly, and the sky is a deep cornflower blue filled with puffy white clouds that drift lazily by. It feels like the kind of day where nothing could be wrong in the world, and yet, my mother's life is in tatters.

Not just hers. Mine, as well.

Even though I've tried to push all thoughts of Beck from my mind,

I can't help but dwell on the scene I walked in on. For a moment, I had wondered if I'd stumbled into the wrong office. It didn't seem possible that Beck would be sitting on the couch, legs outstretched while Dr. Hayes knelt between them.

It was pretty damn obvious what was about to go down.

Her.

Ugh. I just puked in my mouth.

Even though I told Beck we were done, he's been calling and texting non-stop. I finally blocked his number. There's nothing he can say to make this right. The thought of them fooling around behind my back makes me sick to my stomach.

Mexican for lunch no longer seems like such a good idea.

I blink back to the present when Mom says, "I fell apart after Brianna died, and I never recovered."

None of us did.

"Mom, we don't have to talk about this if you don't want to."

She dabs her eyes with a napkin. "Maybe if I'd been able to move on, this wouldn't have happened. Your father and I wouldn't have drifted apart."

I lean forward, closing some of the distance between us. "This isn't your fault. Did he ever tell you that he was unhappy?" When she shakes her head, I continue. "Instead of talking about what was really going on, he threw himself into work and—"

"His secretary?"

A wave of shock washes over me. "*That's* who he's been seeing?"

She nods and shrugs. "I'm not proud to admit this, but I parked outside his work the other day and watched them walk out together. They were holding hands. Then he helped her into the car, and they left."

Mandi?

He's been having an affair with his secretary?

That's such a cliché, it's almost embarrassing.

I don't know what to say other than, "I'm sorry, Mom."

"You know what burns my ass the most?"

That's a loaded question.

When I remain silent, she continues. "That I would buy her gifts every year for Administrative Assistant Day."

Yeah…I could see how that would chafe.

"Apparently, my gifts weren't good enough since she helped herself to my *husband* instead."

Yikes.

The waitress returns with my Diet Coke and Mom's margarita.

"Just in the nick of time," she mutters, swallowing down half of it in one thirsty gulp. "Have you spoken to him yet?"

I shake my head. Like Beck, he's reached out. And like Beck, I've avoided his calls and texts. There is nothing he can say or do that will change the disgust and disappointment coursing through me. If he wasn't happy in his marriage, he should have done something about it instead of sneaking around behind Mom's back.

"As furious as I am with him," she says, "I don't want to cause a wedge in your relationship. No matter what happens between us, he *is* your father, and he loves you."

It's almost a relief when our lunch arrives. Mom needs something solid in her stomach to counteract the tequila. She's been snacking on the chips and salsa, but it's not enough.

I use my fork to push around the beans and rice on my plate. "I'm not ready to talk to him right now. He didn't only walk out on you, he walked out on me, too."

She reaches across the table and snags my hand. "He left me, honey. Not you. He loves you more than anything."

That may be so, but I'm too angry to deal with him right now. It doesn't escape me that the only reason he came clean about the affair is because I caught him in the act. And even then, he chose to lie before begrudgingly admitting the truth. He could have also let me know about the decision he arrived at before talking to Mom so I could have been prepared, but he couldn't be bothered to do that either.

So, no…I'm not interested in speaking to him now that he's shacked up with his whore and living his best life. Maybe some time down the road, but not right now.

Mom points her fork at my plate. "You haven't eaten much. Aren't you hungry?"

I shrug. "Not really. Don't worry, I'll take it home for dinner."

She glances at her own untouched plate. "Yeah, me neither."

I'm concerned about her driving home, especially since she didn't eat much. "Do you want to come back to my place for a while?"

"No. I forgot to mention it, but I've decided to stay with Aunt Amy for a few days. She'll help me find a lawyer and walk me through the process. I'm feeling a bit overwhelmed at the moment."

Aunt Amy has three divorces under her belt, so she's an old pro at this. "I'm sure that will be helpful." I pause before asking point-blank, "Are you all right to drive?"

"I'm fine," she snorts and waves her hand. "It takes more than one and a half margaritas to knock me on my ass."

My lips bow up at the corners.

That's probably true.

When I've finished picking over my enchilada, I set my fork on the table. "I'm going to run to the bathroom before we leave."

"All right, honey. I'll pay the check."

"Thanks, Mom. Lunch was nice."

"Not really," she chuckles, "but I love spending time with you."

I shimmy around the table and wrap my arms around her shoulders. "Maybe we can do this more often."

"I would love that," she says, leaning into my embrace.

I run to the bathroom at the back of the restaurant. Once inside, I take care of business and wash my hands before applying a bit of lip gloss. As I'm about to head out, the door swings open, and I do a doubletake as Dr. Hayes walks in.

Everything inside me freezes.

"Mia! I wasn't expecting to run into you today." She pauses, carefully looking me over. "How are you feeling?"

Huh?

My brows slam together until I remember emailing her yesterday about the stomach virus I'd come down with. It wasn't a *total* lie. The idea of sitting in her class all the while remembering what she looked like on her knees between Beck's legs makes me want to throw up.

"Much better, thank you." When an uncomfortable silence settles over us, I clear my throat and inch toward the exit. "I should really get back to the table."

As I take another step toward the door, her fingers wrap around my wrist. I glance at her hand in surprise.

A hesitant smile curves her pink-stained lips. "Could we talk for a moment before you run away?"

I shake my head. "Now probably isn't a—"

"I won't keep you long." She steps closer. "I promise."

Good time.

Ugh. Talking with Dr. Hayes is the last thing I want to do. It ranks right up there with talking to my dad or Beck.

My shoulders slump as I mumble, "I guess."

Her hand falls away from my wrist. It's odd that she can stand here and act like everything is perfectly normal. As if I didn't see her getting ready to blow one of her students.

The guy who was supposedly my boyfriend.

Pain blooms in my chest before I quickly stomp it out. I refuse to give Beck another moment of my time. I've given him way too much as it is.

Her attention stays locked on me as she leans against the counter. "I wanted to apologize for what you walked in on the other day. It was highly unprofessional of me to engage in a personal relationship on campus."

I blink, knocked off balance by her apology because honestly, it doesn't sound like much of one. "Isn't it inappropriate for you to be involved with one of your students?"

Her smile never falters. "It was consensual."

The little bit of food I've eaten for lunch threatens to revolt. "Was it?"

"Of course. Do you think any twenty-one-year-old male in his right mind would turn down sex with one of his professors?" She shrugs. "Consider it a perk of my position," she laughs. "I keep getting older, but the guys stay the same age. It's fabulous."

Gross.

The conversation I had with Beck at the library a couple of weeks ago forces its way into my consciousness. He'd tried telling me that Dr. H had been acting a little *too* friendly, and I'd brushed off the conversation. A pit settles in my belly as I consider the possibility that I was wrong. Maybe he wasn't as willing of a participant as I'd assumed.

As much as I don't want to discuss the topic, I have to get to the bottom of it. "How long has your relationship with Beck been going on for?"

"I wouldn't really call it a relationship." A smug smile plays around the corners of her lips. "More like a pursuit."

"On your part?" My breath becomes wedged in my throat as I wait for her answer.

She gives me a wink. "I love the thrill of the chase."

After I'd walked in on them in her office, Beck had once again claimed she'd come on to him. I wince, remembering my reaction. Instead of believing him, I had accused him of being a liar and walked away.

When another silence falls over us, Dr. Hayes reaches out to squeeze my arm. "I'm glad we could clear up this misunderstanding, Mia. I'll see you in class tomorrow?"

I blink out of those thoughts before shaking my head. "No, I'm sorry. It turns out I won't be able to TA for you after all."

"Excuse me?" She straightens as her voice fills with disbelief. "You're going to leave me high and dry for the rest of the semester because you walked in on a private moment behind closed doors?"

"No, that has nothing to do with it. The reason I can't work for you is because I've lost all respect for you. Ever since freshman year Composition, I've admired you. I thought you were someone worthy of emulating. But you know what? I was wrong. How can I look up to someone who uses their position of power to make sexual advances toward a student? What you did to Beck was sexual harassment, plain and simple." I cock my head and narrow my eyes. "You realize he could file a complaint against you with the university."

Her eyes bulge as her mouth drops open. "It was consensual," she whispers again.

"Is that what you tell yourself when you hit on guys half your age and make them feel like they have to trade sexual favors for grades?"

She makes a choking sound deep in her throat but remains silent.

"Yeah, that's what I thought." With nothing left to say, I push out of the bathroom and head to the table where Mom is waiting. My hands are shaking so badly that I have to press them together to make them stop.

Mom rises to her feet when she sees me. "Are you all right?" Her brow furrows as she searches my face. "You look awfully pale."

"I don't think the enchiladas are sitting well."

"Uh-oh." She wraps an arm around my waist and steers me through the restaurant. "We better get you home before they hit."

My lips lift. "Thanks, Mom."

I lean against her shoulder as we push through the doors and into the bright fall sunshine. Only then, do I suck in a shaky breath and force down all the emotions that churn dangerously inside me.

Beck was telling the truth, and I didn't believe him.

I groan with the realization that I probably threw away the best relationship I've ever had. And there might not be a way for me to get it back again.

MIA

"You really said that?" Alyssa gapes before shoveling the last of my enchilada into her mouth. It's been sitting untouched in the refrigerator for days. *"To Dr. H?"* she mumbles around a mouthful of tortilla, cheese, and chicken.

I swing away from her as she sits on the couch in our living room. "Yup."

"Damn, girl!" she hoots, slapping her thigh. "You are seriously my hero!"

I tunnel my fingers through my hair and groan. Days later and I'm still reeling from the encounter in the bathroom at El Toro.

"No, I'm not." I spin toward her again as I continue to pace. A mixture of nerves and nausea makes it impossible to sit still.

My bestie shakes her head. "Are you kidding me? Everyone on campus has heard the rumors about Hayes. It's about time someone called her out on her bullshit."

"I've heard the gossip, too," I admit, "but I never suspected there was any truth behind it." I blow out a slow breath. "If I hadn't seen it happen with my own eyes, I still wouldn't believe it." Which only makes me feel like more of an asshole because I sat there in the library and brushed off Beck's concerns. Then I called him a liar and pretty much told him to fuck off.

"What are you going to do? File a complaint with the university?"

"I don't know." My teeth sink into my lower lip before worrying it. "I need to talk with Beck. He's the real victim in all this. I'm not sure if it's my place to say anything."

"When are you going to do that?"

"I have no idea." I drop onto the leather armchair across from the couch. A mirthless chuckle escapes from my lips. "After the way I treated him, it's doubtful he'll ever speak to me again." I lift my fingers to massage my temples. A headache brews behind them. "And I can't blame him for that."

The look she gives me is full of pity. "Yeah, blocking him on your phone and all social media probably wasn't the best move. You kind of went nuclear on his ass."

I wince. Her assessment of the situation isn't wrong. I have no idea if there's a way to come back from this.

A soft knock on the apartment door has both our heads whipping toward the entryway.

Alyssa's eyes widen. "Do you think that's him?"

"Why are you whispering?" I glance at the door. "Do you really think he can hear us?"

She sticks out her tongue before jumping off the couch and jogging toward the door.

We're both surprised when she swings it open only to find Colton on the other side.

I crane my neck to see what's going on. Their voices drop, becoming hushed. Their heads are bent together as if sharing secrets, but that can't be. Alyssa hates Colton with the passion of a thousand burning suns. I strain my ears to hear what's being said but can't make out anything other than whispered tones.

Well, well, well...isn't this an interesting turn of events.

I'm tempted to sidle up to the pair and stick my nose where it doesn't belong. When Alyssa shoots a furtive glance over her shoulder, I don't bother to hide my interest in their conversation.

Wait a minute…is Alyssa *blushing*?

That can't be. The girl doesn't have a bashful bone in her body. Not only is this exchange becoming more fascinating by the second, but it's taking my mind off Beck and the disaster I made of our relationship.

She swings toward me. Her gaze darts around the living room, landing everywhere but on me. "So…we're going to grab something to eat."

"Really?" I point to the empty food container on the coffee table that she practically licked clean. "You inhaled an entire enchilada."

"I have a big appetite." Her eyes narrow. "Are you trying to food shame me?"

My shoulders shake with laughter. "Not at all."

If it's possible, more color seeps into her cheeks.

Damn, but I really need to find out what's going on between them. Because obviously something is. And the bitch hasn't mentioned one word.

Looks like I'm not the only one keeping secrets.

"I'll see you later," she mutters, swiping her purse from the credenza near the front door.

"Yes, we'll definitely—"

The sentence isn't even out of my mouth before she slams the door shut behind her, leaving me to my own devices.

I wave a hand at the empty doorway. "No, no, that's all right, I'll stay here," I call out, raising my voice to add, "thanks anyway for the invite!"

With a sigh, I allow my body to sink into the chair before staring at the ceiling. I need to figure out how I'm going to handle the situation with Beck. No matter what happens between us, I need to apologize.

There's a knock on the door as my phone chimes with an incoming text. I jump from the chair and glance at the message. It's from Alyssa.

Heads up.

My brows slam together.

Could she be more cryptic?

I need a decoder to figure it out.

Or maybe I can buy a vowel.

I pad to the front door and pull it open. My heart stutters before beating into overdrive at the person I find standing in the hallway.

"Dad." My fingers bite into the handle. I'm so tempted to slam the door in his face. Especially after the lunch with Mom. "What are you doing here?"

He's the last person I expected to find knocking on my door.

Make that the second last.

Looking strangely nervous, he shrugs and stuffs his hands into the pockets of his slacks. "I thought I'd stop by so we could talk."

"Oh…I wish you would have called first."

His lips ghost into a thin smile. "Maybe if you would have answered my calls, stopping by unannounced wouldn't have become necessary."

"Yeah," I mutter, "I guess."

When I don't budge from the doorway, he says, "Are you going to invite me in?"

Begrudgingly, I step aside, giving him room to pass. Once he's inside the tiny entryway, I close the door and head into the living room before dropping onto the chair. He follows me in, settling on the couch across from me.

He looks around the room, taking in all the little details that have been added. Both of my parents helped me move in, but he hasn't been back to see the finished product. "I like what you've done to the place, it looks nice."

"Thanks." I shift on the chair as an uncomfortable silence settles over us.

We both fidget, looking everywhere but at each other.

This is beyond awkward.

What sucks is that my father and I have always had a close relationship. He's the one who introduced me to tennis. When I was a kid, he would take me to the courts, and we would spend hours hitting balls and working on my serve. I have a lot of great memories of my dad that revolve around tennis. It's difficult to swallow that he blew it all to shit with one traitorous action. I'm not sure if it's possible for us to get back to that place again. The man sitting across from me doesn't resemble the one who filled those memories.

Nerves stretch tautly across my skin as he releases a sigh before dropping his gaze to his clenched hands.

"I'm sorry, Mia."

"For what?" Now that the shock of his visit has dissipated, fury rushes in to fill the void. I can't stop dwelling on my lunch with Mom and the anguish and humiliation he inflicted upon her.

"For lying," he says, "and hurting you. Most of all, I'm sorry you found out about my affair the way you did. I should have handled the situation differently."

My eyes narrow. "So…you're sorry for hurting me and that I found out the way I did but not for cheating on your wife and breaking up our family." Maybe I'm being a little harsh, but that's too damn bad. I refuse to make this easy on him.

His shoulders slump under the weight of my words, and suddenly, he looks much older than his forty-eight years. "I've been in love with Mandi for a long time." He searches my eyes before admitting, "And now that we don't have to sneak around, it's like a huge weight has been lifted from my shoulders. Everything is out in the open, and I'm no longer stuck…"

Did he seriously just say that?

It's only after his voice trails off that I realize my eyes have widened, and my mouth is hanging open.

"Wow." Slowly I shake my head. "I guess it all worked out for you, *Dad.*"

"I didn't mean it like that," he says, attempting to backtrack. "It's just a relief not to be living a lie. The last two years have been stressful."

I bet.

His words are like a punch to the gut.

"You've been sleeping with this woman for two years?"

He jerks his head into a nod.

"That's it then?" I stare at him as a fresh wave of shock washes over me. "You're not going to try to fix your marriage?"

Guilt flickers in his eyes before they skitter away. "No. Our marriage has been over for a long time." He clears his throat. "I'm sure your mother would agree with that."

"It might have been nice if you'd had a conversation with her about it before you slept with someone else."

He hangs his head. "You're right. I shouldn't have allowed the situation to spiral so far out of control. I take full responsibility for that. After Brianna died, your mother and I drifted apart. When you left for college, I realized how unhappy I was in our marriage. I thought about leaving at that point, but your mother was still in such a fragile place. So, I waited and hoped things would get better." He shrugs helplessly. "But they didn't."

I press my lips together, refusing to say anything. If he's looking for sympathy, he won't get it from me.

"Is it so difficult to understand that I wouldn't want to spend the rest of my life in a loveless marriage?" He waits for a beat before continuing. "Your mother and I have become more like roommates than anything else. Old friends who are stuck together, making the best of a situation." He searches my eyes. "But the thing is, I love Mandi. She makes me feel young and hopeful again. This is my second chance at happiness, and I need to take it before it passes me by."

I'm rendered speechless by everything coming out of his mouth.

Who the hell is this guy because I sure as hell don't know.

"Mia? Did you hear me?"

I jerk back to our conversation and shake my head to clear it. "No, sorry." I'm on information overload. I can't process anything else.

He leans forward, and excitement leaps to life in his eyes. "When you're ready, I'd like to introduce you to Mandi."

He wants to introduce me to the woman he left my mother for?

The same woman he's been cheating with for two years?

I don't even know what to say. Wrapping my lips around words feels impossible. I can only sit and stare at him.

"She has two kids. They're still in middle school, but you're going to love them." He pauses, enthusiasm growing in his voice. "They can't wait to meet you."

I shake my head. "No."

Is he insane?

Or am I the one who has completely lost it?

I can't tell anymore.

He tilts his head. "No?"

"I'm nowhere ready to meet the woman you left Mom for, and I have no desire to meet her kids either."

Surprise flickers across his face before he mumbles, "Well, I didn't mean this very minute. I was thinking more like a month or two. Christmas is right around the corner, and I was hoping we could have everything smoothed over by then."

Nope, it's definitely him. He's lost his ever-loving mind. He'll be lucky if this is *smoothed over* by the following Christmas.

"Sorry to burst your bubble, Dad," I shove a hand through my hair, surprised I have to explain myself to him, "but I don't think that will happen."

Happiness drains from his eyes. "I guess you'll let me know when you're ready to be part of my new life."

You know what?

I have zero desire to be part of his *new life.*

In fact, he can take his *new life* and shove it where the sun doesn't shine.

How can he be so oblivious to the damage he caused?

It's like he wants to sweep it all under the rug and pretend it never happened so he can move on with someone else and start his *new life.* Meanwhile, Mom and I are trying to pick up the tattered pieces of our old one.

It's a relief when Dad rises to his feet.

"I suppose I should go." He shoves his hands into his pockets. "You probably have homework or studying to finish up."

I nod, unwilling to tell him any different.

Neither of us speaks as we walk to the entryway. The man beside me no longer feels like my father. He's nothing more than a stranger. Once we reach the door, he pulls it open and pauses. "You'll keep in touch?"

Even though it's a lie, I nod. Maybe, at some point in the future, we'll be able to get our relationship back on track, but it'll take time. Whether or not he realizes it, he's inflicted a lot of pain that I need to work through.

When he wraps his arms around me, I stand frozen, unable to return the embrace.

"Remember that I love you, Mia. None of this is your fault."

I suck in a sharp breath before gradually blowing it out. If I don't keep a tight rein on my emotions, I'll lose it. Not for one damn moment did I ever think I was to blame for the destruction of his marriage. The fault for that lies *entirely* with him.

Once Dad releases me, his lips lift into a smile. After he disappears down the hallway, I close the door and sag against it.

This has officially become the week from hell.

With a sinking heart, I realize it's not over yet.

BECK

The spiral I throw lands perfectly in Colton's hands. Whatever problem he had been struggling with earlier in the season seems to have worked itself out.

Thank fuck, because that's the last thing we need right now. We have four games under our belt and eight more to go. It's still early, but we have an undefeated record.

When Coach blows his whistle, signaling the end of practice, I unsnap the chin strap and pull off my helmet, letting it dangle from my fingers. Colton jogs toward me, meeting me as we head off the field.

Grinning from ear-to-ear, he holds out his hand for a fist bump.

"Looking good out there," I tell him. "Nice to see you got your groove back."

"Damn right I did, baby!" He flashes a grin as relief oozes from every pore of his body. "And not a moment too soon with the Alabama game coming up."

Already I know it'll be a tough one. Both mentally and physically. We're neck and neck with Alabama. After next Saturday, one of us will be first in the conference, and I'm going to do everything in my power to make sure it's us.

I'm glad Colton finally got his head out of his ass and into the game. I don't know what's changed, and I don't particularly give a crap. All I care about is that he's squared away. Seems ironic that as soon as Colton manages to pull it together, my shit falls apart. Although, I'll be damned if I let it mess with my game.

I keep telling myself that maybe, in the long run, it's better this way. For a long time, I thought Mia was the one. Turns out that's not the case. The bitch of it is everything had been going so well. I'd really hoped…

I shut down that line of thinking before it can spread like a contagious virus and infect my bloodstream.

Colton rams his elbow into my side, and I glare. "What the fuck, dude?"

He lifts his chin toward the bleachers. "What's Mia doing here?"

Huh?

My gaze sweeps over the stands before landing on her dark head in the second row.

"I don't know," I mutter, trying to ignore the way my heart lurches at the sight of her.

"Guess you're gonna find out," he says.

When she realizes I'm staring, she rises to her feet before moving down the cement stairs and stepping onto the track that circles the field.

Once we pull up to her, Colton stops and grins like a Cheshire cat. "Hey, Mia. Wasn't expecting to see you here."

The way his voice simmers with humor makes me want to knock him upside the head.

She smiles, but it's not a full-blown one that reaches her eyes. There's a wariness holding her back. "Hi."

Silence falls over us before she clears her throat. "Beck, do you have a moment to talk?"

You know what?

I don't need this bullshit right now.

Not with the upcoming games.

Not with the NFL Scouting Combine and Draft.

For years, I let this girl mess with my head, and I can't afford to do it any longer.

I always thought there might be a chance for us, but I was wrong. It took me awhile, but I finally got it through my thick head.

We weren't meant to be.

End of story.

That being said, do I have more time to waste on Mia Stanbury?

Hell, no.

"Sure."

Goddamn it.

Colton grins before taking off. "All right, bro, I'll see you in the locker room." And then he's jogging to catch up with Devon Baker. They disappear through the tunnel and into the stadium.

The team walks past, and a few guys slap me on the back as they head to the locker room. There's a lot of laughter and good-natured ribbing. Now that practice is over, everyone has perked up.

Sweat runs down the back of my neck before getting absorbed into the material of my jersey. I'm exhausted from two hours of drills. All I want to do is get out of these pads and hit the showers.

I squint against the sun as it dips behind the stadium. "What did you want to talk about?"

Mia wrings her hands as her gaze flits around the field. She looks like she's being devoured by nerves. Part of me wants to reach out and put her at ease, but I refrain from touching her. Instead, I keep my arms locked at my sides. She made it perfectly clear the last time we spoke that she wants nothing to do with me.

So, as hard as it is, I wait.

Her anxiety continues to ratchet up as her tongue darts out to smudge her lips. I stare at her perfect cupid's bow of a mouth, unable to stop myself from tracking the movement. My dick twitches against my jock, and I shift impatiently, wanting to get this over with.

Why the hell is she here when all she's done is avoid me for the last couple of days?

I almost laugh. What the hell am I talking about?

Mia has spent most of her life trying to evade me. I should be used to it by now. After what we shared, I thought everything had changed.

Guess I was wrong.

It isn't the first time, and it won't be the last.

"I'm sorry, Beck," she blurts. "I owe you an apology."

My gaze jerks from her mouth to her eyes. Out of everything she could have said, that's the one thing I wasn't expecting. "What are you apologizing for?"

She sucks in a deep breath before steadily releasing it back into the atmosphere. "I should have believed you about Dr. Hayes."

I tilt my head and narrow my eyes. "What makes you so sure I *wasn't* lying?"

The question gives her pause, and her knuckles turn bone white as she locks her fingers together. "I spoke with her, and she admitted to hitting on you."

Well, color me surprised.

When I remain silent, Mia continues in a rush, "I walked in on a situation and jumped to the wrong conclusion instead of giving you a chance to explain, and for that, I'm sorry."

A thick lump of emotion settles in the middle of my throat. "Not only did you accuse me of screwing around with my professor, but you thought I was cheating on you. When I tried to explain, you shut me down and walked away." I step closer so she has to crane her neck to hold my stare. "You should have known better, Mia."

"I know," she whispers, her breath escaping in harsh pants, "I'm so sorry. Can you forgive me?"

"Ever hear the expression—too little, too late?" I continue to push into her personal space until we're so close that the tips of her breasts press against my chest pads.

"Yes." Her face falls as she nods. "Even if you can't forgive me, I needed to apologize for hurting you."

When she tries to retreat, I drop my hands onto her shoulders to keep her in place. My face hovers inches from hers.

"So that's it?" I pause. "All I get is a lame apology for breaking my heart?"

Her dark eyes fill with tears. "I don't know what else to say other than I'm sorry."

"Maybe you should start by telling me that you love me."

She blinks in confusion before her eyes widen. *"What?"*

I lower my mouth until it can ghost over hers. Goddamn, but I've missed her kisses. Actually, I've missed everything about this girl. The last couple of days have sucked. "Tell me that you love me."

When a whimper slides from her mouth, my cock stirs.

"I love you, Beck." Her attention stays focused on me. "Even when I didn't want to, I did."

Emotion explodes in my chest. "Say it again," I demand, needing to hear those three little words.

She smiles, and the tension haunting her eyes dissipates. "I love you."

As soon as my lips settle on hers, she opens until my tongue can slip into her mouth as I wrap her up in my arms. I pull away long enough to mutter, "Know what you're going to do next?"

A bemused expression settles on her face as she shakes her head.

"Unblock me."

Laughter bursts from her as she presses her forehead against my chest. "I'm sorry. I shouldn't have done that."

"Damn right, you shouldn't have," I grunt.

"It will never happen again."

"I'm going to hold you to that promise." I press another quick kiss against her. "Looks like you have a long night ahead of you."

She pops a brow. "And why is that?"

"Make-up sex." A grin curls its way around the edges of my lips. "And lots of it."

Silent laughter shakes her shoulders. "Is that so?"

"Yup." Before she can say anything else, I bend down, wrap my arms around her thighs and hoist her over my shoulder. She lands against me with a squeal before grabbing hold of my jersey as she dangles upside down. I reposition my hands, sliding one to her ass and the other around her legs to hold her in place.

Thankfully, this time, she's not wearing a thong. No one gets to see the goods except me.

"Beck!" she shrieks. "What are you doing?"

"That should be obvious. I'm taking you home where you can apologize in the privacy of my bedroom." The thought has my cock stiffening right up. "I hope you don't have plans for the rest of the night because you'll be otherwise engaged."

"Please tell me that you're going to shower," she laughs, "because you kind of stink."

She's right, I smell terrible. That's what a couple of hours of practice will get you. Man sweat, baby.

But now that she's mentioned it…

"That can be part of the making up you owe me. What do you think about that?"

"Only that I love you, Beckett Hollingsworth."

I squeeze her ass as we walk through the tunnel. "Right back at you, babe."

EPILOGUE

BECK

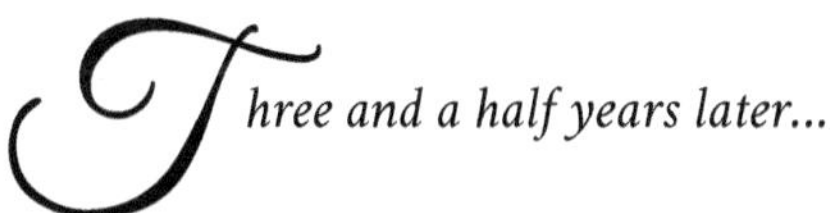

hree and a half years later...

"MIA HOLLINGSWORTH," the Dean of the Law School announces as she walks across the stage in her cap and gown.

I jump to my feet and stick my fingers between my lips, whistling like crazy. Mia grins as her gaze seeks mine out in the thick crowd of observers. "Way to go, Mia!" I holler at the top of my lungs. I don't give a rat's ass if she's embarrassed. She worked damn hard for this moment, and I want everyone and their mother to know how proud I am of her.

Speaking of mothers...

I wrap my arm around Julia and give her a squeeze as we share a grin. My parents occupy the seats next to her. On my left is Mia's father, Dan, and his wife, Mandi.

When Mia told me that she planned on inviting both of her parents to the graduation ceremony, I thought she was nuts. Or maybe drunk. She insisted everyone was in a better place now. Considering that a fight has yet to break out, she might be right.

Three years seems to have mellowed Julia's bitterness toward her ex-husband.

And his home-wrecking new wife.

I won't lie, the first year was a rough one. Dan ended up paying through the nose in order to expedite the divorce proceedings. It turns out Mandi was preggers.

Yeah…

That news went over like a lead balloon with his daughter. And who can blame her for that? There was a long stretch of time where they didn't talk. It's only been within the last year that Mia reached out and rekindled their relationship. It's been slow going. We're talking baby steps. But they seem to be on the right path.

I glance at my mother-in-law. I'm happy to report that she's doing much better. With the settlement from Dan, she went back to school for interior design and is working full-time at a design house. Once the divorce proceedings were underway, she began therapy and is now in a more Zen place.

Believe it or not, Julia has even dipped her toe in the dating pond.

And the guy she's seeing?

Has absolutely nothing to do with finance.

For today, everyone has put their differences aside, and we're all getting along like one big dysfunctional family. If we're lucky, all these good vibes will last throughout lunch. No one wants to ruin this day for Mia.

Dad is working on opening another law office in San Francisco since that's where I was drafted as their backup quarterback. First-round, baby. Don't worry, I worked my way up to starting QB after my rookie season.

As soon as the commencement ceremony ends and the auditorium empties, we all head outside to wait for my wife.

Yup, you heard that right.

After a year of dating, I proposed and put a ring on it. Then, before Mia's third year of law school, we got hitched. And it's been wedded bliss ever since.

Just kidding. Nothing is perfect, but it's pretty damn close. I can't imagine my life without this woman filling it.

I search through the sea of faces until I find my wife. The moment she sees me, a huge grin breaks out across her face, and she runs, hurtling herself into my arms. When I swing her around, she giggles before pressing her lips against mine.

"Congrats, babe, you're officially a lawyer!"

Her face lights up with joy. It's the best damn expression. One I'll never tire of.

Sure, maybe it took us a while to get our shit together, but it happened. And what I mean by that is—I chased her until I wore her down, and she finally had no other choice but to give in and marry me.

That's a joke. The Grinders R Us visit aside, we all know I didn't stalk her…right?

Right?

Moving on. No matter how it worked out, Mia Stanbury—AKA Mia Hollingsworth—is officially mine, and I don't have any plans to let her go. If I'm doing my job right as a husband, she'll have me locked in for the long haul as well.

"I love you, Beck," she whispers before pressing her lips against mine.

I squeeze her to me and hold her close. "Right back at you, babe."

BONUS EPILOGUE

BECK

Eight years later...

"I'm so glad you talked me into this," Mia says from where she's stretched out on a plush lounger on the white sand beach as bright sunlight beats down on her nearly naked body.

We've only been here a couple days, but already her skin is glowing. She looks like a goddess with her face tipped toward the sky and her long, dark hair pulled up into a messy bun at the top of her head. The only piece of clothing she wears is a teeny tiny bikini bottom that covers the necessities.

I can only stare at her and wonder how the hell I got so lucky.

How is this gorgeous woman my wife?

No, I'm serious.

She's smart, gorgeous, and the best damn mother to our little girl, who is currently staying with Mia's mom and spending a little one-on-one time with her nana. Alexis is three and is the spitting image of her mama. We jokingly refer to her as Mia's mini me.

Honestly, I look at my daughter and it's like someone reached inside my chest and ripped out my beating heart. Not in a million years could I have imagined feeling this kind of intense love for another human being.

As much as I miss the munchkin, I'm enjoying having my wife all to myself for the week. I'm still playing for San Francisco, and Mia practices law at my father's firm. Although, she's scaled back and works from home if she's not meeting with clients. When it's the off season and I'm not traveling, I take over kiddo duty so she can put in extra hours at the office if she needs to. We're partners, and I never want her to feel as if she has to sacrifice her career goals in order to have a family.

Especially when there's another on the way. We've already seen the ultrasound pictures, and this one is a boy.

Mia suggested Beckett Junior, but I'm not so sure the world is big enough for two Beckett Hollingsworths.

Plus…people might call him BJ for short.

He'd either love us or hate our fucking guts.

Unable to resist the lure of her, I rise from where I've been lounging until I can hover over her nearly naked body and cage her in.

"I'm glad you're enjoying it. You needed a little R and R before the baby arrives."

One hand settles on the rounded curve of her belly before I lean down and take her mouth. As soon as I lick at the seam of her lips, she opens. Our tongues tangle as she tilts her head, allowing me greater access. All I want to do is plunder her sweetness.

When a whimper escapes from her, I deepen the kiss. Our teeth scrape as need spirals through me and my cock stiffens up.

I'm so damn hungry for her.

Although, that's nothing new.

There has never been a time when I haven't been greedy for my wife.

Her arms loosely slide around my neck to hold me in place.

As if that's necessary…

Once her lips are swollen from my kisses, I nip at her chin before sliding downward. When I suck the sensitive flesh of her throat into my mouth, she arches and bares the slender column as her naked breasts thrust upward. Now that she's pregnant for a second time, she's way more than a handful, and I fucking love it.

I kiss my way along her collarbone, making sure to adore every single sun-kissed inch, before circling her nipple with the tip of my tongue. Her fingers tunnel through the short strands of my hair and the nails trail along my scalp as I draw her stiff little bud into my mouth and greedily suck it. Then, I give the same ardent attention to the other side. She writhes beneath me as I continue to arouse her body, stoking the flames to life until they're blazing out of control.

Christ, this woman is sexy.

Especially when her belly is swollen with my child.

Even better than that?

Pregnancy turns Mia into a horndog. She can't get enough.

I release her nipple with a soft pop before whispering against her heated skin, "Feel good, baby?"

"Mmm, you know it does."

She's right, I do. We've been together for eight years, and there are times when I think I understand the needs of her body better than she does.

As I kiss a trail over her burgeoning belly, my fingers gently knead her breasts, and she stretches like a contented cat beneath my touch. I give both nipples a little tweak before trailing my hands to the twin ties secured at each hip.

"Beck..."

"Yeah, baby?"

I glance up and meet her heavy-lidded eyes.

"We shouldn't. Not here on the beach." Her voice turns breathless. Even though she's wary, I can tell just how turned on she is by the idea of making love outside.

"Why not?" One pluck at the knot and the strings quickly unravel.

"Someone could see us."

I glance up and down the deserted beach. The sand is pristine and untouched. The turquoise water is so clear that you can see straight down to the bottom, even when out deep.

"We came here for some privacy. So we could make love anywhere we wanted." Colton and Alyssa were here six months ago and told us all about the place. The luxury accommodations weren't cheap by any means, but they're entirely worth it.

Mia has to realize that there's no way I'd want someone else catching even a glimpse of her naked. Or while we're having sex. Her body and orgasms belong to me. No one else will ever get to see what she looks like when she comes.

I was her first, and my plan is to be her last.

"I know, but..."

Her voice trails off when my fingers release the second bow and there's nothing to hold the tiny scrap of material in place. My gaze arrows to the shiny black triangle as I peel it away and press a kiss to the top of her bare pussy.

Even though that wasn't nearly enough to satisfy me, I meet her gaze with a raised brow. "Should I stop?"

She chews her bottom lip for a heartbeat before shaking her head. "No."

The edges of my lips curl into a knowing smile. "Didn't think so."

With that, I rip the fabric away and drop it to the sand next to the lounger before settling between her supple thighs and spreading them wide.

One look at her perfection and my mouth waters for a taste. Pregnancy has made her pussy full and ripe. Already there's wetness glistening on her lips. I trail my thumb over her soaked center from the top to the bottom and then up again. It only takes a few lazy strokes for her to squirm beneath me. All of her previous reservations fall to the wayside.

I might be intent on tormenting her, but I'm torturing myself as well.

Unable to hold back for another second, I lower my mouth to her honeyed flesh and take a long lap of her softness. She arches beneath my touch, widening her legs even more so that every delicate inch is exposed.

So.

Fucking.

Beautiful.

Not to mention mine.

No matter how many times I've done this, there's no way I'll ever get enough.

I know how she likes to be eaten. I know exactly what turns her on and makes her forget her own name until she's screaming out mine.

It's the best damn sound in the world.

And I take pride in my work.

Pride in keeping my woman well satisfied.

I spear my tongue deep inside before nibbling at her clit. When her back arches and her muscles tighten, I know she's seconds away from coming. I focus all of my attention on licking her flesh before sliding a finger in her pussy, curling it in order to hit that magic spot inside that will have her going off like a shot.

As soon as the guttural cry escapes from her, it's swept away by the warm breeze that slides over us. It's only after her body stops shuddering and she turns limp that I press a kiss against her engorged clit.

Then her belly.

Each breast.

And, lastly, her mouth.

She opens so that my tongue can plunge inside to dance with her own.

I pull away just enough to say, "Turn over, baby."

By the way she continues to stare at me, it's obvious that she's still riding high on endorphins.

I nip at her plump bottom lip and tug it with my teeth to get her attention. "Now. I need to take you."

Her eyes clear just enough for me to see the fire leap within them at my rough command. There aren't many places I'll get bossy with Mia, but the bedroom is one of them. It turns us both on.

My arms slide around her, helping to move her into position until she's on all fours on the oversized wooden sunbed, ass high in the air.

My gaze slides over her backside, touching on every delicate inch.

Fuck.

If I thought I was turned on before, it's nothing compared to what

I feel with her pussy on full display, all wet and waiting. That's all the prompting I need to shove my board shorts down my hips and thighs until they're puddled around my bare feet before stepping out of them and closer to the lounger. With one last look, I glance around the beach to make sure it's vacant.

Thankfully, it is.

There's not a soul in sight.

At this point, I'm not sure it would matter.

I'm so fucking hard. I'm like the horny teenage boy I used to be when I claimed her virginity after high school graduation. Twelve years hasn't changed that. I've spent my entire life longing for this girl.

The one who lived right next door.

The one I never thought could belong to me.

Sweeping those thoughts away, I hunker down until I'm eyelevel with her pussy and thrust my tongue deep inside her slick heat. That's all it takes for a moan to escape from her.

I tongue her softness, intent on driving her just as insane as I am.

I'll be damned if she doesn't come for a second time.

Maybe even a third.

Have I mentioned how much I love vacation sex?

Best.

Sex.

Ever.

Quick mental note to book another stay in a year or so.

Hell, let's just make it an annual thing.

I give her one last leisurely lap before rising to my feet and wrapping my fingers around my dick, bringing the head to her soaked entrance. Even though I'd like nothing better than to slam into her and take her hard, there's no way I'm doing that. It's carefully that I ease inside her body until I'm buried balls deep and my groin is pressed against her ass.

My hands settle on her hips, drawing her closer as I stare at the place we're intimately connected. I have the perfect view of her gorgeous rosebud. I grit my teeth and thrust inside her sweet heat.

Her pussy clenches my dick like a tight fist. Already, I know I won't last long.

For fuck's sake, I'm thirty years old. It shouldn't be like this.

She arches her spine and presses even closer.

Holy mother of god...

If she doesn't come soon, I'm gonna—

Another strangled cry escapes from her and she chants my name over and over. When her pussy clenches my thick length, it's game over. That's all it takes for me to follow her off the precipice and into oblivion. I squeeze my eyes tightly closed as I pump inside her body.

I come so hard that I see stars.

It's only after my cock softens that I slump over her with a satisfied huff. My hands slip around her ribcage to palm her breast before stroking the elongated nipples as my teeth sink into the top of her shoulder.

Even though she's six months pregnant, the need to mark her as my own thrums through me.

"I love you, baby," I whisper.

"I love you, too."

I pull out before running my hand over the rounded curve of her ass and giving it a swat. Nothing hard. Just enough to elicit a gasp as she turns to meet my gaze.

The love shining brightly in her eyes is like a punch to the gut.

It's a love that is echoed fiercely within my own.

Unwilling to give her up just yet, I scoop her into my arms, holding her close before swinging around toward the vast stretch of ocean that fills the horizon.

"Beck! What are you doing?"

"Taking you to the water. Play your cards right and I'll make love to you there as well."

She threads her arms around my neck before resting her head against my chest and sighing in contentment.

This life...

I have no idea how the hell I got so lucky.

I have a beautiful wife and little girl. Another kiddo on the way. A family who we can count on. And a career that fulfills me.

I have no idea what else is in store for us, but I sure as shit can't wait to find out.

The End

THE BOY NEXT DOOR

COLTON

Summer before freshman year of college...

MY LIPS QUIRK at the corners as I glance around. It's fucking madness and I wouldn't have it any other way. This is *exactly* the way you kick off summer vacation. Leave it to Beck Hollingsworth to throw the mother of all graduation parties. The three key ingredients for a kickass party are present—scantily clad chicks, plenty of free-flowing booze, and last but not least, parents conspicuously absent from the festivities. Never let it be said that Beck doesn't know how to do it up right. After all, this isn't his first rodeo. This guy has thrown some over-the-top, police-called-to-break-it-up, someone-almost-drowns-in-the-pool parties over the years.

There's a girl tucked under each arm as they stare adoringly up at me. Albeit drunkenly. A few more crowd around me, circling like sharks, waiting for an opportunity to home in on the action. Delicate hands stroke over my bare chest. Another female presses her breasts against my back as nimble fingers slide their way around my waist and wrap around me.

One thing is for sure, I'm going to miss these girls when I leave for college next month. This is a carefully curated group I've trained since freshman year. I have rules when it comes to the opposite sex.

Rule number one—I don't do relationships.

If that's what you're looking for, find your pleasure elsewhere. If you think you can parley a one-night stand into a bone fide relationship, you've got the wrong guy. I have zero interest in getting serious or forming attachments.

Rule number two—what happens at a party, stays at a party. Don't bring that shit to school Monday morning. As long as everyone walks away feeling good at the end of the night, there's no reason to expect anything more. I'm damned careful to cull out the ones who are secretly looking for more.

Needy and clingy chicks need not apply.

Rule number three—

"Colton," a female voice purrs in my ear, "let's go upstairs."

My gaze flickers to Ella Sullivan. She's become a fan favorite over the years. Pretty face. Banging body. And has demonstrated an impressive stamina when it comes to blow jobs.

She's got that elusive trifecta going on.

"Yeah, Colton," Marissa Dix adds, trying to get in on the action as she presses her sweet titties against me, "let's get out of here. It's way too crowded."

Did someone order a threesome for the evening?

Yes, please.

What I've found is the more, the merrier. Added bonus, it's a lot harder to try and say that you were under the impression we were exclusive when you sat there and watched me bone your friend Saturday night.

I'm about to let these girls have their wicked way with me when I catch a flash of long blond hair from the corner of my eye. Before I can stop myself, my head whips in that direction. It's like an automatic reflex.

Every muscle goes whipcord tight.

Alyssa Williams.

What the hell is she doing here?

I'd hoped she would remain conspicuously absent from tonight's festivities. If there's one chick I avoid at all costs, it's the blond firecracker. My gaze slides to the girl she's dragging through the crowd like a ragdoll. By the stubborn set of Mia's jaw, my guess is that her bestie wasn't given much of a choice in regard to making an appearance. She looks like she's here at gunpoint. Now *that* brings a smile to my face. The dark-haired girl is Beck's next-door neighbor. She hates the dude with the passion of a thousand burning suns.

Possibly more.

Interestingly enough, Mia avoids Beck in much the same way I avoid Alyssa which hasn't been easy since my dick has decidedly different ideas on the matter. Even now, it's stirring in my boardshorts with interest, trying to rise to the occasion. Unfortunately for me, Alyssa has no concept of the word *no*. Even though I shoot her down on a regular basis, she continues to come at me hard every chance she gets.

And that, my friends, only makes me want her more. She's a girl who knows what she wants and goes after it with a single-minded determination. And what she wants, is me.

Damn, if that isn't hot.

I'd like to say that it'll be easier once I leave for college but that won't be the case given that Alyssa is also attending Wesley University this fall. At least there are ten thousand students on campus. With any luck, evading her will be a hell of a lot easier than it has been in high school. Everywhere I go, there she is.

As ridiculous as it is, air gets wedged in my lungs as Alyssa's blue gaze steadily combs over the sea of drunken classmates before locking on mine. I steel myself for that little zip of electricity to sizzle its way through my blood. It takes everything I have inside to will down the growing erection.

Just the sight of her is enough to get me hard.

One of the girls wrapped around me like a python pretends to accidently graze my wood with her fingers before making an appreciative noise deep in her throat and pressing closer.

If only she realized that my state of arousal had nothing to do with her.

Then again, she probably wouldn't give two shits.

"Colton, baby," another female purrs before cupping my cheek and manually turning my head until I have no choice but to rip my gaze away from Alyssa. Once I meet her eyes, a seductive smile wreathes her face. "I thought we were heading inside."

A couple of seconds ago, that's exactly what the plan had been. Unfortunately, that's no longer the case. As much as I wish it were otherwise, these girls pale in comparison to the blond, blue-eyed dancer.

"Not yet," I mutter before shifting my stance, only wanting to shake these chicks off as my gaze fastens on Alyssa again. Once I find her, everything settles inside me.

Over the years, I've done my damnedest to steer clear of any attachments. When I fuck, I don't want to feel anything. I'm not into emotions. It's a physical release. Pure and simple.

My gut tells me that it would be different with her. Which is exactly why I steer clear like my life depends on it.

With a critical eye, I dissect her one feature at a time.

What the hell is it about that girl?

I've spent more time trying to figure out that conundrum than I'm comfortable admitting. Even to myself.

Sure, she's gorgeous with a curtain of shiny blond hair that hangs down her back. Dark blue eyes that are, more times than not, lit up with mischief and laughter. I'll be honest, she's not my usual type. I like a big booty and nice round titties. Alyssa is long and lithe with a dancer's body. She's muscular and athletic with high, tight breasts.

She's beautiful.

But beautiful girls are a dime a dozen around here. And if they aren't naturally alluring, they add extensions, fake lashes, and have learned to apply influencer-level makeup to give the illusion. I could swing my dick around and hit five of them right now.

Whatever this is with Alyssa, it's more than skin deep. I can't put my finger on the attraction, but it's been there since I can remember.

We're talking way back in middle school when I first noticed the opposite sex. Luckily, it was right around the same time that they became aware of me.

Except for Alyssa. She was too damn busy dancing.

It was probably better that way.

Sometime during sophomore year, her sights locked on me and she's been giving chase ever since.

It's exhausting to keep someone at a distance that you really don't want to hold off. There have been times when I've been tempted to just give in and get together with her. I have a feeling it would be nothing short of amazing. The attraction between us has always been combustible. It sputters and sparks to life whenever we're in the same room together. The more I deny it, the more it ratchets up. Deep down, I know she's the one girl who has the ability to weasel her way into my heart and that's the last thing I need or want.

A look of determination settles over her face as she shoves her way through the thick sea of half-naked bodies gyrating to the beat of music pumping on the patio.

Fuck me, but that's sexy.

The girl makes no bones about wanting me.

The closer she gets, the harder my heart jackhammers against my ribcage. As much as I want to run and hide to protect myself, I'm no longer sure that's a possibility. It feels like a losing battle.

We're like two runaway trains barreling down the same track, destined for a head-on collision. There's no averting disaster.

Part of me wonders if I even want to.

I've spent so much time denying her, denying myself. The closer she gets, the more I feel my self-control waver. She pushes girls aside.

"Hey!"

Alyssa doesn't bother to glance in the brunette's direction as she stumbles. Nope, she's one hundred percent focused on me.

Whatever happens tonight, I know I'll regret it in the morning and yet, that's not enough to stop this.

I step away from the other girls just as Alyssa halts in front of me. She tilts her head as a look of challenge enters her eyes. I straighten to my full height which is a good ten inches taller than she is and stare down at her. She has to raise her chin to hold my stare.

When electricity crackles and snaps between us and the boisterous voices fade, I know that I'm in trouble. It's just the two of us.

Fuck.

ALYSSA

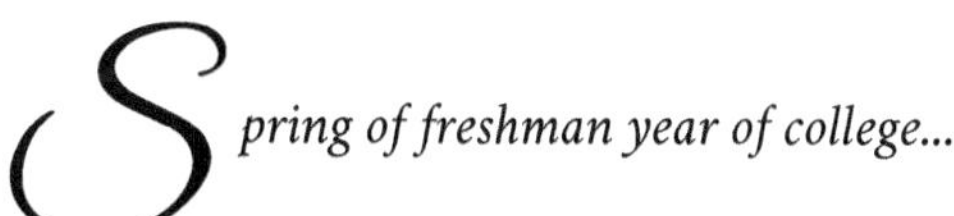

Spring of freshman year of college...

"Do you have any idea how badly I need coffee?" At this time of the morning, I'm barely coherent. A girl walking in the opposite direction knocks into me as we make our way through the throng of student traffic moving across campus. I bare my teeth, ready to snap. "Watch where your going!"

"Easy, tiger," Mia says, grabbing my arm. "Unfortunately for you, we don't have time to stop."

"Ugh." I'm so blurry-eyed, I can barely see straight. I was up until the butt crack of dawn this morning working on a paper that needs to be turned in for this class. If it had been any other instructor, I would have shown up at their office and attempted to charm my way into a twenty-four-hour extension.

But with this guy?

No way. Professor Mendelson refuses to accept late work. I've heard horror stories about him. And so far, I can say with absolute authority that they are all true. He's already made a couple of students cry. In front of everyone. So, I do my best to fly under the radar where he's concerned.

Plus, I've been spending a ton of extra time in the studio rehearsing a dance solo I choreographed for the annual showcase at the end of the semester. Between that and keeping up with my classes, I'm exhausted.

"Hey, isn't that Colton?"

Just like that, I blink out of the thoughts I've become mired in. My head whips up and any haze clouding my eyes instantly evaporates. "Where?"

Colton Montgomery sightings have become increasingly rare on campus. There are times when I have the sneaking suspicion that he's deliberately avoiding me.

I mean, how crazy is that?

"Well," Mia chuckles as we continue to traipse across campus, "that certainly woke you up. Probably more than a straight shot of caffeine to your veins."

The girl isn't wrong.

Trust me, I kind of hate myself for the infatuation I have with the blond football player. I've been crushing on him for four years. Deep down, I was hoping there would be so many new guys at college, that I would forget all about him.

That, unfortunately, hasn't turned out to be the case.

Sure, I've met a lot of guys in the two years I've been at Wesley. In classes, at parties, and during football games. I even allowed a friend to talk me into a blind date with her cousin. That, by the way, turned out to be a huge disaster. Not one single guy has been able to obliterate Colton from my mind.

It sucks.

I haven't figured out how you get over and move on from someone who wants nothing to do with you. It's painful. And a little bit humiliating. I can have anyone I want...with the exception of Colton. He's made his disinterest clear.

And yet...here I am. Still lusting after the guy.

What I need is a twelve-step program.

Like an addict, my gaze roves over the crowd before zeroing in on him like a heat-seeking missile. He's a little taller and broader than everyone around him. His hair is cut short on the sides and left long on top so that it flops over his forehead. It's a constant struggle to keep the golden strands out of his blue eyes.

I've been tempted on more than one occasion to do it for him.

That is if I could get close enough.

I narrow my eyes as hot licks of jealousy burst to life inside me. It's not even nine o'clock in the morning and he's surrounded on all sides by jersey chasers. My God, it has to be at least three deep.

"I bet he's slept with every girl on campus." I grumble in irritation.

"Everyone but you," my bestie oh-so-kindly points out.

The reminder isn't necessary.

I can only grunt in answer.

The only time we've gotten together had been at one of Beck Hollingsworth's over the top parties. I thought for sure we were going to go all the way. We'd been in the pool. The making out had turned decidedly hot and heavy. I'd taken off my top and panties (don't judge me, I'm a girl who goes after what she wants) in an effort to move things along.

Trust me when I say that the boy knows exactly how to use his mouth. It had been amazing. Amazing enough for the rowdy party around us to fall away. Just when I thought we would seal the deal, Colton had pulled the plug and left me high and dry.

Well, not so dry.

More like wet and sexually frustrated.

I've heard many-a-story surrounding the sexual exploits of Colton Montgomery. None of them ended with him walking away. It's funny —in a not so amusing kind of way—that the one guy who has a reputation for being a manwhore won't even look at me much less have sex with me.

Go figure.

"And me, of course," she tacks on quickly.

My jealousy melts away as I flash her a grin before looping my arm through hers.

Mia Stanbury has zero interest in meathead jocks with a penchant for sleeping with every girl they come in contact with which means she's definitely not into Colton or his best friend, Beck. Although, I'm pretty damn sure the guy has a major thing for her. In fact, I have my suspicions that something might have happened between them at Beck's graduation party, but Mia has never mentioned a word about it no matter how much I've interrogated her. And you better believe that I asked all sorts of questions.

As we walk past Colton and his entourage, I can't resist throwing one last look in his direction. After all, who knows when I'll see him next. Electricity sizzles through my veins as our gazes collide. It takes everything I have inside to keep moving forward. Only when I'm past him, does the air rush from my lungs.

And that's when I realize that until I can find another guy who makes me feel the way Colton does, I won't be able to move on from him.

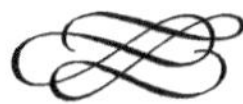

COLTON

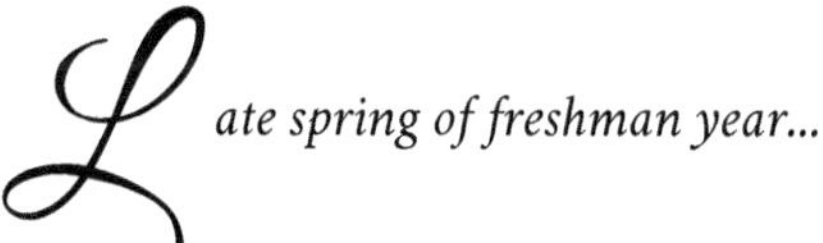

ate spring of freshman year...

THE SOFT STRAINS of stringed instruments fill the theatre as I crack open one of the double doors and carefully slip inside the darkened space. A few people seated in the back turn and stare as I settle on a seat in the last row.

I've arrived in the middle of someone's performance. The ballerina leaps across the stage before halting. With her arms stretched out in front of her, she holds the pose before slowly folding in half and sweeping her arms across the floor. The spotlight shining on her dims as the music fades into nothingness. There's a moment of silence before applause rings throughout the packed auditorium.

Did I miss it?

Is the show over?

I'd planned on getting here earlier, but Coach kept us an extra thirty minutes. We might not be in season, but practice and lifting starts up again in late winter and goes through the summer. Honestly, there is no down time. Especially when you play Division I college sports. It's more like a job. I wish I'd known that when I signed my NCAA paperwork senior year of high school. Some of these guys, like Beck, plan on turning pro. So, for them, they need to be constantly working out and improving their game.

After much thought, I decided not to continue playing football. The plan is to work for my father after I graduate from college. Then, I'll probably go on to business school. We'll see. That's yet to be determined. As much as I love the game, I don't feel like getting my brains beat to shit on a daily basis or feeling like a seventy-year-old man when I haven't even hit thirty.

Senior year will be it for me.

I plow a hand through my still-damp hair as the curtain drops.

Fuck.

Fuck.

Fuck.

The showcase has been on my radar for months. Just like it was last year. I can't believe I missed her performance. I'm halfway to my feet and ready to sprint out of the auditorium when the heavy curtain rises, and the violin section of the orchestra take up their instruments. My heart stutters as my gaze fastens on her. Carefully I lower myself back down onto the seat. The last girl had been wearing the full ballerina getup. You know, pink leotard, tights, puffy tutu, hair slicked back into a bun, small crown decorating her head. Kind of overkill, if you ask me.

Alyssa, on the other hand, is outfitted in a tight, long sleeved shirt that bares her midriff and a black matching booty shorts. Her hair is pulled back into a ponytail and she's barefoot.

Her arms are raised above her head and her chin is tilted upward as if staring at something only she can see. Even from this distance, the expression on her face is one of intensity. Almost as if she's alone, unaware of the hundreds of spectators watching her every movement.

It's only when the tempo of the violins change, and other instruments join in, giving more depth to the music, does Alyssa break her pose. Her movements are graceful. Deep and sweeping. She soars across the space, using every square inch of the stage. My breath catches, becoming trapped in my chest as I lean forward. My gaze greedily follows every movement. Every arc and bend. Every spin and dip. It doesn't take long before she becomes one with the music, telling a story through movement to the audience. Her expressions change and contort. She is poetry in motion.

It sounds stupid, but it's true.

Alyssa lights up the stage. Everything about her is captivating.

It doesn't take much for the audience around me to fall away. And then it's like she's dancing solely for me.

The first time I saw Alyssa dance was in high school. Jenna, my stepmother, dragged my father and me to a performance of the Nutcracker at Christmas. I hadn't been happy about it, but I love Jenna. As far as stepmothers go, she's a keeper. A hell of a lot better than my biological mother who took off when I was five years old and I haven't seen her since. Even though I try not to think about Candance, the fact that she couldn't be bothered to stick around when I needed her the most bothers me.

How could it not?

Dad married Jenna two years later and she's been a permanent fixture in my life ever since. So, if she wanted me to experience a little culture? Fine, I would do it. Once the lights dimmed and the curtain was raised, I'd popped an earbud in and settled back in my seat, fully prepared to waste the next two hours of my life. Instead, Alyssa had danced her way across the stage. I'd pulled out the earbud and sat spellbound, unable to look away.

I'd let Jenna make the outing a tradition and didn't bitch once about going. Maybe in real life, I couldn't stare at Alyssa the way I wanted to, but in a darkened theater, I could spend a couple of hours feeding the intense need I felt for her. The craving that was deep inside. The one I continued to deny myself on a daily basis.

The best part, the most reassuring part, was that she would never be the wiser.

COLTON

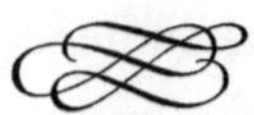

September of sophomore year...

"Dude, why the hell did you drag my ass here?" Beck doesn't bother to wait for a response as he glares around the wide-open space. "You know I hate this place. It's too damn quiet."

A librarian sitting behind a long stretch of counter in the middle of the second-floor scowls at us before raising a finger to her lips. "Shhhh!"

Beck stiffens beside me as his mouth sinks at the corners. "That woman just shushed me."

I glance at the older lady who is now full-on glaring at us. "Yup, that's her job."

"Why the hell did you bring me here?" His grumbled words are barely decipherable. "Is it payback for something I did to you? If so, I'm sorry. All right? Whatever it is, I apologize. And I'll never do it again." There's a beat of silence. "Can we leave now?"

I roll my eyes. What a damn baby. "Just give me a few minutes. I need to check out a few books for an econ project."

"Sounds boring."

He's not wrong. Most of the time, economics is dry and tedious. And micro-econ makes me want to hurtle myself off a cliff. It's a necessary evil for the finance degree I'm working toward.

As we wind our way through a few of the stacks, looking for the business section, Beck grinds to a halt. I stop and raise a brow. I swear to God, if he's about to bitch and complain again, I'm going to punch him in the face. Then he can bitch and complain about that.

Instead, his gaze is riveted on something in the distance. He's like a bird dog who has spotted, well...a bird. Normally, Beck is a laidback kind of guy. Nothing riles him up and he doesn't take life too seriously. I'm pretty sure that his father, Archie, tried to beat it out of him but it didn't work. Beck is who he is and that's not going to change.

"Beck, you want to get out of here, then let's move."

He doesn't respond.

Hell, I don't even think he heard me.

From past experience, there's only one thing capable of harnessing his interest to this degree. Or maybe I should say—*one person*.

I scope out the surrounding area until my gaze lands on Mia Stanbury.

Yup, it's just as I suspected.

Beck's had a thing for the dark-haired girl ever since I can remember. Even though they grew up together and are next door neighbors, she refuses to give him the time of day. I'll admit that it's kind of funny. There's nothing he won't do to get her attention.

He doesn't bother to glance at me. "I'm going to see what Mia is up to while you dick around."

"Dude—"

He walks away before I can spit out the rest.

Typical Beck.

I shake my head and watch as he beelines for the table she's camped out at. She's so focused on the books spread out around her that she doesn't realize she's being stalked until he's hovering over her. It takes a moment for her to blink to awareness before a scowl settles over her pretty features.

Yup, just the reaction I was expecting. He should have been expecting it, too.

I'm not sure why he bothers. She is never going to give him the time of day. It's been that way since freshman year of high school. There are plenty of girls at Wesley who would give their left tit to sleep with him.

What's the point of getting hung up on a girl who wants nothing to do with you?

Trust me, we've had this conversation on multiple occasions.

What I've learned about Beck Hollingsworth is that he's stubborn. When he wants something, he goes after it until it happens. Apparently, he's going to try and wear Mia down.

Good luck with that, dude.

I shake my head before taking off.

Hopefully, by the time I need to find the books I'm looking for, Mia will have shot Beck down and we can get the hell out of here. Although, something tells me that trying to drag Beck away from Mia might be a losing battle.

It takes about five minutes to locate the books I'm hunting for. With a big breath, I blow off the dust covering them before pulling each one out and thumbing through the pages. One peek at the table of contents is enough to confirm that this project will be just as painful as I first suspected.

Fucking economics.

With my books in hand, I swing around, ready to find Beck. With any luck, Mia will have torn him to pieces, and he'll be licking his wounds. As I retrace my steps, I catch sight of blond hair from the corner of my eye and turn my head. My footsteps falter when I spot Alyssa sitting at a table buried in a corner of the business section. It's not exactly the most popular place for obvious reasons, but I guess if you're looking for a quiet area to work, this would be it. For just a moment, I take her in. Her long blond hair is piled on top of her head in a messy bun and she's wearing a shirt that hangs off one shoulder. There are black glasses perched on her nose.

A zip of unwanted attraction ricochets through my heart. I don't think I've ever seen Alyssa wear glasses before. She looks all kinds of sexy in them. And studious.

Fuck.

I like to give Beck shit for being hung up on Mia, but the truth of the matter is that I've been stuck on Alyssa for just as long. Fooling around with her after high school graduation was a huge mistake. One I regret. If I thought it would help evict her from my head, I was wrong. More like the opposite. One taste was never going to be enough.

Instead of giving in to the feelings, I've steered clear of the west end of campus where the dance building and her dorm as located. If I catch wind that she'll be at a party, I hit a different one. That's been my tactical plan ever since.

Has it helped to stomp out my feelings for her?

Nope. Not a damn bit. When I do run into her, the intensity is like a tidal wave crashing over me, threatening to suck me under. Instead of cautiously backing away, I take an unconscious step in her direction. Before I can think better of it, more distance gets eaten up between us. Even though my brain is shouting at me to turn around and walk away, instinct takes over, propelling me forward.

This is the one girl who continues to override my feelings of self-preservation. I've never understood how she's managed to get around it. Alyssa stirs emotions inside me that I'd rather not have. There's something about her that draws me like a moth to a flickering flame. As much as I want to put her behind me, I can't. She's always there in the back of my head. When I'm with other girls, it's Alyssa I envision.

She's the one girl who makes me feel something. It's the very reason I continue to deny myself.

Which is...yeah, it's all kinds of fucked up and I damn well know it.

When Alyssa flashes a smile across the table, my gaze shifts and I realize she isn't alone. I straighten to my full height, only now noticing the guy parked across from her.

Jameson Daniels.

He's a teammate.

What the fuck is she doing with him?

His lips hitch at the corners as he reaches across the table and brushes his fingers across her knuckles.

Oh, hell no!

That is so not going to happen!

Not on my watch!

Before I realize it, I'm stalking across the space. It only takes a handful of long-legged strides before I'm pulling up alongside their table. Alyssa blinks out of her Jameson-induced haze as her gaze flickers toward me. Ever since that girl turned fifteen, she's been after me. I've never seen her so much as look at another dude.

A potent concoction of jealousy infused anger vibrates through every cell of my being. It takes every ounce of self-control not to tackle this asshole to the ground and get him away from her.

"Hey." I'm almost impressed at my ability to keep my fury from bleeding through that one syllable. I want to rip his head off and shit down his throat. I want Alyssa to know that she belongs to me. Whether we're together or not.

She's mine.

She's always been mine.

"Hi." Her gaze stays pinned to mine as she leans back against the chair. The movement has her fingers slipping free from his outstretched hand.

I release a pent-up breath the moment they're no longer touching. I'd hate to beat the shit out of one of my own teammates, but I'll do it. I don't like him touching her. Hell, I don't like anyone touching her.

Anyone but me.

Fuck.

I plow a hand through my hair.

Only now does it occur to me that I have no idea if she's gone out with other guys. Whenever we run into each other, her attention has always been focused on me. Even if I'm surrounded by other girls, she'll fight her way through the crowd to get to me.

And you know what?

That's exactly the way I like it.

I like her single-minded determination where I'm concerned. I like knowing that even though I'm holding her at a distance, it's me who she wants.

Does that make me an asshole?

Maybe it does.

But...what if that's not the case. What if she's been going out with other guys? What if she's no longer interested?

Icy cold tendrils of fear slither down my spine. I can't have Alyssa for myself, but I don't want anyone else to have her either.

I don't know what to do.

Whether Jameson realizes it or not, he's treading on my territory. "Daniels."

With reluctance, he sits back and folds his arms across his chest. "What's up, Montgomery?"

Instead of responding to the question, I ask one of my own. "You two know each other?" I wince at the bite of jealousy that threads its way through my gruff voice.

"We have psychology together," Alyssa says, beating him to the punch and drawing my attention to her.

Fuck this. I need to get her away from him right now. I jerk my head toward the stacks where we can have a little more privacy. "Let's talk."

Her brows skyrocket across her forehead before she does the unthinkable and shakes her head. "Sorry, maybe another time. We're in the middle of something."

I'm a little thrown off by her behavior.

First of all, I'm damn well aware of what they're in the middle of and that's exactly what I'm attempting to break up.

Second, is Alyssa really telling me no?

Me?

Is this the same girl who would have spread her legs for me at one of Beck's pool parties? Let's get serious here—or any other time I wanted?

"Look, Mont—"

"Shut the hell up," I glance at Jameson and snap, "this doesn't concern you. So stay out of it."

His eyes widen. I don't think he could be more surprised if I actually tackled him to the floor in the middle of the library. Jameson Daniels might be a senior, but I don't give a flying fuck. Alyssa is mine and he's encroaching on my territory. By the end of this, he'll know it and stay away.

Alyssa's mouth falls open. Whatever she was expecting, that wasn't it.

Since they're both in a state of shock, I take this opportunity to pull her away. Alyssa has always been something of a wildcard, I don't bother to pretend that it's not part of the attraction I feel for her. Once she finds her bearings, she'll probably rip me a new one.

I grab her hand and yank her to her feet before flicking a glance at Daniels to make sure his ass stays glued to the chair. Even though I can tell he's tempted to get in my way, he doesn't move a muscle. The guy has always struck me as a pussy, so this isn't a total surprise. All bark and no bite.

"Colton," she says in weak protest.

"You've got two minutes, Montgomery," Jameson mutters.

Or what? What's he going to do?

He's already proved that he doesn't own a pair of balls.

Instead of jumping further down his throat and getting into a physical altercation in the middle of the library, my grip tightens on her. That one touch has the brightest part of my anger and jealousy diminishing. Alyssa has always had this effect on me. She settles something deep inside me. Something I've never wanted to inspect too closely. Only now do I realize that I might have to. If the only alternative I have is to lose her, then there might not be a choice in the matter.

Not bothering to answer Jameson, I wind my way through the stacks, looking for a private place we can converse without interruption.

"Colton!" She tugs on her hand, trying to pull it free. "Stop! You just can't come here and hijack—"

Want to bet?

When I grind to a halt, she slams into me from behind before stumbling a step. I swing around. My hands lock around her slender shoulders as I turn her body. She has no choice to scramble backward. Her eyes widen as her spine hits the bookshelf and she realizes there's no where else to go. She's effectively trapped.

And at my mercy.

I'm close enough that our chests touch with each rise and fall of her breath. Our gazes stay locked as my lips hover over her parted ones. Her warm breath feathers across me. The scent of her is intoxicating. I've spent so much time keeping her at a firm distance that being this close drives me insane. It takes everything I have inside to keep my self in check.

I want this girl in the worst possible way.

I've always wanted her.

Now that I've allowed myself to finally touch her, I'm finding it difficult to control myself. The floodgates have opened and there's no way to close them again.

"What are you doing?" Her voice shakes as her hands press against my chest as if she's capable of holding me off. The heat of her palms burns through the thin cotton of my T-shirt, singeing the skin beneath it. Tattoos that will forever be a reminder of the day I lost my battle.

"This."

I step closer, pressing our bodies together until I can feel every rise and fall of her chest against mine. Her breath catches at the contact right before my lips crash onto hers. For a heartbeat, maybe two, I wonder if she'll fight me or try to push me away. Fuck, I wouldn't put it past her to bite me. Her body goes stiff before finally melting against mine as if she's wanted this for as long as I have. But that's not possible.

When my tongue sweeps across the seam of her lips, demanding entrance, she opens, and I delve inside. Her fingers curl, sinking into the cotton fabric of my shirt. The crescent shape of her nails bite into my flesh, grounding me to the present, to the moment unfolding between us. It's only now that I'm exploring her mouth do I realize how much I've wanted this. How did I ever think that one taste of her sweetness almost a year and a half ago would be enough?

I lose all sense of time as our tongues mingle and dance. I've missed the taste of her. No matter how many girls I've been with, they've all paled in comparison. Needy little noises escape from her and it only drives me on.

When I finally lift my mouth, we're both breathing hard.

There's a dazed expression filling her face. "I don't under—"

"Go out with me."

Every bit of haziness disappears as her eyes widen. I have to admit that the words shock the hell out of me as well. I stiffen and wait for panic to crash over me. Instead, I'm filled with relief.

"You want to go out on a...*date*?" The question is forced out as if every syllable is foreign on her tongue.

Again, I steal myself for an avalanche of panic to bury me alive. When that doesn't happen, I release a pent-up breath as the corners of my lips bow up. "Yup, I do."

Her brows draw together as she carefully searches my eyes. "You don't date." There's a pause before she tacks on in a harder voice, "You fuck around."

Guilty.

That's what I've always done. Although not for the reasons she thinks. I've spent years running away from the one girl I've always wanted, and I can't do it any longer.

I don't want to.

Only now do I realize that she might not give me a chance. I've lived the life of a manwhore, fucking whatever girl I wanted all in an attempt to forget the one in my arms. It didn't work. And I can't bare the thought of her with anyone else.

For all I know, she's over it.

Over me.

Fear pools in my gut.

Fine. I'm up to the challenge. It'll just take my powers of persuasion to change her mind. I press closer before ghosting my mouth over hers. She tilts her head as if trying to give me better access. The way her breathing hitches and her lips part, tells me that she wants me.

Wants this.

Instead of giving us what we both want, I whisper, "Let me take you out."

Her teeth sink into her bottom lip as indecision flashes across her face. I loosen my grip on her shoulders before gliding my fingers down her bare arms until arriving at her hands and interlocking our fingers. Then I drag her arms over her head and pin them to the bookshelf.

"Give me a chance."

A groan slips free from her as I bury my face against her neck, licking and nipping her flesh. My cock stiffens in my jeans. I've never wanted anyone the way I want her. And I'm so damn tired of fighting this need I feel for her.

"Okay." The word falls from her lips in a breathy little sigh.

It takes everything I have to beat back the beast inside and not take her right here in the library. I want to brand Alyssa as mine. I want every guy on this campus to know that she belongs to me.

"Good." My lips curve. "Now get rid of Daniels."

ALYSSA

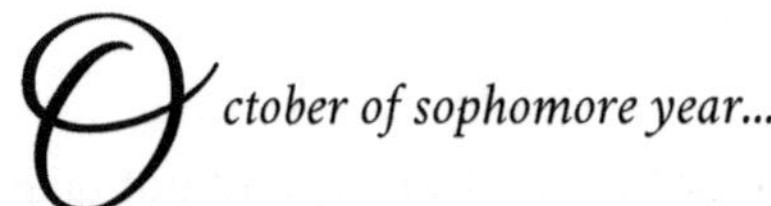

October of sophomore year...

MIA and I push our way through the crowded student section at the stadium, searching for a place to park our asses. It's game day and I'm here to root on my man. Even though it's mid-October, the temperature is still seasonable and I'm able to wear Colton's red and black jersey over a turtleneck. He gave it to me a couple of weeks ago. It's a big deal. Only girlfriends get to wear player jerseys to the games or around campus. After he left my dorm room, I screamed at the top of my lungs.

While wearing his jersey, of course.

Sometimes I have to remind myself that this isn't a dream I'll wake from. It's my reality. I'm dating Colton Montgomery. Every time I think it, a little bubble of joy explodes inside me.

This relationship has come out of nowhere and taken me completely by surprise. Sure, I'd always hoped we'd get together, but did I really think it was going to happen? No way in hell. How could I when Colton went to such great lengths to avoid me? First in high school, then at college. If we were paired up together for a class project, he found a way out. If I arrived at a party, he slipped away. If he spotted me on campus, he'd take off in the opposite direction.

It might have taken me a while, but it's not like I can't take a hint. Just when I'd decided to put Colton Montgomery behind me and move on with my life, he came out of nowhere and swept me off my feet.

Me!

I'm still in a state of shock.

Colton can have any girl he wants. And he has. But he's never been one to get serious. He likes to play the field.

And yet...here we are.

We're, for lack of a better term, getting serious.

Although, trust me when I say that I'm taking it slow. It's all about baby steps with this guy. Even though Colton came after me, he's like a skittish animal I need to approach with both caution and patience. So far, I've let him set the pace and that seems to be working. I'm taking it day by day and letting our relationship unfold naturally. If I get too serious, too quick, he'll bolt. I can see it in his eyes.

"You're getting an awful lot of looks," Mia murmurs from beside me. "I wouldn't be surprised if one of these bitches shanks you in the bathroom just to wrestle that jersey from your cold dead body."

I snort. She's not wrong about that. I can practically feel the coveted stares and hear the whispers as we move up the stadium stairs in search of seats. There are a lot of thirsty bitches around here waiting for an opportunity to steal my man. Especially now that he's done the unthinkable and committed to one specific female.

Me!

Yeah, I still can't get over it.

Any moment, I'm going to break out into a little happy dance. Although, I think Mia would slap me upside the head if I did.

Even though Colton is only a sophomore at Wesley, he's been a hot commodity since stepping foot on campus freshman year. Not only is he good looking, he's a first-string wide receiver for the Wildcats. The idea of dating a guy like him is much akin to capturing a mythical unicorn. The girls who don't want to strangle me, come to me for advice. As if there's a secret formula to my success. If only they knew the truth.

I have no idea what happened to make him change his mind.

For the first couple of weeks, I was overly cautious, waiting for the bottom to fall out. Waiting for him to wake up and say that he's not interested in being with one girl when there are a ton of them willing to spread their legs. I was almost afraid to sleep with him, figuring that's when he would break things off.

Instead, six weeks have slipped by and we're still together. Gradually I'm figuring him out. I used to think that he was just a guy who enjoyed screwing as many girls as he could. After getting to know him —the real Colton Montgomery—I think there's more to it than that. He's surprisingly more guarded than I realized. It's almost as if Colton puts up a facade for everyone around him. Only now am I starting to peel back the layers to the man lurking beneath. It makes me wonder what happened in his past to make him erect so many walls. I'm afraid to ask. So, I don't. I remain silent in hopes that he'll open up on his own when he's ready.

For the time being, I'm content to take this relationship one day at a time. I'm enjoying getting to know Colton on a deeper level. He's not the guy I assumed he was. There's so much more to him. It only makes me want to dig deeper and strengthen the tentative connection we've forged.

Mia points to two open spots in the middle of the row. We slide past a dozen people before settling on our seats with our drinks and popcorn. We wave to a few friends before the band performs their rendition of our school song and the players jog onto the field in a wave of red and black. Even though there's ninety guys on the team, my gaze cuts through them, locking on number twenty-five. My heart flips over in my chest as I watch him. The pads only accentuate the broad set of his shoulders. My gaze drops to his ass. I'm not going to lie, the red stretchy pants do wonders for it.

Mia knocks my shoulder with her own. I tear my gaze away from Colton and glance toward her.

A knowing grin simmers around the corners of her lips. "I know what you're looking at."

My lips curl around the edges. "Can you blame me?"

She straightens in her seat and cocks her head as if giving serious consideration to the question. "Nope. The guy has a mighty fine ass."

Yes, he certainly does.

The ref flips a coin, and Alabama takes possession of the ball. I munch on my popcorn and watch the first play of the game. My father is a die-hard football fan. It doesn't matter if it's the NFL, college, or high school. In our house, it's a religion. Friday, Saturday, and Sunday are days of worship in the Williams household. That meant loads of BBQ chicken wings, pigs in a blanket, chips, and bottles of cold beer. Not exactly dancer-friendly food. But Mom always made sure to have a veggie platter with hummus and lots of fresh fruit.

After about five minutes, a ref blows a whistle, throws up a flag, and stops the action.

"What happened?" Mia asks, brows drawing together as she watches at the field.

"There's a penalty for holding," I tell her.

When she continues to stare in confusion, my lips twitch. "It means that one of our offensive guys grabbed hold of the other team's defensive player while trying to block him. You can't do that. Now there's a penalty and we lose ten yards."

Her brows pinch together. "It's like you're talking English, but I still can't understand a word you're saying." She touches her face. "Am I having a stroke? Am I able to smile? Wait a minute...aren't I the one who shouldn't be making sense if I'm stroking out?"

I burst out laughing. "Neither of us are stroking out. Although, if these refs don't get their heads out of their asses, I just might." I point to the field and explain, "Now we're further from the end zone which makes it more difficult to score a touchdown."

She nods but continues to look baffled by what's happening. "Why does football have to be so confusing?"

I pat her shoulder. "It's a good thing your pretty."

Mia snorts. "Shut up. You know I've never been a fan of the game. Too slow and boring."

"Yup. Which is exactly why I appreciate you tagging along with me today."

"You'll owe me," she shrugs, "that's all."

"I'm almost afraid of what you'll extract as payment."

She sends me a chilling grin. "Don't worry, I'll come up with something that you'll hate."

I don't doubt it. She'll probably force me to stay in one weekend and binge watch Gilmore Girls. She knows I can't stand that damn show. Usually, I'm the one dragging her ass to parties when she would much rather stay home.

An hour and a half later, the buzzer sounds, ending the second quarter of the game and signaling halftime. My gaze settles on Colton as he jogs off the field. His gaze coasts over the student section before zeroing in on me and I feel the connection down to my toes. He grins before tapping his fist against his chest and pointing toward me.

A sigh escapes from my lips before I can stifle it.

Are there little red and pink hearts dancing above my head? Because I think there might be. If I'm not careful, I'll fall head over heals in—

"You're falling for him, aren't you?"

It's not a question. More like a statement. And not a happy one either.

As tempted as I am to downplay my growing feelings, I don't want to do that. Mia has been my best friend for nearly a decade. We've always been straightforward with one another. Even though she won't like the answer, I can't bring myself to lie. "Yeah," I track his movements until he disappears inside the tunnel, "I am."

Mia worries her lower lip before gnawing on it. Concern flickers across her expressive features.

When she remains silent, I blurt, "He's not the guy you think he is."

"So what you're telling me is that he's only been pretending to be a player out for one thing all these years?"

I wince as my shoulders slump and some of my happiness dims.

It's a complicated question. One I don't have an answer for. "I don't know." That's what I'm trying to figure out.

I focus on the band now marching in formation on the field. It's so much easier to focus on the halftime show than meet Mia's searching gaze.

Her arm snakes around me as she leans her head on my shoulder. "The last thing I want is for you to get hurt."

I huff out a breath as some of my defensiveness melts away. It's not like I don't understand her concern. We both attended high school with Colton. He's always been the king of hookups. The guy is nineteen years old and this is the first time he's been in a relationship. I would be an idiot not to be cautious where he's concerned. But that doesn't mean I can hold back my feelings or pretend they don't exist.

"I won't get hurt." I know that Mia has my best interest at heart. When it comes down to it, all she's trying to do it look out for me. "We're taking it slow."

"Girl, please," she says with a snort, "you don't know the meaning of the word slow."

My lips tremble at the corners. She's right. Where Mia carefully weighs each move that she makes, I've always been more of a leap before looking kind of girl.

Has it gotten me into trouble?

Yup. But that's the way I live life.

"I think you're already in love with the guy." There's a beat of silence before she adds with in a serious tone, "You've always been in love with him."

Instead of acknowledging the truth of her words, I press my lips together and remain silent.

She's right. I'm in love with Colton.

This is the problem with having a best friend who knows you so damn well. She's able to figure out all your dirty little secrets. Even the ones you try to hide from yourself.

COLTON

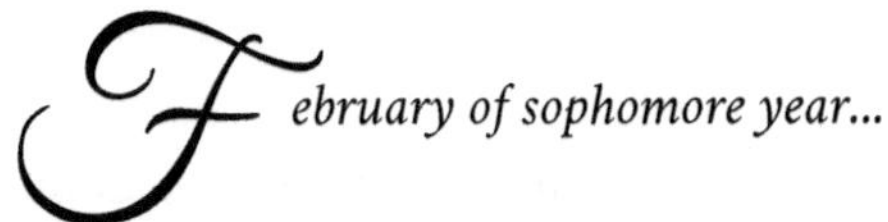

ebruary of sophomore year...

ALYSSA IS WRAPPED up in my arms as my mouth roves hungrily over her neck. She arches, allowing me better access to her delectable flesh. A little moan escapes from her as she shoves the key in the lock of her room.

Once.

Twice.

After three failed attempts, she whispers, "You need to stop that, or I'll never get this door open and we'll end up having sex in the hallway."

I don't care where we screw, as long as I can get inside her. My cock is so damn hard that it's all I can focus on. The moment I slide deep inside her is always one of pure nirvana. I've never experienced anything like it before. There's a little voice inside my brain that wonders if I ever will again. Since that's not an entirely comfortable thought, I shove it away before I can inspect it too closely.

"Colton."

My name comes out sounding more like a breathy sigh and it does the impossible and makes me harder.

I'll be honest, I couldn't stop even if I wanted to. Her skin is way too damn sweet. I want to gobble her up in one tasty bite. I've had my fair share of chicks over the years, but I've never craved anyone the way I do her. It's like she's a drug pumping wildly through my system. Sometimes it feels like way too much, way too soon. And that scares the shit out of me. There are times when I'm struck with the urge to pull away so I can regain my bearings, but I always stop short of actually doing it. Deep down, Alyssa has managed to crawl under my skin. I don't want to lose what I've found with her.

My teeth sink into the delicate skin of her bared throat. My fingers reach around her ribcage before sliding up to her breasts. I glance down the hall to make sure that it's empty. Since the coast is clear, I tweak her nipples through the thin shirt she's wearing. "What's wrong, baby girl? Is there a reason you can't focus?"

She whimpers in answer as I continue playing with her.

Alyssa is so damn responsive to my touch. It's just one of the things I love about her. Sex with her is like...

I don't even know how to describe it.

There's a high I get when I'm inside the heat of her body. And the more I have, the more I want. It's never enough. This must be what addiction feels like. To crave something all the time. Even if that thing is a person. Even when you're balls deep, you can't help but wonder when you can be there again.

"If you keep doing that I'll come."

She's not kidding either.

So.

Damn.

Responsive.

Her whispered words go straight to my dick and make me throb more than I already am.

Why the hell did I ever fight against this in the first place? Hands down, it's the best decision I ever made.

"Hey," someone yells from a couple doors down, breaking into the thick fog blanketing me, "get a room!"

"What do you think we're trying to do?" Alyssa bellows back, unapologetic about our PDA.

My lips quirk as a chuckle slips free. Reluctantly I lower my hands until the thumbs can graze over the soft outer swells of her breasts and my index fingers settle beneath her bra.

Once upon a time, I'd thought her breasts were too small.

Needless to say, I was wrong about that. Maybe her cup doesn't runneth over like some girls, but it doesn't matter. Alyssa's tits are fucking perfect.

Everything about her is.

"Colton," she groans for a second time, writhing against me, all the while trying to jam the metal in the lock.

"What, baby?"

"You're killing me."

"Good. I want to ruin you for all other guys." The words slip free before I can stop them. My heartbeat jackhammers. It's the closest I've ever come to declaring my feelings for her.

"I think you already have."

On the fifth attempt, the key slides home and the door handle turns.

"Thank God," she mutters as we stumble inside the space. I've been dying to get my hands on her for days now. Since Alyssa rooms with Mia and I live with Beck, carving out time to be alone is a challenge. I'm not going to lie, we've done it in my car and at the library. The potential thrill of being caught turns us both on. She's definitely a girl after my own heart.

Next year, the plan is to move into an apartment or house off-campus. I'll have my own room. Then I can sleep with her wrapped up in my arms every damn night. If that thought leaves me slightly shaken that for the first time ever, I'm thinking that far ahead into the future when it comes to a female, I ignore it and refocus my attention.

"Are you sure that Mia won't be home for a while?"

A smile curves her lips as her eyelids lower to half-mast. "Yup, she has class for another two hours."

"Perfect."

"I know."

"Hey, Alyssa," a girl hollers from down the hall, "do you have—"

"Nope!" she yells without even glancing in her direction, "I'll catch you in an hour."

"An hour?" I grumble, nipping at her earlobe, "is that it?"

Her lips twitch. "Make it two hours," she corrects, slamming the door shut without waiting for a response.

The moment we're locked inside her tiny dorm room, we tear at our clothes as if starving for one another. Jackets are the first to be shed. Then shirts and her bra. Shoes and socks come next. Somewhere in the mix, jeans and leggings are added. It's a frenzy of fabric thrown in every direction until we're both stripped bare and falling onto the single twin bed.

Alyssa chuckles as my mouth lands on hers. She opens immediately until our tongues can tangle. It's like this every damn time. It never gets old. I'm so fucking hot for this girl.

After we got together, I half expected we'd screw a time or two and then monotony would set in. If I'm being completely honest, I'd secretly hoped it would be like that. All I really wanted was to fuck Alyssa out of my system so I could move on and she'd stop lurking in the back of my brain.

But that didn't happen.

If anything, it was the complete opposite. I can't get enough of her. The more I have, the more I want.

Hands down, being inside her body is the best damn feeling in the world.

Nothing else compares.

Hot licks of need spike through me, making me impatient. With the way I'm feeling, there's no time for foreplay. Alyssa understands this and widens her legs until I can settle between her thighs. As I thrust my tongue inside her mouth, my dick sinks simultaneously inside her.

An appreciative groan rumbles up from deep in my chest. There is no greater feeling than her welcoming heat squeezing me tight. She always laughs when I tell her how much I love her pussy. I fucking revere it.

Eight strokes later and I'm coming with a vengeance.

Thank fuck she's right there with me.

Six months later and every time still feels like the first.

How the hell am I ever going to get enough of this girl?

Her teeth sink into her lower lip to stifle her moans. I keep my gaze pinned to hers and watch as wave after wave of pleasure crashes over her delicate features. I don't think I've ever seen anything as beautiful as the look on Alyssa's face when she orgasms. Her ecstasy only intensifies my own. I'm ashamed to admit that in the past, it was my satisfaction that came first. I've always been a selfish bastard when it came to sex. As long as I got my rocks off, it was all good.

Alyssa has changed that.

Her pleasure means everything.

With a huff of breath, my muscles loosen, and I collapse on top of her. Her arms slip around my neck as she pulls me close.

A chuckle fills my ears as her body shakes. "More than an hour, hmmm?"

Yeah...that didn't go according to plan. I'm lucky if that lasted five minutes.

Maybe four.

"That was round one," I grunt. "I've got a few more inside me."

"Well," her lips brush across the side of my face, "I certainly hope so."

"Give me a few minutes and I'll be ready to go." I roll to my side and take her with me which is no easy feat in the narrow bed. Somehow, we manage to switch positions so that my back is to the mattress and her naked body is draped across my chest.

Is there a better feeling than this?

If so, I haven't found it yet.

As our harsh breathing fills the dorm room, a strange contentment settles over me. I wrack my brain, trying to remember the last time I felt this insanely peaceful. As if all was right in the world.

But I can't.

I don't think I've ever felt like this.

If so, it was when I was a kid. Like four years old. Before Mom decided to cut and run. As soon as that ugly thought mushrooms up in my consciousness, I squash it and blink back to the here and now. Alyssa grazes my chest with her fingers before circling the tip around my nipple. I glance at her, surprised to find her watching me. There's a sleepy look in her eyes and a softening around her lips as if she doesn't have a care in the world.

In this precise moment, I feel it, too.

The crack she's managed to find in my heart opens wider. More than it ever has.

Our gazes lock and hold as she whispers, "I love you."

And just like that, those feelings of peace and contentment vanish into thin air as if they had never been there to begin with. Everything inside me stills as my breath gets clogged at the back of my throat. It feels like I'm being suffocated from the inside out. My heart thumps a painful staccato, filling my ears like the roar of the ocean until I can't hear anything else.

There's a cautiously hopeful look on Alyssa's face. I open my mouth to say something.

Anything.

But nothing comes out.

One heartbeat passes.

Then another.

The happiness filling her eyes drains away before dying a painful death.

As much as I want to echo the sentiment, the words refuse to budge from my lips. Instead, my mouth turns cottony. Deep down, I knew this conversation was inevitable and I'd even hoped I would be able to parrot the words back to her.

But I can't do it. I can't force them free.

When I say nothing in response, she turns her head away before resting her cheek against my chest so that I can no longer see her expression. But the movement isn't nearly quick enough for me to miss the pain my silence has caused her.

ALYSSA

 *ne week later...*

I CROSS one leg over the other and fold my upper body to my thighs, stretching my arms until they can sweep across the floor. Gradually I inhale, filling my lungs with oxygen and expanding my chest to capacity. I hold it for a couple of seconds before forcing every molecule from my body. Repeating the process, I focus on my breathing. I can almost feel the break down of lactic acid that has built up in my muscles during the intense sixty-minute practice. After a few more deep breaths, I sit up and shift my legs before crossing the left in front of the right and bending forward to deepen the stretch. Once my calves and thighs have been stretched, I straighten my legs in front of me and fold at the waist before widening my legs and moving through a second series of stretches.

Francois Dupre, our guest instructor, is a French import. His pedigree is impressive. Classically trained, danced as the lead with the French Ballet, travelled the world. Most of the female dancers have a massive crush on him. A few of the male dancers do as well. I can't blame them. He's dreamy with black wavy hair and intelligent cocoa-colored eyes. His body is long, lean, and muscular from years of training.

As if he hasn't already commanded everyone's attention, he claps his hands. "Excellent work," he says in heavily accented English. "We meet again on Friday."

A few sighs escape as three girls pop gracefully to their feet before rushing toward him. Once he's flanked on all sides, tittering laughter rings throughout the spacious room.

I glance at Zoe, who is finishing up her stretches next to me, and roll my eyes. "What a bunch of whores," I mutter under my breath.

The corners of her lips tremble before she grins and spears a glance toward the growing swarm outfitted in Lycra. "Apparently they haven't figured it out that Monsieur Dupre has no interest in someone with lady parts."

I snort and shrug. "Perhaps they're hoping to persuade him differently?"

"It won't work." She closes the distance between us before admitting, "I already tried."

"You did not!" I gasp.

"Of course, I did." Her gaze slices to him as she lifts a shoulder. "I mean, come on. Just look at the man." Her voice goes a little dreamy. "Can you even imagine what he looks like beneath his clothes?"

An image of Colton pops into my head. As delicious as Monsieur Dupre is, I only have eyes for one man. And it's not our dance instructor. "He turned you down?"

"Yup. He said his boyfriend would have a problem with it," she admits with a laugh. "I told him that I'd be more than happy to be the star of that little show."

"Shut up!" I swat her arm as my eyes pop wide. *You didn't!*

"Please, girl. You know me better than that." She grins and shoots another glance in our teachers' direction. "Do you have any idea how hot that would be?"

Ummmm...maybe?

"Anyway," she continues blithely, "it was a no-go."

I rise to my feet and lift my arms above my head before bending to the left, holding the pose, and then repeating it on the other side until my muscles feel limber.

After she's done stretching, Zoe slips off her beat up shoes before stuffing them inside her dance bag. I do the same, grabbing a bottle of water and raising it to my lips. Once the container has been drained, I stuff it in the bag and pull on an oversized T-shirt. Black leggings come next before shoving my feet into a pair of boots and stuffing my arms into my jacket. "Ready to go?"

She nods as we wave to our instructor, who is still surrounded by a handful of students, and exit the studio. Even though I'm tired from a full hour of dancing, I feel amazing. My muscles are fatigued and pliable.

No matter what happens in my life, dance is the one thing I can count on. I can always lose myself in the choreography. When my parents went through a rough patch and were at each other's throats, dance is what got me through the hard times. If I couldn't escape to the studio, I was able to shove earbuds in, crank up the music, and lose myself in the movement while locked in my bedroom.

What would I do if I couldn't dance?

Who would I be without it?

I don't have an answer to that. It's an integral part of who I am.

Even though I'm nowhere near good enough to dance profession-ally, my dream is to one day open up my own studio. During high school, I started teaching ballet and jazz classes. It's something I enjoy. I've been lucky to find a studio here in town where I can pick up a few classes to teach on the weekends.

Am I under any illusion that it will make me rich?

Nope. But I don't care.

Dance makes me happy.

Dance makes the world happy.

As we walk through the crowded corridor, Zoe chatters about the annual showcase. Each performer choreographs a three-minute routine to highlight their talent. Wesley has a fierce program with dancers from around, not only the country, but the world. Guest instructors are brought in from the most elite programs. A number of dancers end up performing in companies, on Broadway, or dancing backup. I feel fortunate to be here, studying alongside and learning from such a talented group of people.

"Hey, you want to grab lunch?" she asks. "After such a grueling practice, I'm starving."

I pull on my fingerless gloves. "Sure. I could eat." Truth be told, I can always eat. It's a continuous battle.

What can I say?

I'm part Italian and have a serious love affair with pasta. I'm sure that it will be my downfall.

As we push through the glass doors into the bright January sunshine, my phone chimes with an incoming message. I slip the cell from the pocket of my white puffer jacket and glance at the screen.

My heartbeat quickens as Colton's name pops up.

Six months.

It seems almost unbelievable that we've been together for half of a year.

Last week, unable to hold all these feelings inside, I'd dropped the *I love you* bomb after sex. I couldn't help myself. It had needed to be said and I wanted Colton to know how much he means to me.

Yeah, it had been disappointing when he didn't return the sentiment, but it's fine. I know he cares. He shows me in a hundred different ways each and every day. Little things that make my heart beat into overdrive. Like opening the car door for me, stroking his fingers gently through my hair, clasping my hand when we walk across campus, or showing up at my dorm in the morning with a steaming cup of coffee.

Even though we've been together for half a year, we're still taking baby steps. At some point in the not-so-distant future, I'm hoping Colton will come to the realization that what we have is special and he loves me. I know enough about football to realize that it's all about the long game with Colton. I'm nothing if not patient and persistent.

My finger swipes across the screen and my gaze skims over the message as Zoe and I jog down the cement stairs until we're in front of the William Dutton fine arts building. It takes a moment for the words to sink in. As they do, my footsteps falter and I grind to a halt. My gaze stays glued to the text bubble as all of the oxygen evaporates from my lungs, leaving me to feel as if the wind has been knocked from me.

"Alyssa?" With her brows pinched together, Zoe swings around before hoisting the strap of her bag onto her slender shoulder. "Are you coming?"

People knock into me in their haste to flee the building. A few grumble and tell me to get out of the way. When I remain silent, Zoe's fingers lock around my wrist before dragging me off the pathway and out of the rush of student traffic.

She waves a hand in front of my face to capture my attention as concern floods her voice. "Alyssa?"

I blink and refocus on the words—willing them to morph into something else—before giving my head a little shake.

Is this a joke?

"Are you all right?" Zoe's voice softens as she carefully searches my face.

Even though I'm falling apart on the inside, I force myself to remain calm. "Ummm, sorry to bale," I mumble, unable to rip my gaze away from the screen. "but there's something I need to take care of. Go on without me, okay?"

Her lips sink further into a frown as she shifts her weight. "Are you sure?"

"Yeah." I glance up as my head continues to spin. "Sorry to flake on you like this."

"I don't know what's going on, but if you need me to come with you, I will."

I shake my head. "Thanks, but no."

"All right," she says, sounding dubious, "if you're sure."

"I am."

"I'll see you on Friday?"

"Yup." Barely am I aware of Zoe walking away and leaving me alone. Instead of reading over the message again, I stab the call button and hold the phone to my ear. A pit the size of Texas settles in my belly as it goes straight to voicemail.

What the fuck?

Is Colton really doing this to me?

After six months together, it seems almost unfathomable. Anger crashes over me as I stab the red end button and hit redial. When it goes straight to voicemail for a second time, I realize that he has no intention of picking up my call.

He's really doing this.

He lit a match, threw it over his shoulder, and burn our relationship to the ground.

COLTON

My elbows are perched on my knees as I sit on the bench in the locker room and stare sightlessly at my clasped hands. They're clenched so tightly together that the knuckles have turned bone white.

Did I do the right thing?

Or was it all a huge fucking mistake? One I can't take back because let's face it, there's no way to come back from a breakup through text. That's signed, sealed, and delivered.

Here's what I know—relief flooded through me as soon as I hit send.

And that's got to mean something...right?

I straighten my shoulders and try to convince myself that I did what needed to be done. That, unfortunately, doesn't stop the self-doubt from mushrooming up inside me. I feel like the world's biggest asshole for handling it in this manner. I damn well know that Alyssa didn't deserve to be broken up through text message, but I also realize that I wouldn't have been able to go through with it if I'd had to stand before her and look her in the eye.

So, yeah...I pussied out and texted her instead. And now, I'm acting like a little bitch by not picking up her calls or responding to her texts.

She's tried calling at least half a dozen times and sent a slew of messages asking what the hell is going on. Each one has escalated in both anger and disbelief. I can barely stand to read them. The pain is palpable.

A heavy hand lands on my shoulder and knocks me from those thoughts. Blinking away the melancholy, I glance at Beck as he loiters beside me. He's dressed and ready to get the hell out of here and I'm still sitting here with a towel draped across my hips. I drag a hand over my face and attempt to pull my shit together.

"Everything good?"

The two of us have been friends since elementary school. We played on Pop Warner football teams together, then high school, and now college. Beck is one of the most talented quarterbacks in the country. He's been breaking state and NCAA records for years. Even as a sophomore, there's no doubt in my mind that he'll end up playing in the NFL. If Beck had his way, he would enter the draft next year, but his father has other ideas. And in the Hollingworth household, Archibald rules the roost.

I shrug off his hand. "Yup."

My world is only imploding...no biggie.

Although, it's by my own hand, so I'm not really sure if that's something I can bitch about.

"Then move your ass and let's go. Sanders is having a little get together. I need to chill out for a while."

A party?

No, thanks. There's no way I can deal with that right now. Not with all this emotion churning inside me.

"Go on without me," I mumble, unwilling to reveal what's really going on. "I've got some shit to take care of."

He smirks. "Is that what we're calling getting laid now a days?"

Yeah, it's doubtful that will be happening any time soon. Instead of forcing out the words, I rise to my feet and yank a pair of boxers out of my locker before dragging them up my thighs. Joggers and a red Wildcats T-shirt come next. Once dressed, I grab my sweatshirt and athletic bag, ready to take off. I just want to go home and lick my wounds. Sure, they're self-inflicted but that doesn't make a damn bit of difference at the moment. Beck and I are the last ones to leave as he pushes out through the locker room door. I follow behind, sucked back into my thoughts.

The whole did-I-make-a-mistake-or-not is eating me alive. The bitch of it is that I'll probably never know.

"Oh," he says, moving into the corridor of the athletic center, "hey, Alyssa."

My head snaps up at the sound of her name so fast that I almost give myself whiplash as my gaze collides with icy blue eyes. All it takes is one look at the fury vibrating off her in heavy waves to know that I won't escape this confrontation unscathed. I swallow down my growing nausea. This is exactly the kind of altercation I'd been hoping to avoid.

When she remains silent, lips pressed together in a tight line, Beck's quizzical gaze flicks to mine. Whatever he sees painted across my face is enough of a tipoff for him to abandon this sinking ship poste haste. Can't exactly say I blame him for it. I'd probably do the same thing if I were in his position. He jerks a thumb over his shoulder and takes a swift step in retreat. "So...I'm going to take off."

Instead of glancing at Beck, Alyssa's gaze stays pinned to mine.

"I'll catch you at the dorm," I mutter, dread pooling at the bottom of my gut.

"Yup." With pent-up longing, I watch as he disappears down the hallway like the hounds of hell are nipping at his heals.

An uncomfortable stillness crashes down on us.

One heartbeat passes.

Then another.

Now that we're alone, I mentally brace myself for the oncoming explosion. But Alyssa doesn't do the expected. Instead, she stares silently, scouring my face for answers I refuse to give. Hurt seeps into her eyes, mingling with the fury. A fresh wave of guilt crashes over me, nearly swallowing me whole.

Fuck.

It would be so much easier if she'd just go off the deep end. Then I could mentally shut down and tune out the theatrics while she got everything off her chest.

But this?

The silent recriminations aimed in my direction?

The pain that radiates off her as if it's a living breathing entity?

That's impossible to tune out.

How can I when I'm the architect of her agony?

When I'm the one to blame for giving in and allowing this to get so out of hand?

Ever since middle school, I've yearned for this girl. Longed to reach out and touch her. Be close to her. Make her mine. Although, she'd never know it from my behavior. I've done everything in my power to ignore Alyssa. To keep her at a distance. To push her to the outer recesses of my brain so I wouldn't have to think about her. So that I'd finally stop wanting her.

Dreaming about her.

It didn't work.

Nothing worked.

Even when I broke down and asked her out, I knew this is exactly how it would end between us. When it comes down to it, I can't give Alyssa what she wants. What she deserves.

No matter how tempting it is, I can't love her, and I refuse to let her in.

So where does that leave us?

Exactly in this place that neither of us want to be.

More than anything, I wish Alyssa had just been a fuck. One I could forget about. But she was never that.

Whether she realizes it or not, that's the problem.

"Why?"

One shaky word falls from her lips, but it's more than enough. It's like a burning arrow shot right through the center of my heart.

Even though it's tempting to look away, I force myself to steadily hold her gaze. It's vital to bear witness to the harm I've inflicted. It'll serve as a permanent reminder to never let my guard down again. The damage wreaked isn't worth it.

My gaze roams over her. So badly do I want to close the distance and pull her into my arms. She might only be five foot six, but Alyssa is a towering pillar of strength. I don't think I've ever met another girl like her. It's doubtful I ever will again. She's brave, confident, and ballsy. It's a wicked combination that drew me in from the very beginning.

It's the only reason that she's standing before me now.

Had I really fooled myself into believing that this girl wouldn't track me down and demand answers?

I should have known better.

More than anything, I wish everything could be different between us. I wish I weren't so fucked in the head. But, like everything else in life, wishes don't mean jack shit.

"Colton?" she bites out, holding up her phone. "Why would you do this?"

I jerk my shoulders. There's no way I can tell her the truth. That would mean opening up and letting her in. Like slitting my wrist and bleeding out emotionally. And that, I'm unwilling to do. So, I go with something believable. "I dunno, just kind of feels like this relationship has run its course." When her eyes widen, I force out the rest, needing a clean break. I can't have her coming back, trying to repair this. I need to blow it up. "There's only so much monotony I can deal with."

Her mouth tumbles open as she sucks in a sharp breath. *"What?"* Whatever she was expecting me to say, that wasn't it.

When her eyes turn glassy, I glance at the cement block wall beyond her. If I don't, I'll drop to my knees and beg for forgiveness. And I can't allow that to happen.

"We had a good run. Six months is practically an eternity as far as I'm concerned. But I'm over it. I need to mix things up. Explore my options."

"You," there's a beat of silence as if she's having a difficult time wrapping her lips around the words, *"want to sleep with other people?"*

No.

"Yeah." I shift my weight, impatient to get this over with. Bile rises in my throat as I throw the question back at her and hold my breath. "Don't you?"

Any color that had been filling her cheeks, drains away as she slowly shakes her head. "No, I don't."

I tighten my hands into fists to stop myself from reaching out and consoling her. My words are ripping her apart and it's excruciating to watch. Any moment, I'm going to crumble. "Look, Lys—"

"Don't call me that," she growls from between clenched teeth. "I will never be that to you again."

I jerk my head into a terse nod. "It's better to walk away before someone gets hurt."

A gurgle of strained laughter bubbles up from her throat. "Yeah, it's too late for that."

As much as I fight to keep the words locked deep inside, I blurt them out. "I'm sorry." It's probably the only thing that's come out of my mouth that's actually true.

"Are you?" She tilts her head and stares at me as if she has no clue who I am. It's the first time she's ever looked at me that way. It takes effort to keep my expression blank. Almost bored. "You know what hurts the most?"

All of it.

There's nothing that doesn't hurt.

I brace myself before shaking my head.

"That you thought so little of me and my feelings that you couldn't be bothered to have an honest conversation." Again, she holds up the phone. "Instead of acting like a man, you sent me a lame-ass text." Alyssa falls silent, almost as if digesting what she's just expressed. "If I hadn't hunted you down, you probably would have ghosted me."

As much as I hate to admit it, she's right. That's *exactly* what the plan had entailed.

"It seemed easier that way," I mumble, feeling like a grade-A asshole. It's almost impressive the depths I've managed to jackhammer.

"Easier for who?" she snaps, voice escalating, echoing off the cavernous cement walls.

Since that seems more like a rhetorical question, I don't bother to respond.

"Where did this come from?" Her brows draw together in bewilderment as if silently going over the autopsy of our doomed relationship. "I thought you were happy."

"I was." The emotion churning in her eyes is enough to break me. I hate myself for doing this to her. "And now I'm not."

"Just like that." There's a pause. "Like a light switch. Happy." She snaps her fingers as the brightness in her eyes returns. If she loses the battle with her tears, I won't be able to stand it. "Unhappy."

"Yeah," I force out glumly, nearing my breaking point.

"I don't know what to say." She shakes her head. "Just...wow."

When I remain silent, Alyssa takes a step forward, closing the distance that separates us. Sorrow is written across every line of her expression. "I realize there's nothing I can say that will change your mind." She forces out a bitter laugh. "And I won't even bother to try. I refuse to beg and grovel for some guy who is willing to throw me away like a dirty Kleenex."

No, that's not Alyssa's style. She has way too much pride and self-worth for that.

Instead of allowing the tears to trek down her ashen cheeks, she blinks back the wetness and glances away. "You know what sucks the most?" Before I can answer—not that I was going to—she continues, "I really loved you. Even though you didn't say it back to me, I thought you loved me to."

A thick lump of emotion settles in the middle of my throat making it impossible to breathe. Death would be preferable rather than witness the way she's laying herself bare.

A frown tugs at the corners of her lips as her gaze slices to me. "That's the reason, isn't it?"

I gulp down the icy shards of fear and try to keep it all buried deep beneath the surface before it can undo the chaos I've inflicted on this relationship. "What are you talking about?"

Understanding dawns across her face as she examines my eyes. If she searches hard enough, deep enough, she'll unearth all my secrets. "That scared you, didn't it?"

The floodgates open and fear rushes through every cell of my body. I shift, tempted to flee from not only this building, but her. My chest clenches and pain throbs through me with every sharp intake of breath.

Maybe Alyssa believes that she loves me, but she doesn't.

How could she when my own mother wasn't able to?

There has to be something seriously wrong with me if she was able to walk away without a second look.

Doesn't Alyssa understand that I can't be the man she wants me to be?

I'm incapable of giving her what she needs in life. Even for the short term. She deserves better. I know it, even if she doesn't. It's only a matter of time before she realizes it and leaves. And that, I can't withstand.

Once was more than enough.

The fear of this happening is enough to have the blood running through my veins turn icy. It also gives me the little push I need to end this once and for all. "Come on, girl, you had to know this was a long shot when we got together. It was a gamble." I shrug, wanting to appear nonchalant. "You rolled the dice, and it came up snake eyes. You should be giving me props for remaining faithful this long. As much as I've enjoyed your unicorn pussy, this whole exclusivity thing isn't for me." I reach out and stroke my fingers along her jaw. It doesn't escape me that this will be the last time I touch her. "I wouldn't mind keeping you in my back pocket and having a taste of it every once in a while."

As the last word falls from my lips, she knocks my hand away before shoving both palms against my chest and knocking me back a step with an angry grunt.

"Fuck you, Colton! You really are an asshole, you know that?"

Yeah, I do.

And now, thankfully, she knows it, too.

ALYSSA

There's a gentle tap on my arm.

"Lys?"

I blink out of my thoughts and refocus my attention on Mia. "Hmmm?" If she asked a question, I have no idea what it was. I really need to snap out of this funk.

Sympathy flashes across her face as she loops her arm through mine and tugs me to her. "Aww, girl. I'm sorry. I know this must be tough." There's a pause. "You want me to beat Colton's ass? For you, I'll do it."

Even though it takes effort, I force out a snort. "Nah. He's not worth it." My lips quirk at the corners at the idea of Mia getting into any kind of physical altercation. She's never so much as had a disagreement. She's always walked the straight and narrow, but that behavior intensified after her sister, Brianne, died in a car accident. Sometimes I get the feeling that Mia is trying to distract her parents with all of her accomplishments. Straight A's, tennis tournaments, squeaky clean image and reputation. It must be exhausting to be so perfect.

I wouldn't know. I'm far from it. More than that, I have zero inclination to pretend I am.

"Damn right, he's not," she agrees.

I glance up at the sun as it shines brightly in the cerulean-colored sky. There's not a cloud in sight. Even through my sunglasses, the harsh illumination hurts my eyes. It's beautiful out. Normally, a day like this, even in the winter, would make me want to tip my face to the sky and soak up all the rays.

That's not the case today.

If I didn't have dance class, I would be buried beneath a mound of blankets in my bed. It's been more than a week since Colton blew apart my whole world. I still find it hard to believe that he broke up with me.

Through text.

Text!

The lousy bastard.

Who the hell does that?

Colton Montgomery, that's who.

I give my head a vigorous shake, attempting to knock those insidious thoughts loose. Dwelling on the situation won't do any good. And it won't make the pain magically disappear. Although, it would be kind of nice if it did. I'm tired of thinking about it. Tired of feeling depressed and pissed off.

Mia squeezes my arm and I realize that I've once again become trapped in my thoughts. "Sorry," I mutter, embarrassed by my own inability to pull myself out of this depression, "what did you say?"

"I asked if you want to grab dinner tonight. Maybe pizza?" Her voice escalates with excitement. "Oh! There's a new Thai restaurant downtown that just opened. I've been dying to try it out."

I grimace at the idea of eating either. It's enough to make my belly revolt.

"No." Instead of admitting that I don't have much of an appetite, I say, "I'll probably hang out at the studio for a while and work on choreography. The showcase will be here before you know it and I need all the extra practice I can squeeze in."

It doesn't escape me that without dance, there wouldn't be a reason to drag my ass out of bed in the morning.

Or ever.

Am I being a tad melodramatic?

Perhaps. Unfortunately, it's the truth.

"Listen," Mia's voice turns hesitant, "I know you said you didn't want to talk about the breakup—"

"Good," I cut in promptly, before she can meander too far down this pain-ridden road, "then we understand each other perfectly."

Her face falls and her shoulders wilt. A heavy silence descends as we continue along the cement path that winds through campus.

It's on the tip of my tongue to apologize when she murmurs, "It might help you get over the breakup if you talk about it."

Absolutely not.

I shake my head. Revealing just how much Colton hurt me won't do a damn bit of good. It'll only make me look like an idiot for believing he was anything other than a player. Mia is my closest friend and I usually tell her everything, but I couldn't bring myself to share his parting words with her. It was way too humiliating.

Fuck him and his unicorn pussy comment.

Even the memory is enough to bring a hot sting of embarrassment to my cheeks.

Relief floods through me as the fine arts building comes into view. I appreciate Mia trying to be there for me, but all I want to do is forget about Colton. I want to forget we were ever together or that I gave him the time of day. The only way that will happen is to stop talking about him. Or even thinking about him. I want to focus all of my energies on things that matter. Like dance. Even the thought of losing myself in the choreography and movement is enough to loosen the constriction around my chest, making it easier to breathe.

I keep my attention locked on the brick building. "I appreciate the offer, but I'm good."

"Okay," she mutters, not sounding the least bit convinced. "If you're sure."

"I am." Somehow, I even manage to hoist my lips into some semblance of a smile. It's not one that stretches across my face, but still, I deserve credit for the effort.

A sigh escapes from Mia's lips before she shrugs. "If you change your mind, know that I'm hear to listen." Just when I think that we've put the whole ugly matter behind us, she adds, "Bottling all that emotion up inside isn't healthy."

"Maybe not, but it's a hell of a lot better than sitting around and crying over a guy who isn't worth one damn tear."

I wouldn't mind keeping you in my back pocket and having a taste of it every once in a while. No strings attached, of course.

"That's not what I learned from Dr. Haskel."

Those quietly spoken words have everything inside me softening. Mia attended therapy with her parents after Brianne's death. Even though I would never ask Mia, I can't help but wonder what good it did. It sure as hell didn't bring Brianne back. And her family, for all their plastic smiles and pretending, are still fractured. Her dad works a gazillion hours a week and is barely around. Julia, her mother, drowns herself in alcohol, anti-depressants, and shops like there's no tomorrow. Maybe she secretly wishes that there wouldn't be. I can't necessarily blame her for that. What could be worse than losing a child?

Guilt explodes in me like a gunshot as I pull Mia into my arms and hug her tight. She's like my sister from another mister and nothing will ever change that. Not time, distance, or assholes masquerading as boys. "I realize you're trying to help, I really do, but I don't want to talk about Colton. Like at all. Let me process this breakup in my own way."

Her muscles loosen and I feel the precise moment she reluctantly relents. "But you're not working through anything. All you're doing is pretending that Colt—"

When I give her a hard look, she rolls her eyes and flattens her lips. "All you're doing is pretending that the jerk who shall not be named was never in your life. How is that healthy?"

Healthy?

I want to laugh. Or maybe cry.

Processing this breakup in a healthy manner is the least of my worries. I'm more concerned about spiraling into a deep depression that I won't be able to claw my way out of. The truth of the matter is that I'm hanging on by my fingernails. I've crushed hard on Colton for years. What he did was devastating. Toward the end, I'd given him my love and it hadn't been enough. Instead, he'd tossed it back in my face and decided that he'd rather screw as many girls as possible.

Yesterday, I'd spotted him across campus by the Union, surrounded by a fawning crowd of groupies. Clearly, they were all rejoicing his newly minted single status. I'm sure panties have been dropping left and right in celebration.

I'd caught him mid-laugh with a smile curving his lips. Unconsciously, my feet had stopped moving as my heart cracked wide open. For the briefest of moments, our gazes had collided before he glanced away, dismissing me on the spot. The rejection, along with the way he'd moved on so effortlessly, cut right to the bone. How I'll get through the rest of this year—not to mention the next two—I have no idea.

I never thought I'd say this, but graduation can't come fast enough. I need to get as far away from him as possible. I'd briefly flirted with the idea of transferring universities, but that's not really feasible. Wesley has the best dance program in the state, and I don't want to leave Mia. More than that, I refuse to let him chase me away.

So, for the foreseeable future, I'm stuck here with the jerk who shall remain nameless.

"I'm not pretending," I mutter. "I'm choosing to move on and forget about him."

"Same thing."

"Not at all." Before she can argue, I add, "I really need to get moving." I give her a quick kiss on the cheek. "I'll see you tonight, all right?"

She nods. "Yup. Whatever I end up ordering, I'll make sure there's enough for you."

"You're the best." With that, I haul ass toward the fine arts building. Mia might think that I'm running away from my feelings, but she's mistaken. I'm simply putting them behind me and moving forward. Nothing wrong with that, is there?

Once inside the studio, a puff of air leaves my lips, and my shoulders relax from around my ears. I don't realize how tight my muscles had become until they loosen. I drop my bag along the wall and peel off the scarf and jacket. I'm twenty minutes early and there are only a few other students in the room warming up at the barre or stretching on the floor.

The next to come off are the leggings and shirt until I'm stripped down to a black leotard and tights. I grab my shoes from my bag and slip them on my feet before settling on the floor and stretching. There's something comforting about the routine. Sunlight pours through the floor-to-ceiling windows as a tinge of sweat hangs in the air.

"Bonjour," Monsieur Dupre says as he saunters through the entryway. He's dressed entirely from head to toe in black. And yes, he looks hot as fuck in a way that only attractive European men with an overabundance of confidence can pull off.

My hand rises in a wave as a smile trembles across my face when I think about Zoe propositioning him.

And his partner.

One of the girls on the floor hisses my name and I blink back to awareness. She jerks her head toward the corner of the studio where our instructor waits. "Sorry." I press a hand to my chest. "Did you call me?"

"A word, *s'il vous plaît.*"

"Of course." I pop to my feet and pad over to him.

A slight frown tugs at the corners of his lips as he takes me in. "You are well?"

I shift uncomfortably under his relentless stare. "Umm, yes." I'd rather shove bamboo beneath my fingernails than admit that I'm upset over a guy. The number one rule in the studio is that outside bullshit stays where it belongs. *Outside.* We don't bring it into this space.

"Excellente." Before I can return the question—Monsieur Dupre is a stickler for etiquette—he says, "I assume you have submitted an application for the London Contemporary Dance School study program."

I suck my bottom lip between my teeth and give my head a little shake. "No, I didn't." When he had first mentioned the highly sought-after program a few months ago, I'd kicked around the idea but never applied. I'd been drunk on my relationship with Colton and the idea of leaving Wesley for an entire year hadn't been high on my priority list. I'm embarrassed to admit that I'd prioritized him above dance. Clearly, that had been a mistake.

Especially since all I'd been to him was unicorn pussy.

My nails bite into my palms as I straighten my shoulders. That's a costly mistake that I will never make again.

His perfectly sculpted brows pinch together. "Why not?"

There's no way I can tell him the truth. The man would probably mutter in French before banishing me from the program all together. "I didn't think I stood much of a chance against the competition." Which is somewhat true.

"The deadline is next week," he clips out with a glare that makes me feel three inches tall. "Turn your application in."

Properly chastised, I bob my head. "Yes, Monsieur."

When he remains silent, I scurry back to my spot on the floor. My heart pounds a steady tempo as I give serious consideration to the program in London.

Do I really have anything to lose by throwing my hat into the ring?

Not really. The odds of me actually making it through the selection process is miniscule and it'll give me something to focus on.

So...I guess it's a win-win.

ALYSSA

ne month later...

THE MUSCLES of my belly spasm as I click on the email and skim over the first line. I'd mentally prepared myself for a—*we regret to inform you...blah, blah, blah.*

Instead, it reads—*Congratulations! You have been selected...*

I blink and read over the first line with more care, but the words remain the same. It still says congratulations.

Holy shit! How did this happen? I didn't think I had a shot in the dark of being selected to attend LCDS. There were only a handful of spots and the competition was killer. Without Monsieur Dupre practically forcing me to apply, I wouldn't have bothered.

A potent concoction of excitement and fear bubble up inside me.

As that thought swirls through my head, the door to the dorm opens and Mia steps inside.

Her lips lift into a smile when she spots me at the desk near the window. "Hey! I didn't expect you back so soon."

"We were let out early," I tell her. "I just walked in ten minutes ago."

With a huff of breath, she tosses her bag onto the bed before pulling off her jacket. "It's freezing out there." Her cheeks are pink from the walk across campus.

"Yeah," I agree, gaze flicking to the window and the thin blanket of snow that covers the ground, "it is." As far as I'm concerned, spring can't come soon enough.

Mia drops down onto the bed next to her bag before pulling out her phone. "I'm glad your here. I found a few more apartments for next year that we can check out. I know it's still early, but we should try to find something before all the good ones get snapped up."

Shit.

Mia and I have talked about living off-campus since we were freshman. We've already checked out a few places, but they were located further away from the university than we wanted. It has to be within walking distance since parking on campus is a nightmare.

I gnaw my lower lip as my gaze darts to the laptop screen. Only now do I realize that I hadn't bothered to mention the LCDS exchange program to her.

I mean, why would I?

It's not like I had a snowball's chance in hell of getting selected.

Except...I've actually been accepted. And I would leave in July. That's only five months away. My belly drops to the bottom of my toes. It's like I'm sitting at the tippy top of a roller coaster. Unconsciously, my hand settles over my lower abdomen. In that moment, I realize that it's not even a question in my head if I'll accept.

There's no way I can turn down such an amazing opportunity to dance. Honestly, this couldn't have happened at a better time. Escaping from Wesley for the year is exactly what I need to get my head on straight and stop thinking about Colton. I can finally purge him from my system. There's got to be a few hot guys in London who can help with that, right?

Excitement bursts inside me.

My gaze settles on Mia again and some of my pleasure fades.

How am I going to break the news to her? I feel like a real jerk for baling on her. We've had these plans for years. But...I can't stay here. For my own mental health, I need to do this. I need to get away from Colton. I need to break the hold he has on me once and for all.

"There's something I need to tell you," I blurt, unable to hold it inside any longer.

"You still want to look for something off-campus, right?" With a frown, she glances around the tiny space. "Because I don't think I can live in the dorms for another year. I need out."

"Yeah." I fall silent, uncertain how to break the news about the exchange program. "I mean, no."

Her brows snap together as she straightens on the bed. She has no idea where I'm going with this. "Oh my God, you want to live in the dorms again? Aren't you tired of such cramped quarters? It's like we're on top of each other all the time." Mia stares at me like I've grown a horn on my head. And why wouldn't she? I've been bitching about the dorms since day one. If we could have moved off campus after freshman year, I would have but it's university policy that freshman and sophomores live in the residence halls.

Ugh. I'm making a complete mess of this.

I suck in a deep breath and hold it in my lungs for a moment before slowly forcing it out again. Maybe it would simplify matters if Mia reads the email herself. Before I can rethink my decision, I grab my laptop from the desk and plop down next to her. "I received this today."

She shoots me a puzzled look before her gaze settles on the computer screen. A few beats of silence pass as her eyes widen and she glances at me. I can almost see the wheels in her head spinning. "Wait a minute," her voice rises with each word, *"you're doing a study abroad program next year?"*

My shoulders collapse. "I only applied because Monsieur Dupree insisted. I didn't actually think I'd make it." Hesitantly I force out the words, "Are you angry?" This month has been difficult enough, I don't think I could stand that.

"Angry?" As she shakes her head, some of the shock falls away. "Of course, I'm not mad. Although, I wish you would have given me the heads up when you applied."

"I didn't think I even had a shot."

She frowns, anger sparking to life in her eyes. "That's the most ridiculous thing you've ever said. Why the hell wouldn't you get accepted?" Barely does she give me a chance to open my mouth before she continues, "You're an amazing dancer. They're lucky to have you."

Thick emotion wells in my throat as I set the computer aside and pull Mia into my arms. This right here is exactly why this girl is my bestie. Why she will *always* be my bestie. I couldn't ask for a more supportive friend.

"As much as I'm going to miss you, I think it's an amazing opportunity."

"Really?" Hope rises inside me like a balloon.

"Hell yeah! I wish I could come with you! I'm jealous!"

"You'll visit!"

She laughs. "Try and stop me. Maybe I'll just squat in your apartment. Or dorm. Or flat. Or whatever the heck they call it over there."

That would be amazing. I wish it was a possibility. A pang of sadness fills me when I think about not seeing Mia's smiling face everyday. It's funny, my mother tried to warn me about living with Mia when I announced senior year of high school that we were going to room together at college. She said that it was a good way to lose a friend. But that never happened. We're closer than ever.

And a year of separation won't change that.

As much as I've insisted that I'm over Colton, it's more wishful thinking on my part than anything else. It's been five weeks since the blond football player dumped my ass and he's been spotted at several parties with his harem. Every time one of my so-called *friends* catches sight of him, I'm sent a barrage of photo evidence regarding how easily he moved on from our relationship. I finally had to tell them to stop. Every damn picture was like a paper cut. Painful, yet not enough to kill me.

Mia reaches over and lays a hand across mine before giving it a gentle squeeze. "Even though I'll miss the hell out of you, it's too amazing of an opportunity to pass up."

She's right. It is.

Now that everything is out in the open, a fresh wave of excitement crashes over me.

I can't believe how lucky I am.

I get to dance in London for a whole year!

COLTON

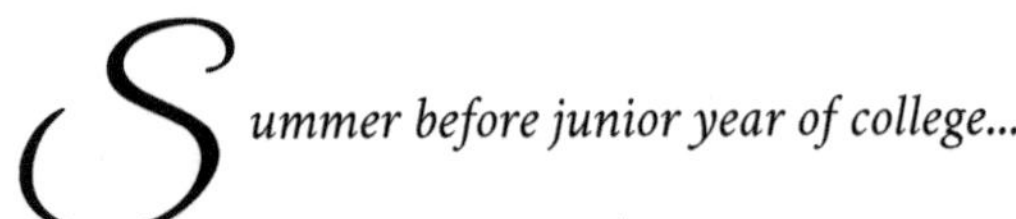

*S*ummer *before junior year of college...*

I PULL my metallic grey 840i convertible BMW into Beck's circular driveway before shifting into park and leaving the car to idle. I shoot Beck a text to let him know that I'm outside waiting before drumming my fingers impatiently on the sleek leather steering wheel.

A couple of minutes tick by and there's no sign of Beck. His truck is parked in the drive and there are lights on inside the house, so I know damn well that he's home.

For fuck's sake, where the hell is that guy?

Irritation pounds through me. We've got plans tonight and I'm impatient to get to them. We're supposed to meet up with a couple of chicks from high school. I fire off another text.

Let's move!

There's nothing but stereo silence from his end. It's enough to rile me up. Muttering under my breath, I slam out of the vehicle and stalk up the wide stairs to the massive front door before rapping my knuckles against the heavy wood.

No answer.

I ring the bell. It chimes throughout the house.

This is seriously ridiculous.

I peek in the side window but don't see any signs of life. My fingers go to the ornate handle and wiggle it, but it doesn't budge. Beck's parents are out of town for a couple of weeks, travelling somewhere in Europe.

Honestly, it would serve his ass right if I took off and left his ass to sit home. I would have zero problems entertaining the girls on my own. Wouldn't be the first time. Won't be the last.

As soon as an image of Alyssa pops into my head, I shove it away and curse under my breath. The girls are supposed to help me forget, not remind me of her.

It's totally fucked up.

I glance around the darkened front yard before stalking around the side of the house. For all I know he's hanging out by the pool. The guy's got a pretty sweet setup out back. As I step through the black iron gate, a splash of water comes from the pool. No wonder he didn't respond to the texts. I open my mouth to tell him to get his ass in gear when I realize that he isn't alone.

He's got company of the female persuasion.

Looks like the party started without me.

Fucker.

Since the couple in the pool is going at it pretty hot and heavy, they don't notice me stalk closer. Close enough to get a good look at who he's making out with.

Well, well, well...isn't *this* an interesting turn of events.

Since I'll be damned if Beck is the only one who gets a little action this evening, I say in an overly loud voice, "Dude, I thought we had plans."

The couple splinters apart before Mia Stanbury blinks at me looking all sorts of dazed and confused. I can't help the shit-eating grin that slides its way across my face. Not in a million years did I ever think I'd see the day that she willingly allowed Beck to lay hands, not to mention lips, on her.

The emotion that tumbles across her expression when she realizes she's been sucking face with her arch nemesis—and that I'm here to witness it—is almost comical.

At least, I'm entertained by it.

"Why, hello there, Mia," I say, humor simmering in my voice, "can't say I expected to find you here."

When I was with Alyssa, I couldn't get the dark-haired girl to join us if she thought there was even a remote possibility that Beck would make an appearance and now look at her...

I'm a huge fan of irony.

And this situation is chock-full of it.

Beck keeps his arms locked around her. Clearly, he's not in any hurry to let her go.

"Colton," she mutters through stiff lips. Even with only the pool lights for illumination, color blooms in her cheeks. Any moment she'll burst into flame.

I stuff my hands in the pockets of my shorts and rock back on my heels as if I've got all the time in the world to stand around and shoot the shit with them. I can't resist rubbing the situation in her face. "So, what have you crazy kids been up to?"

I didn't think it was possible for more color to scald her face, but that's exactly what happens. She looks like an overripe tomato. I'm tempted to laugh but I'm sure Beck will kick my ass if I do. Although, it might be worth it.

"Wait in the car," Beck snaps, "I'll be out in ten."

I have no idea what prompts me to say it, but the words are shooting out of my mouth before I can stop them. "You gonna come out with us, Mia?" I pause for a beat. "I doubt the chicks we're supposed to hookup with tonight will appreciate that, but, oh well." I shrug. "Sucks for them."

Her eyes widen as she presses her hands against Beck's chest, attempting to escape from his embrace. Fury flashes across his face as he levels a hard-edged stare at me.

Fine, I'll admit that it was a dick move.

"Dude," Beck growls, clearly pissed that I just blew up his plans, "get the fuck out of here before I beat your ass."

I hold up my hands in a gesture of surrender. "Whatever. Don't get your panties in a bunch." Now that my work is done here, I swing around and head for the car. Although I can't resist calling over my shoulder as I pass through the gate, "You got ten. Wrap this shit up and let's go."

Not waiting for a response, I stalk to the front of the stone mansion. He gets fifteen minutes and then I'm out of here.

Anger simmers in my veins as I slide onto the butter-soft leather. I'm not oblivious. I know Beck has been carrying a torch for Mia. I'm also well aware that he'll probably beat my ass for jacking up his night once he gets out here.

After ten more minutes, I fire off a third text. I'm losing my patience. Scratch that, I'm fresh out. Hell, for all I know, he and Mia are still getting it on. Although, she was pretty pissed off when I walked away, so that's doubtful.

You know what?

Fuck this shit.

I'm out.

I jam the key in the ignition as Beck opens the door and slides onto the seat beside me. "Took you long enough," I bite out. "I was just about to take off."

"Too bad you didn't do that when you realized I was busy," he shoots back, clearly irritated with me.

"Give me a fucking break," I snort. "We both know Mia can't stand your damn ass. What were you gonna do? Fuck her in the pool? You might not realize it, but I did you a solid. That girl would have hated you even more than she already does."

He presses his lips together and glares.

He knows I'm right.

The tension gathered inside me finally loosens when he fails to respond. A grin slides across my face as I cup my fingers to my ear. "I'm sorry, what's that?" I pause for a beat, knowing damn well he won't say a word. *"You're welcome, Colton? Thanks for saving me from myself?"*

"I wouldn't go that far," he mutters, slouching on the leather and staring straight ahead.

"Please. I couldn't get Mia to come out with us if there was even a slight chance you would show up." I cock my head. "Doesn't that tell you something?"

Of course it does, but Beck is nowhere near ready to acknowledge it.

"Just drive," he mutters.

"You know I'm right," I say smugly, starting up the engine and squealing out of the driveway before punching the gas. "I hate to be the one to break it to you, but it's never gonna happen with that girl. You need to move the fuck on."

He slouches further onto the black leather. "Maybe," he bites out, "you should do yourself a favor and take your own advice for a change."

My jaw tightens as I stare at the ribbon of road stretched out in front of us. "Don't think I'm not trying," I mumble. "Every damn night, I'm trying to get over that girl." There's no point in specifying which one I'm talking about. He damn well knows.

Just like he knows why I've been in such a pissy mood for the last five months. It doesn't take a rocket scientist to figure out.

"You screw so much," he continues with humor tinging his voice, "that I'm surprised your dick hasn't shriveled up and fallen off. Remind me to buy you some balm for your birthday."

A hint of a smile lifts my lips, although it doesn't quite reach my eyes. "Don't I know it, brother."

A heavy silence falls over us as I crank the steering wheel and turn onto the main stretch of road. It's on the tip of my tongue to ask about Alyssa. I haven't seen her around in a while. And she blocked my ass on her socials. Which...I can't exactly blame her for. But tell me how I'm supposed to stalk that chick if I can't see what she's up to?

I try to swallow down the words but they refuse to budge. It's only a matter of time before they burst free.

One second.

Two.

Thr—

"Did Mia mention Lys at all?"

Fuck me.

I've done my best to wipe Alyssa from every part of my life. Evicting her from my head and heart are another story. It sucks.

Beck scrutinizes me silently before tossing me a crumb. Not that I deserve it with the way I've been acting. He's a better friend than I am. "Guess she's studying abroad in London for the year."

His answer takes me by surprise. I blink and stare straight ahead as my lips tug down at the corners. "No shit?"

"Yup."

My heart constricts. It's like there is a vise squeezing it.

"Huh." That's all I'm capable of forcing out.

It's weird to think of Alyssa not being here. At the same school. In the same town. In the same damn state. Hell, the country. Even when I was trying to ignore her, she was here. I could keep an eye on her. I caught glimpses of her on campus when she didn't know I was looking.

And now she's gone.

A heavy pit settles deep in my gut. I'm so fucking tempted to ask where she went. This time, I keep the question buried deep inside. In the months since our breakup, I've done my damnedest to move on. It hasn't worked. So maybe...maybe this is for the best.

Out of sight, out of mind, right?

Let's hope that turns out to be the case.

If not, I don't know what the hell I'm going to do.

ALYSSA

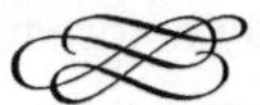

arch of junior year...

JACK GRABS HOLD of my hand and laces our fingers together before flashing me a cheeky smile as we take in the shops on Oxford Street. The skies are overcast, but the weather is seasonable for this time of year in London, which means it's about fifty degrees. We're both bundled up in jackets. I can't help but return the easy expression.

Effortless.

That would be the perfect word to describe my relationship with him.

He's handsome, charming, and so very British.

I've turned into something I never expected to be—a cliché. I could listen to him talk all day long. And I flipping love when he uses words like—bullocks, bloody, and knackered. It makes me laugh every time. And the guy knows it, which is why he does it. He gets a little twinkle in his dark eyes when my lips start to twitch.

And he's a footballer.

Well, I mean soccer player. In England, it's called football and it's huge. Like nothing I could have imagined. Everyone is crazy for either Manchester or Liverpool. Having been born and bred on American football, I never paid much attention to professional soccer. A few high school games here and there but that was the extent of it.

When Jack realized I was totally clueless about the sport, he took the time to explain the rules and over the months, I've grown to enjoy it. It's fast paced, and the fans are rabid. I would pit them against the most diehard football fans any day. He even bought me a scarf to wave at the matches we've attended when the team jogs onto the pitch.

Watching him sprint across the field certainly isn't a hardship. He's thick and muscular and reminds me nothing of a certain someone else.

We met at a pub while I was out with my roommate. Much to Jack's chagrin, I friend zoned him pretty quickly. After that, I noticed we were ending up at a lot of the same parties and before I realized it, I was spending more time with him, getting to know him on a deeper level.

It's been...nice.

Different than what I'm used to. I don't have to chase Jack to get his attention. I already have it. He seems to have eyes only for me. From the start, he's made his intentions clear. He doesn't play games and he's not out screwing every girl who spreads her legs.

It's a refreshing change of pace.

We've been teetering on the brink of...*something* for the last couple of weeks, but I'm not ready to delve into another relationship. Especially when my time in London will be drawing to a close. Even though I try not to dwell on Colton, there are times when he invades my brain, slyly wrapping himself around my heart and squeezing. He's turned out to be a difficult habit to break. Even when we're an ocean apart.

But then again, what did I really expect? I've had feelings for the guy ever since sophomore year of high school. It's unrealistic to assume they would simply disappear over night because I wanted them to.

The moment I realize where my mind has wandered to, I shove

those thoughts away and squeeze Jack's hand, wanting to ground myself in the present. Colton has been relegated to my past and that's exactly where he needs to stay. Jack, on the other hand, is my present.

Possibly future.

Even though everything remains uncertain, I'm excited to figure it out.

COLTON

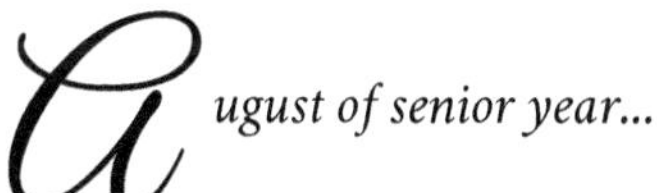

ugust of senior year...

"HOLD THE ELEVATOR!" I call out and force myself to jog through the lobby of our new apartment building. Sure, I could take the stairs, we only live on the third floor, but I'm wiped. We've been practicing on the turf under the blazing hot sun twice a day for the last couple of weeks. Every muscle is screaming at me. A fifteen-minute soak in an ice bath wasn't nearly enough to undo the damage Coach inflicted this morning.

Just as the metal doors are about to close, they bounce open again. I quicken my step, jumping on board, a huff of relief escaping from my lips. My plans for the afternoon involve my queen-sized bed and a long nap to recharge before heading back to the field for round two.

"Thanks." I glance at the lone occupant inside. There are three oversized boxes stacked in her arms, obscuring her face. All I'm able to make out are curvy hips and long, sun-kissed legs peeking out from the bottom of her black athletic shorts.

A quick glance at the control panel reveals that the button for the third floor has already been hit.

"No problem," she says, shifting the boxes around in her arms to get a better grip.

As tired as I am, I can't just stand here and let her struggle with the containers by herself. Without a doubt, I can be an ass but my stepmother, Jenna, did attempt to drill a few manners into my head. "Looks like you've got quite the load there. Want some help?"

"Nah," she says with a soft grunt as she shifts the load again, "I'm in the homestretch."

"You sure? I don't mind helping."

"Nope, it's all good."

I lean against the wall of the elevator and fold my arms across my chest. "Must be moving day."

"Yup," she confirms.

I glance at the panel again. "You've just moved into an apartment on the third floor?"

"Right again," she says with a laugh. It's deep and throaty.

My brows draw together as I wrack my brain. There's something oddly familiar about her voice. Fuck...I really hope we haven't hooked up. That always makes for awkward run-ins. Before I can investigate the situation any further, the elevator jolts to a halt and the doors slide open, spitting us out onto the third floor. I slap my hand against the frame of the elevator so the doors can't slide shut as she steps off the platform and into the hallway.

As she takes a few steps, the top box wobbles, and I spring into action, grabbing it from her. Maybe she doesn't want my help, but she's getting it.

"Thanks!"

Our gazes lock and my footsteps falter, surprised at who I find buried behind the containers. "Mia."

Her gaze widens as her body freezes. She looks equally stunned. "Colton." There's a pause as she forces out a greeting. "Hey."

Silence descends as we stare. It's like neither of us know what to say. Just when the situation turns awkward, she clears her throat.

"So...you live here?" A hopeful note tinges her voice and I realize she's probably hoping that turns out not to be the case.

Unfortunately, I'm going to have to burst that bubble.

"Yeah." I point to the end of the hall. "Last door on the left."

Her lips sink at the corners as she stares reluctantly in that direction. "Oh."

Mia and I grew up together. I've known her since elementary school. We've never had a problem with each other although, she definitely became more standoffish after my breakup with Alyssa. Not like I can blame her for that.

I guess that's what happens when you dick over someone's best friend. You become a permanent fixture on their shit list.

I jerk my head in the same direction. "You're that way, too?"

"Yeah." Her lips do more than just sink at the edges. They bow into a full-blown frown. Every emotion and thought is there to see as it flickers across her expressive face.

We both know why this has the potential to be a powder keg of a situation.

Don't ask about her, asshole.

Don't you dare do it.

It's been eighteen months since our breakup, but who's counting?

By now, I should have moved on. Alyssa Williams should be nothing more than a blip in my past. One of the many girls that I've fucked. But that's the last thing she'll ever be. No matter how much I've tried to eradicate her from my brain, she's still there, gnawing away gleefully at the back of it.

What I've gradually realized during the time Alyssa has been gone is that she will never be *just* a girl.

She'll always be *the* girl.

The one I forced away because I was too chicken shit to open myself up and risk getting hurt again. If I have any brains whatsoever, I'll assist Mia to her door and pretend that there isn't a past that sits uncomfortably between us.

Easier said than done.

"So...Alyssa?" I wince as the words shoot from my mouth. "She back yet?" The possibility of her staying in London has my heart constricting painfully in my chest. I hate to admit it, but I've been mentally counting down the weeks until her return.

I'm not even sure what the point in doing that is. After the way I blew up our relationship, it's doubtful she'll even look at me, much less engage in idle conversation.

I just need to lay eyes on her. I've been starving for the sight of her.

It's not a surprise when Mia's face shutters and she glances away. Her lips press into a tight line and I wonder if she'll brush off the question.

Hell, maybe she'll tell me to get bent. Anything is possible.

After a long stretch of silent moments, she grumbles, "Not yet."

"But she'll return to Wesley for the fall semester?"

She huffs out a breath. "Yeah."

If Mia thinks I'm at all deterred by her reluctant responses, she's dead wrong. "Is she gonna live here with you?"

The dark-haired girl's brows slide together as she glares. "Yeah. Are you finished with your grand inquisition?"

Once I've got confirmation of Alyssa's return and living arrangements, everything inside me loosens and I can finally breathe again. Air rushes into my lungs. Until this very moment, I didn't realize how oxygen deprived I'd become. It feels like I've been submerged beneath the water indefinitely. Only now am I able to fight my way to the surface and breakthrough to the other side.

Mia mutters something indecipherable under her breath and stalks down the hallway before I can continue grilling her for information. Since my legs are almost twice as long as hers, it only takes a moment to catch up. She stops one door short of mine before shifting the boxes in her arms and attempting to dig around in her front pocket.

"Here, give them to me."

"No thanks," she huffs.

"Come on, Mia. Don't be stubborn."

She shoots me another glare before giving in. "I suppose giving in is the quickest way to get you to leave."

"There, you go." I flash her a grin. "Looking at the positives."

She snorts before rising to her tiptoes and stacking the containers on top of the one I'm already holding. Then she slides the key from her pocket before shoving it in the lock and turning the handle.

With her back against the open door, she holds out her arms. "I can take it from here."

"I got it. Just tell me where you want them." Not waiting for a response, I saunter past her.

She points to the living room/dining room combination. "Set them down anywhere over there."

I do as she asks before straightening to my full height and glancing around the apartment. There are boxes stacked everywhere. I'm overwhelmed just looking at it. She'll be putting things away for weeks. Even though I know she'll turn me down flat, I can't resist throwing the offer out there. "You want some help with all this? I've got a few hours to kill before I need to head back to the stadium."

She blows out a lengthy breath all the while surveying the cardboard shanty town she's got going on. For a moment, I almost wonder if she's considering the offer. But then she shakes her head. "No, it's fine. I'll just take it a little bit at a time."

I cock my head before shifting my weight from one foot to the other. "You sure? I'm willing to help."

Her voice softens, losing some of its hard-edge. "I appreciate the offer, but no."

Since I wasn't expecting a different outcome, I shrug. Hell, I'm kind of surprised she didn't toss me out on my ear as soon as I set the boxes on the floor. "All right then." I meander to the door. "Guess now that you live here, I'll see you around the building."

As I cross over the threshold, Mia's voice halts me in my tracks. "Colton?"

I turn and meet her steady gaze. "You should know that Alyssa has moved on."

And just like that, I'm shoved beneath the glassy surface of water and can't breathe again. Mia's words shouldn't hurt. In fact, I shouldn't feel anything where Alyssa is concerned. Or maybe it's relief that should be pounding through me.

That's exactly what I wanted, right?

That's why I shoved her away.

Unable to utter a sound, I jerk my head into a tight nod before slipping from the apartment and into the hallway.

COLTON

"We're late," Beck mutters, hastening his step as we move through the lobby of our apartment building before pushing through the glass doors and into the bright sunshine, "and I'm in no mood to run suicides."

Yeah, me neither. We've done more than enough of that this summer. My body already feels battered and bruised and it's only August. Coach came back in July when training camp started up with all these new workout regimes. I'm not sure if he's trying to scare the freshman, but I don't like it.

Not one damn bit.

Added to that, it's hot as hades out here. And it will feel a thousand degrees hotter running plays on the turf. There are times when the field actually looks hazy in the afternoon sun. A few of the guys have already passed out. That's Division I football for you. Pussies need not apply.

I'll tell you this, it makes me glad that I decided not to enter the draft. As much as I love football and I'll miss the sport, I'm ready to move on with my life. I glance at Beck. He doesn't feel that way. He'll be entering the NFL draft this year and more than likely, he'll go in the first round. I can't wait to see what team he ends up with.

I'm knocked out of those thoughts when a female voice catches my attention. My head whips up, knowing exactly who it belongs to.

Alyssa.

My footsteps falter as the air gets clogged in my lungs.

I don't know how it's possible, but she's even more beautiful than I remember. For the moment, she's unaware of my presence and I'm able to eat her up with my eyes. My gaze touches every part of her. From the top of her blond head to the tips of her toes, I catalogue all the little details that have changed. The sleeker haircut that frames her face. The willowy form that now looks longer and leaner. No longer does she resemble the girl I remember. The one who chased after me throughout high school and the first couple years of college. There's something different about her. An air of sophistication that wasn't there before.

From all the luggage being dragged up the walkway, my guess is that Mia just picked her up from the airport.

"Well, this should be interesting," Beck mutters under his breath.

It's almost laughable that I'd thought our time apart would have dulled the emotions that have always simmered beneath the surface where she's concerned. If anything, they're stronger than ever and trying to break free. For the first time in eighteen months, my blood pumps through my veins with renewed energy.

It takes a heartbeat for her to become aware of my presence. Her gaze settles on me and the easy-going expression falls away from her face as if it had never been there in the first place. Her blue eyes turn stony. If I'd thought more than a year of separation would have dulled her anger toward me, I was woefully mistaken. That realization is slammed home when Alyssa grabs hold of Mia's arm and yanks her to a halt.

There's no disguising the wrath in her voice as she snaps, "What the hell is *he* doing here?"

I couldn't look away from her if I tried. She bristles as I continue to stare.

"Right," Mia glances nervously between us before admitting quietly, "I, ah, meant to tell you about that."

"About what?" Her expression turns stormy as if she's bracing herself for bad news. "What didn't you tell me about?"

"They also live here," her friend blurts, shifting her weight.

There's a beat of silence before Alyssa says through stiff lips, "I really hope you're joking."

"Sorry, Lys," the dark-haired girl whispers. "When I signed the rental agreement, I had no idea they lived here or that we're neighbors."

Alyssa's eyes widen. Any moment, they're going to fall out of her head. *"What?"*

Mia winces as her friend's voice cracks through the air.

I don't realize I'm on the move or that I've closed the distance between us until I grind to a halt a few feet away from her. The temptation to reach out and pull her into my arms is almost overwhelming. It's been way too long since I've been able to do that. Unfortunately, I know exactly how that would go over and it's not well. I'd probably lose my balls in the ensuing skirmish. After twenty-one years, I'm kind of partial to them.

Alyssa watches me through narrowed eyes. Color flares to life in her cheeks, giving them a flushed look. My mind tumbles back to the other times when her cheeks would fill with color. Only then, it had nothing to do with being pissed off.

Her lips compress into a thin line. When she remains silent, it becomes apparent that I'll have to be the one to make the first move. Which is just fine with me. In a way, it feels like I've been waiting for this moment for a long time.

"Hey, Lys." Everything warms inside me as her gaze holds mine. All I want is to feel the intensity of her gaze on me. Even if it's filled with anger. I don't care. I have no idea if I can make this right between us but as I stand before her, I realize just how much I want to.

Need to.

If it were possible to wipe away the past and start fresh, I would do it in a heartbeat.

Am I delusional enough to think a simple conversation will undo the mistakes I've made?

Hell, no.

This is Alyssa Williams we're talking about. She has a temper. So, what I'm expecting her to do is bite my head off. Kind of like a female praying mantis after they've mated. I'm willing to swallow my pride and let it happen. Anything that will get us on the rocky road to making amends.

Much to my surprise, that's not what happens.

Instead, she says, voice full of ice, "Did you hear that?" Eyes wide, she glances around as if searching for someone. "It almost sounds like a ghost from boyfriends' past."

My brows rise as a frown pinches my face. I'm...not quite sure how to react to this, but all right. She wants to give me the silent treatment? I guess I deserve it.

I glance at Mia to get a read on her expression. She jerks her shoulders and for a second, my heartbeat stutters as her words from two weeks ago ring unwantedly through my head.

You should know that Alyssa has moved on.

What if that's true?

Can I necessarily blame her for trying to find happiness with another guy?

Nope.

All this girl wanted to do was love me and I stomped on her heart and ran away like a little bitch. Truth be told, I'm embarrassed by my own behavior.

My tongue darts out to moisten my lips as I make a second attempt to break through her icy veneer. What I don't know is how deep her cool exterior runs and if it's possible to drill down past it.

"It's really good to see you, Lys." When she continues to avoid eye contact, I decide to take my life into my own hands by stepping closer and pulling her into my arms. For a sliver of a moment, my mind tumbles back to what it felt like to hold her any damn time I wanted.

I guess what they say is true—you don't realize what you have until it's gone.

Her body goes whipcord tight as a growl of protest emanates from deep in her chest and then she's fighting her way out of my arms like

I'm a serial killer trying to wrestle her to a white van. Once she breaks free, she shoves me away before straightening her clothing and spearing me with a steely-edged glare that would shrivel the balls off most guys. With a huff, she turns her attention to Beck, who watches the current show we're treating him to with an amused expression.

I'm sure he's loving this. Usually, it's him making an ass out of himself. And yeah, when the shoe is on the other foot, I get a lot of enjoyment out of it.

"Hello, Beckett. It's nice to see you." Now that Alyssa is no longer addressing me, her voice softens considerably as she flashes a mega-watt smile in his direction. A kernel of unwanted jealousy explodes in my belly even though I know damn well that I have nothing to be concerned about. Alyssa and Beck have been friends for years. But still...I don't like her looking at him like that. Especially when she can barely be bothered to give me the time of day. "Did Mia happen to mention the welcome home party I'm having this Saturday at Bang Bang?" She continues to ignore me like I'm not even standing here. The temptation to lay my hands on her pounds through me. This time, instead of giving in to the urge, I keep my hands to myself. "Feel free to stop by if you're not busy."

Humor ignites in Beck's green gaze as he slants a look toward the dark-haired girl. "Nope, she didn't mention it." Yeah, there's a reason for that. Mia can't stand Beck. It's doubtful she would spit in his mouth if he were dying of thirst. Then again...I did catch them swap-ping spit in Beck's pool a year ago. So, it's altogether possible I'm wrong about that.

Mia's lips sink into a frown as she gives her best friend a bit of side-eye. Alyssa doesn't bother to glance in her direction. My guess is that the invitation is payback for moving into the same apartment building as me.

"Hmm," Alyssa continues with a small frown, "that's strange. She must have *forgotten* to mention the party to you the same way she *neglected* to mention that a certain someone who shall remain name-less is my new neighbor."

Yup. Most definitely payback.

Mia's eyes narrow as she arrives at the same conclusion.

Unable to remain silent any longer, I blurt, "Hey, what about me? Don't I get an invite?"

By the sparks of blue anger that flash in her eyes, I'm guessing that would be a negative. When she remains silent, I give her my most charming smile—the one that can melt the panties right off a girl—and make a second attempt. "How about for old times' sake?"

I get zero reaction.

Any power I'd once had over her has vanished. Even though I'm the one who opened my hand and let her go, she's slipping through my fingers when I want more than anything to snatch her back and hold her tight.

Alyssa cocks her head and glances around owlishly. "It's so strange the way I keep hearing something."

Anger and frustration bubble up inside me. Maybe I have no right to feel them or even be irritated by her behavior, but that doesn't stop the emotions from flooding through me.

Tired of being ignored, I say, "Really, Lys?" I pause for a beat before adding something I *know* will solicit a reaction out of her. "You're acting like a child."

Boom. Mission accomplished.

If I'd wanted her attention, I certainly have it. She goes off like a firework on the fourth of July. Thunderclouds erupt on Alyssa's pretty face as she wheels around to face me. Two steps bring her close enough to drill a finger into my chest.

Well...at least she's touching me of her own volition. That's got to be a step in the right direction.

Or not.

Fury vibrates off her in heavy, suffocating waves. *"I'm the child?"* Her voice escalates with every word that she bites out. "That's rich! You dumped my ass because you couldn't keep your dick in your pants! Don't you *dare* turn this around on me!" The people passing by on the sidewalk in front of the building stop and stare. "You and I are *not* friends. We will *never* be friends! I was an idiot for thinking you were anything other than a *manwhore!*"

When I remain silent, the air around us crackles with explosive energy. It's like an impending lightning storm. Any moment, I'm going to get fried.

Guilt nearly swallows me whole as tears prick Alyssa's eyes, making them appear glassy. She blinks back the moisture, refusing to let it fall, and glances around as if only now realizing that her outburst has drawn an unwanted audience. A dull red color seeps into her cheeks.

She meets their inquisitive stares with a snarl. "Move it along! Show's over, there's nothing to see here."

An apology sits on the tip of my tongue. Before I can get it out, Mia grabs Alyssa's luggage and drags it to the building. Beck scrambles to open the glass door before the two girls disappear inside the lobby. And I'm left standing like a dumbass with my dick in my hand.

Fuck me.

Once the door closes firmly behind them, Beck glances at me with a raised brow.

"Well," he says, running his fingers across his jaw, "that didn't go well."

I grimace at the understatement. "Nope, it sure as hell didn't."

Any hope that my past transgressions might be forgiven go up in flames.

More like a dumpster fire fueled by a drum of gasoline.

ALYSSA

*O*h my God! What the hell was that?

Emotion churns through me as Mia shoves the key into the lock and twists the handle before dragging my bags inside our brand-new apartment. The confrontation with Colton has left me feeling shaken and out of sorts. Was I really under the delusion that it was possible to ease back into life at Wesley? I could take my time, adjust a bit, and find my bearings before having to come face-to-face with. I glance at my phone, noting that I haven't been back on American soil for a full hour before we had a run-in.

Ugh.

That encounter couldn't have gone any worse.

After a couple of months in London, I'd all but convinced myself that I was over him. That I'd detoxed the guy from my heart.

Only now do I realize that it was wishful thinking on my part. If I had, I wouldn't have gone off the rails like a complete psycho. I wince, remembering the avid faces watching from the sidelines. A few spectators had been on the verge of grabbing a bowl of popcorn and pulling up a lawn chair to enjoy the show.

Jerks.

On the positive side, it's doubtful I'll have to worry about Colton pestering me in the near future. Or anyone else who witnessed that debacle. I'm sure my new neighbors will give me a wide berth and avoid me like a case of the clap.

One year. That's all I've got to endure. Then we'll go our separate ways never to see one another again.

Hopefully.

The adrenaline pumping wildly through my veins minutes ago dissipates, leaving exhaustion behind to fill the void. It takes every last bit of strength to muscle my luggage into the small entryway and slam the door closed.

With a huff of breath, I glance around our new digs. I'd been so excited by the photos and virtual tour Mia had sent me. It seemed almost unbelievable that we had all this space to ourselves. No more dorm life! Or teeny tiny flat.

Now I would happily exchange this place for a dorm. I have no idea how I'm going to coexist in the same building with Colton Montgomery.

I trudge into the sun-filled living room before collapsing onto a chair. Another wave of exhaustion crashes over me. Looks like the jetlag is about to catch up with me. I don't think I've slept in twenty-four hours. There was just too much packing to do and too many people to say good-bye to. As excited as I was to return, I was sad to leave all the friends I'd made behind. Especially since I have no idea when I'll see them again.

Almost gingerly, Mia settles on the couch across from me. A flicker of unease fills her expression as concern gathers in her eyes. "I'm really sorry, Lys. I meant to tell you about Colton on the ride home from the airport, but I just didn't know how to do it." She jerks her shoulders. "When I toured the building and then signed the rental lease a few weeks later, I had no idea he lived here."

My gaze meanders to the patio door that leads to a small balcony. I'd been over the moon when she'd stepped outside with her phone and panned the area. The idea of being able to sit outside on a balmy night and study in the fresh air seemed almost extravagant. And now?

Not even that little perk is able to bring a smile to my lips because all I can think about is that Colton will be here too. I'll run into him in the hallways. I'll have a first-class seat to the groupies he entertains.

That thought makes me sick to my stomach.

A humorless chuckle bubbles up in my throat.

Had I really convinced myself that I was over him?

Or that I'd moved on with my life?

Ha!

"It's fine." Now that the brightest part of my anger has drained away, guilt rushes in to swamp me. "Sorry for being a bitch and inviting Beck to the party."

She shakes her head as a groan slips free.

It only makes me feel worse. Renting an apartment in the same building as Colton was an unfortunate coincidence. Me inviting Beck to the welcome home party, however, was not.

I clear my throat and add in a hopeful tone, "It's always possible that he won't show up."

Mia snorts before leveling a knowing stare in my direction. "I think we both know he'll be there."

She's right, we do.

Beck has always had a not-so-secret thing for my bestie. Mia, on the other hand, wants nothing to do with the guy, which is a challenge since they grew up together, live next door to one another, and their parents are good friends. So, she gets stuck with him during holidays and family vacations.

As easy on the eyes as Beck is, I can't blame her for keeping him at a distance. Mia has experienced enough pain in her life to invite more.

Beck has been attracting attention of the female persuasion since he was in middle school for both his talent on the football field along with his good looks. Think bottle green-colored eyes, wavy dark hair, and ridiculously high cheek bones that look like they were chiseled from stone.

Sure, Colton has his own fan club when it comes to the ladies at Wesley, but so does Beck. The guy has never lacked for female attention. And Mia isn't into that. I might have been gone for a year, but I can't imagine that much has changed where Beck Hollingsworth is concerned.

Unlike me, Mia knows better than to try and tame a bad boy.

"We could always look for another apartment and if we find something, try to get out of the lease," she says, breaking into my thoughts.

Yeah, I guess that's a possibility.

I glance around the decorated space. I like what Mia has done with the place. Already, after only being here for two weeks, the place looks homey. It would be such a pain in the ass to move again. Not to mention, I really do love that balcony.

Am I going to allow Colton Montgomery to chase me away?

I refuse to give him the satisfaction.

Decision made, I blow out a long breath and shake my head.

Mia's shoulders loosen from around her ears as a tentative smile curves her lips. "Don't worry, I'm sure we'll barely see him. You're busy with dance and he's got football. You'll be like two ships passing in the night."

You know what?

She's right.

I've got nothing to worry about.

And if Colton has any brains whatsoever, he'll avoid me like his life depends on it.

COLTON

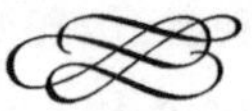

"Montgomery, get your ass off the field!" Coach barks when I fumble yet another pass. "Kwiatkowski, take his place!"

Fuck.

Fuck.

Fuck.

I need to get my shit together before I get permanently pulled. Instead of making eye contact with Beck, I stare at the turf and jog off the field. I already know what I'll find in his eyes and that's a—*what the hell is going on with you* look. I can't blame him for it either. The last couple of practices have turned out to be a complete shitshow. Passes I should be catching with ease are getting dropped, missed, or slipping through my fingers. On one of the last plays, I actually tripped over my own damned feet. If you didn't know better, you'd think I'd never even seen a football before. It's embarrassing as fuck.

Ever since I first stepped foot on the field, my game has been consistent. I don't have high-highs or low-lows. I'm a solid player. Dependable. Coaches know this. My teammates know it. Beck knows it, as well. I'm always in position, ready to catch whatever my QB throws my way.

Except today.

And yesterday.

Not to mention the day before that.

Now that I think about it, my game has been off for the last week. Specifically, since my run-in with Alyssa outside the apartment building. She's dominated almost all of my thoughts. I can't stop thinking about her. Or searching for her. I'm like a stalker, hanging around the building, trying to catch sight of her.

Most people, the ones who know jack about football, think the game is all brute strength and physicality, but that's not true. It's mental. And that's where I'm falling short. My head is no longer in the game. It's wrapped up in my ex. Unless I can turn things around on the field, I'll be riding the pine for the immediate future. And that's never happened before. Not even when I played Pop Warner and started off with pads that swallowed me up.

Coach ignores me for the remainder of practice while Kwiatkowski, our second-string wide receiver, runs through a handful of plays with Beck. And wouldn't you know it, the junior receiver catches every damn pass thrown to him. It only compounds the feelings of powerlessness already wreaking havoc on me. I've been first-string since I stepped foot on campus freshman year. My spot has never been in question.

Now it feels like I could lose everything I've worked years for in an instant. By the time Coach blows his whistle at the end of a two-hour practice, my head is a fucking mess. I need to get out of here and figure out how I'm going to fix this problem.

Once in the locker room, I keep to myself. I've had a shitty practice and I'm not in the mood to joke around with these assholes. Even though I remain silent, Beck doesn't take the hint. Instead of giving me a wide berth, he drops onto the bench and peels off his jersey before tossing it in the locker.

I feel the heaviness of his gaze burning a hole through me. He might not give voice to all the questions swirling around through his brain, but I hear them loud and clear just the same. Beck and I have been playing ball together since we were kids. We recognize each other's tells and quirks. Half the time, I know what play he'll run before he does. The guy never has to seek me out on the field, I instinctively know where I need to be and get into position. As far as football is concerned, we have some kind of weird mental connection. It's what makes us so good on the field.

It's just another reason the last couple of practices are fucking with my head even more than Alyssa. Sure, everybody is entitled to an off day. It goes with the territory. But this has turned into more of a slump and that scares the fuck out of me.

Especially with the season looming right around the corner.

What if I can't turn it around?

This is my last year at Wesley. The goal had always been to go out on a high note with a winning season. I want to bring home a conference championship before taking my rightful place alongside my father in the personal finance company he founded. These are my glory days, the ones I'll look back at with longing and fondness when I'm stuck behind a desk for twelve hours a day, trading stocks, and shoring up client portfolios. At this rate, I'll be glad they're over.

I keep my gaze focused straight ahead. The last thing I want to do is field any questions or talk about the obvious elephant in the room. Everyone knows that once you do that, it becomes real. There's no shoving the genie back in the lamp. With rough fingers, I rip off my jersey and shove it in my locker. Agitation wafts off me in heavy, suffocating waves. I'm all but choking on it.

The rowdy locker room turns quiet as Coach stalks through with his Wesley Warriors ball cap pulled low over his eyes and a clipboard clenched in his hand. Air gets wedged in my lungs as I wait for what I know is coming next.

"*Montgomery,*" he barks, "get your ass in my office as soon as you're dressed."

I jerk my head into a tight nod but keep my lips pressed together.

Fuck.

Coach Taylor glares at the group of half-naked guys and barks out a few more victims. When he's done, he slams the door to his office with so much force that it rattles on its hinges.

Devon Baker, a three-hundred-pound lineman, laughs, "Better bring some lube with you, Montgomery. Doesn't look like he's in the mood to give it to you gently."

Like I don't know that?

I glare at Baker before giving him the finger.

Our first game against Tennessee is in two weeks. If I can't pull my shit together, there's no way Coach will allow me to step foot on the field. They're a tough team with a powerhouse of an offense. The thought of cooling my ass on the bench while Kwiatkowski takes my place makes me gut sick.

Beck clears his throat, drawing my attention to him. "So—"

"Don't even say it, man." I fall silent and rip off the remaining pads. It's like they're choking the life out of me. I've never felt that way before. I don't understand why I'm failing at something I've always excelled at. Always taken pleasure in.

"Say what?" he asks nonchalantly, continuing to strip off his clothes.

Even though it's uncomfortable, I admit through stiff lips, "That my game is off." For the first time since we've entered the locker room, I give Beck a bit of side-eye to get a read on his expression. It's just like I suspected. Concern mingled with confusion. Exactly what I don't want to deal with. I've always found it easier to suppress my feelings and shove them deep down inside where they can't see the light of day.

Keep it moving.

That's always been my motto.

Acknowledging the truth is like a sucker punch to the gut. Expected, but still a surprise.

It started out with a day. Just a momentary blip and then I was back on track. There wasn't anything to be concerned about. A few days later, I fumbled a play. It was a misstep. A mistake that, if made during crunch time, could cost us a win. It was all downhill from there. The mistakes have been piling up. Every practice has turned into a shitty one. Each time I step onto the turf, I give myself a pep talk, telling myself that this is the one that turns it around.

That hasn't happened.

By the time I'm walking off the field, I'm berating myself for yet another shit practice. For stupid mistakes that not even the most incompetent incoming freshman would make. For not having my head in the game where it belongs.

I do my best not to think about the reason this is happening. My hope is that if I ignore it long enough, it'll fix itself. That's what I've done all my life—ignored the bad shit and kept it moving and I've been just fine. So why isn't it working now? Why are the wheels falling off when I need them to stay put? This can't be how I go out.

It just can't be.

I need to get it figured out and fast before it becomes any more of a problem.

Beck shrugs, downplaying my plunging spiral. "Wasn't going to mention it."

I almost snort.

Yeah, right.

"Good," I say with a grunt. Unable to help myself, I shoot an anxious glance toward Coach's office. My voice drops before I reluctantly admit, "For once in his life, Baker is right. I'd better grab some lube. Coach is going to ream my ass."

Beck flicks his gaze toward the inner sanctum.

Nik Taylor is one of the toughest coaches you'll find in Division I football. He runs his program like a tight ship. If he's willing to give one hundred percent to his team, he expects his players to do the same in return. If you're not willing to bleed for the guys standing shoulder to shoulder with you on the field, there's no place for you on this roster. Even though I have no intention of entering the NFL draft, I still wanted to play for the best. With the best. Against the best.

Now I don't feel worthy of playing alongside these men. It's the worst fucking feeling in the world.

"Please," Beck snorts. "Baker is a bonehead. Don't listen to a word that comes out of his yap."

That might be true, but I have a hunch that he's spot-on about the lube.

Coach isn't going to put up with stupid mistakes on his field. I'm scared shitless that he's going to pull me. If Coach doesn't believe in me—a man I've played for my entire college career—how can I believe in myself?

"Look, bro," Beck continues, interrupting those depressing thoughts, "we all have off days. Don't stress about it."

I think by now, we both realize this is more than just an *off day*. It's a string of unfortunate events.

"Easier said than done," I mumble.

With nothing else to say, we silently strip off the rest of our gear before hitting the showers. Now that Coach has cloistered himself in his office, the locker room once again turns rowdy. Everyone has caught their second wind. Guys are talking about all the parties happening off-campus this weekend. The team has been at Wesley, practicing twice a day since the beginning of July. We've spent hundreds of hours running through plays on the field, lifting in the gym, scrimmaging, and watching game film. With the start up of school next week, this is the final hoorah. Everyone wants to cut loose and party their asses off before we have to buckle down for the season.

Once Beck hits the shower, I slump onto the bench with a huff and stare pensively at my hands. I just want to get this ass chewing over with and move on with my life. Best case scenario, this will be a pep talk. Worst case, Kwiatkowski is moving up in the world. A cold sweat breaks out across my brow at the possibility. A couple guys have already come and gone from the enclosed space and yet, I remain paralyzed on the bench.

"Get a move on it, bro," Beck prods, returning with a towel slung around his waist. "I got shit to take care of."

"Go on without me," I mutter. "I have a feeling this is gonna take a while."

Beck pulls on a pair of athletic shorts before shoving his feet into slides. "Does this have anything to do with Alyssa?"

"Fuck if I know." I drag a hand over my face not wanting to admit my suspicions to him.

There's a long pause before he says, "You could always try talking to her."

Ha! The only problem with that bit of advice is that I actually value my life and aren't looking to end it prematurely.

"Yeah, I don't know about that. It didn't go so well the first time." For fuck's sake, he was there. He witnessed the shitshow that ensued when I tried to make nice. At one point, I'd actually thought she might inflict bodily harm. "That girl could give Coach a run for his money in the ass reaming department."

One side of Beck's mouth hitches with reluctant humor.

"You heard her," I add, just in case he's a little slow on the uptake. "Alyssa wants nothing to do with me. In fact, she'd rather I not breathe the same air as her." I shake my head, chuckling grimly under my breath. "If Lys had her way, she'd rather I didn't breathe at all."

It's funny, I can't remember a time when Alyssa *wasn't* chasing after me. Throughout high school and then college. I'm sure I sound like a giant dick, but there was something comforting about the knowledge that she was waiting in the wings and only had eyes for me.

And now?

Now she wants nothing to do with me. If it were possible for her to smote me on the spot, she'd do it in a heartbeat, without a single thought or care. Then she'd step over my cold dead body on her way out the door.

Beck interrupts the whirl of those thoughts. "Can you blame the girl?"

Nope.

He knows how everything went down between us sophomore year.

Maybe sending a text message to breakup with her wasn't the smartest idea. Actually, there's no *maybe* about it. Alyssa had confessed her love, and I freaked out and cut her loose. At the very least, I should have sat her down and had an adult conversation. Instead, I'd taken the easy way out and it backfired in my face.

I focus on my clasped hands instead of meeting his curious stare.

"Nope, not at all." Only now, as the uncomfortable silence settles around us, do I realize the locker room has thinned out. Most of these guys are ready to get their weekend started. This is the last place they want to hang out.

Even though I don't want to give voice to the words, I'm powerless to stop them from escaping. "You going to Alyssa's party?"

Beck shrugs as guilt flickers in his gaze before it skitters away.

Why did I even bother to ask? Damn right, he's going. Beck has a major boner for Mia. And there's no damn way that she won't be at her best friend's party. So, yeah...Beck will be all over that. And technically, an invitation was issued.

"You could always crash the party," he says with a chuckle.

I snort out a laugh.

Can you even imagine?

It would only give Alyssa a chance to finish what she started the other day and that would be ripping off my balls and shoving them down my throat.

As appealing as that sounds—no, thanks. I like my balls exactly where they are and that's firmly attached to my body.

"Somehow I don't think that would go over well." The only thing my presence would accomplish is to piss Alyssa off even more than she already is. And I'm not sure that's the way to proceed in this situation.

Just like football, I need a little bit of time to figure out the best course of action.

"Have you considered giving her a gift she really wants?" When I raise a brow in question, Beck smirks. "Like your balls on a silver platter?"

I wad up my sweaty practice jersey and throw it at Beck's face. He bats it away before it can make contact.

"You're a dick," I laugh, my muscles loosening.

He grins and the thick tension that had been gathering strength like an impending storm dissipates. "Tell me something I don't know."

ALYSSA

"Welcome home, bitch," Mia shouts, attempting to be heard over the pulsing beat of techno as we clink our shots of Fireball and toss them back. The smooth liquor slides down my throat, warming me from the inside out.

"Holy shit, that's terrible!" my bestie sputters, coughing as tears gather in her dark eyes. "No more shots. I'm tapping out."

Undeterred by the pronouncement, I laugh and order another round. I'm nowhere near done. Everywhere I look, there are friends who have shown up to help celebrate my return to Wesley. I'll admit that while packing up my bags and preparing to leave London, part of me considered extending my student visa for another year, but in the end, I decided the best thing I could do was come home, finish out my degree, and graduate on time. Maybe, if I still feel the same way in the spring, I'll return.

And then there's Jack. Even though I'd taken everything at a glacial pace where he was concerned, it had just started to heat up between us. I'm not sure what will happen with that situation. Probably nothing. We're an ocean apart. It's difficult enough to maintain a relationship when I'm on the same continent with a guy, let alone a six-hour international flight away.

I glance at my best friend, the girl who planned out this amazing night, and realize that coming home was the right decision. Even though I made some amazing friends—ones who will be in my life forever—I'd missed my bestie something fierce. We've been friends for as long as I can remember. There's a history between us that can't be denied or erased. I was there when her sister died and the hard times her family went through. She's been the shoulder I leaned on when I broke my ankle freshman year of high school and wondered if dancing would ever be the same. She was there when I struggled through math courses in high school and college.

We've have one last year together before our lives truly begin and we end up heading in different directions. I'm both excited and scared by the prospect. Above all, I'm glad Mia is by my side.

I have no idea what I would do without her.

Luckily, I'll never have to find out.

My gaze runs over the length of her. She looks smoking hot in a black dress that hugs every single curve. Unlike me, the girl has an hourglass figure. Tonight is all about showcasing it. Maybe I had to twist her arm, but it was well worth it.

The drinks have already gone to my head and I'm in my element. When the music changes and the bass starts thumping, reverberating off the walls, I squeal and grab Mia's hand, dragging her to the dance floor. "I freaking love this song!"

This night is all about fun. I want to let go and enjoy the drinks, music, and good friends who have come out to celebrate my return. I shove my way through the press of writhing bodies before carving out a tiny space for us. My hands go in the air as I lose myself in the beat. It's not difficult. The DJ has some serious skills. Each song bleeds into the next as we shake our asses, singing along with the lyrics. Mia grabs my hand and twirls me around. A smile stretches across my face as I laugh, enjoying myself like I haven't in a long time. Friends come and go as the music plays on.

I have no idea how long we stay out on the dance floor. The only way I realize that time has passed is when I become parched. I close the distance between us and shout, "I need to use the bathroom."

Her cheeks are pinkened from all our exertion, but I can tell she's having a blast. Sometimes Mia has a hard time cutting loose. She wants to be the perfect kid and student, forever walking the straight and narrow. It's good for her to let go and just have fun. She needs it. "Want me to come with you?"

"Nah." With a shake of my head, I wave her off. "I'll be back in a sec, stay here so I can find you again."

A strobe light of color bounces off the walls as I push my way through the thick crowd. I catch flashes of people I know and wave as I continue on my way. It turns out to be a five-minute wait for the restroom. I chat with a few friends in line and catch up on their lives. Once inside, I do my business and touch up my lip gloss before fluffing my hair. It's long and loose, floating around my shoulders. I probably should have put it up with all the ass shaking I'm doing, but I'm having way too much fun to give a damn.

On the way back to the dance floor, I detour to the long stretch of bar for another drink. I'm dying of thirst. If I were smart, I'd get an icy cold bottle of water and hydrate. But tonight, I'm not going to be smart. I'm going to suck down as many drinks as I want and keep the party going to the wee hours of the morning.

As I shoulder my way through the throng, I prop my elbows on the smooth surface and catch the eye of a smoking hot bartender mixing cocktails with the precision of a professional. His hair is inky black in the dim lighting and his eyes are dark, almost onyx in color. He must feel my perusal because he glances in my direction and flashes me an easy smile before handing over two green glass bottles of beer and making his way toward me.

The closer he gets, the sexier I realize he is. Physically, he ticks all the boxes.

Tall—*check*.

Easy on the eyes—*check*.

Large hands—*check*.

Knows how to make a cocktail—*check*.

This guy is perfect one-night stand material. And with his dark hair and eyes, he doesn't remind me of—

Nope. Not even going to go there.

I refuse to let him ruin my night.

The sexy bartender lays his palms on the counter before leaning toward me. "What can I get for you, birthday girl?"

His voice is deep and smooth. A little shiver careens down my spine. It's another check.

I can't resist dropping my gaze to the hands spread wide a few inches from where I stand.

If I'm going to bag him and tag him, I need to play this right. I know how it works in a place like this. Girls are probably throwing themselves at him all night long. I need to stand out. Make it worth his wild.

"Birthday girl?" I raise a brow, wondering if he's confused me with another chick. There are certainly a ton of them here. If that's the case, it doesn't bode well for me.

"Sure. People have been buying you shots all night long." A beguiling set of dimples flash as he grins. "Props to you. I'm surprised you're still standing. You must have one hell of a tolerance."

"Oh." I laugh and shake my head, realizing that he's been eyeing me for a while. That definitely makes things easier. "It's not my birthday. Just a little celebration for my return. I was away last year."

"Huh." His dark eyes sparkle. "Well then, welcome home."

"Thank you." I twist a curl around my finger and angle my body to give him a good look at what I have to offer.

"Sounds like it's my turn to buy you a shot."

"No more shots," a deep voice grumbles, interrupting our conversation. All my flirty vibes evaporate in the blink of an eye. "Although, she'll take a bottle of water."

I stiffen and swing around. Even though I know exactly who'll I'll find standing beside me, it's still a surprise when my gaze collides with bright blue ones. A shiver of awareness scuttles down my spine at his proximity.

The last time I saw him outside our apartment building, I was too furious to take him in and notice all the little changes a year of separation has wrought. As much as I'm loath to admit it, Colton looks better than ever. The maroon T-shirt he's wearing hugs his biceps before stretching tautly across his chest. Somehow, his shoulders are even broader than they were a year ago. My mouth dries as an avalanche of memories crash over me. I remember what it felt like to slide my fingers across all that steely strength. I tighten my hands so that I don't reach out and touch him.

What the hell am I doing?

It takes effort to jolt myself out of those insidious thoughts. For as long as I can remember, Colton has had this kind of effect on me. I lose all conscious thought when he's near. I'd hoped my year spent in London would help me to forget about him—or, at the very least, get over him—but that doesn't seem to be the case.

When it comes to Colton Montgomery, my heart and body have a mind of their own. With punishing force, I crush the fragile emotions attempting to take root inside me.

Never again.

I will never willingly give my heart to another man who is unable to hold it carefully in his hands.

You know that saying—when someone shows you who they are, believe them?

Yeah...I need to take that more seriously.

Fool me once, shame on you.

Fool me twice and I deserve everything I get for being a dumb ass.

I'll be damned if I allow Colton to ruin this night for me. He no longer has a place in my life. He made sure of that when he dumped my ass and walked away.

"You don't get to tell me what to do," I snap before turning my full attention to the guy behind the long stretch of counter. The hunky bartender's gaze bounces cautiously between us.

I grit my teeth, hoping my ex-boyfriend will slink off and stop trying to cock block me.

"Hey, Shane," Colton says. "How's the knee holding up?"

"It's better. Had surgery on it in May and have been rehabbing it ever since." He adds, "Pretty sure my football days are over."

"That sucks, man."

I press my lips together until they feel bloodless as Colton commiserates with my potential one-night stand. Although, the chances of that now occurring have dwindled into the single digits.

Hunky bartender shrugs. "It is what it is."

"Truth," Colton agrees.

This is the point where I wonder if they'll take a moment of silence for Shane's knee.

Instead, the bartender slants a tentative look in my direction. "Is she with you?"

I open my mouth to tell him that I'm my own person and can answer that question for myself when Colton beats me to the punch.

"Yup."

Is he being serious right now?

We aren't together.

We will never be together again.

"Got it." Hunky bartender doesn't bother to spare me another glance. All flirty banter has now ceased. "One bottle of water coming right up."

My mouth hangs open. Before I can gather my wits, a bottle is placed in front of me and then he's moving on to greener pastures. Or, in his case, readily available one-night stands. All possibility of losing myself in him tonight have been blown to shit by my ex.

The big jerk.

Anger bubbles up inside me like a geyser.

Who the hell does he think he is? He can't just saunter in and ruin all my plans for the evening. He wasn't even invited here! It's a struggle to keep all of my emotions in check. The last thing I want is to lose my shit and create yet another spectacle.

Been there, done that.

A few apartment residents still give me side eye when our paths cross in the lobby or elevator. I've now been dubbed the psycho chick who should be avoided at all costs.

When I finally have a thin veneer of civility in place, I growl, "What are you doing here?"

Colton shifts his stance, angling closer. Too close for comfort. "I came to see you."

"Why?" Why would he bother? Didn't I make myself perfectly clear the other day?

"I hate how things were the last time we ran into each other. I don't want it to be like that between us."

A gurgle of disbelief bubbles up in my throat as my eyes widen. "Did you really think it would be any different?"

Guilt flickers across his expression before he plows his fingers through his blond hair. "I don't know. Maybe I'd hoped that enough time had passed, and we could start over. Maybe even be friends."

You know what I think?

That he's lost his damn mind. A year isn't nearly enough time to dull the pain he carelessly inflicted. I had loved him with all my heart, and he'd stomped it to smithereens as if I hadn't meant anything to him. The truth is that I probably hadn't. Him settling down had been an experiment. An epic failure, at that.

Why bother pretending? So he can feel better about himself?

No, thanks.

Hard pass.

"You and I will *never* be friends." Needing distance between us, I take a hasty step away. I'm not usually one to retreat from a skirmish, but in this instance, it's all about self-preservation. I'm making a tactical decision. The sooner I get away from Colton, the better off I'll be. The sight of him dredges up unwanted emotions inside me.

That's the last thing I need.

Just as a breath of relief slips from me, Colton's hand shoots out. His fingers wrap around my forearm, halting me in my tracks, making escape impossible. His touch sends a jolt of electricity sizzling through my veins.

There used to be a time when I melted beneath his hands. Honestly, all he had to do was flick those gorgeous blue eyes my way and my insides turned to jelly. It takes every ounce of resolve to fight the attraction and remain strong. Even though I'm trembling inside,

I'll be damned if I give him the satisfaction of seeing how easily he's able to affect me.

Still.

Still!

It's disheartening.

Colton's tongue darts out to moisten his lips and my core clenches in response. Do you have any idea the amount of pleasure he's capable of giving with that mouth? My guess is that he took the year I was gone to further hone those skills.

That disturbing thought is like a bucket of frigid water dumped all over my libido.

"Lys, please?" He tilts his head, gaze boring into mine. "Can't we hash this out?" He tugs me closer, reeling me to him. "Maybe come to an understanding we can both live with?"

No.

Absolutely not.

After the way he threw our relationship away like dirty Kleenex, it's demoralizing to realize how much I still want him. I need to cut this off at the knees. I'm all to aware that conversation has the potential to lead to other things and I can't take a chance of getting sucked back into his orbit. "There's nothing for us to discuss. You broke up with me sophomore year." I throw in a careless shrug, wanting him to think that I'm indifferent. "We've both moved on."

If only that were true.

Emotion flares in his eyes. He pulls me so close that I have to crane my neck in order to meet his gaze. "You sure about that?" Tension ratches up in the air. "Because it kind of feels like there might be unfinished business between us."

"There is absolutely nothing between us." I gulp down the rising emotion attempting to break loose. "You made damned sure of that."

A soft puff of breath leaves his lips as sorrow fills his eyes. "I'm sorry, Lys. I got scared and hurt the one person I shouldn't have."

No.

No, no, no.

I refuse to listen to his bullshit excuses. More than that, I won't allow him to burrow beneath my skin again. He had his chance, and he blew it. Spectacularly.

It takes all of my strength to twist out of his hold. Relief floods through me when his hand falls away, plummeting back to his side. Mindful that he could spring forward and detain me at any moment, I take a tentative step in retreat. When he remains still, eyes locked on me, I take another. And then a third. The more distance I'm able to put between us, the better I feel.

"It doesn't matter. None of it does." Even though my whispered words are drown out by the music and chatter that surrounds us, I know he hears them.

Before he can take up any more of my time, I swing away, shoving my way through the press of bodies. I need to get as far from Colton Montgomery as possible.

But will it be enough?

Somehow, I don't think so.

COLTON

That went the way I expected it to.

Right down the tubes.

Although, she didn't lose her shit like the other day, so I guess that's progress.

If I had any brains at all, I'd chalk this endeavor up as a lost cause and cut my losses before I can make matters worse. Hell, had I been thinking clearly, I wouldn't have shown up in the first place. I'd leave the past where it belongs and allow Alyssa to move on with her life which is what she keeps insisting she wants to do.

But I can't. Not when I sense that buried beneath all the hurt and anger are emotions fighting to break free. Until I make sure that there's nothing I can do to rectify the situation, I can't move on.

Decision made, I hang out at the bar. Shane keeps me well stocked with water. As tempting as it is to guzzle down half a dozen beers, or a few shots, I've become enough of a shitshow without inviting more problems.

Two hours later, Alyssa is still on the dance floor, shaking her ass for all it's worth. I'm barely able to take my eyes off her. She's mesmerizing. That girl has enough moves to give a corpse major wood. The lights flicker and the music continues to pump as she rolls her hips and lifts her hair with slim hands as if putting on a private dance.

Although, it sure as fuck isn't for me.

I drag a hand over my face. It's killing me to watch her out there. And yet, looking away isn't a possibility. I'm all but starving for the sight of her. Every time an asshole slides in front of her, I have to grit my teeth and talk myself out of stalking over there and ripping her away. I've lost track of how many shots she's tossed back, but it's a lot. Too much. It's a surprise that she's still able to stand upright, let alone twerk in that tiny silver dress that barely covers her ass.

Alyssa hasn't glanced at me once since stalking away. It's like I don't exist. At this point, I'm not sure there's anything I can say or do mitigate the damage I've inflicted. A pit settles at the bottom of my gut at the realization that I might not be able to fix the damage I so needlessly inflicted.

"You want another?" There's a pause. "Although, I'll be straight with you, man—you have anything more and I'm gonna have to take your keys away. I can't allow you to drive home in your inebriated condition."

I snort out something that barely passes for a laugh. "Nah, I'm good."

Shane leans against the bar as his gaze cuts through the crowd to Alyssa. Her blond head is like a halo glowing under the strobe lights. I pull my gaze away and glance around. Unfortunately, I'm not the only one who has noticed. Dudes are circling her like hungry sharks.

"How long have you two crazy kids been together?" he asks, cutting into my thoughts.

Instead of admitting the truth, I narrow my eyes and glare. "Long enough."

Shane played football until an ACL injury took him out last season. He's always been a fan favorite with the ladies. As much as we're friends and teammates, I'm not an idiot. The interest was apparent in his eyes when they were talking earlier.

He nods toward the dance floor. "You sure she knows that?"

"It's complicated," I grumble, not wanting him to get any ideas.

Although, by the looks of it, it's much too late for that. I don't want to knock them from his head, but I will if I have to.

"It always is, brother."

Before I have a chance to respond, he takes off, heading down to the opposite end of the bar to help a customer.

Alyssa's friends come and go. There's dancing and more shots. I caught sight of Beck earlier in the evening but now, he's nowhere to be seen. I glance around and realize Mia is also missing from action.

Hmmm. Interesting.

An hour and two more bottles of water later, Alyssa hugs a few girls and gives them a quick wave. A cheerful light fills her eyes as a smile stretches lazily across her face. She looks pleasantly buzzed as she saunters past the bar. Her feet grind to a halt as her gaze collides with mine and all the lightheartedness filling her expression dissolves. The edges of her pink slicked lips sink into a frown as her brows jerk together. "You're still here?"

I straighten to my full height before closing the distance between us. Alyssa might be tall, but I've got a good eight inches on her. The closer I get, the more she lifts her chin to maintain eye contact. "I didn't want to leave you alone. I wasn't sure how you were getting home." And it sure as shit wasn't going to be with another dude.

"I'm hardly alone." She waves toward the people still filling the club. "So, feel free to take off."

I shake my head. "I'll head out when you do."

A puff of exasperated breath escapes from her lungs. "Then you can go now because I'm leaving."

The physical pull is more than I can withstand, and I take another step in her direction. We're so close that I could reach out and yank her into my arms. The temptation to do that pounds through me like a steady drumbeat. Except I know how it'll end. And that's not well. It'll only piss her off more than she already is. "I'll take you home." I just want to get her into my car and away from all these guys still scoping her out.

"No, thanks." She searches the crowd for an alternative. "I'd rather Uber it home."

Sorry, that's not happening.

"We're headed to the same place. It's a ten-minute drive. I think you can withstand that much time alone with me."

"Wanna bet?" When she attempts to slip past me, I mirror the movement, and block her escape.

Anger sparks to life in her eyes, banishing the mellowness that had been filling them minutes ago. "Get out of my way, Colton."

"We can do this the easy way or the hard way. It's your choice." Unfortunately, I can already tell how this is going to play out. I'm still holding out a glimmer of hope that she'll surprise me and make it easy on the both of us.

Her lips form into a snarl. "You're out of your damn mind if you think I'm going anywhere with you! I'd rather—"

"The hard way it is," I say with resignation, stepping closer before hunkering down and hoisting her up. She grunts as my shoulder connects with her midsection.

For one blissful moment, she's silent as her slender body hangs stiffly over mine. Knowing the surprise will wear off quickly, I hightail it to the exit. Two steps later, all hell breaks loose.

"*Colton Davidson Montgomery!*" She pounds on my back, trying her damnedest to inflict as much pain as possible with her fists. "Put me down this instant or I'll scream my head off!"

Thankfully, the club is dark, and the music is still pumping around us. Other than a few drunken glances speared in our direction, no one pays us much attention as I stride toward the door.

Which is for the best.

This would be a difficult situation to explain.

The second I hit the paved lot, I beeline toward my BMW parked a couple rows back.

"Goddamn it! You have no right to kidnap me!" Even though she continues to pound her fists against my back, she's not inflicting any real damage. Hell, the hits I take in practice are worse than this. The best-case scenario is that she's releasing all of her bottled-up frustration.

When she wiggles against my shoulder, nearly falling off, I smack her ass with the flat of my hand. "Stay still before you hurt yourself."

"Ow!" She sucks in a sharp, disbelieving breath. "You son of a bitch!"

"Then stop fighting me. All I'm trying to do is take you home."

"I don't wan to go anywhere with you! I can find my own way home!"

With one hand holding her in place, I reach into the front pocket of my jeans and grab my keys before hitting the button on the fob.

Now comes the tricky part. How to maneuver Alyssa into the vehicle without her fighting me and possibly getting hurt. I yank open the door and lower myself down until her high heels scrape against the pavement. With my breath wedged in my lungs, I release her before straightening to my full height. My gaze stays locked on her. It wouldn't surprise me if she tried running—even in those heels—or punched me in the face.

A gentle breeze slides through the riotous tangle of her blonde hair, blowing it around her shoulders as a wild light flashes in her eyes. Her hands bunch impotently at her sides. She's gorgeous in all her towering rage. Even though it's totally perverse, my cock stiffens to half-mast.

The slinky silver dress clings to every slender curve. Barely does it hit mid-thigh. I'm sure if she bent over, I'd catch a glimpse of her panties.

And she better damn well be wearing panties.

"How dare you!" she growls. The words are low and menacing as her body shakes with barely contained anger. "You have no right to pick me up and cart me out of a club like a sack of potatoes." Her gaze arrows to the two-story brick building across the parking lot.

Her face is so easy to read. Every thought flickering across it for me to see.

"Don't even think about it," I tell her. "You won't get far." There's a pause as I tilt my head. "Unless you're looking for me to lay hands on you again."

She gnashes her teeth before baring them like a rabid animal. *"I hate you!"*

All of the sexual tension simmering in the air between us dissipates. "I know, Lys. There's nothing else I can say other than I'm sorry."

Wetness pricks her eyes. Instead of allowing the tears to fall, they pool in her blue depths, shimmering like crystals in the darkness.

That's all it takes for my heart to crack wide open.

"I don't give a fuck about your apologies," she whispers. "You can shove them right up your ass for all I care."

As she takes a hasty step in retreat, her heel hits a crack in the asphalt and her eyes flare wide as she falters. When her arms pinwheel, I spring forward, wrapping my fingers around her shoulders in an attempt to steady her.

Our gazes collide.

I gulp. "Are you all right?"

She shakes her head. "No." Before I can ask what's wrong, she continues, "Do you have any idea how much you've hurt me?"

My throat closes up until it feels like I can't breathe.

When I remain silent, she continues, "Any at all?"

The pain that seeps into her vivid blue depths is enough to kill me. "Yeah, I do. I wish it were possible to go back and change everything about the way we ended." The truth is that I wish I hadn't ended it at all.

"That's not possible. You can't change the past. You can only put it to rest and move on and that's what I've done."

"I don't believe that." More like I don't want to believe it. "I think you still want me."

Just like I still want her.

My gaze drops to her mouth. Those pouty lips that were made for all kinds of sin. I miss kissing them. I miss them wrapped around my cock as she stared up at me from her knees. Even dredging up the memories makes me throb with need.

It's as if she can sense the thoughts running rampant through my head. "Don't."

Her tongue darts out to smudge her lips. Everything in me tightens as I lower my face to hers. We're so close that I can feel her warm breath drift over me. It only drives the fierce need I've always had for her.

"Don't what?" I murmur, ghosting my lips over her soft ones. It takes every ounce of self-control not to close the distance between us and take what I want.

"Kiss me."

"Why not?"

She tilts her head toward mine almost as if angling it to give me better access. "Because...I don't want it."

Losing the battle with myself, I nip at her lower lip before sucking the fullness into my mouth. A whimper escapes as I tug her against me until her breasts are smashed against my chest. A sultry taste that is distinctly hers explodes on my tongue. After all the time and distance that I forced between us, to have her this close is like a wave crashing over me, dragging me to the bottom of the ocean. I'm drowning in the taste and feel of her and I don't care. I don't care if I ever make it to the surface again.

Even though it goes against every single impulse pounding through me, I pull away enough to say, "Are you sure about that?"

ALYSSA

Why is it that when he lays hands on me, all rational thought falls to the wayside? Colton Montgomery has been my Kryptonite for as long as I can remember. It's disheartening to realize that nothing has changed in that regard. No matter how strong I think I am, this is all it takes for me to crumble.

His hands coasting over me, singeing my flesh. His mouth...

A shiver works its way through me.

I've kissed a handful of boys since our breakup and none had the capacity to make me feel like this. Not one of them made me forget myself. Not a single person made me feel as if I would shrivel up and die if they didn't take my mouth with theirs.

But that's exactly the way it is with Colton.

It's disheartening to realize that a year and a half of separation did nothing to lessen the attraction that churns within me. I want him now as much as I ever did. And I have no idea how to change that. How to kill the feelings still simmering beneath the surface.

"Tell me to stop," he growls against my lips. "If that's what you want, you need to say the words."

My lungs fill with air as my head swirls from a potent concoction of Colton infused alcohol. It's dizzying. I open my mouth to tell him exactly that, but the words die a quick death on my tongue, refusing to be summoned.

I need him to step away and give me a little bit of breathing room so rational thought can once again prevail. When he's this close, corrupting every sense, sending every nerve ending into chaos, it's impossible to think straight.

My guess is that he won't give me the time or distance to find my bearings and come to my senses.

In fact, I know he won't.

Not unless I demand it of him.

And...I'm unable to do that.

After nearly a year and a half of separation, not only do I secretly crave his touch, I need it. With a groan, I tilt my face toward his. That's all the indicator he needs to proceed. His hands slide from my shoulders to my face where they cup my cheeks. His thumb slowly strokes over my lower lip before his mouth slants over mine. One sweep of his tongue across the seam of my lips is all it takes for me to open. His tongue slips easily inside to mingle with my own. The first taste of him has fireworks exploding inside my head before sinking like a heavy stone to my core.

One kiss and it feels like I could self-combust from the pent-up desire simmering beneath the surface for all this time.

"You have no idea how much I missed this," he mutters against me.

Oh, but I do because I feel the same.

His fingers disappear from my face, slipping over the tops of my shoulders, grazing my arms and ribcage, before settling on my ass. He cups each cheek in the palm of his hands before squeezing them as if testing the weight and feel of them. Electricity sizzles through me at the contact. A groan bubbles up inside me, fighting to break free.

I haven't felt this turned on since...

Well, since Colton.

And that is all kinds of depressing.

As much as I know that this will end badly, the knowledge isn't nearly enough for me to push him away. It's nothing more than a fleeting thought. Here and gone before I can fully grasp it.

Or act on it.

I'm so caught up in the feel of his hands and mouth wreaking havoc on my body that I don't immediately realize he's turned me around and walked me backward until my spine hits the shiny metal of his BMW. He pins me in place. The thick length of his erection digging into my belly, leaving me to gasp for breath. I remember all too well what it felt like to have Colton driving deep inside my heat. The mere thought is enough to weaken my knees. If he weren't pressed against me, I'd fall to the ground before melting into a puddle of goo.

How can something so bad feel so damn good?

He nips at my mouth before drawing away. Without thinking, my fingers dig into his T-shirt, attempting to drag him to me. Instead of backing away and giving me the distance I so desperately need, his mouth hovers over my ear, ghosting over the curve of it. Shivers scamper down my spine before he sucks the lobe into his mouth. His teeth sink into the soft flesh and a whimper of need escapes from me.

The fire he ignited in my core bursts into flames as his lips caress their way down the column of my neck. Sucking and licking at my sensitive flesh, drawing it into his mouth and feasting on it. His mouth singes a hot trail across my collarbone before nipping at the tops of my breasts. My chest rises and falls in rapid succession as his hands sweep along my sides before settling on the gentle swells. With a flick of his gaze, he tugs at the slinky material until one breast is bared to the warm night air that swirls around us.

A deep groan rumbles up from his throat as his mouth fastens onto my nipple. Not once do I consider the possibility that anyone could exit the club and spot us.

How can I when Colton is attacking every single one of my senses?

I tilt my head toward the bright star-filled sky and allow the pleasure to crash over me like a tidal wave. Once he's licked and sucked at one tiny bud, he pulls the material up and covers me before lowering the other side and showering it with the same ardent attention.

"I fucking love your tits."

His words echo in my head.

This isn't the first time he's claimed this. I always laughed when he made the declaration because let's face it, my breasts are fairly non-existent. Wesley's campus is overflowing with girls who are, well...overflowing in that department. But Colton never seemed to mind. When we were in bed, he spent hours worshipping them. And I loved it. They might be small, but they're incredibly sensitive and easily stimulated.

I have no idea how much time elapses before he lifts his mouth from me and slides the material back into place before popping to his feet and pressing his muscular body against mine.

"I've missed you, Lys."

The deep rasp of his voice as he calls me by the nickname makes me melt. It always has. But especially now with his hands all over my body. Other than Mia, he's the only one who calls me that.

"I've missed this," he adds, his mouth descending. As he pushes into me, forcing me to flatten against the metal of the vehicle, my spine curves. Each vertebra bends under his strength. His fingers lock around my wrists before dragging them upward, over my head, and pinning them to the roof. I'm so cognizant of his thick erection digging into me. Of my breasts pressed beneath the steel of his chest. I'm overwhelmed by his presence.

More than anything, I wish I didn't like the dominance, but I do.

So much.

Just because I can be assertive and know what I want, doesn't mean that I don't enjoy submitting and made to feel as if I've been rendered powerless. To have my senses eclipsed by physical strength wielded in a manner that isn't an attack but one that makes me feel emboldened by my own sexuality. It's nothing more than an illusion. A trick of the imagination. It requires a man to walk a fine line and Colton knows exactly how to do it.

And that, like everything else he does, is a turn-on.

As much as I hate to admit it, there were too many nights since our breakup when I laid awake in my bed, unable to find sleep, as thoughts of him swirled unbidden through my head. The way he touched me. Stroking my flesh to life. Sliding deep inside my heat until there was no choice but to shudder with orgasm. Inevitably, my fingers would slip beneath the elastic band of my panties before stroking my lower lips and circling my clit until I was gasping out his name.

Every time I caved to the temptation, I told myself that it was because I would never feel Colton's touch again. He was like a ghostly specter hovering over me, dredging up painful yet delicious memories. Which is precisely why this feels more like a dream than anything else. Tomorrow morning, I'll be chalk-full of regrets and recriminations but tonight?

Tonight, I'm going to blot out common sense and enjoy this experience to the fullest.

By the time he pulls away to nip at my chin with sharp teeth, my lips feel bruised and swollen. As loath as I am to admit it, Jack's kisses were *nothing* like this. They didn't stir anything beneath the surface. They were a pleasant distraction I'd hoped would grow into something more. As soon as that thought bursts into my brain, I force it away.

Jack is sweet, kind, and nice. He's one of the most caring and considerate people I've ever met. We built a solid base of friendship before it grew into something more. And even then, when it turned romantic, I insisted on taking my time and easing into a relationship. But we never generated this kind of...

Combustible energy that feels like it has the potential to destroy everything in its path.

That's exactly how it feels when I'm with Colton. There's no other way to describe it.

He's all I can see.

All I'm able to think about.

It's addictive.

It's the rough scrape of hands sliding beneath the hem of my dress as it rides up my thighs that grounds me in the here and now. The tips of his fingers dance across my flesh, inching their way beneath the fabric. Air gets trapped in my throat when they stroke over my panties, grazing my lower lips.

The warm August air wafting over my flushed cheeks isn't nearly enough to cool them. I'm not sure if anything can extinguish the heat that has exploded to life in my core. As he drops to a crouch in front of me, I know exactly how this scenario will play out. I also know that I'm not going to prevent it from happening. I don't have that kind of strength. If I'm being completely honest with myself, I don't want to stop it.

I want him.

And I want this.

I'll deal with the ramifications of my stupidity tomorrow.

Colton's hands slide upward, lifting the dress with them until my panties are exposed to him. He leans forward, brushing a soft kiss against the cotton. His fingers hook into the elastic band on each side of my hips before dragging the fabric down my thighs, past my knees, until it's stretched taut between my ankles. I expel a shaky breath from my lungs as anticipation coils like a spring deep in the pit of my gut.

Actually, the excitement unfurling inside me is much lower.

It's carefully that he lifts one foot, removing the scrap of material serving as protection before repeating the movement with the other side. Silently he pockets the panties in his jeans.

His face hovers no more than six inches from the heat of my core. Every inhale has him breathing me in before exhaling a warm puff of air against my bared flesh. A thick shudder works its way through me as his gaze stays focused on me.

"You're so fucking beautiful," he rasps.

My heart jackhammers a painful staccato against my ribcage. My gaze stays locked on him, watching every move, taking in every detail about this moment. Wanting to etch it into my memory so that I'll be able to take it out anytime I want to revisit it.

Time stretches between us until it becomes almost unbearable. I shift restlessly beneath his hands. When he finally leans forward, I expect him to attack in much the same manner he did a handful of minutes ago, devouring me in one hungry gulp. Instead, he buries his nose against me before inhaling deeply. It's as if he's trying to breathe in my very essence.

My soul.

"No matter how much pussy I attempted to lose myself in after we broke up, it was never you."

My breath hitches at the admittance.

Slowly, gently, as if we have all the time in the world, as is we're not standing in the back of a crowded parking lot, he rubs his face against me. The slight stubble on his cheeks abrades my delicate flesh, releasing a thousand tiny shivers inside the confines of my belly.

My spine arches as I give in to the feeling he has created deep inside me. The havoc he's wreaking on me.

Just when I don't think I can take another moment of this sweet torture, his lips press against me. My skin is so over sensitized and achy, I want to scream with the storm brewing inside me, pushing to the surface. The first flick of his velvety softness sends me soaring and I groan, my head rolling back as my eyes shutter so I can focus on his touch.

He draws one plump lip between his teeth and nibbles at it before repeating the maneuver on the other side. His tongue thrusts into my throbbing heat, falling into a devasting rhythm. Just when I begin to spiral, he backs off, allowing his soft breath to drift over me as if trying to cool my lust. Before I can utter a word, he circles my clit with his tongue, pushing me relentlessly toward orgasm.

I'm moments away from splintering apart when he eases back for a second time. Frustration explodes inside me. I can't take much more of his teasing. My fingers curl with the need to claw at him, to pull him against me and finish what he started. I open my mouth to protest when he lifts one heeled foot from the ground and plants it on his shoulder so that I'm spread impossibly wide. Even though the night air is warm, it cools my damp flesh, and a shudder works its way through me at the erotic image we must make.

"Fucking gorgeous." As he presses forward, my leg bends, opening me even more. Exposing every pink delicate inch of me for him to feast upon.

And he does.

The first swipe of his tongue nearly sends me hurtling over the edge of insanity. My fingers tangle in his hair to hold him in place as he nibbles at me. With his face buried against my heat, he pushes me relentlessly toward orgasm until I have no choice but to hurtle over the edge.

Stars explode behind my eyelids as my heart beats wildly. Wave after wave crashes over me, threatening to suck me under. If I die like this, I would have zero regrets. My pussy continues to throb against him as he focuses on my clit. A moan threatens to break free. I have to pin my lower lip with my teeth to keep all the sound buried deep inside where it belongs.

It's only after Colton has wrung every last drop of pleasure from me does he rise to his feet and press his body against mine. If he didn't, I would slide to the pavement. My bones feel limp. My mind slightly dazed.

"You're even more delicious than I remember. I've missed your sweet taste."

With that, his lips slant over mine and I find myself lost in a sea of turbulent emotion.

ALYSSA

 groan escapes as I roll onto my side. The motion has my head throbbing to life behind my eyelids.

Correction—my entire body throbs to life.

What the hell went down last night?

It takes a moment to jumpstart my brain.

Ah, that's right...welcome home party at Bang Bang. That much, I remember. And shots. My God, the shots. What the hell had I been thinking?

Apparently, I hadn't been.

I crack open an eye and glance around.

Thankfully, I'm in my own bedroom. That's a relief. I remember getting flirty with one of the bartenders. And dancing. The music had been on point. One amazing song after another.

And wait a minute...

My brow furrows.

Colton. The party crasher. He'd put the kibosh on any possible fun with the hunky bartender, which had been annoying. If only I could have ignored his presence, but that's never been an option. Even though I'd spent the night dancing, I had been acutely aware of his brooding presence at the bar. From the corner of my eye, I watched him stare at me with a single mindedness that had shivers careening down my spine.

Does that mean I made sure to put on a show so that he could see exactly what he was missing?

Damn right I did.

Guess I pushed it too far because I remember him hoisting me over his shoulder and carrying me out of the club caveman-style.

If only I hadn't put up a fight. Maybe then, everything smoldering in the air between us wouldn't have detonated the way it did.

A groan of embarrassment slips free.

Oh my God! Did I really let him go down on me in the parking lot?

Yeah. Yeah, I did.

I search the murky depths of my brain. I don't remember anyone stumbling across us but let's face it, I was out of my mind. There could have been a full-on crowd cheering us on and I wouldn't have been cognizant of it.

Even thinking about the orgasm that had streaked through me is enough to make me throb to life with painful awareness.

Oh, the horror of it all.

I grab my pillow and drag it over my head before letting loose a scream. I've done exactly what I said that I wouldn't. I allowed Colton Montgomery to lay his hands on me.

Needing to escape from the onslaught of memories that continue to flood into my brain, I throw off the covers and ease my way from the bed before staggering out of my room. I make it a few steps into the short hallway before spotting Mia as she shovels a spoonful of cereal into her mouth. She looks none to worse for the wear which is the opposite of me. I feel like a steaming bag of dog shit some derelict teenager lit on fire.

Bitch.

I lift my hand to my hair and realize that it's sticking up from every conceivable angle. And I didn't bother washing off my makeup last night. I probably bear a striking resemblance to a rabid raccoon.

"Hey," she chirps, spoon paused midway in the air, "how are you feeling?"

"Stop shouting," I wince before grabbing my head so that it doesn't roll off my shoulders. "Please, I beg of you."

"That good, hmm?" A smile simmers across her lips as a teasing light enters her eyes. "Let me guess, you're looking for a little hair of the dog that bit you?" There's a pause. "I'm sure we have a bottle of tequila around here somewhere. Want me to get it?"

"God, no." Even the thought is enough to make my stomach heave. "I'm never drinking again."

Mia snickers as if she doesn't believe me. Hell, I'm not even sure *I* believe me but with the way I'm currently feeling, it seems like an excellent idea moving forward.

Once my belly stops spasming, I point to the kitchen. "I need massive amounts of Tylenol and Gatorade.

I stagger into the other room before returning with a humongous bottle of the orange sports drink. My fingers tremble as I fumble with the cap.

"Why did you let me drink so much," I accuse, successfully prying off the top and chugging a quarter of it.

Oh God.

Instead of settling my gut, it only makes it churn even more. I press my fingers against my mouth before releasing a loud belch.

"If memory serves, I told you several times to slow down, but you weren't in the mood to listen. At one point, you called me a buzzkill." Leave it to Mia to throw that in my face. When I fail to respond, she asks, "Exactly how many shots did you have?"

"I lost count after eight." That thought is enough to make me sick. I shake my head to clear it before frantically waving a hand. "Please, I can't even think about that. It'll make me sick. Never mind, I'm already sick." Getting up was a mistake. I point to my room. "I'm going back to bed. Wake me up tomorrow. Or maybe the day after that. Hopefully, I'll have bounced back by then."

I stagger a few steps when an image materializes in my mind and I swing around to face Mia. As I do, my head spins. Damn, but this is seriously miserable. With my free hand, I grab my head. "Wait a minute. Were you busting a move on the dance floor with Beck or was that a tequila-induced dream?"

Because at this point, anything is possible.

With a wince, she quickly averts her eyes. But not before I catch the guilt that flickers in their dark depths. Instead of answering, she busies herself by shoving another spoonful of cereal into her mouth.

Huh. Well, isn't this a rather interesting turn of events.

Seconds tick by without a response. My hangover dissipates just a bit as I take another step and jab a finger in her direction. I wrack my brain for anything more. The images are fleeting and blurred at the edges, but there's no way they're a figment of my drunken imagination. "Yeah," I pipe up, instantly warming to the subject, "you two were *definitely* dancing. His hands were all over you. And you, *ya little hussy,* were totally enjoying it."

Her face goes up in flames as she squirms on the couch. Her eyes turn a little hazy and I'd give almost anything to know what's running through her brain.

I wave a hand in front of my bestie's face. "Hello? Earth to Mia. Come in, Mia."

She blinks, snapping back to attention and our conversation. "Sorry."

"Please tell me I wasn't hallucinating. Because if that's the case, I really *am* going to lay off the booze."

She's silent for a long moment before begrudgingly admitting, "No, we danced together." Emotion flickers across her face but she remains silent. As tempting as it is to give her the third degree, I'm in no frame of mind to do it. I'll just tuck away this bit of information for safekeeping.

Instead of answering the question, she raises a brow and attempts to turn the tables on me. "Is there anything *you* would like to tell me about?"

"Huh?"

Her gaze turns knowing. "I saw you at the bar with Colton."

Instead of admitting the truth, I grumble, "Can you believe that guy had the audacity to show his face after I purposefully went out of my way *not* to invite him?"

"Umm, maybe?" She pauses. "Any interesting conversations?"

Colton is the last person I want to discuss. Even with Mia. I want to forget about what happened last night. Nothing good will come of it. No one has ever hurt me the way he did. And I'll be damned if I give him a chance to do it again. I force my feet into movement before dropping down onto the armchair and squeezing my eyes shut. "He wants to be friends," I mutter. "Don't worry, I was extremely clear about where he can shove his friendship."

All right...perhaps I could have been clearer in my stance.

Mia's lips bow into a smile. "Maybe that was the closure you needed to move on. Feel any better about getting it out of your system?"

Nope. Not one bit. Because at the end of the day, all I did was open up a can of worms.

"Surprisingly, no."

"I'm proud of you for giving him a piece of your mind. That took balls," she tells me. I'm sure Mia assumes that I gave him a repeat performance of my psycho tirade from in front of the building.

Unfortunately, nothing could be further from the truth.

I snort, wishing that's what had happened. "As far as I'm concerned, he can shove those up his ass as well."

"Sounds like his ass is a crowded place," she says with a chuckle.

Unable to help myself, I crack open an eyelid. My shoulders shake before we both burst into laughter. "Yeah, it does."

COLTON

The apartment door closes behind me with an audible click as I hitch my backpack onto my shoulder. As I turn, ready to head to campus for the next couple of hours, my gaze collides with Alyssa's as she steps into the hallway as well.

For a moment, time stands still and we both freeze in place. Memories from Saturday night burst through my brain at lightning speed.

Alyssa in my arms, backed up against my BMW as my mouth feasted on hers. Her long legs had been splayed wide as I pushed her relentlessly toward orgasm in the parking lot of Bang Bang.

It had all happened so damned fast. One minute, she's raging at me and the next, my hands are on her with our mouths fused together. The energy we always generate exploded upon impact. Whatever this is between us, it's so much more than sexual chemistry. If that's all it were, it would be easy to relegate her to the past and move on with my life. She would be like all the other girls I've slept with and forgotten about. With Alyssa, it goes so much deeper than that. Maybe too deep. Certainly deeper than I'm comfortable acknowledging.

Unsure what to do, I lift my hand in a cautious wave.

Even from this distance, Saturday night sits uncomfortably between us.

As I give her a tentative greeting, she jerks out of her paralysis and flees down the carpeted hallway like the hounds of hell are nipping at her heels.

It's tempting to huff out a laugh. Had I really thought that kissing her into submission would work?

Maybe.

Although, I really should have known better. If I'm being brutally honest with myself, pushing her up against my vehicle and going down on her in a public parking lot probably didn't help matters either.

What am I saying?

Of course it didn't. Just look at her—she can't get away from me fast enough.

What I should do is cut my losses and leave her the hell alone. Clearly, that's what she wants. And yet, I can't do that. After holding Alyssa in my arms again and kissing her, I'm unable to fool myself into believing it's possible to move on to a life without her.

Decision made, I do the only thing I can and give chase.

Instead of waiting for the elevator to stop at our floor, Alyssa pushes through the metal door and disappears into the stairwell. I pick up my pace and push through the opening before it has a chance to fully close. As I peer down the stairwell, she glances up and our gazes collide before she quickly flicks them away and hastens her step. With my hand wrapped around the railing, I move faster. A few steps down, my shoe slips and I tighten my grip around the railing to steady myself. I can just picture it now—breaking my neck in an ill-fated attempt to catch up with Alyssa. More than likely, she'd feel as if it were sweet irony for my past misdeeds.

Who knows...maybe she'd even be right.

Thirty seconds later, I throw open the door and glance around the empty lobby. Not that I actually thought she would wait for me, because let's face it—hell would have to freeze over in order for that to occur, but it would have simplified matters.

As I push threw the glass door into the fresh air, I catch sight of her striding down the cement walkway. She gives a quick wave to another girl before hastening her pace as I jog to catch up with her. Her long blond hair is pulled up into a ponytail that swings from side to side as she moves. My gaze roves down the slender line of her back before arriving at her ass. My fingers itch to palm the supple cheeks again. My cock stirs in agreement.

Fuck me.

Since the direction of those thoughts isn't helping matters, I jerk my gaze away. New plan—I'm going to do my best not to manhandle her. If I'm going to have any chance of winning Alyssa over again, I need to employ a different tactic.

As I pull up beside her, Alyssa slants a look in my direction. Her lips sink at the corners before she jerks her attention straight ahead and proceeds to ignore me as if I'm not there. If she thinks that's going to work, she's underestimated me.

"So," I say, testing the waters, "long time, no see."

She presses her lips into a flat line before muttering, "Not nearly long enough."

Well...at least she offered up a few begrudging words. That's something, right?

Since she hasn't bared her teeth and growled, I ask, "Did you have a good time Saturday night?"

A tick or two passes by before she finally says, "Yup. It was nice to see everyone again."

Wow. Look at us, communicating like adults.

Since I'm unwilling to drop the conversational ball, I add, "I had a great time, too."

"Did you now?" Her gaze narrows as it slices to me. "Didn't you spend the night sitting at the bar all by your lonesome?"

"I meant that I had a good time after I carted your ass to the parking lot." The way her eyes flare tells me that I probably should have restrained myself and kept the comment to myself. Although that knowledge doesn't stop me from tacking on, "I'm pretty sure you enjoyed it, too."

She sucks in a sharp breath before hissing, "We're not going to talk about the parking lot because absolutely nothing happened."

Like hell it didn't.

"Oh, I'm pretty sure it did."

A punch of color flags her cheeks. "You're mistaken about that."

"Am I? Cause I'm pretty damn sure I took off your panties and spread you—"

"Enough!" She grinds to a halt before wheeling around to face me. Anger leaps to life in her eyes as she takes a step forward, closing the gap between us until she can drill a finger into my chest. "I don't want to talk about what happened in the parking lot! In fact, I just want to forget about it. Got it?"

"That's unfortunate." My gaze settles on her parted lips and I'm so damned tempted to remind her just how good it can be between us. Instead of doing exactly that, I reach out and trail my fingers along the soft curve of her jaw. With a grimace, she quickly bats my hand away. "We were always good together."

"Maybe so," she concedes, "but that was a long time ago." I open my mouth to argue when she continues, "I will *never* be stupid enough to get involved with you again."

I almost wince at the pain that flashes in her eyes.

After our breakup, I did everything possible to push Alyssa to the outer recesses of my mind. I fucked every female who would spread her legs for me. And yet, it was never enough. It wasn't *Alyssa*. Every girl was a paper-thin imitation of the only one I'd ever cared about. She's dominated my thoughts since her return. Laying my hands on her Saturday night only amplified all of the emotion coursing through me.

I have no idea if there's anything I can do or say to get her to forgive me for past transgressions, but I have to try. Even though she wants me to leave her alone, I find myself unable to do that.

Believe it or not, my intention this morning hadn't been to piss her off even more than she already is. I'd only wanted her to acknowledge that she's still attracted to me. Maybe even has feelings for me. If I can get her to admit that, then there's a glimmer of hope we can pick up the pieces and move forward. "Lys—"

"Don't call me that," she snaps.

"Alyssa," I correct, only wanting to soothe the fire I've unwittingly stoked to life. She swings away before I can finish. Unwilling to throw in the towel just yet, I huff out a breath and jog to catch up with her as she stalks toward the university.

A heavy silence settles over us as we walk side by side before stopping at a crosswalk. Campus looms on the other side of the street. Alyssa shifts impatiently as if she'll burst out of her skin any moment. I'm sure she's counting down the seconds until she can shake me loose. As I wrack my brain for something to say, something that will turn the tide of this doomed interaction, her phone dings with an incoming text. Without sparing me a glance, she pulls the slim device from her bag before glancing at the screen. I crowd closer, trying to catch a glimpse of the message.

Jack.

Who the fuck—

"Who the fuck is Jack?" I grunt as a surge of jealousy rushes through me.

Alyssa scowls as if only now becoming aware of me—almost as if she legit forgot I was hovering beside her—before pocketing the phone without responding to the message. "None of your damn business."

Wanna bet?

As difficult as it is, I keep that thought to myself. I don't need to aggravate her any more than I already have. It's almost impossible to believe there was ever a time she chased after me. You sure as hell wouldn't know it from this disastrous interaction.

Even though I'm the one who fucked up our relationship, I don't want her dating other dudes. If that makes me an asshole, then so be it. I can live with that. What I can't abide is another guy touching what's mine.

Maybe Alyssa doesn't realize it yet, but that's exactly what she is.

Mine.

She's always been mine. I was just too much of a dumbass to understand it and hold her close. Instead, I pushed her away.

"Look, I—"

As soon as the light changes, Alyssa scrambles across the street. It only takes a few long-legged strides to catch up with her. It feels like that's all I've done. Chased after her in an attempt to get this girl to hear me out.

"How about we meet for lunch," I suggest, knowing our time together is limited now that we've reached campus.

Her gaze stays focused on something in the distance only she can see. "Sorry, I'm busy."

I narrow my eyes. "I didn't give you a specific time or date."

"It doesn't matter," she says in a clipped tone before scowling. "Where your concerned, I'm busy for the foreseeable future."

Damn, but she's a tough nut to crack.

"Lys—" When she skewers me with a glare that could send a lesser man up in flames, I hastily correct myself. "Alyssa. I meant to say *Alyssa.*"

Impatience wafts off her in heavy waves as she grinds to a halt and swings toward me. She peers around before dropping her voice. "Whatever you're trying to accomplish here, I'm not interested. I'm really not." There's a pause as she steps close enough for me to feel the heat of her body. It takes everything inside me not to reach out and grab hold of her just to prove her wrong. She still wants me. I see it buried beneath the fury in her eyes. Not only is she intent on battling me, but herself as well.

For the first time since Alyssa returned to Wesley, I wonder if it's possible to break through the thick walls she's erected. Doubt trickles in before I stomp it out. I'm a lot of things, but a quitter isn't one of them.

"Here's the thing, you had me. I was *yours.*" Pain flickers across her face before it's once again masked behind an icy exterior. "But you threw me away because you wanted to fuck your way through this campus."

No. That's not true.

"You need to move on and allow me to do the same. Just because you have regrets, doesn't mean that I do. Or maybe this is all a game." She shrugs. "I have no idea and I don't really care one way or the other."

Does she really think I'm capable of that kind of heartlessness?

That I could mastermind some kind of game to pull her in again before kicking her loose?

Even though I can't necessarily blame her for being suspicious, her opinion of my character makes me gut sick.

When I remain silent, at a loss as to how to reach her, a pleading look enters her eyes, and it crushes me.

Alyssa has no idea why I pushed her away. She believes the bullshit I fed to her. What I need to do is tell her the truth. It had absolutely nothing to do with other girls and everything to do with my feelings for her.

I open my mouth, ready to lay it all on the line. I don't care if we're on the edge of campus and there are tons of people rushing past us on their way to class. I don't care if we're getting curious stares from onlookers. Our gazes stay fused together as everything around me falls away.

"Colton!"

The high-pitched voice has the moment disintegrating as I'm jolted back to reality. Alyssa blinks to awareness before taking a hasty step in retreat. Alyssa flicks an uninterested glance at the girl waving and calling my name before her lips lift into a bitter smile. "Seems like your fan club has found you. Take a good look. That's what you dumped me for." With that, she walks away and there's not a damned thing I can do to detain her as I'm swarmed by a handful of girls.

Fuck.

My gaze stays glued to Alyssa as she disappears through the crowd. Any hope that I could get her to hear me out bursts into fiery flames before dying a quick death.

ALYSSA

*H*ands down, this has been the week from hell.

Not one damn thing has gone right for me.

All right, perhaps that's a slight exaggeration.

Classes were good. Most of them are dance which makes the day pass by in the blink of an eye. And I was able to secure my old job at a small studio in town teaching a few classes to four and five-year olds. Yeah, they're squirrelly and have way too much energy, but they're adorable as hell and make me laugh. And I need the cash. Unlike Mia, my parents don't have a fat portfolio filled with stocks and bonds. They do just fine, but it helps them out if I have my own spending money.

So...if everything is going just fine why aren't I able to shake the feelings of irritability and discontent? It's almost as if something is brewing inside me and I have no clue what it is. And that makes me nervous.

Jack has Facetimed a handful of times since my return, but our relationship doesn't feel the same. It's almost as if I was able to blot everything out when I was in London and now that I'm once again at Wesley, it's impossible to do that. It only adds to my growing confusion.

What I will say is that it's nice to be back with Mia. I really did miss my girl. And dancing again for Monsieur Dupre has been amazing. I didn't realize how much I'd learned and grown in London. But he's noticed. And that means everything to me.

My brain continues to spin as I yank open the apartment building door and walk through the lobby. Instead of waiting for the elevator, I decide to take the stairwell. As soon as I arrive at the third-floor landing and push through the metal door, the sound of music assaults me. My jaw unconsciously locks as I tighten my hands. The trimmed nails bite into my flesh, leaving little crescent-shaped imprints on each palm. Even though I'm at the far end of the hallway, I can already guess where the booming bass is originating from.

Colton and Beck's apartment.

In less than two seconds flat, the annoyance that had been simmering beneath the surface becomes full blown anger.

The music grows in intensity with every step I take toward my apartment. By the time I shove the key in the lock, I'm ready to explode. With a slam of the door, I stalk into the living room. Mia is at the small dining room table with her laptop and earbuds. My guess is that they have to be noise cancelling otherwise there is no way she could work through this racket. I shoot an irritated glance toward the wall we share with our neighbors. For a handful of seconds, I consider contacting the building manager to complain before deciding against it.

Although, if this continues much longer, I'll be more than happy to make that phone call.

Mia glances up from her computer screen and gives me a wave. The smile curving her lips disappears as she takes in my expression. She pulls out the earbuds and sets them on the table next to her laptop. "Hey! How was school?"

"It was fine." I send another glare toward our noisy neighbors before waving my hand in their direction. "How long has this been going on for?"

"Hmmm. Maybe an hour or so?" Mia shrugs. "It's not that big of a deal. It kind of goes with the territory when you're living in an apartment building with a bunch of college kids. The weekends get noisy."

My lips sink further into a scowl. "Someone should really talk to them about this." When her brows rise, I add, "It's so rude! I can barely hear myself think."

"I'm sure it won't last much longer. I'll bet they're just pre-gaming it before hitting the parties."

"I don't care what they're doing. They should have more consideration for the people who have to live next to them."

"Well, I can see someone is in a mood."

I drag a hand down my face.

Honestly, I don't know what's wrong with me. I lived in the dorms for two years. The weekends were exactly like this and it never bothered me in the least. Hell, most of the time, I was the one leading the charge.

Even though I suspect the reason for my pissy mood, I'm not ready to acknowledge it to myself or Mia. Instead, I do my best to shake off the bad vibes before they can totally ruin my night.

"Sorry." I drop my bag onto a chair. "It's been a long week. I'm just tired and still adjusting from moving back here." That's a reasonable explanation for my behavior, right?

Mia pops to her feet before closing the distance between us and pulling me into her arms. Because my bestie knows me so well, she cuts right through the bullshit and gets to the heart of the matter. "I know it hasn't been easy living next to Colton, but I'm glad you're back. There's no way I would have wanted to go through senior year without you."

Her earnest words make the tension rushing through me evaporate. "Me, too." As tempting as it had been to stay in London, there's no way I would have gone through with it. Mia and I only have this year to spend together before we go our separate ways. Her to law school and me to...well, something with dance. I'm not nearly good enough to make a living as a professional dancer but I would love to one day open my own studio and teach.

"So, any plans for the night?" she asks before pulling away. "Isobel and Kara are going to Bang Bang. Apparently, they didn't get enough last weekend. Izzy said something about a hot bartender."

As soon as she mentions the club, an image of Colton pops into my brain. The way his lips had devoured mine before coasting over my body and settling on—

Nope.

There is no way I'm going there.

I quickly shove the memory away and shake my head. "I'm in the mood for that."

"Really?" Her brows slide together. "You love shaking your ass on the dance floor."

She's right. Under normal circumstances, I love getting out there and busting a move.

Presently?

Not so much.

And that has everything to do with a certain someone who shall remain nameless. Although his goddamn music is reverberating off my walls which makes it difficult to *not* think about him.

"That's fine with me. Let's see." She taps her finger against her chin. "I heard Lambda Chi Alpha is having a huge bash. We can always stop by and check it out."

"Yeah," I mutter, glancing away before sucking my lower lip into my mouth and chewing on it thoughtfully, "maybe."

Usually, I'm the one trying to cajole Mia into going out for the night and cutting loose, not the other way around.

Disconcerted by the role reversal, Mia lays a hand across my forehead. "Are you feeling all right? You're not acting like yourself."

I snort out a laugh and try to shake off the strange emotions that have taken root inside me. It's become an all-too-common occurrence. I've had to do this too many times since my return to Wesley. As much as I don't want to admit it, this has everything to do with Colton. I hate that he has so much control over my life when I want nothing to do with him. If only there were a way to purge the guy from my system. That's exactly what the thirteen months spent in London was supposed to accomplish.

Clearly, that didn't happen.

"I'm fine." I suck in a breath before releasing it. "You know what, maybe we should go to—"

My voice ends on a squeak when there's a loud crash against the interior wall that connects with the guy's apartment and then the music is cranked up which, quite honestly, I didn't think was possible.

Mia raises her voice in order to be heard. "Maybe we should go out and grab something to eat."

I grit my teeth and try to hold onto the last shreds of my temper, but it's no use. "I'm not going to be forced out of my own apartment! I've had enough, I'm going over there!"

"Oh, God." Even though she mutters the words under her breath, I hear them loud and clear. "This isn't going to end well."

"Not for them it won't," I agree.

Before she can stop me, I stalk out of the apartment. Twenty steps bring me to their door. I raise my fist and pound on the wood. Now that I'm right outside their apartment, the music is obnoxiously loud.

This is ridiculous!

Ten seconds tick by without answer. I grit my teeth and rap my knuckles harder.

Fuck!

I hiss out a breath before shaking my hand.

Oh, I am so going to let them have it!

After another twenty seconds, the door finally swings open and I find Beck on the other side. There's a cheerful smile on his face. "Hey, Alyssa! Wanna come in? We're pregaming it. Lotta parties happening tonight." He points at me. "You should really come out with us."

My eyes narrow before I bare my teeth. A low growl rumbles up from my chest.

There's a pause. "Give me a sec." He holds up a finger before turning away and yelling into the crowded apartment, "Colton, it's for you!"

Instead of waiting, I push past Beck and stomp into the crowded apartment. Jeez. There must be at least thirty people jammed in here. I recognize a number of guys from the football team. For each one, there's at least two girls hanging on them.

Unless you're Colton Montgomery.

Then you have at least four groupies pawing at you.

A punch of unwanted jealousy surges through me before I can stomp it out. That thought is so disturbing, that I quickly shove it from my brain. As soon as our gazes collide, he rises from the couch he's parked on. Without a word to the jersey chasers attempting to maul him, he cuts easily through the crush of people. His towering presence has them scattering out of the way. It only takes a moment for him to reach me.

Before he can say anything, I snap, "We need to talk."

Carefully he searches my face. "Okay."

When he doesn't move, I growl, "In private." Any moment, I'm going to lose my shit.

"Um, yeah." He glances over the throng before locking his fingers around mine and towing me through the cluster of people laughing and drinking in the small apartment.

Even though I steel myself for it, the moment he makes contact, a little zip of electricity sizzles through my veins. If there's a way for me to turn off this unwelcome attraction, I haven't found it.

It's only after he shutters us away in the privacy of his bedroom and clicks the lock into place that I wonder if marching over to give him a piece of my mind wasn't the best idea. He leans against the door, barring my escape, before crossing his arms against his wide chest.

Yeah...this definitely wasn't a good idea. I should have taken Mia up on her offer to grab something for dinner and gotten the hell out of here instead of taking matters into my own hands.

"What's up?" he asks, interrupting the frantic whirl of my thoughts.

My mouth goes bone dry as I try not to notice how good he looks in the fitted navy-colored T-shirt that hugs both his chest and biceps. It occurs to me that this is exactly how I got in trouble last weekend.

I clear my throat and glance away. "The music is really loud."

Unconsciously, my gaze flickers back to him. It's like I can't *not* look in his direction.

"Yeah, sorry about that. Things got a little out of control. I'll turn it down. No problem."

His apology takes the wind out of my sails. I shift my weight, unsure what to say.

One brow hikes up across his forehead. "Is there anything else?"

"No." I shake my head as my teeth sink into my lower lip.

The room turns quiet as he pushes away from the door and deliberately closes the distance between us. Every step sends my heart jackhammering painfully against my ribcage until I'm positive he's able to hear it above the pumping beat of the music emanating from the other room. Every nerve ending inside me goes on high alert.

My eyes flare wide. As much as I long for his touch, I realize that if he does, it will be my downfall. As much as I want to be over Colton, I'm not. I hate myself for the attraction that hums like a live wire between us. The callous manner in which he dumped my ass should have killed every fragile emotion inside me. It's disconcerting to realize that it didn't. My feelings are as strong as ever. Even if they're tinged at the edges with fury.

What's worse is that his intentions are written clearly across his face. And still, I'm powerless to stop it from happening. It's demoralizing.

My hands tighten into fists. "Don't," I whisper, knowing that it won't do me a bit of good. As much as I don't want this—*him*—there's a part of me clamoring for his touch.

The moment he touches me, I know that the battle is already over.

His hands gently cup my cheeks as he tips my head and searches my eyes. "You shouldn't have come here."

Yup. I'm already berating myself for my stupidity but there's nothing to be done about it now. I walked right into the lion's den, thinking I would come away unscathed. That won't happen.

Barely do I get a chance to suck in a breath before his mouth crashes onto mine. With one sweep of his velvety softness against my lips, I'm opening until he's able to plunge inside. Our tongues tangle and its enough to wipe away the knowledge that this is a disastrous idea. My palms go to his chest. Instead of pushing him away, my fingers curl into his shirt, attempting to drag him closer. A growl rumbles up from deep in his chest.

Our lips fasten together, teeth scraping against one another, as our tongues continue to tangle. All of the protests inside my head go silent as a barrage of sensation floods through me. As much as I try to convince myself that Colton is no different from any of the other guys I've been with, I realize deep down inside this is a lie. Colton is unlike anyone else. There is something elemental between us. Electric. Cataclysmic. Every time we come together this knowledge is slammed home almost painfully, making it impossible to ignore.

I have no idea how to go about altering this truth. Hell, I don't even know if it's possible. All I understand is that when I'm locked in his arms and his mouth is claiming mine, I feel more alive than ever before.

And that, in a nutshell, is the problem.

How do you go about eradicating an emotion so powerful?

I don't have an answer.

His hands fall from my face, gliding over my chest and belly before arriving at the button of my jeans where they hesitate. He pulls away enough to growl, "I want you, Alyssa. Saturday night wasn't nearly enough."

A groan bubbles up in my throat because he's right. Even as I lay stretched against his car, the warm night air hitting my damp flesh, I realized it. If Saturday night did anything, it was only to stoke all those dormant emotions I had buried back to life.

Jokes on me.

They're more alive than ever and clamoring to break free.

"Do you want this?" he asks when I remain silent.

Say no!

Push him away!

Do something!

"Yes."

As soon as the word escapes from my lips, the snap of my fly is released, and the zipper tugged down. My fingers skim across his flat abdominals, hovering for a moment, before dipping inside his athletic shorts and wrapping around his hard length.

Oh, God.

Memories of what it felt like to have him surging inside me bursts into my consciousness and my panties dampen. We always fit together perfectly like two pieces of a puzzle.

As soon as the zipper is lowered, his hand delves inside my panties and parts my lower lips before thrusting deep inside. A gasp escapes from me as a second finger joins the first. My muscles contract around him as pleasure floods through every cell of my body.

"You're so fucking wet." He pumps his fingers, picking up the pace. "I've missed this so much."

Even as the words reverberate throughout my being, I refuse to parrot them back to him. Already I've given him so much more than I wanted.

My fingers tighten around his cock. Somehow, it becomes even harder, feeling like steel. Another punch of arousal hits me as I remember what it felt like to take him in my mouth. To have his fingers tunnel through my hair and watch him spiral out of control.

"That feels so damn good," he whispers hoarsely as I stroke his shaft. "I need to be inside you, baby."

The endearment is like a fist tightening around my heart, squeezing until it becomes painful.

Don't do it!

Don't say the words!

This is bad enough!

Allowing him inside your body will only make it worse. It'll be like he's branding you all over again.

"I want that, too."

"Thank fuck."

He breaks free from me before crouching down and ripping away both the panties and jeans. Once those have been tossed to the floor, he brushes a kiss against my bare pussy before rising to his feet and lifting me off mine. A moment later, we're tumbling onto his queen-sized bed and he's landing between my legs. There's something comforting about his heavy weight pressing down on me. If I close my eyes, it would be so easy to trick myself into believing that everything was the same.

That we were the same.

With his shorts in place, his thick erection presses against my heat and a shiver of need careens through me.

His movements still. "Are you sure?"

Yes.

No.

Oh God.

I jerk my head into a tight nod. For better or worse, this is going to happen. Colton and I are like two trains on the same track, speeding toward one another. A head on collision was inevitable. He slips his hand between us and yanks away the material covering him. In one swift movement, he thrusts deep inside me.

Yes!

A whimper falls from my lips as a feeling of fullness suffuses me. It's been more than a year and a half since Colton has been inside my body. A powerful concoction of pleasure infused pain jolts through me as he buries himself to the hilt. Once he bottoms out, he holds himself perfectly rigid. His girth stretches me impossibly wide. I used to tease him about having such a thick cock, but it's absolutely true. I feel truly owned when he's inside me like this and my pussy is pulsing around him, attempting to adjust to his size. He brings every nerve ending to life.

"Shit," he grits between clenched teeth, "I forgot the condom."

"I'm protected."

Thank God.

I've never allowed anyone but Colton inside my body without one. This is exactly what this guy does to me and I wish with all my being that he didn't. He makes me throw my better judgment out the window.

A grunt of relief falls from him before he pulls out almost completely before thrusting back home again. As he does, a tidal wave of pleasure crashes over me and I forget all about the fact that he's not wearing a condom.

He repeats the movement.

And then again.

With each thrust of his hips, ecstasy swirls through me, building until containment feels impossible.

"Fuck, baby," he growls, "I'm going to come."

As soon as he bites out the words, an orgasm streaks through me and I chant his name over and over again. Stars explode behind my eyelids and for one glorious moment, it feels like I'm going to pass out. I can't remember the last time I experienced such an intense orgasm.

Colton arches his back, continuing to thrust inside me, riding out the wave until his muscles turn lax. As his head falls forward, he buries his face in the hollow of my neck. His warm breath wafts across my flesh as I squeeze my eyes closed.

I can't remember the last time sex felt so completely mind blowing.

Actually, that's a lie.

It was with Colton.

Huffing out a breath, I force my eyes open and stare sightlessly at the ceiling. I've always been someone who takes responsibility for my actions. Colton didn't force me to have sex. Nor did he make me do anything I didn't want to in the parking lot of Bang Bang.

I allowed this to happen.

Wanted it.

And now I'll be the one who lives with the consequences.

It's almost as if Colton can sense the disconcerting thoughts crashing around inside my head as he props himself up on his elbows and watches me. "Am I hurting you?"

"No." I shake my head, realizing that if there's anyone inflicting pain, it's me.

His voice turns cautious. "Are you all right?"

Rather than meet his inquisitive stare, I keep my attention focused on the ceiling. I need to think about an extraction plan. "I'm fine."

His cock is still buried deep inside my body. There's a part of me that doesn't want him to pull out. Even though I'm not looking at him, I feel the weight of his stare. It's inescapable. "You don't seem fine."

A sigh escapes as my gaze flickers toward him. Now that the ecstasy has faded, an odd kind of regret rushes in to fill the void. "This shouldn't have happened."

"Don't say that," he whispers, actually sounding wounded by my words which is laughable considering that he's the one who threw me away. He buries his face against the side of my neck for a second time and a shiver scampers down my spine when his warm breath feathers over my flesh. "Give me another chance."

My heart stutters.

No.

Sex is one thing, handing over my heart is an entirely different matter. "Why would I do that when I don't trust you not to hurt me again?"

His breath catches as a heavy silence falls over us.

And that, my friends, is all the answer I need.

COLTON

I check my phone for the umpteenth time for any missed messages.

Unfortunately, it's just as I suspected.

Nada.

I reached out and texted Alyssa a few times, but it's been stereo silence from her end which isn't a total surprise. Nothing I do seems to make a difference or help to turn over a new leaf. If anything, my actions have only pushed her further away. At this point, I have no idea how to bridge the gap between us.

It's been more than a week since she barreled over and we had sex. I find myself hanging around the apartment building, trying to catch sight of her, but she remains elusive. Almost as if she's trying to evade me.

Actually, that's *exactly* the tactic she's employing.

That girl wants nothing to do with me and there doesn't seem to be a damned thing I can do to change that. I hate to admit it, but I'm on the verge of giving up. I can't force Alyssa to give me the time of day. There are times in life when you fuck up and are able to fix the mess. This isn't one of those times.

My head is full of the blond-haired dancer as I walk across campus on my way to my last class of the day. It's a business course and boring as hell. Although I suspect that has more to do with the professor. He's a middle-aged dude with a monotone voice. No matter how many energy drinks I guzzle, it's not enough to keep me from dozing off.

As I pass by Grinders R Us, the local coffee house on campus, a flash of long blond hair catches the corner of my eye and I find my head whipping in that direction. My footsteps falter as I spot Alyssa sitting at a table inside. Her lips lift into a smile as she tucks a stray lock of hair behind her ear. A bolt of electricity surges through me as my attention zeros in on her, eclipsing everything around me. I wrack my brain, trying to remember the last time Alyssa looked at me like that.

It was more than a year and a half ago before I blew our relationship to hell. Back then, there were times when I would catch her staring at me like I was a fucking god. I loved it. Craved it. In the end, I took it for granted, thinking that she would always feel that way. Turns out that's not the case.

I don't realize I've sidled up to the picture window until my nose hits the glass.

"Fuck," I mumble, rubbing the tip with my fingers and taking a hasty step in retreat.

Is this really what it's come to?

Me stalking some girl in the middle of campus in broad daylight?

Don't answer that.

No other female has ever twisted me up inside like this.

Every instinct I have is screaming at me to go inside and claim my girl. But how can I do that when it's become increasingly clear that Alyssa wants nothing to do with me? The mature thing to do would be to respect those feelings and move on.

As I force myself to take a reluctant step away from the window, a burst of laughter escapes from her lips as a hand reaches across the table and settles on hers.

What the hell?

And then I'm right back where I started, pressed against the glass. Only now do I realize that she's not alone. There's a guy parked across from her. All thoughts of backing off and giving Alyssa her space evaporate as I hightail it into the coffee shop and stomp over to where the happy couple is lounging. Even the thought of another guy touching her is enough to set me off.

You know what scares me the most?

That she actually might move on.

As soon as I pull up alongside the table, Alyssa glances at me. The smile falls from her face as her eyes widen. "Colton."

"Hey." My narrowed gaze slices to the guy across from her.

A heavy silence blankets the three of us, turning the atmosphere in the shop oppressive.

Alyssa shifts on her chair before clearing her throat. "Um, Levi, this is Colton."

Levi?

What the hell kind of name is that?

Unbothered by the way I glower at him, the dark-haired guy sits back in his chair as a relaxed smile lifts the corners of his lips. "Oh, hey. You're Colton Montgomery. Nice to meet you, man."

"Yeah," I mumble, even though I don't mean it. "Same."

"The Wildcats are having a great season so far." He chuckles, "I probably shouldn't admit this, but I have a lot of money riding on you guys winning a conference championship."

"Is that so?" I grunt in response. Like that matters to me? I'm almost tempted to tank the season just so this guy loses money.

Fuck him.

Of course, that's not going to happen. I'm still playing like shit, so my ass hasn't seen very much of the field. Kwiatkowski on the other hand, is living his best life.

Asshole.

I shove that thought from my head not wanting to dwell on it. I've got more pressing matters at the moment.

Namely, this guy.

Levi.

I try not to snort.

"Yeah," he continues, "I was just telling my buddies that—"

Dismissing him, I shift my weight and focus on Alyssa. I don't give a fuck what this guy was yapping to his buddies about. "Can I talk to you outside?"

"Oh." She peeks at Levi from beneath her lashes. "Well, I—"

"Great." Not taking no for an answer, I grab her hand and pull her to her feet. She rises with a squeak of protest.

"Um, we're in the middle of something here," Levi says, straightening on his chair.

No, douchebag, you're not.

I swear to God, if he gets in my way, I'm going to punch him. Now that I'm practically benched, I got nothing to lose.

Alyssa must see the determination on my face because she quickly says, "It's fine, Levi. I'll be back in a minute."

Yeah, that's not going to happen either.

"Are you sure?" His gaze bounces reluctantly between the pair of us as a frown settles on his face.

No more easy-peasy smile, is there?

"Yup." Alyssa gives me a bit of side eye. "It's all good."

Levi grumbles something indecipherable under his breath and slouches against the chair looking fairly impotent, like he realizes that he should be making more of a fuss since I've swooped in and hijacked the girl he was with, but then again probably knowing better than to mess with me. My guess is that I outweigh him by a good fifty pounds.

Now that it's been decided, I haul Alyssa out of the shop and around the corner away from the prying eyes of student traffic. Plus, I don't want the dude inside to come out and find us.

"Colton," she growls, "was that really necessary?"

You bet your damn ass it was.

When I advance on her, she scoots backward until there's nowhere for her to go. Her shoulder blades hit the brick building. My fingers lock around her wrists before dragging them over her head and shackling them against the wall.

The pulse beneath her delicate flesh of her throat flutters wildly as she whispers, "What are you doing?"

"This." And then my mouth is crashing onto hers. I couldn't stop myself if I tried. The urge to brand her as my own throbs through me.

For a moment, her body stiffens before melting beneath me. The taste of her is the only thing powerful enough to calm the beast raging inside. It's desperate to claw its way from beneath my skin.

The irony is that I've spent so many years not wanting to feel anything, afraid to let anyone in, including this girl. *Most especially this girl.* My deepest, darkest fear is that they'll disappear from my life. It's not something I like to acknowledge. But it's the reason I pushed Alyssa away after she told me that she loved me.

She didn't love me.

How could she when my own mother couldn't do it?

When she turned her back and walked away without a second glance?

The last thing I wanted was to let someone in and have them take a knife to my heart. By the time I'd broken up with Alyssa, it had already been too late. Somehow, when I hadn't been looking, she'd gotten into my blood. And nothing I've done since has eradicated her from my brain.

From my heart.

Now I feel things that I'd rather not.

All because this tiny female insisted on clawing her way inside me and burrowing deep.

And now she wants to walk away? Push me aside? Move on without me? Forget I ever existed?

I refuse to allow that to happen.

It's only when she turns soft and pliant, that I take the kiss deeper, so deep I have no idea where she ends, and I begin. When I finally lift my mouth away, we're both breathing hard. I rest my forehead against hers. The only time I feel sane is when she's in my arms.

Unfortunately, I'm the last person she wants touching her.

"Who's the guy?" I ask gruffly, unable to forget about him.

As if waking from a dream, she blinks away the thick haze clouding her eyes. "Just someone from a class."

My eyes narrow. "Was it a date?"

Her body stiffens. Just when I think she might not answer, she says in a clipped tone, "We were grabbing a coffee after class."

"Do you like him?" I can't stop myself from bombarding her in a spray of questions. I honestly don't know what I'll do if she's developed feelings for him. How can I combat that?

"We're just friends."

A puff of relief escapes from me.

Even though I have no right to tell her what to do, the words burst free before I can rein them back in again. "I don't want you with anyone else. And I sure as shit don't want any other guys touching you."

"Colton..." Emotion flickers in her eyes before she glances away.

"Look at me," I growl.

Her widened gaze slices to mine as I repeat, "I don't want anyone else to touch you." When she remains silent, I run the tip of my nose along the curve of her jaw. "I don't want anyone else inside your body."

"Please," she whispers. Not only is she intent on fighting me, but herself as well. I hear the struggle in her voice. And I get it. I truly do, but still...

"Give me another chance, Lys." Before she can shoot me down, I add, "That's all I need to prove that I've changed. That I'm not the same guy you left behind."

A rush of air escapes as her body wilts against mine. "I don't know."

Her wrists are still pinned against the brick wall as I ghost my mouth over hers. "Just one."

When I make another pass, never quite touching her lips, she groans and tilts her head, as if silently offering them up to me.

"You've got my word that I won't fuck it up this time."

"I don't want to be hurt again, Colton."

The honesty of her words nearly breaks my heart. I did this to her. And I'll have to live with that for the rest of my life. "I'm sorry, baby."

I hold my breath as indecision flickers across her features. "Okay. But you only get one chance, and if I want to walk away, if I want you to leave me alone, you do it. No questions asked."

Even though it's a frightening thought. It's all I got. "One chance is all I need."

ALYSSA

*A*m I really this stupid?

Ugh. Don't answer that. I'm well aware of the answer.

It was foolish to allow myself to get persuaded into this date with Colton.

Persuaded...ha!

I have no resistance when it comes to that guy. All he has to do is lay his hands on me and my brain leaks right out of my ear. It's disheartening.

For the hundredth time today, I pick up my phone and stare at it. I should cancel. That would be the smartest thing to do. Just as I type out a message, there's a knock on the apartment door, and my head snaps up as my belly crashes to my toes. I place my palm against my lower abdomen as if that will keep it in place.

It's too late. He's already here.

I straighten my shoulders. One date. One chance. That's all I agreed to. If he fucks it up in any way, I can walk away with a clear conscious. When my heart clenches at the idea of us really being over, I brush it aside and tell myself that it's for the best. Colton isn't the kind of guy I need in my life. He's just the one I'm attracted to.

For a moment, I force myself to relive the way he broke up with me. The text message that popped up out of nowhere. And then waiting outside his locker room when he refused to take my calls. A dull ache fills me as I remember the ugliness of his words.

Come on, girl, you had to know this was a long shot when we got together. It was a gamble. You rolled the dice, and it came up snake eyes. You should be giving me props for remaining faithful this long. As much as I've enjoyed your unicorn pussy, this whole exclusivity thing isn't for me. I wouldn't mind keeping you in my back pocket and having a taste of it every once in a while. No strings attached, of course.

It's the rap of knuckles against wood that knocks me out of those troubling thoughts as I force my feet into motion. When I'm standing in front of the door, I inhale a shaky breath before reaching out and twisting the knob.

Even though it's not a surprise to find Colton standing on the other side of the threshold, my heart skips a beat.

Instead of his normal jeans or athletic shorts and a T-shirt, he's wearing a pale pink polo and chinos that hug his thighs. There's an oversized silver watch wrapped around his left wrist. A sprinkle of hair covers his bare forearms.

My mouth turns cottony as I take him in.

Why does he have to be so damned sexy?

I gulp as a fresh burst of nerves explode inside me. I am in so much trouble. This was a mistake. One I never should have agreed to. Already I know that there's only one way this will end and that's badly.

For me.

No matter what happens, I'm going to get hurt. And I'm nowhere near healed from the last time.

The way his gaze skims over me feels very much like a physical caress. "You look beautiful."

Heat seeps into my cheeks as I glance away. It's difficult to hold his stare. The possessiveness that fills his eyes makes me uncomfortable. "Thanks."

As much as I didn't want to dress with Colton in mind this evening, that's exactly what I found myself doing. Even though it's mid-September and the weather is seasonable, I know the temperature will drop and it will grow chilly. I decided on a thin, loosely knit, cream-colored sweater with three quarter length sleeves and a short red skirt with a white tear drop pattern. I've paired silvery sandals with the outfit. It's a little summer and autumn mixed together. Even though I've only just returned to the States, there's been quite a bit of sun and my skin has turned a nice, tanned hued.

If I was looking for confidence, this outfit gives it to me. Although maybe that approach has backfired because the appreciation is clear in Colton's eyes.

"Let me get my purse and we can go."

"Sounds good."

I give myself a silent pep talk as I grab my purse off the dining room table and return to the entryway.

Nothing will happen that I don't want.

Unfortunately, that knowledge isn't as comforting as it should be given the fact that I fold like a cheap house of cards each time he lays hands on me. Thankfully, we'll probably head out to a party. Colton will be swarmed by groupies and I'll be on my own for the duration of the evening. Then I can tell him he had his chance and blew it. I remember all too well what it was like to go out with him. He has a zealous fan club and from what I've witnessed in the weeks since my return, they're as enthusiastic as ever. It's a comforting thought. One that calms the nerves dancing in the pit of my belly.

He steps aside as I stride into the hallway and close the door behind me.

A couple of hours and this will be over with.

As I move toward the elevator, he says, "We're not heading that way."

How's that possible? It's the only way to the exit.

I halt in my tracks before swinging around to face him. "I don't understand." How is he taking me out on a date if we're not leaving the building? It doesn't make sense.

One side of his mouth hitches at the confusion that must be written across my face. "I made dinner at my apartment."

My mouth turns cottony at the idea of being alone with him. "Oh." Well, shit. This isn't good. "Um...I thought we would hit a party."

Heat fills his eyes, and his voice drops. "I'd rather be alone without any distractions."

I gulp down my growing unease.

Yeah, that's exactly what I'm afraid of.

I shift uncomfortably from one foot to the other before blurting, "I'm not going to have sex with you."

"It's just dinner, Lys." A chuckle escapes from him. "That's all this is."

It's never *just* dinner.

Not with Colton.

Not with the way my heart is hammering under my chest.

And Beck won't be there to run interference either. His family is having an anniversary celebration this weekend for his parents. Both he and Mia returned home, albeit separately. Like they would ever travel together? Ha! Not likely. My bestie wasn't looking forward to it.

Colton holds out his hand for me to take. "Are you ready?"

Nope! Not at all.

Instead of admitting the truth, I jerk my head into a nod and tentatively place my fingers in his. A sizzle of awareness shoots down my spine as his larger ones close around mine. Why does it have to be this way between us? After everything that happened, why is he still able to affect me like this?

A horde of butterflies erupt in the pit of my belly with every step that brings me closer to his apartment. Any moment, their going to find an escape hatch and break loose.

Once the door is opened, he ushers me inside. I pause in the entryway and glance around. The place is dimly lit, but it smells—I cautiously sniff the air—really good.

Familiar.

When I realize what it is, I spin toward him. "You ordered chicken parmigiana?"

His smile widens. "Nope, I made it."

My eyes widen. "What?" Since when does Colton cook?

He laughs at my surprise. "Trust me, it wasn't easy. I had Jenna on the phone for an hour, walking me through the steps."

I...have no words.

"Why would you do that?" I whisper, trying to wrap my head around this.

"It's your favorite." He shrugs. "At least it used to be." The question lurks in his eyes.

"It still is," I begrudgingly admit. I love Italian to begin with but chicken parm is my absolute favorite. I've had it at every Italian restaurant I've ever visited. Some have been amazing while others have just been good.

When I continue to stare in puzzlement, he places his hand on the small of my back and propels me gently inside the apartment. Ten steps brings me into the dining room. The set up is exactly the same as ours. Two bedrooms to the left with a bathroom in the middle and a small living room straight ahead. Outside there's a balcony big enough for a cafe-style table or two chairs. The kitchen is to the right with all the essentials, minus a dishwasher, crammed into the tight space. A breakfast bar surveys the living room/dining room combination. While my apartment is decorated and homey with artwork and photographs, the guy's apartment is bare. More utilitarian in nature. It's a place to drop their bags at the end of the night and crash.

"Want a glass of wine?" he asks, interrupting my perusal.

Holy crap. He's offering me wine?

Well, he's certainly pulling out all the stops. It's a little frightening. At least, I'm frightened by it. As much as I shouldn't give in and have a drink, I need something to steady my nerves.

"Go ahead and sit down." He points to the table which is already set with plates and silverware. "Everything is ready."

On wooden legs, I force myself to the table and awkwardly take a seat on the chair. My fingers fidget restlessly in my lap. Colton returns with two glasses of red wine before offering me one.

Once I have mine in hand, he raises his glass and offers a toast. "To new beginnings."

Another burst of nerves explode inside me. With stiff lips, I echo the sentiment and raise the glass to my mouth before gulping down at least half the contents. If this behavior continues, I will never make it through the night.

If he notices my unease, he refrains from commenting. Instead, he returns to the kitchen and brings out a colorful looking salad filled with lettuce, tomatoes, cucumbers, and croutons before doling out our servings. There's a bottle of Italian dressing already on the table. I pour just enough to give the greens taste. Normally, I try to eat carefully. What I've discovered over the years is that there is no way to hide a few extra pounds in a skintight leotard.

As much as I hate to admit it, if the dinner Colton made tastes half as good as it smells, I'll be going back for seconds. I haven't had this dish since I left for London. As delicious as the food was across the pond—hello, fish and chips with malted vinegar—I missed a few favorites.

And this was definitely one of them.

Colton keeps the conversation flowing, peppering me with questions about my study abroad program. As I finish off the salad, I lift my glass to take a sip and realize it's empty. He quickly refills it without asking.

Oh God, I really shouldn't.

While I silently debate a second glass, Colton brings out the main dish along with a plate filled with buttery-looking garlic bread. It's become my nemesis because I love it so much. Carbs and dancing don't mix. Well, they do because they give you energy which is needed to dance. But processed carbs are a big no-no. That being said, it doesn't stop me from grabbing a slice oozing with butter and herbs and placing it on my plate along with the chicken dish he serves.

I haven't even taken a taste yet and already my mouth is salivating.

"Be honest, did you really cooked all this?" I'm finding this scenario a little difficult to wrap my head around. The Colton I remember never went out of his way for a girl. The truth is that he didn't need to impress the female sex, they chased after him regardless. All he had to do was sit back and soak up the adoration. And yeah, I was right there, in the thick of it all, vying for his attention.

Even when we dated sophomore year, girls continued to hang on him. They propositioned him. Even now, I've seen for myself that his fan club has grown in size. So why is he bothering with this?

Why is he bothering with *me?*

"I did." His gaze stays locked on mine from across the table as he takes a sip of his wine.

Unable to hold the intensity of his gaze, mine drops to his lips as arousal explodes in my core where it settles uncomfortably. I shift on my chair. It does nothing to alleviate the growing tension.

"Lys."

I blink out of the daze and glance at him. What I find smoldering in his blue depths only adds to the growing tension brewing inside me. I've had too much wine and not enough food. That has to be the problem.

As I reach for my fork, he extends his hand across the table, laying it over mine. Awareness crackles in the air between us. "I'm trying to be good here, Alyssa, but when you stare at me like that, it makes me think you want me as much as I want you. I'm trying to take this slow and prove that I'm not the same guy I was before." He pauses. "But you're making that awfully difficult."

All of the saliva in my mouth dries. I tell myself to look away but can't do it. Colton Montgomery is like the sun. And I find myself pulled into his gravitational force even though I've done everything in my power to avoid it.

"Do you want a water to drink?"

"Yes, please." My voice comes out sounding more like a croak.

As soon as he disappears into the kitchen, I drag a hand over my face and order myself to pull it together. Barely do I get a chance to huff out a breath before he's returning and handing over a bottle. With trembling fingers, I twist the cap off and guzzle down half of the cold liquid. It does nothing to alleviate the fire burning inside. Any moment, I'll go up in flames and there's not a damn thing I can do about it.

How can I put Colton in my rearview mirror and move on with my life when he's doing everything possible to pull me back in again?

This would be so much easier if he was the jackass who broke up with me in a text. He's trying to chip away at the walls I've erected and if I'm not careful, he'll smash right through them.

By the time I finish my chicken parmesan and set down my fork, I'm a jittery mess and sliding headfirst into a food coma. I need to get out of here before my resolve softens.

"Thanks for dinner." I wave a hand toward the table and my demolished plate. "This was amazing." Who knew that Colton Montgomery actually had mad culinary skills? If the word got out, he'd be even more of a hot commodity than he already is.

"Thank you for agreeing to come over."

I jerk my head into a nod and rise from my chair. "I, ah, should—" *go before anything happens.*

With stealth-like grace, he pops to his feet. One step is all it takes to close the distance between us. "Don't go just yet. I have dessert."

I shake my head, tempted to make a mad dash for the door. "I couldn't possibly eat anything more. I'm stuffed."

"Fair enough." His fingers swallow up mine as he takes my hand. "How about we watch a movie, and we'll have dessert in a little bit?"

No way. That's a terrible idea.

He sweetens the deal by saying, "I'll even let you pick out the movie."

Say what now?

I hate to admit just how tempting the offer is simply because when we were together, I had to force Colton into watching a rom-com or anything sappy. I'm sure you can imagine what I had to promise in return...

I narrow my eyes, deciding to test the waters. "Amy Schumer has a new one out."

His jaw ticks as he sucks in a sharp breath before steadily releasing it back into the world. "Amy Schumer?"

My lips tremble at the corners. "That's right. I remember how much you enjoy her as an actress."

Even though he remains silent, I can see that he wants to argue with me about enjoying her movies. With any luck, he'll turn me down flat and I can scamper back to my place.

"Okay," he says with a shrug. "We'll watch it."

Well, damn.

I glance at the couch and realize I've made a tactical error in judgment. Unfortunately, it's much too late to back out of it now. Plus, I've wanted to watch this movie and haven't had the time. School and dance have kept me busy which is good. Less time to dwell on Colton.

I almost wince at that unchecked thought as it pops into my head.

Reluctantly I grab my bottle of water and beeline to the overstuffed chair in the corner while Colton runs the plates to the kitchen.

This seems like the safest option. I'll be an island onto myself. As I nestle onto the chair, I'm actually feeling pretty proud of my strategic maneuver. I've beat him at his own game, and I get to watch a movie I'm interested in. Seems like a win-win to me.

I keep my face carefully blank as he saunters into the living room. He'll be forced to sit on the couch all by his lonesome. I'm sure he wasn't expecting that.

Ha!

I'm tempted to crow—*checkmate* but keep my giddiness to myself.

Instead of heading to the couch like I expect, Colton stops in front of me. I'm about to ask what he's doing when he leans down, slides his arms around my body, and scoops me up. A yelp of surprise escapes from me as he settles on the chair before resituating so that I'm snuggled against him.

This is definitely not what I had in mind.

"Good choice." Humor simmers in his deep voice as he grabs the remote off of the small table beside him. Unsure what to do, I remain stiff as he cues up the movie.

And here I'd thought I had outsmarted him.

Turns out he's the one who outmaneuvered me.

"Relax," he whispers as the opening credits flash across the screen.

Yeah...easier said than done.

How can I relax when he's stretched out beneath me?

Even though I keep my gaze trained on the television and attempt to focus on the movie, I can't. Unable to sit still, I squirm until his hands settle on my waist, gently pulling me toward his chest. His legs are stretched out in front of him as mine hang off the side of the chair while he cradles me in his arms. The position is entirely too comfortable and after a while, my muscles gradually loosen as my head fits perfectly against the hollow of his neck. The woodsy scent of his cologne inundates my senses, lulling me into a contented state.

A sigh escapes from me as Colton absently strokes his fingers through my hair. Only now do I realize how much I've missed the quiet moments we spent alone. There were a ton of parties, but it was the nights we spent shuttered away from everyone that were my favorite because I had Colton all to myself. It wasn't necessary for me to share him with his teammates, friends, or other girls. He was all mine.

No matter how many guys I went out with, none of them came close to provoking these kinds of feelings within me.

Not even Jack.

Midway through the movie, I realize that I have absolutely no idea what's going on. I'm not even sure what the plot is. The only thing I'm capable of focusing on is the way his fingers are stroking over me. I'm so tempted to purr and stretch like a cat basking under the warmth of the sun.

Every caress fuels the flame of desire he has carefully kindled to life deep in my core. I have to fight the temptation to turn in his arms and straddle him. I want to pepper kisses along his shadowed jawline. I want to nip his earlobe between my teeth. Part of me wants to sink to my knees and take him in my—

Crap.

As those thoughts invade my brain like a swarm of locusts, I jolt to awareness before scrambling off his lap. "I need to go." The words come out ridiculously breathy as need bubbles up inside me.

Thankfully unaware of my inner turmoil, his brows jerk together as he points to the television. "But the movie isn't over yet."

I wave a hand. "Yeah, I know, but I really should go." Even though I have no idea what time it is, I add, "It's late."

He glances at the silver watch adorning his wrist. The one I'd found so damn sexy when he picked me up earlier. It does nothing to alleviate the arousal crashing around inside me. "It's only nine."

"Yeah, but I'm exhausted." I feign a yawn but stop short of stretching my arms over head. "It's been a long week."

As I BACK AWAY TOWARD the dining room area, Colton rises to his feet. "Do you want to have dessert before you leave?"

Hell, no.

I shake my head and pat my belly. "I'm still full."

Disappointment fills his eyes. "Well, at least let me wrap it up and you can take it home with you. Maybe have it for breakfast tomorrow morning."

Argh. He's being entirely too nice. I almost can't take it.

"You really don't have—"

"It's not a problem. Give me a couple of minutes to get it packed up."

Colton disappears into the kitchen before I can decline the offer for a second time. Shifting restlessly, I wring my hands, only wanting to escape before the images that had been rolling through my head minutes ago have any chance of coming to fruition.

A few minutes later, he's returning with a transparent container filled with chicken parmesan and a small white box I assume holds the dessert.

Relief floods through me as I nip my purse from the counter and hold out my hands for the boxes. "Thanks, you really didn't have to do that."

"I wanted to," he murmurs before nodding toward the door. "Come on, I'll walk you home."

A chuckle bubbles up from my throat. "Don't worry about it, I think it's safe enough for me to walk twenty feet."

He cocks his head as his gaze searches mine. "Escorting you to your apartment has nothing to do with safety."

And just like that, my belly hollows out and my chest constricts. It takes everything I have inside not to melt into a puddle of goo.

As tempting as it is to argue, I don't bother. I know a losing battle when I see one. Instead, I scramble out of his apartment, striding down the hallway as fast as humanly possible. The faster I get to my door, the sooner I can escape to my own space. No matter how quickly I move, Colton is right beside me. His long legs are no match for my shorter ones. I'm acutely aware of his presence next to me. The warmth that emanates from him. His aftershave that tickles my senses. It's almost too much to bear. Any moment, I'm going to come undone. And I can't allow that to happen.

A puff of air breaks free as I find myself standing in front of my door. With a smile plastered across my face, I spin around and thrust out my hand, only wanting to get this over with. More like get away from the tangle of emotions he's rousing inside me.

Further inspection isn't necessary to realize that they're dangerous and counterproductive to everything I've been trying to accomplish since my return to Wesley.

He steps closer and the distance between us gets swallowed up. I tilt my head in order to maintain eye contact as his warm breath drifts over me. Why does it have to feel so intoxicating? It takes effort not to strain forward and inhale a big breath of him.

I clear my throat and glance away, needing to somehow break the tentative connection that has formed between us. "Thanks again for dinner."

My gaze jerks to him as his fingers slip beneath my chin. "I'm glad we could spend time together. It was nice."

How is it that he's only a breath away?

A shiver slides through me as I press my lips together, reluctant to agree. As much as I hate to admit it, he's right. It was...enjoyable.

When I remain silent, he raises a brow in askance.

"Yes, it was," I admit begrudgingly.

He tips my chin higher. "Nice enough to do again?"

No way. Being with him is sweet torture and there's only so much I can take before I eventually break.

When my tongue darts out to smudge parched lips, an answering groan rumbles up from deep in his chest. Just when I expect him to lean in for a kiss, my fingers scramble behind my back, locking on the handle and twisting. When the door springs open, I realize that I didn't lock it earlier and nearly fall inside the entryway. The motion is enough to break the spell he has effortlessly woven around me. I stumble back a step before he reaches out and steadies my body.

Before he can detain me any longer with his voodoo magic, I snatch the containers from his other hand and take a hasty step in retreat, slamming the door in his face.

"Thanks for dinner," I yell through the thick wood that separates us.

"Anytime," he says in reply, humor dancing in his voice.

I don't give a damn if he's laughing at me. At my awkward attempts to keep him at bay. The only thing that matters is that all of my maneuvering worked.

There's a beat of silence as I tiptoe to the door and cautiously press my ear against the wood. Only when I hear his from down the hall slam shut do I release a pent-up breath of relief before swinging around and collapsing against it. Curiosity gets the better of me as I stare at the small white dessert box before giving in and opening the top.

What I find inside has my throat closing up.

Chocolate covered strawberries.

My favorite.

Damn him.

ALYSSA

For what feels like the hundredth time, I roll onto my back and stare at the ceiling in the darkness that fills the bedroom. Even though I glanced at the clock on the nightstand less than two minutes ago, my gaze flickers in that direction again. It's after midnight. If it were simply a matter of closing my eyes and allowing my mind to wander until sleep took over, I would do it in a heartbeat. Instead, every time I close my eyes, an image of Colton materializes in my mind. No matter how much I try, I can't stop thinking about him.

I can't deny that this Colton...the one who prepared dinner for me tonight is different than the guy I dated a year and a half ago. It's not that I don't think people can grow and change. Of course, they can. I'd like to think that I've matured somewhat over the years. But am I necessarily ready to take the risk only to wind up hurt again?

That's a complicated question with an even more complicated answer.

The unnerving part is that it shouldn't be. After the way he treated me, I should be completely immune to his charms. But Colton has always been my Kryptonite. That, unfortunately, hasn't changed.

A month ago, when I was living in London, life had seemed so much clearer.

Now?

Now I'm a confused mess.

If I had any brains whatsoever, I'd stay as far away from Colton as I could get. And even that wouldn't be enough distance.

He's been carefully chipping away at my resistance and I'm afraid that tonight might have truly weakened me. What I can't do is allow him to realize that.

Just as I flop over onto my side and squeeze my eyes tight, willing myself to find sleep, my phone chimes with an incoming message. Even before I look at the screen, I know who it's from. It's like he can sense my vulnerable state even though we're nowhere near each other.

Don't do it!

Don't you dare do it!

Ignore him.

I hold out for roughly ten seconds before rolling over and reaching for my phone.

I had a great time tonight. Hope you realize I won't give up easily.

My breath escapes in a rush as I pour over the message half a dozen times.

His words scare the hell out of me. Deep down inside, I know they're true. He won't give up. Colton will continue to pursue me until I give in. As tempted as I am to do just that, I'm terrified he'll hurt me in the end.

The day he broke up with me, it felt as if someone reached into my chest, wrapped their hand around my beating heart, and ripped it free. There's no way I can go through that again.

Colton meant everything to me. More than I imagined possible. Until he threw it all away. Until he threw *me* away. The darkness that had fallen over me had been all-encompassing. I'd had to fight my way free and that had taken time and determination.

To allow Colton back into my life again simply because he says he's changed has the potential to undermine all the progress I've made. It also means taking a chance that he'll crush my heart without a second thought. I've known him since we were kids. He's never been the kind of guy to get serious with one specific girl. Until me.

And look how that turned out?

It had been a disaster.

But there's something about Colton.

If I'm being truthful with myself, there's *always* been something about Colton.

Instead of placing the phone on the nightstand where it belongs, I carefully type out a response.

I had a good time, too. Thank you.

Am I going to ignore the second part of the message?

Absolutely.

As soon as I press send, another text pops up within seconds.

I meant everything I said, Lys.

I release the pent-up breath from my lungs as everything weakens inside me. He knows the nickname pulls at my heartstrings and he's using it against me.

I need time.

Then that's what I'll give you.

I chew my lower lip and set the phone down before turning my back to it.

Another hour drags by and I'm still wide awake. Even though my body feels tired from a long week of classes, dancing, and teaching, I can't turn off the thoughts that continue to churn through my head. I can't stop my body from craving the one guy who pushed me to my limits.

I roll over and snatch the phone again. Even though I know it's a mistake, I type out a message and hit send. My heart riots painfully under my breast as I wait for a response. One minute slowly stretches into two and still, there's no answer. For all I know, he's sleeping and won't get it until the morning.

God knows it would be better that way.

A fresh wave of humiliation crashes over me. I should have held strong and not given in.

Ugh.

Irritated with myself, I drop the phone on the nightstand and roll over. No more thinking about Colton. He needs to go back to being a stupid mistake I made in my past and nothing more.

Detachment, that's exactly what I need.

It's the light knocking on the apartment door that has my eyes springing open. My heart leaps as I throw off the covers and roll from bed before padding through the hallway and living room into the entryway. It's only when I reach for the lock that I hesitate and consider the consequences of my actions.

Is this truly what I want?

To allow Colton in again?

Not just the apartment but my heart?

My life?

It takes effort to still the nerves that churn inside my belly. Maybe I'm unsure that's the best course of action, but something is urging me to take a cautious step in that direction.

As I twist the lock and open the door, I'm hit with a punch of arousal. "Hi."

The corners of his lips lift as he echoes the sentiment, "Hey."

His blond hair is tousled, and I'm ridiculously tempted to plow my fingers through the strands that are longer on top and shaved on the sides. A Wesley Wildcats T-shirt stretches across his chest as black athletic shorts hang from lean hips.

When I remain silent, too busy eating him up with my eyes, he asks, "Can I come in?"

I blink out of those thoughts as a punch of heat hits my cheeks. The most I can hope for is that it's too dark inside the apartment for him to witness the effect he has on me. The last thing I want to do is stroke his already inflated ego or give him anymore confidence.

Especially where I'm concerned.

In silence, I step aside, allowing him entrance. As he brushes against me, the familiar woodsy scent from earlier this evening wafts around me, cocooning me in the past. In the memories I still hold dear. All I want to do is close my eyes and inhale a big breath of him.

Instead, I lock the door to the apartment behind him.

If Mia were here, there's no damn way I would be doing this. My bestie cautioned me about getting together with him the first time. She was afraid that he would hurt me and sadly, she was right.

A groan bubbles up in my throat as I reevaluate the merits of my decision. Let's face it, choices made after midnight are generally questionable by nature. Maybe I haven't been drinking, but this falls neatly into that category.

I've been hesitant to tell Mia what's been going on with Colton. Mostly because I've been too busy denying that I still have feelings for him. If I utter the words out loud, that will only make them more real. Even now, as he stands inside my apartment at one o'clock in the morning, I'm unsure if I'm ready to take that leap.

Whether he realizes it or not, this is the guy who changed everything for me. My life can be neatly broken up into two segments. A *before Colton* and *after Colton*. I'm way more cautious than I was before. What Colton taught me is that I'm not as bulletproof as I once suspected.

And yet, that's still not enough to stop me from grabbing his hand when he hesitates in the dining room. A sizzle of awareness shoots through me at the innocuous contact. The energy we always seem to generate is part of the attraction. I'm like an idiot moth to a flickering flame that will ultimately lead to its demise. That knowledge isn't enough to stop the onslaught of emotions from hurtling to the surface.

Sometimes I wonder if he feels it too or if it's all one-sided. Given the easy manner in which he walked away makes me suspect that it's all me.

Once inside my room, I release his hand, allowing mine to fall back to my side.

He grabs the hem of his shirt and drags it partway up his rock-solid abdomen before pausing. "Is that all right if I take off my shirt and shorts?"

My mouth turns bone dry as I jerk my head into a tight nod.

He yanks the soft cottony material over his head before dropping it carelessly to the floor. The shorts get removed next. Once they are added to the small pile, he stands in front of me wearing nothing more than form-fitting boxers. Even in the shadowy darkness of the room, I'm able to make out the hard ridges and contours of his muscular body.

I stand rooted in place, simply drinking him in. Colton's body is spectacular. Football and a rigorous weightlifting program have molded his physique into a thing of beauty. Instead of being bulky like a lineman, he's long and lean. His body was built for quickness and speed.

As I shake myself out of those thoughts, I realize that he's studying me with an equal amount of intensity. My muscles tense as air gets trapped in my lungs making it impossible to breathe.

His gaze is like a physical caress and my body reacts accordingly. When my nipples tighten, poking through the thin fabric of the tank top, I lift my arms self-consciously to cover them. Before I can fully wrap them around myself, Colton reaches out, halting the movement. "Don't. I want to look at you." There's a pause as his voice turns rough, sounding as if it's been scraped from the bottom of the ocean. "I've missed this."

Hesitantly, I lower my arms and stand ramrod straight, allowing him to look his fill. I've never been embarrassed of my body. I've spent my entire life in a leotard. I'm used to scathing remarks from teachers. I've become almost deaf to the criticism.

But this...

I want Colton to like what he sees. The appreciative gleam filling his eyes tells me that he does.

This time, when he extends his hand, it never occurs to me not to take hold of it. With one tug, he pulls me toward the bed. He climbs in first before turning on his side. Once he's settled, I crawl in next to him until our bodies are perfectly aligned. His bigger one curling protectively around my smaller one. One of his arms bands around me, locking me in place. For the first time in what feels like forever, contentment fills every fiber of my being.

Now that Colton is holding me in his arms, I realize this is the reason I couldn't fall asleep. I needed him here with me. Even though I've spent all this time fighting against him, trying to break free of the hold he has on me, it turns out that I've been fighting myself as well. It's a relieve to finally drop the pretense.

At least for the night.

COLTON

Harsh sunlight filters through my eyelids and I wake with a satisfying stretch. It's been a while since I've felt this well rested. Like I slept for twenty-four hours straight. As soon as I shift, I realize that I'm not alone. There's a warm body snuggled up against me.

Well, fuck.

It takes a moment for my sluggish brain to conjure up the events from last night.

Alyssa.

Dinner at my place.

Unable to sleep and shooting her a text.

I crack open an eye only to find her sprawled across my bare chest. There is nothing better than waking up with her in my arms. Even though my feelings for her had scared the shit out of me, I regret pushing her away sophomore year. I have no idea if it's possible to get back to a place where she can trust me again, but I'm determined to do everything in my power to give it a shot and prove to Alyssa that I can be the man she needs. All I know is that I need to slow my roll and not come on too strong.

If I push too hard, she'll run. And I can't blame her for that. She handed over her heart for safekeeping and I stomped it to smithereens.

A strange contentment fills me as I watch her sleep. Even though I want this moment to last forever, I know it won't. As soon as she wakes, the protective armor she cloaks herself in will fall back into place and she'll continue to hold me at a firm distance.

Unable to resist touching her, I stroke my fingers over her golden head. Alyssa has beautiful long hair. I love having it swathed across my body. I love wrapping it around my fist and tugging it. I told myself when we were together that it was pure and simple fucking. She'd always been up for anything. Whatever I wanted to do. However I wanted to use her body, she let me do it. She was sexually adventurous. Always willing to push the limits.

But the last time we had sex, and she admitted that she loved me, was different. Softer. Somehow more meaningful. No longer could I pretend that it was nothing more than mindless screwing. It scared the shit out of me. I freaked out and pushed her away. I made damn sure to blow up our relationship so that I could walk away.

Not once did it occur to me that forgetting about her and moving on would be impossible.

A soft sound escapes from Alyssa as she shifts against me. My fingers still. I'm nowhere near ready for this interlude to end. For a few more minutes, she drifts in and out of sleep before finally opening her eyes and turning her head until our gazes lock. Slowly she blinks away the sleepiness.

I remain silent.

She's so fucking beautiful that my throat has closed up on me.

"Morning." Her body stills. Her top was shed during the night, leaving her as bare chested as I am.

I clear my throat along with the thick emotion trapped inside it. "Sleep good?"

"Yeah, I did." Her voice is deep and sexy.

Ever since I was a freshman in college, I've made it a rule never to spend the night with a chick. Fucking is one thing. Sleeping in someone's bed and having an awkward convo the morning after is quite another.

Alyssa has always been the exception to that rule. She's the only girl I've spent the night with. The only one I've held in my arms for hours at a time. The only one I've woken up with in the morning. I have no idea if that's the case for her. I've done my best to blot out the fifteen months that we've been apart. As much as I want to ask, I can't summon the words. I have no right to delve into her past when I'm the one who pushed her away and shattered her heart.

"Me, too."

Even though I'm afraid to push my luck, the question escapes before I can rein it in again. "What are your plans for the day?"

Her drowsiness falls away as she watches me carefully. "Homework. Maybe some grocery shopping."

As we stare at each other, it feels like I'm standing on the edge of a precipice. One leap and I could plummet to my death. The fear of being rejected is terrifying. "Maybe we could spend it together?"

Indecision flickers in her eyes as she gnaws her lower lip and glances away. "I don't know. Is that necessarily a good idea?"

My hands go to her cheeks, forcing her to meet my stare head on. "I told you that I'm not going to give up on you. Or us. We can take this as slow as you need. Just give me time to prove that I'm not the same guy I was before. That's all I'm asking."

My heart jackhammers almost painfully as silence stretches between us. I've done everything I can think of to change her mind. And maybe...maybe it won't be enough. "Lys?"

She draws in a breath before whispering, "Okay."

Relief rushes through me, leaving me to feel almost giddy. Before I can think better of it, I give in to the impulse rushing through me and lock my fingers around her delicate wrists before flipping her over onto the mattress. A squeak of surprise escapes from her as I drag her arms over her head and pin them to the headboard. Heat flashes in her eyes.

I'm all about taking this slow, but I also want to feed the need she has. And I know exactly what Alyssa needs because I feel it as well.

"Colton..." A fine tremble works its way through her voice as she shifts restlessly beneath me.

"Yeah, baby?" My lips ghost over hers, never giving in to the baser urges clawing beneath the surface of my skin. More than anything, I want to rip her panties away and bury myself deep inside her tight heat.

But I can't do that. The next time we have sex, she'll be mine.

"You said that we could take this slow."

I press my mouth to hers before murmuring against her lips, "And so I will."

With that, I release her wrists and pull away just enough to stare down at her. She's so fucking beautiful with her blond hair spread out across the snowy white pillowcase. Her blue eyes are wide and watchful as a deep flush stains her cheeks. A thin scrap of material is all that bars her core from me. My cock stiffens as a punch of arousal hits me full force. The urge to plunder her sweetness roars through me. It takes every ounce of restraint to beat back the need I have for her.

Even though I'm no longer holding her captive, her arms remain above her head as she shifts beneath my gaze. Her breasts are high and tight with little pink nipples that beg to be played with. The temptation is too much to take and I lean down, capturing one perfect bud with my lips. A whimper slips free from her as I suck it greedily into my mouth. After a few moments of torture, I allow the hard tip to pop free before drawing its twin between my lips. When I bite down gently on her flesh, a hiss of pleasure escapes.

Her fingers thread their way through my hair as if to hold me in place. My dick is rock hard. Any moment, I'm going to explode in my boxers which hasn't happened since...well, never. It just goes to show how this girl affects me. The truth of the matter is that she always has. Only now am I coming to terms with it.

Alyssa shifts impatiently beneath me and I know without a shadow of a doubt that if I stripped her bare and mounted her, she wouldn't stop me. No, she'd probably beg for it.

But then I'd be breaking my promise to take it slow, wouldn't I?

And I can't do that.

If I've learned anything over the past couple of weeks, it's that Alyssa will go into avoidance mode in the blink of an eye. She's tried pulling a disappearing act after both times we were together. So, no. I'm not about to give her a reason to turn tail and run from me for a third time.

I just have to remember that slow and steady wins the race. Especially when it comes to this girl.

It's with a shit ton of regret that I allow her nipple to pop free from my mouth. Both breasts are rosy from all the attention. Unable to help myself, I pluck the tiny buds between my fingers, continuing to toy with them. Her eyelids feather closed as she arches her back as if silently offering them up to me.

"I love your breasts." I tug at the stiff little nipples, pulling and tweaking them in tandem. It's pleasure infused pain at its very best. What I love most is that this turns her on just as much as it does me. With one last playful tug, I release them.

If I don't shift gears now, it'll be too late, and I'll end up spreading her thighs and doing exactly what I know we shouldn't. "How about I run out and grab us some coffee?"

Alyssa blinks a few times as if that's the last thing she expected to pop out of my mouth. *"Coffee?"* Her lips wrap around the word as if it's foreign. *"Now?"*

"Yup." I roll from the bed and stretch.

Her gaze roves over my body before settling at my groin. I glance down to see what has captured her interest and realize that I'm sporting a massive boner.

Yup, that's exactly what this girl does to me.

She props herself up on her elbows, all the while staying laser focused on me.

Damn but she makes a pretty picture lying there all naked and flushed.

I really need to get out of here before I jump back into bed with her. I grab my athletic shorts and yank them up my thighs before tugging on my T-shirt. Now that I'm dressed, the situation feels much safer. It's like I've got a protective shield in place.

Once I've got my slides on, I retreat from the space. "Is a mocha frappe still your preferred drug of choice?"

Her lips tremble at the corners as she relaxes against the mattress. "Yeah, it is."

There's a sliver of comfort in the knowledge that while some things are completely different, others stay the same.

"Okay. I'll be back in fifteen."

With that, I disappear from the bedroom and out of her apartment. I make a quick pitstop at my place and grab my wallet before heading to my BMW parked in the lot. As I slide behind the wheel and shove the keys into the ignition, the vehicle purrs to life. That's three hundred and thirty-five horses waiting to break free under the hood. I rev the engine before pulling out and heading up the street about half a mile before swinging around the corner. There's a little coffee shop off the beaten path where the locals stop for java. I have no idea if Alyssa has frequented the place, but I know her penchant for coffee and I'm pretty sure she'll enjoy it. At this time on a Sunday morning, the shop is fairly quiet and I'm in and out in a matter of minutes. All I want to do is get back to Alyssa and spend the day together. I don't give a crap what we do, I just want to be with her. I want our relationship to feel like it did before I blew everything to shit. Even if it's just fleeting moments.

As I park the convertible in the lot, I grab our containers of coffee along with the fresh baked almond scone I picked up for Alyssa and head inside the lobby before beelining for the elevator. Normally, I would take the stairwell, but my hands are full. Using my elbow, I hit the button and wait for the car to arrive. Once it does, I hop onto the platform. I almost shake my head when I find myself whistling a song.

Whistling, for fuck's sake.

I can't remember the last time I whistled. Or felt this happy. And it has everything to do with Alyssa.

"Hold the lift!" someone yells from the lobby as the doors slide shut.

Without thinking, I wedge my foot between them. The metal bounces off my rubber shoe—which by the way, hurts like a mother fucker—before sliding open. A dark-haired guy with a suitcase jumps onboard. He's slightly winded as if he's just run a mile. Although that's doubtful since he's wearing pressed khakis and a crisp light blue-colored button-down shirt.

"Thanks, mate!"

Hmmm. Interesting.

British accent.

"No problem. Seems like you're in a hurry."

Once we're inside, he glances at the control panel but doesn't press anything else which means he's also getting off on the third floor. I've lived her since July and I've never seen this guy around.

He cracks a smile. "I've come straight from the airport." Before I can ask, he offers, "I'm here to visit a friend."

A prickle of unease blooms in the pit of my gut as I study him with a little more care.

"Oh?" I try to keep my tone nonchalant. "Your friend is on the third floor?"

"Yes." Once the doors slide open, he glances at the drinks in my hands before placing a palm across the metal threshold. "After you."

"Thanks." I roll my shoulders, trying to shake off the thick tension that has gathered there before stepping into the carpeted hallway. The air gets clogged in my throat as I give him a bit of side eye, waiting to see which direction he heads in. If he turns to the right, then I don't have—

Fuck.

Not only is he walking in the same direction as I am, but he's pulled up along side me. With every step that brings me closer to Alyssa's apartment, my anxiety grows, morphing into more of a heavy stone. While I asked Alyssa questions about her time in London, I painstakingly avoided the topic of people she might have dated. It's not like I wanted to know.

The British dude glances at the silver numbers alongside each apartment door. Just when I think he'll pass by her place, he grinds to a halt and rechecks the numbers. "Here we are." He flashes me another smile. "Thanks again, mate."

My footstep faulters as he raps his knuckles against the wood and waits. Within seconds, the door swings open and Alyssa stands on the other side of the threshold. Thank fuck she's wearing more clothing than when I walked out twenty minutes ago. She's pulled on a white T-shirt and tiny red shorts. The shorts are teeny tiny and do absolutely nothing to cover her long lean legs. A growl rumbles up from deep within my chest.

Alyssa's movements still as her lower jaw drops open. It takes a moment for her to blink out of the stupor she's fallen into. "Jack?"

Jack?

Why the hell does that name sound so familiar?

Wait a minute. Is this the dude who was texting her?

Fuck.

Fuck.

Fuck.

"Surprise! I was in Chicago for an interview and decided to make a slight detour." He let's go of the suitcase handle and opens his arms wide.

Every instinct is screaming at me to rip her away from him. Bile bubbles up in my throat until it feels like I could choke on it. My hands tighten around the contains of coffee as she steps into his embrace. I take a step forward before grinding to a halt.

What the fuck am I going to do?

There was a time when Alyssa belonged to me, but that's not now.

Her eyes find mine as he presses a kiss against her cheek.

All I know is that I can't stand here and watch this happen right in front of my face. Even though it goes against every impulse, I turn away and force my feet into motion. It takes effort to put one foot in front of the other. The walk to my apartment feels like it lasts forever. As I slip the key into the lock and turn the handle, I glance down the hallway only to find it empty.

ALYSSA

y mind continues to cartwheel as I press my hands to my mouth and stare at Jack as he sits on the couch across from me. "I still can't believe you're here," I whisper for what feels like the hundredth time. "Why didn't you tell me that you were going to visit?"

His smile grows wider until his blue eyes crinkle at the corners. "I wanted it to be a surprise."

Laughter bubbles up in my throat. "Mission accomplished." I'm having a hard time wrapping my head around this new turn of events. When I'd opened the door, I had fully expected to find Colton waiting on the other side.

Instead, I found Jack.

And Colton.

Oh God...

A shiver scampers down my spine as I remember the look on the blond football player's face. I'd just stood there, staring at Jack. Totally shellshocked. I'll have to deal with the Colton situation later.

It takes effort to shake off those thoughts and focus on the guy in front of me. Even though it's only been a month since I left him behind at Heathrow, it feels like forever. Only now do I realize how

467

much I've missed our friendship. Facetime and texting are not the same as being in the same room and spending time together.

"How long are you here for?" I'm hoping that it's at least a few days. Maybe even a week. I'm sure Mia wouldn't mind the unexpected guest. They met in London when she visited over Christmas break and struck up an instant friendship.

The wattage of his smile dims. "Twenty-four hours."

"Really?" My heart sinks. "That's it?"

"I'm afraid so." He shrugs. "I couldn't take any more time away and need to be back by Tuesday. Even though it's a quick turnaround, I couldn't come to the States without taking a slight detour to see you."

"I'm glad you did. I've missed you."

"I've missed you, too. Maybe I can convince you to come back for a visit."

Even though I left behind quite a few new friends, I haven't even considered returning so soon. Sometimes it still feels like I'm trying to acclimate to life at Wesley. Plus, I'll be graduating in this spring. I kind of need to get my act together and figure out a plan.

And then there's Colton. At every turn, he's there, pushing at me, refusing to back off. He's taken over more and more of my thoughts.

Jack must see the flicker of emotion as it crosses my face. He tilts his head and gives me a considering look before asking lightly, "The guy I rode up with on the lift, is he a friend?"

And there it is.

The dreaded question.

Heat suffuses my cheeks.

Jack knows all about Colton.

Everything.

The good, the bad, and the heartbreaking. I wasn't shy with the details. Perhaps I shouldn't have been quite so honest with him, but I had needed to work through all the crap in my head and Jack had been a good listener. Plus, I had needed him to understand that as much as I liked him, I couldn't move forward with a new relationship when I was still so hung up on a different one.

I blow out a long breath unsure where to even begin.

His voice softens as he searches my eyes. "Come on now, is it really that bad?"

Ha! he hasn't got a clue. Although that's because I've been reluctant to fill him in on the details. I'm well aware that Jack is hopeful that the time will come when I'm ready to move on.

Needing to be honest, I admit, "No. The guy in the hall was Colton."

His brows rise across his forehead. "Ahhh."

There is a wealth of meaning held in his voice.

I snort. "Yeah."

He shifts as a serious light enters his eyes. "Are you all right?"

My heart squeezes almost painfully under my chest. Of course this would be Jack's response. There is no sign of anger, jealousy or even disappointment.

Just concern.

It only makes me feel worse.

Why couldn't I fallen head over heals for this guy?

He's perfect. Kind and considerate. And he treated me so well. I never have to guess where I stand with him. He lets me know. How's that for mature?

"You know that no matter what, I'll always love you, right?"

It takes effort to blink the wetness from my eyes. Before I realize it, I'm flying out of the chair and hurtling myself at him. As soon as I land against Jack's chest, he wraps his arms around me and presses me close. I squeeze my eyes tight as the citrusy scent of his aftershave soothes my senses.

When he presses his lips to my hair, I lift my face to meet his eyes. One hand comes up, the fingers settling under my chin before tilting it upward until our mouths can align. It's only a light sweep but it's enough.

Enough to know that Jack will never make me feel the way Colton does.

Jack is a safe port in a storm but he's not the man I long for. He doesn't send my pulse skitter or send my body into overdrive.

He is steady and calm.

And I'm probably the biggest idiot in the world for not giving him a real chance.

But I can't. It wouldn't be fair to Jack. He deserves to have someone be head over heals in love with him and that's not me.

It can't be me when I already feel that way about someone else.

COLTON

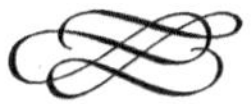

"*D*ude, what the hell is up with you?" Beck mutters, barely glancing away from the seventy-inch television and the video game he's in the middle of.

"Nothing." I swing around, pacing to the other side of the living room.

He snorts but stays laser-focused on the combat game unfolding on the screen. Gunfire erupts from the surround sound in a spurt of noise. "Whatever you say, man. Got practice today at three."

Fuck.

My head is too full of Alyssa and the British prick that came out of nowhere for me concentrate on anything else. I might as well plant my ass on the bench now because it's doubtful I'll see the playing field anytime soon.

Here's the way I see my day unfolding—stew about Alyssa for a couple of hours, head to practice, more than likely fumble a few plays, get my ass chewed out again by coach, and end it all by feeling like complete asshole.

I drag my fingers through my hair.

It's been more than twenty-four hours since that dude showed up at her door. After dumping the coffee I picked up earlier, I'd paced a hole in the floor all the while considering the merits of stalking over there and claiming that girl as mine.

Except...she's not really mine.

Like at all.

I don't actually have any right to question what she does or who she spends time with. I lost that privilege when I broke up with her. For all I know, she had a relationship with this guy in London. That thought is enough to make me want to punch my fist through the wall.

And do you think I slept one damn wink last night?

Fuck, no. Of course I didn't.

All I could think about was the two of them in bed together. His hands on her body. Stroking her the way I've imagined a thousand times.

"Can you sit your ass down for five damn minutes? You're really throwing off my game."

I glance out the slider door. The skies are a dark leaden gray. I'm no meteorologist, but my guess is that it'll pour any moment. "I'm going for a walk."

"Excellent idea." He shakes his head. "And they say that *I'm* the one with ADHD."

Not bothering with a response, I pocket my keys from the breakfast bar and stride out of the apartment, slamming the door closed behind me. Emotion continues to rush through my veins. I don't like it. I don't like feeling out of control. Now that I've actually made some headway with Alyssa, it feels so much worse to have it ripped out from under me.

As I stalk through the narrow hallway, I grind to a halt in front of her door. My hands tighten into fists that hang uselessly at my sides.

You know what?

I need answers. Maybe I don't deserve them, and I have no right to them but that doesn't mean that I'm not going to try and figure out what the hell is going on.

Is this guy a friend or more?

Is this a short visit?

Where the hell did he sleep last night?

It had better not be where I slept the night before. That's all I got to say. Or we won't have to worry about him. He'll be dead.

Before I realize it, my fist is raised and I'm straightening my shoulders. Before I'm able to knock, the door is yanked open and Alyssa is standing in front of me.

"Oh," she says in surprise, falling back a step. It's difficult to tell just who is more surprised. Although, I'm thinking that it's her. "Colton." Confusion flickers across her face. "What are you doing here?"

That's an excellent question. I hadn't gotten that far in my thought process and have to improvise on the fly. It's not like I can just demand to know what's going on. "I was just wondering if you were heading to class."

"No, I'm going to skip today and drive Jack to the airport."

Jack—or as I like to call him, the British prick—wheels his suitcase into the entryway and proceeds to stand entirely too close to Alyssa. It's on the tip of my tongue to tell him to back the fuck off.

Before I can snap out the words, I realize what she said.

He's leaving.

My brows shoot up. "Don't skip class, I've got a couple hours to kill before practice. I'll drop him off."

Alyssa blinks, looking uncertain. Already I can tell that she wants to argue with me. "Umm..."

"It's not a problem. You shouldn't be missing a dance class, anyway." I glance at the dude who is still standing entirely too close. "Right, Jack?"

His eyes narrow. "Of course."

She shoots a cautious look over her shoulder before biting down on her lower lip. "Are you sure you don't mind? I hate the idea of not seeing you off."

"It's fine." Now that she's no longer looking at me, his lips lift into a smile. I don't like the way his eyes soften when he looks at her. "And your friend is right. You shouldn't miss class."

"Colton," I say, interrupting their conversation.

Jack's blue eyes harden as they shift to me. "Yes, I'm aware of who you are."

Hmmm. Apparently my reputation precedes me. That's probably not a good thing. I can imagine the stories Alyssa told him about. I have the feeling that Jack and I are going to have a coming to Jesus meeting in the car.

Worry ignites in her gaze as it bounces between us. "You know what, maybe this isn't such a good idea after all. I'll just—"

"It's all good." Not taking no for an answer, I grab the handle of Jack's suitcase and wheel it into the hallway. I'll be damned if this guy spends another minute alone with Alyssa. The thought of him being off US soil in a matter how hours has a massive amount of relief pumping through me.

"All right," Alyssa mutters, still looking uncertain. "I need to change before heading to class." She gives me a bit of side eye before stepping closer to the dark-haired guy.

They both ignore me as he takes her into his arms. Everything inside me riots painfully as I stand by and watch. My jaw locks as I grind my back teeth together. It takes every ounce of willpower not to rip her from his embrace. He turns his face and presses a kiss against her cheek before murmuring something in her ear that I can't quite hear. I'm on the verge of breaking up this little lovefest when they finally pull apart.

"I guess this is goodbye," she says, sadness filling her voice.

"For the time being. And we'll still continue to talk. I'm only a phone call away."

Not if I can help it.

I clear my throat. Even though I have no idea what time his flight is, I say, "We should probably get moving. Wouldn't want you to miss your flight."

Not bothering to wait for a response, I drag the suitcase down the hall to the elevator. The sooner I get this guy away from Alyssa, the better off I'll feel. Even if I have to drive him to the damn airport myself. I'm not looking forward to the next thirty minutes of my life. I have the feeling that it's going to suck balls.

I punch the button and tap my foot, shooting impatient looks down the hall and wait for the car to arrive. Once it does, I roll the suitcase inside. The door tries to close four times before he finally gets his British ass into the elevator. The ride to the lobby is made in absolute silence. The stroll through the lobby and into the parking lot is no different. With every step we take, the oppressive tension rachets up between us until it's enough to choke on.

When I finally stop in front of my 840i, his expression lightens. "Nice roadster."

"Thanks," I mutter. Under normal circumstances, I'd showoff some of the features. That's not happening.

In one swift movement, I pop open the trunk and toss his luggage inside before slamming it shut and clicking the locks. We both slide inside before I started up the engine and pull onto the street, heading toward the metropolitan airport about thirty miles away. Normally, it's a forty-minute drive with traffic. I plan to have him there in under thirty.

See if I don't.

Not only does it take effort to unlock my fingers from around the leather steering wheel, I have to unclench my now aching jaw. I dredge my brain for something to say. Something that will fill the uncomfortable silence that has settled between us. I glance at him from the corner of my eye. The British prick sits ramrod straight as if someone shoved a two-by-four up his ass.

What the hell does Alyssa see in this guy?

He's dark-haired where I'm blond. He's slightly shorter than I am in height. You bet your damn ass I noticed that. Sure, he's broader. Beefier. His physique is more suited to a brawler where I was build for speed on the football field.

I clear my throat. "Short trip."

Yeah. That's the best I got at the moment. Even though I've separated him from Alyssa, jealousy continues to eat away at my insides. I hate that he holds a special place in her heart. More than that, I hate that he's trying to oust me from hers. I can see it in his eyes. That's exactly what he's trying to do. And I'll be damned if I allow it to happen.

His blue eyes flicker toward me. "Unfortunately, I need to return by Tuesday. It prevented me from tacking on a few more days and making a proper holiday of it."

Unfortunate for who?

Not me.

His eyes narrow as if I spoke the thoughts out loud. He shifts in the butter-soft leather seat and says in a clipped tone, "I know all about you."

My brows shoot up. "Excuse me?"

"You're the wanker Alyssa dated before studying in London."

I press my lips together. I might not be familiar with the term wanker but I'm pretty sure it's not good. By the disgusted expression marring his face, I can imagine that Alyssa revealed all the gory details. What sucks is that there's nothing I can say to defend myself.

It's all true.

I'm a wanker.

My finger tighten around the wheel until the knuckles turn bone white. "I'm not the same guy I was before. I've changed." More than anything, I want that to be true. I'm fighting not to be the guy who was frightened away by three words.

His upper lip curls as he snorts, "Well, I certainly hope not." Even though we're roughly the same height, he's mastered the way of looking down on someone and making them feel tiny. I don't like it. "Did she mention that we dated?"

The acidic taste of bile rises in my throat as I stare straight ahead. I can't even look at him. I don't want to see the smug look on his face. I'm afraid that if I do, I'll jerk the car over to the side of the road and beat the piss out of him for laying his hands on her.

"You realize that she's perfect, right?"

Does he think I'm a complete dumbass? Of course I do!

When I remain silent, he continues. "She's the kind of girl that makes you start thinking long term."

I want to punch my fist through the windshield.

Why the fuck is he telling me this? To rub my face in the fact that I had the one girl worth having and I let her slip away?

"The moment we met, I realized there was something special about her."

My foot presses down on the accelerator and the engine revs as we shoot through traffic.

"But she held me off. Couldn't move on from you."

That last piece is probably what saves his damn life.

"It wasn't until the last month that we became romantically involved. Although, she never gave it a chance to get deep. And when it was time for her to leave, we decided that a long-distance relationship probably wouldn't work. Too many unknowns with the future. But you know what?"

I have to steal myself for what he'll say next. He doesn't make me wait long.

"I would have been more than willing to give it a crack. Alyssa is well worth it."

Barely am I able to suck in air through the thick lump that has been wedged in the middle of my throat. Why had I thought taking him to the airport was a good idea? I'm tempted to pull over and dump his ass along the side of the road. But then he'd still be here, and I can't have that.

"You know why I didn't put up more of a fight?"

Goddamn it! I just need him to shut the fuck up and let me drive. I glance at the speedometer. I'm going about ninety.

"Because I knew she was still in love with you. A man who doesn't deserve her."

What the fuck?

My head whips in his direction.

"I'd hoped that Alyssa would return home and realize that she was over you. Then we could pick up where we had left off, albeit from a distance." His blue eyes darken as he shakes his head. "But she still fancies herself in love with a wanker."

I hit the turn signal and crank the wheel, zipping off the exit ramp.

Everything he's just confessed churns inside my head as I enter the airport area and turn toward international departures. Once I find the terminal, I pull to the curb and cut the engine. For a long moment, I stare at the steering wheel. I have no idea what to say to the guy sitting beside me. The one who has been very blunt about his interest in Alyssa.

The thing is...I can't blame him for it. And I sure as shit can't blame him for attempting to win her over. Or back. Or whatever the hell they had going on. I would do the same damn thing if I were in his position.

I have two options here. I can tell him to get fucked or—

I swivel in my seat until I can look him in the eyes. "I know that I hurt her."

His gaze hardens. Apparently, I'm not telling him that he doesn't already know. "Damn straight you did."

"But I'm not the same guy that I was before. I'm trying to prove that to her."

"Maybe so, but what's to stop you from hurting her again?"

Because...I love her.

I always have.

But I'm not about to tell him that. I haven't gotten that far with Alyssa. She's the one who deserves to hear the words first. Not him.

My jaw clenches. "I guess you'll have to take my word for it."

"Not good enough."

I shrug. "It's going to have to be."

Jack presses his lips into a tight line. It's obvious that if he didn't have to catch a flight, he'd gladly take the time to kick my ass. And part of me feels like I deserve. All right, fine...I deserve it. What I did to Alyssa sophomore year was shitty. I'm not denying that. But people make mistakes. And somehow, they redeem themselves. That's all I'm trying to do.

"You hurt her again and I'll be on the first flight back to kick your arse."

"It won't happen."

"Better not," he grumbles before exiting the BMW without another word. I pop the trunk so he can grab his luggage before doing the same. As I slam the door closed, I stuff my hands into the pockets of my jeans before grinding to an awkward halt where he waits.

"I wish I could say that it's been a pleasure, but it hasn't."

I almost snort. "I suppose that's one thing we can agree on."

The corners of his lips quirk slightly before he clears his throat. "I had better go."

"Yup." I jerk my head into a nod. The sooner the better as far as I'm concerned. I can't get him out of here fast enough.

"I'm sure this won't be the last time we see each other."

My brows lower. If I can help it, it will be.

When I remain silent, a genuine smile curves his lips. it's as if he knows exactly what I'm thinking. "I'm not going anywhere."

With that last parting shot, he leaves me standing behind my car.

Fucker.

ALYSSA

Zoe wraps her arm around me as we push through the glass doors of the fine arts building. "Have I told you how much I missed your ass?"

"Only about a dozen times, but I'm all ears if you want to tell me again."

"Well, I did. Who else can I be catty with, if not you?"

A gurgle of laughter bubbles up from my lips.

Zoe enjoys ripping the other dancers to shreds. She always has the lowdown on everyone. She knows who is sleeping with who and who is cheating on the other. Dancers, as a rule, are a cutthroat bunch. And the ones at Wesley are no exception. They'd stab a bitch in the back without blinking.

And a couple of times, I've been that bitch.

Zoe is actually one of the few I've found who has my back. And I have hers. Next to Mia, she's the person I'm closest to.

I glance at the sky, surprised to find the sun peeking through the clouds. Earlier this afternoon, it had looked like it would be dark and gloomy with impending storm clouds. Luckily, that's turned out not to be the case. I'm tempted to close my eyes and let the sun's warmth stroke over my face.

"Hmmm," Zoe says, as we jog down the wide stone steps, "isn't that Colton Montgomery over there?" Her voice turns speculative. "I wonder what he's doing hanging out on this side of campus."

Those words jolt me out of those lazy thoughts and my head whips around as I search the crowd for his blond head. It doesn't take long to find him. He's standing off to the side, near a large gurgling fountain. The fine arts building is situated directly across campus from the athletic buildings. Most of the crowd on this side of campus are the artsy bunch. Colton sticks out like a sore thumb. An athletic and handsome thumb, I think begrudgingly. Even here, when he's out of his element, people recognize and swarm him.

Unconsciously, my feet grind to a halt. I'm not even aware that I've stopped moving until Colton's gaze locks on mine. That one look has electricity sizzling in the air between us.

"Damn, girl," Zoe whispers alongside of me where she, too, has stopped, "I could get off on the hungry look in his eyes and nothing else."

Sadly, she's not wrong. I feel it like a physical caress straight down to my toes.

As much as I've tried to stomp out all of the emotions that have taken root inside me where Colton Montgomery is concerned, it hasn't done me a bit of good. They're still there, alive and well. Thriving.

"Wait just a minute," she hisses, "you two aren't together, are you?"

I shake my head. "No."

"Are you sure? The look in his eyes are all sorts of possessive."

Nope. Not at all.

A shiver scampers down my spine as I realize that she's not wrong.

As much as I don't want that knowledge to thrill me, there's no denying that it does.

The outrage in her voice disappears as a soft sigh escapes. "I could use a little of that."

When I stay rooted in place, unable to budge from the spot on the sidewalk, Colton breaks away from the group he's been mobbed by before eating up the distance between us. My heart beats into overdrive with every footstep that brings him to me. Not once does he break eye contact. Even when a few fans call his name.

Only when he's about five feet from where I stand does he stop. Uncertainty flickers across his face. It's an unusual look for him. The Colton Montgomery that I know has always been full of confidence. It practically oozes from his pores. Both on the football field and with girls.

But I can't deny that the last couple of days have been odd. Colton cooked me an amazing dinner Saturday evening. As much as I fought against it, the night ended up with him in my bed. He ran out for coffee Sunday morning and unbeknownst to him, came back with Jack in tow. We haven't had a chance to talk or sort out where we stand with one another.

I'll be honest, the unexpected visit from Jack has me rethinking everything. I've told myself since returning to Wesley that I would steer clear of Colton and yet, how many times have I ended up in his arms? Even though I only have feelings of friendship for Jack, he made me realize that I need to slow down and get some perspective instead of leaping headfirst into a bad situation.

Colton shifts his weight before shoving his hands into the pockets of his jeans. "Hey."

"Hi." The question shoots out of my mouth before I can stop it. "What are you doing here?"

"I came to see you."

A reluctant thrill shoots through me. As much as I don't want to be affected by him, I am. I always have been. "Oh."

Zoe clears her throat and I blink out of the trance that has fallen over me before shaking my head. It takes a moment to collect my thoughts. "Colton, this is my friend, Zoe."

His dark gaze flickers to her. "Yeah, I remember. You're a dance major."

She straightens up. Even though Zoe is taller than I am, Colton still dwarfs her in height. "Yes, that's right."

Colton met Zoe dozens of times when we were together, but I

didn't expect him to remember. It was a long time ago and Colton comes in contact with tons of people each week.

"I hope you don't plan on jacking around with my girl again," my friend says.

Surprised by the comment, my mouth falls open and I gasp, "Zoe!" She can be blunt to a fault. Most of the time it's a good thing. Every once in a while...not so much.

"What?" She glances at me as a fierce look glows in her eyes. "He'll answer to me if he does." She looks a little like Xena: Warrior Princess. Trust me, she can be just as fearsome. It makes me glad that she's on my side.

"You'll have to get in line," Colton mutters under his breath.

"What?" My brows draw together, not understanding the remark.

"Nothing."

His attention returns to Zoe. "I have no intention of hurting Alyssa, if that's your concern."

A reluctant thrill shoots through me.

She presses her lips together and gives him the stink eye. "That's exactly what I'm worried about. You did some real damage."

Before I can utter a squeak of mortification that they're talking about me as if I'm not even here, Zoe pulls me in for a quick hug and kisses the side of my face. "I gotta run but I'll see you tomorrow in class." She gives his one last stink eye as if to somehow prove that her words carry weight to them.

Silence descends as Zoe disappears into the crowd of student traffic. I wrack my brain for something to say. I'm not quite sure where we go from here. And I'm equally unsure where I want it to go. If anywhere. No matter how attracted I am to Colton, I still don't know if I can trust him. And that's the crux of the problem.

I shift from one foot to the other. "Why are you here?"

He clears his throat. "We're celebrating my stepmother's birthday tonight and I was wondering if you wanted to come with me."

I blink, thrown off balance by the invitation.

What's going on here?

Have I entered some kind of parallel universe?

Even during the time we were together, Colton never offered to let me meet his family. His parents attended a few Wesley football games, and he was careful to keep us separated. At the time, I brushed off the hurt feelings, telling myself it would take time to earn Colton's trust. It was yet another warning sign I had refused to pick up on because that never happened.

"Lys?"

"Ummm," my brow furrows as I blink back to the present, "Why would you want to do that?"

Guilt flickers across his face. "I want you to meet my parents." He steps closer and reaches out to tuck a stray lock of hair behind my ear. "It's something I should have done a long time ago."

I hate that he's telling me everything I want to hear. Everything I wish he would have said before. "What's the point? We're not even together." I force out the rest. "And when it comes down to it, we're not really friends."

"Aren't we?" When I remain stoically silent, he adds, "Friends, at the very least?"

"I don't know." I glance away before I can get lost in his dark depths. They've always pulled me in, making me a little stupid in the head.

"I want to be." He picks up my hand, intwining our fingers. I can't help but stare at them and remember how good it felt to wake up in bed together Sunday morning. "I want more than that, but I'm willing to take this slow and build trust."

Am I stupid for faltering? For believing him? For wanting to take a chance?

Probably.

Colton Montgomery has always been my Kryptonite. Sadly, I don't think it will ever change.

I blow out a breath, afraid to take this leap. Afraid of what it'll mean.

"Alyssa?"

"Okay," I blurt. "I'll come with you."

My heart pounds a painful staccato as a smile spreads across his face. "Really?"

"Yeah."

"Awesome." He lifts my hand to his lips before brushing a kiss across my knuckles. "I promise, you won't regret it."

God, I hope not.

ALYSSA

Three hours and a shower later, I'm seated in the front of Colton's BMW. The top is up, and we're headed north toward the place we both grew up. Although, admittedly, Colton's upbringing was vastly different. Colton grew up in a wealthy neighborhood near Beck and Mia while I was on the other side town, in a more middle-class area.

I can't resist glancing at him from the corner of my eye as I sit in the passenger seat.

Did I make a mistake?

If I did, it's much too late to do anything about it now. I'm along for the ride. There's no backing out. After a couple of miles, the familiar exit comes into view and we depart the highway and turn onto a country road surrounded by farm fields on both sides. I roll down the window and inhale a deep breath of fresh air. There's something so comforting about it that it settles the nerves fighting to break free at the bottom of my belly. I need that right now more than anything. Once on the outskirts of town, Colton turns into the drive of a gated subdivision before rolling to a stop outside an enormous iron entrance. Are they trying to keep people out or the residence in? Maybe a little of both?

Colton rolls down his window and taps a code into the control panel. Once the gate opens, we roll on through.

"Fancy," I whisper from the side of my mouth.

He snorts and keeps driving.

I've been to Mia's house more times than I can remember as well as Beck's because he was threw his fair share of parties in high school. This is the first time I've ever been to Colton's. As much as I want to remain lowkey about the situation, I'm interested to see where he grew up and meet his parents. I'm hoping it will give me more insight into who he is. Lord knows that I need it. I've never understood why Colton behaves the way he does.

Each house we pass—if that's what you want to call these monstrosities—grows in square footage. All have intricate stone masonry and thick wrought iron embellishments. Unable to help myself, I press closer to the passenger side window. Each residence has perfectly manicured lawns and flowerbeds that riot with intense color. Trees and shrubs have been pruned to an inch within their lives.

I used to look at people who lived in these mega mansions and imagine their lives were picture-perfect. I mean, how could they not be? Gorgeous house, fancy cars parked in the drive, trips to warm locales, and the best of everything.

Now I know better.

Money doesn't necessarily equate to happiness. Although, let's face it, it sure as hell makes life easier. I'm not that naive. My parents are comfortable, but they've worked hard to attain that level of financial autonomy. While we've never had an excess of money, I'm lucky they could afford for me to dance. It's not a cheap activity. Between the classes, costumes, travel, competition fees, private classes, it all adds up. It's one of the reasons I've taught in the summers.

I blink out of those thoughts as Colton turns into a long winding driveway. Trees that are in the process of losing their leaves dot the front lawn as a majestic stone structure comes into view. It has to be easily twenty thousand square feet in size. I knew Colton came from money, but I never imagined that it was this kind of wealth.

There's a stone fountain in the middle of the weathered circular brick drive. Colton pulls up to the front door before cutting the engine. For a silent moment he stares at the house as it looms in front of us. I do the same before tentatively glancing at him. A reluctant pit takes shape at the bottom of my belly.

The words shoot out of my mouth before I can stop them. "Are you sorry that you brought me with?" Truth be told, I'm wishing that I had turned down the invitation.

What am I doing here with Colton?

What's the point?

From what I can tell, he's different than the Colton I left behind for London, but is it enough? Or am I just going to end up nursing a broken heart? I can't go through that again.

Surprise fills his gaze as it snaps to mine. "Of course not. I wouldn't have asked you to come with me if I had any doubts." He turns his body toward mine. "And I wouldn't have put you in that position either."

Some of my nerves evaporate as his fingers drift across the curve of my jaw. It's so tempting to sink into his touch, but I hold back, unwilling to give in to the impulse.

"Do they know I'm coming with you?" I really hope so. Or that could make for an awkward situation.

"I called this afternoon before I extended the invite."

I release a breath. Why does this suddenly feel like such a big deal? "What did you tell them?"

One side of his mouth hitches. "Are you asking if I told them you were my girlfriend?"

A shiver dances down my spine as I nod. That's exactly what I'm asking. Two years ago, I would have been thrilled to be introduced to his family as his girlfriend. Now...

That's not the case.

A soft puff of air escapes from his lips. "I told them you were a friend from high school. Can't go wrong with the truth, right?"

I suppose not.

His hand drifts from my face to my fingers which lay twisted together in my lap. He squeezes them. "You ready to do this?"

Nope.

"I think so."

"It'll be fine. Just a couple hours and then we'll head back to campus."

With that, we exit the vehicle. As Colton rounds the hood, he extends his hand for me to take hold of. I hesitate for a heartbeat, unsure what to do. This feels like so much more than he's telling me. As much as I want to keep my heart protected against him, it's becoming increasingly more difficult to do.

When I don't immediately offer up mine, he stands still, hand outstretched. A patient look fills his eyes. It's as if he knows all of the thoughts running rampant through my brain. A tentative connection forms in the driveway. One that is undeniable. Against my better judgment, I find myself placing my fingers in his. As they close around mine, my nerve endings tingle with awareness.

In tandem, we walk up the wide stone stairs that lead to the front porch. It's wide and sweeping. A grand entrance. The mahogany door soars twenty feet in length. Colton grabs the ornate handle as I study my surroundings and swings it open. My feet stutter as I take in the two-story foyer. There is an ocean of white marble as far as the eye can see. A crystal chandelier hangs overhead that resembles a piece of art. Tiny light patterns dance across the shiny flooring. A sweeping staircase with a intricate wrought iron banister leads to the second-floor gallery. Everything is open and airy and reeks of wealth.

Sheesh.

When I turn wide questioning eyes to Colton, he shrugs and calls out before I fire off any questions, "Hello? Jenna?" He pauses as we both listen for signs of life from within this castle-like home. "Dad?"

There's the light padding of feet before a small blond woman with dark eyes walks into the entryway. A warm smile lights up her face as she pulls Colton in for a hug.

For a moment, I'm able to stand back and observe them. She's so petite in size that Colton nearly swallows her up in his arms. There's something sweet about the reunion. About the tenderness that flits across his face.

Once they break apart, the woman turns toward me. Her expression is so warm and welcoming that I'm instantly put at ease. "You must be Alyssa." She takes me into her arms as if we are old friends instead of meeting for the first time. "It's so nice to meet you," she says before drawing away.

"You, too. Happy birthday!"

She smiles. "Thank you. I'm delighted that you could join us. The more, the merrier."

"Thanks for having me."

Colton glances around. "Where's Dad?"

"Oh, he ran out to pickup dinner." She rolls her eyes. "I told him that I was happy to throw something together, but he insisted on grabbing carryout from Marco's."

"I love that restaurant," I say. It's one we frequented as a family when I was a kid. Their eggplant parm is amazing.

"Me, too. It's my favorite." She reaches out and grabs holds of Colton's hand. "You didn't have to come home just for dinner. It's such a long drive."

"I wanted to help you celebrate." His gaze flickers to mine. "Sometimes it's nice to get away from campus, even if it's for a couple of hours."

She releases his hand and waves us to the back of the house. "Let's go to the kitchen while we wait for your father to return."

We pass through the immense foyer before entering an arched gallery. A living room lies beyond that before we finally arrive at the kitchen. My gaze travels around the space. It's probably the biggest kitchen I've ever seen. Everything is white marble, stainless steel appliances, and gorgeous crystal lighting. There's not one speck of dust and nothing is out of place. It looks like something you would see in a glossy magazine spread.

"What can I get for you to drink?" Jenna asks, interrupting the whirl of my thoughts.

"Water is fine. Thank you."

"Are you sure?" She pauses near the long stretch of island. "You're more than welcome to have a glass of wine. We have a well stocked cellar downstairs."

I shake my head. Something tells me that it would be best to keep my wits about me this evening. Not that I'll need it to deal with Colton's parents, but more in regard to him. Already, I feel myself falling hard without any way to stop it. Falling any deeper for this guy is a scary prospect. He told me earlier that we could take this slow. I'm not sure if that's possible.

"I'll have water, too."

Jenna shrugs before padding to the minifridge at the island and pulling out two bottles of water. I grab the one set in front of me and unscrew the cap before taking a sip. Again, I'm given the chance to watch Colton interact with his stepmother. There's an easy banter between the two of them. It's obvious they have a strong connection as she teases him with sparkling eyes. I've known him for more than a decade, and this is probably the first time I've seen him so relaxed. It only makes me realize that even though we spent six months together, he never fully allowed himself to be genuine with me. A pang of sadness blooms inside me.

When his dark gaze catches mine, I see the questions that lurk there. When it comes to my emotions, I've always been an open book. Whatever I'm feeling, the people around me know it. I'm not one to hide them. Perhaps that's the difference between females and males. Or maybe it's because I'm used to expressing my emotions through the art of dance. If you can't do that, you lose your power to connect with the audience.

I'm pulled from those thoughts when the backdoor opens from down the hall before slamming closed and an older man walks into the kitchen carrying two white bags with the Marco's logo stamped across them. He sets them down and immediately leans over to kiss Jenna. "Happy birthday, sweetheart."

He turns to Colton and pulls him in for a hug. It's one of those manly types where they pat each other on the backs before quickly stepping away. And then his gaze falls to me. Before I can stretch out my hand for him to shake, he takes me by surprise by swallowing me up in a bear hug. Warren Montgomery is a big, burly man. He and Colton are of similar height, but Warren is broader in the chest and shoulders. Kind of like a bull. His dark hair and beard have silvered over the years. His eyes, much like his wife's, twinkle with kindness.

"Hello, Alyssa. Nice to meet you. Glad you could join us."

"Thank you for extending an invitation."

His glance flickers to his son. "It's not often that Colton brings home friends from college."

"Dad," Colton grumbles.

Unbothered by the rebuke, he continues, "I heard that you grew up around here and attended high school together," he says, unpacking the covered containers and spreading them out on the massive island.

"I've already set the table in the dining room, Warren. Let's unload the bags in there."

We each grab two or three containers and follow Jenna into the two- story dining room off the kitchen. When all of the dishes have been set out on the table, we take our seats. The table is black and stretches thirty feet in length. There is enough seating for twenty people. Since it's just the four of us, ivory and cerulean-colored China plates have been set at one end. Warren takes his place at the head of the table, Jenna on one side, as Colton and I settle opposite of her. Everything is family style, and we all dig in, helping ourselves.

Warren and Jenna pepper me with surface level questions throughout the meal. They tease Colton every chance they get. They talk about the upcoming game next weekend and how they're looking forward to cheering him on. If I weren't watching Colton so closely, I wouldn't have noticed the barely perceptible tightening of his jaw. I can't help but wonder what that's about.

Jenna turns to me. "Hopefully, we'll see you there."

Admittedly, I've avoided attending football games this season. I've been trying to break free from the hold Colton has over me and sitting in the stands for three hours, watching him out on the field, certainly won't help with that.

"Maybe," I say lightly.

"You know," Colton clears his throat, "if you guys are too busy, you don't have to attend. it's cool."

Jenna's brows beetle together as she scoffs, "We haven't been able to attend any this season." She glances at her husband. "We've missed watching you play. Now that your father isn't traveling so much, we'll be able to make the rest of your home games."

Dread flickers across his expression but it's there and gone before I can question whether it was ever there in the first place. Even though I get the feeling Colton wants to argue, he jerks his head into a tight nod.

As the conversation turns to other topics, I continue to feel thick waves of tension radiating off Colton. I can't help but wonder what's going on with him. Does this have something to do with me? Or football? Since I returned from my study abroad program, I've tried so hard to keep my distance from Colton. If people are talking about him or Wildcat football, I promptly tune them out. Only now do I wonder if there's a problem.

I don't realize that I've reached under the table until my fingers wrap around his hand and he turns his head, gaze locking on mine. As much as I don't want to feel the connection strengthen between us, that's exactly what happens. I'm powerless to stop it from happening. And maybe there's a part that doesn't want to stop it.

After dinner, I help clear the table and wash the delicate dishes. Jenna chats about her job as an elementary school teacher and the upcoming trip they have planned after Christmas.

"So, you and Colton? She watches me from beneath a thick fringe of lashes before picking up a plate and drying it. "You've known each other for a long time?"

It's a question...but then again, not really.

"Yes." I'm not sure exactly what to say or how much. That's for Colton to do. I don't want to lead her in the wrong direction. Or myself, for that matter. Although I wonder if it's already too late for that.

She nods. "Colton doesn't bring many people home. In fact," she falls silent for a moment, almost as if she's searching her brain, "he's never brought anyone home from college."

That doesn't surprise me. Even though Colton has a lot of friends and girls buzz around him like drunken bees, it's all surface level acquaintances.

When I remain silent, she continues, "He doesn't allow a lot of people in." Her lips quirk at the corners. "You must be special."

I shake my head, unwilling to let that little seed get planted in my psyche. "We're just friends."

"Hmm. That's too bad. I think you would be perfect for him."

Once upon a time, I thought the same thing. Now? I have no idea.

As I finish with the last dish, a deep voice clears their throat. I nearly bobble the plate before setting it carefully on the drying rack as my gaze slams into Colton's dark ones. His arms are crossed over his chest as he leans casually against the doorframe.

"Do you mind if I steal Alyssa away?"

Jenna picks up the last dish from the wood rack. "Of course. We'll have dessert in about thirty minutes. Sound good?"

"Yup." When he holds out his hand for me to take for a second time this evening, I don't bother trying to fight it. I gravitate across the kitchen before placing my fingers in his. A spark of energy tingles through my fingertips.

With a gentle tug, he pulls me through the gallery and foyer before we take the staircase to the second floor.

My mind buzzes on sensation overload. Everything that's taken place in the last couple of hours, the emotions he stirs so effortlessly inside me. At the top of the staircase, I'm given a bird's eye view of the entryway. "Your house is beautiful."

"Thanks. My dad built it after he and Jenna got married."

"How long have they been together?"

His brow furrows for a moment. "When I was eight years old. So they've been together for fourteen years. The trip they're taking at Christmas is to celebrate their fifteenth anniversary."

Our shoes click against the glossy hardwood that stretches throughout the hallway. Family photographs dot the walls. I'm tempted to stop and study them, but don't. This is the first time in more than a decade that I feel like I've cracked beneath the surface of Colton Montgomery and are catches glimpses of the man he truly is. I'm loath to push too hard or do something that will shut him down.

He pushed open the last door on the left and I realize with a glance that this must be his bedroom. The walls are painted navy and there is a king-sized bed dominating the space. There's a sleek dresser and desk that matches the dark wood of the bed frame. A small sofa is on the opposite side of the space with a chair making an intimate place to sit and talk. Next to the sitting area is a wall of built-in cabinetry that matches the kitchen. A mini fridge is tucked beneath the counter and a fancy stainless steel coffee marker sits on the marble countertop. Across the room are two doors. I imagine one is a walk-in closet and the other is a private bathroom. It's like a tiny apartment. The walls are dotted with football memorabilia and more photographs. If Colton weren't standing next to me, watching my every move, I'd walk around the space and study it all. It's like a peek behind the curtain.

Unsure what to do, I separate myself from him and settle on the couch. Instead of following me, he meanders to the desk before leaning against it. Energy crackles in the air between us.

I shift on the couch, aware that his gaze is fastened on me. "I like your parents."

"They like you, as well." There's a pause as remorse flashes across his expression. "I should have introduced you sooner."

When I shrug, unwilling to dwell on the past, he pushes away from the desk, closing the distance between us before settles next to me on the sofa. He turns toward me, his arm stretching across the back of the cushion. His proximity has the tempo of my heart picking up speed. When I remain still, his fingers strum the slope of my shoulder. Even though I'm wearing a light sweater, I feel the caress down to my toes. The heat of his fingers somehow burn into my flesh and tingles erupt inside me before careening down my spine. No matter what has happened between us, I can't imagine a time when my body won't react to him in this manner. I might not want it to, but that doesn't seem to matter. It's not something I can control.

My tongue darts out to moisten dry lips as I search my mind for something to say. Something that will get us back on even terrain. The question is out of my mouth before I can stop it. "At dinner, when Jenna mentioned attending your game, you didn't seem happy about it."

The energy that had been intensifying between us dissipates and for that I'm grateful.

His muscles stiffen. Even though he glances away, his fingers stay connected to my shoulder. I can't deny that part of me is thankful for killing the mood. I'm not ready for this to progress into something more.

For a long moment, I wonder if he'll bother with a response. Maybe it's better that way. If Colton can't open up and give me a glimpse into what's going on in his head, then what's the point?

I never set this up to be a test but that's what it's turned out to be.

Just as I'm about to suggest that we head back downstairs, he drags his other hand through his blond hair as his gaze returns to mine. "Coach benched me."

No matter what I thought he might say, that wasn't it. Not by a long shot. I've watched Colton play football all through high school and then the first two years of college. He's an amazing player. Solid. He could play in the NFL if he wanted. But that's not the direction he wants to take.

All of the emotion that had been swirling through me dissolves as I turn toward him. My hand settles on his muscular thigh. "What's going on? Did you get injured?"

It's obvious from the uncomfortable expression that settles on his face that he doesn't really want to discuss the situation.

"I don't know what's going on," he mutters. "I can't seem to pull it together. And I really don't want Jenna and my dad to make the trip when I probably won't see the field. They'll ask questions. And at the moment, I don't have any answers."

Sympathy floods through me as I squeeze his thigh. "I'm sorry."

Even though football and dance are nothing alike, I know what it feels like to be off. To know that you can do better but aren't able to pull it out for whatever reason. It's frustrating because you don't know if it's simply a phase or if you've lost your edge. Is there anything worse than that? It's a mindfuck and once you start to go down that road of self-doubt, it can be tough to mentally get straight again. "Is there anything I can do to help?"

"No." He shakes his head. "It's something I need to figure out for myself."

"If you ever want to talk, I'm here."

"I appreciate that more than you realize." He pauses before blowing out a breath, "I keep telling myself that it's a slump and it'll pass but so far, that hasn't turned out to be the case."

As I rub his thigh, his gaze drops to my hand. We both still before I hesitantly remove it and clear my throat, shifting away from him and fiddling with the hem of my shorts. My gaze bounces around the room. I notice photos of Jenna and Warren. Even one with Beck. They're wearing their high school football uniforms with their arms thrown around each other's shoulders. both are beaming at the camera.

What I don't notice are any of his mother. I remember hearing stories, but I have no idea where the truth lies. When we were together, I was too afraid to ask about her.

The question sits perched on my tongue but I'm unable to release it into the atmosphere.

"What are you thinking?"

My teeth sink into my lower lip as I shrug. The words are so close to bursting free, but I'm afraid to push for more information. I'm afraid he'll shut down and this little bit of intimacy we're sharing will vanish.

With a slight tilt to his head, he narrows his eyes. "Come on, I can tell there's something on your mind. Out with it already."

Air escapes from my lungs in a rush. Even though we're not together and haven't been for some time, Colton can still read me. It's both disconcerting and comforting at the same time.

"There are pictures of Jenna and Warren, but none of your mother." Hastily, I add, "You never talk about her."

Silence descends. It becomes so heavy that it feels stifling. Almost as if I can't breathe.

"No," he mutters, "I don't." His lips curve into a frown as his forehead creases.

The moment stretches uncomfortably between us until it feels as if it could snap.

"I'm sorry," I whisper. "I shouldn't have brought it up."

Colton drags a hand over his face. "Don't be."

In one swift movement, he reaches over and plucks me off the couch before settling me on his lap so that I'm able to sit astride his lap. My knees get buried in the cushions as he holds me firmly in place. The pain that reverberates in his eyes has my heart jackhammering a painful staccato.

"Forget I asked. We can talk about something else." His fingers are wrapped around my waist, holding me in place. The heat of them burns the flesh beneath. It's like a tattoo that will always be there, branding me as his.

"Alyssa, it's all right. You can ask me questions." There's a pause. "I want to open up." He shrugs. "Just be patient with me. I'm not used to talking about her. It's difficult."

That's all it takes to have my heart shattering into a million broken pieces as one of my hands drifts to his shadowed cheek. Even though I'm sitting on his lap, I need this connection to him.

"My parents met when they were young. My dad was attending college and Candance—that's my mother's name—was in art school. The way dad tells it, they met at a party, fell instantly in love, and decided to elope. They got married in Vegas."

Wow. That's actually kind of a romantic story.

Before I can ask any questions, he continues with a shrug. "Two years later, I was born. Unfortunately, Candance was more interested in her art than me. So my dad hired a nanny to take care of me during the day so she could work at her studio. Instead of coming home at the end of the day, she started staying later and later, sometimes spending the night. She would get lost in her work and would lose track of time. I remember being at her studio and watching her work. It was like she wasn't aware of the world around her." His voice trails off as his eyes take on a faraway quality.

I don't realize how tense my muscles have become until I ask, "What happened then?"

He blinks back to present and the haze disappears. "When I was four, she decided that she could be a mother and an artist."

My heart clenches.

His voice turns devoid of emotion even though I see hints of it in his eyes. "She packed her bags and left."

"I'm so sorry." My other hand rises so that I am holding both cheeks in the palm of my hands. "Do you see her? Talk to her?"

He glances away and mutters, "In the beginning, she would send a few cards a year, but then it tapered off." His brow furrows. "Honestly, I can't remember the last time I heard from her. More than a decade, for sure."

My heart squeezes until it becomes difficult to breathe. I can't imagine what it would be like to have a parent walk away. To pick something or someone else over their own flesh and blood. I feel like crap for poking my nose where it didn't belong.

Colton's hand rises from my waist, the thumb softly feathering under my eye. Only when it comes away with wetness do I realize that tears have gathered in my eyes.

"Don't cry."

"I'm sorry," I repeat. For his mother walking away but also for dredging it up.

"Don't be. You can't miss what you never knew."

He swipes at my other eye before locking his hands around the sides of my head and pulling me close until our foreheads touch. Our gazes stay locked as the connection grows between us.

"I'm glad you came home with me and got a chance to meet the people who matter most in my life."

"Me, too." It's meant more than he can possibly know. More than I'm afraid to acknowledge, even to myself. "Thanks for inviting me."

"I'm going to kiss you, Lys."

"Okay."

As soon as the word is released into the atmosphere, he tilts his head until his lips can slant across mine. Unlike the kiss in Bang Bang's parking lot, this one unfolds slowly as if we have all the time int he world to explore one another. When his tongue sweeps across the seam of my lips, I open, allowing him entrance. They tangle as the slide of velvety softness takes me to the bottom of the ocean.

Uncovering this side of him, the one that is able to rip down the walls I've erected to keep him at bay one brick at a time, is exactly what I was afraid of. That knowledge isn't enough to stop me from falling even more in love with him.

COLTON

With my arms folded behind my head, I stare at the ceiling as everything from tonight crashes around inside my brain. If there's one thing that I hate, it's thinking about Candance. She's like Beetlejuice. Say her name three times and she magically appears inside my head, taking up residence like an unwanted squatter.

And that, on top of everything else going on, is the last thing I need or want.

The woman abandoned me when I needed her most. She walked away without ever looking back. There's a giant void in her place. It's one Jenna has diligently tried to fill.

Everything softens within me as I think about my stepmother. Truth be told, she's so much more than that. She's the mother Candance never could be. Or, more to the point, never wanted to be.

I'm not embarrassed to admit that I love Jenna. I appreciate everything she's done for me over the years. Driving my ass around town before I had a license. Helping me with homework when I didn't understand something or needed help doing research. Holding me in the middle of the night when I would cry, missing Candance. Instead of badmouthing Candance, Jenna always tried to explain that people sometimes can't be what we need them to be. And that's neither of our faults.

The times that Candance allowed me to tag along with her to the studio stick out in my head vividly. Probably because they were a rarity. She would set me in the corner with a few toys while she became absorbed in her artwork. Hours would pass and I would try to be as quiet as I could. Even then, at age four, I somehow realized that my silence is the only thing that would win her over.

In the end, it didn't work. No matter how quiet, or how good, she still chose to leave.

By the time Jenna came around, I was so starved for attention, that I glommed onto her from the very beginning. I allowed her to cuddle me to her heart's content. Even though she poured every drop of love into me, it wasn't enough. Candance's rejection eats away at me.

It's fucked up.

Why can't I forget her as easily as she's forgotten me?

I wish it were possible to bury all of my memories of her so deep down in my subconscious that I would never think about her or them again.

Another thirty minutes pass by as I toss and turn before finally throwing off the covers and rolling from the bed. Unable to sleep, I pace the dark room at one o'clock in the morning. It's as if there is a scratch deep beneath my skin that is impossible to scratch.

And the one person I long to see, who could make it better, is asleep in her own bed in the apartment next to mine. She's so close and yet a million miles away. After we left my parents' house around nine o'clock and arrived back around eleven. The car ride back had been a quiet one. Not uncomfortable. It's as if we both had been lost in our own thoughts. I dropped her off at her doorstep. Unable to resist, I'd cupped her cheeks in my hands like I'd done earlier that evening in my room and pressed my lips to hers before quickly step-ping away before anything more could happen. It wouldn't have taken much for me to pick her up and carry Alyssa back to my place. The need to be buried in her tight heat had throbbed through me. if there's anything that could make me forget dredging up painful memories of Candance, it's that.

As difficult as it was, I restrained myself. Alyssa needs me to prove to her that I'm not the guy who walked away from her. And that exactly what I'm trying to do.

Jenna had texted me on the ride home and told me how much she and Dad enjoyed meeting Alyssa. How they hope to see her soon.

Hint, hint.

Little do they know that the decision for our future rests in Alyssa's hands.

As I swing around, ready to pace the length of the room, my phone lights up with an incoming message. I move closer before glancing at it.

Alyssa.

You awake?

That's all it takes for me to pounce on the slim device.

Yeah. Can't sleep.

Me, neither. Want to come over?

Be there in a minute.

I toss down the phone and go to the apartment door, cracking it open and peering outside. Alyssa carefully closes the door behind her before jogging toward me.

"Hi." she sounds just a bit winded.

I return the greeting before opening the door more fully and stepping aside. Once she's inside, I close it and nab her fingers with my own, towing her to my room. With the lock secured, I lean against the door. The urge to take her into my arms is so strong that I tighten my hands, so I don't do exactly that. Instead, I hold back, giving her space, needing her to make the first move.

"Why couldn't you sleep," I ask.

She shrugs, looking as tense as I am. "There's a lot going through my head, I guess."

"Me, too." Instead of making her ask, I add, "Most of the time I'm able to forget Candance ever existed. Tonight dredged up a lot for me. More than I realized."

Her expression turns to one of concern as she closes the distance between us before stopping a foot from where I stand with my back to the door. "I'm sorry about that. I shouldn't have asked all those questions."

Unable to control myself, I give in to the temptation and reach out, tugging her to me. Alyssa's palms go to my chest but don't push me away. "I'm glad you did. I'm trying really hard to let you in, Lys. It's not easy. For all I know, it's too late, but I'm trying."

A puff of air escapes from her lips. "It's not too late."

The tension gathered in my muscles, drains away, leaving me limp with relief. I didn't realize how much I needed her to say those words until she did. They give me hope where I wasn't sure there was any. My arms band around her, drawing her closer until our chests are pressed together. Her arms slip around my neck as she lays her head on me.

Even though the words are scary to admit, especially out loud, I want to share them with her.

I *need* to share them with her.

"Sometimes I wonder where she is," I whisper into the darkness that blankets us. "And what she's doing."

Alyssa lifts her head and searches my face. "Have you ever tried to find her?"

Find her?

Hell, no.

Even the thought is enough to make my palms sweaty. I shake my head. Part of me is deathly afraid of what I'd find. In a way, it would be like opening a Pandora's Box. Once you do that, there is no way to shove everything back inside.

Am I really ready for that?

"Do you want to look her up?" she asks, breaking into the chaotic whirl of my thoughts.

I suck my lower lip between my teeth and chew it.

I don't know...do I?

Sure, part of me is curious. It's been more than fifteen years. Most of which there has been nothing but silence from her end. For all I know, she could be dead. I allow that thought to settle inside me before examining it carefully.

It probably would be easy to figure out. Hell, I could Google her and probably come away with at least some information. Enough to satisfy this growing need inside me.

Then again, maybe the best thing I can do for myself is leave the past where it belongs. In the past.

Why does this have to be so difficult?

"We could do a Facebook search and see if she pops up," Alyssa says.

Yes, I suppose we could. Except that suggestion sends my belly into a free fall. It's a frightening thought. And I'm not used to feeling that emotion course through me. Everything inside me screams to shut it down so I don't have to experience it.

"Colton?"

I blink and refocus on Alyssa. She's the only thing that grounds me in the moment. "Okay."

Did I really just say that? I'm almost desperate to snatch it back out of the air. Instead, I remain silent, muscles coiled tight.

"Really?" Her brows rise as she searches my eyes.

Fuck.

Fuck.

Fuck.

"Yeah," I confirm with a grunt as nausea grows in the pit of my belly. Let's say we find something...it doesn't necessarily mean I can't just hold onto the information. Hell, best case scenario, it's enough for me to put all these uncomfortable feelings scratching beneath the surface to rest once and for good. And in the end, that's all I really want, right?

"You don't have to do this," she says.

But I've come this far, do I really want to back down now? Will I ever find the courage to do it again?

"I know."

She nods. "Do you want to do it now or wait until tomorrow?"

If I wait, I might chicken out. Scratch that, I'll *definitely* chicken out. As far as I'm concerned, it's now or never. "Let's just get it over with."

Her hands slide from around my neck where they've been draped, up my neck, before cupping the sides of my cheeks. She leans up on her tiptoes before pressing her lips against mine. Before I can sink into the kiss, she draws away. "I'll be right here with you."

I jerk my head into a nod as she steps away.

On legs that feel wooden, I walk across the room and grab my laptop from my backpack before we settle on the queen-sized mattress. Alyssa sits close enough for our shoulders and thighs touch. Barely do I acknowledge to myself that this is really the first time she's taken the initiative to be near me since she's returned from London. Almost as if to punctuate that thought, her fingers settle on my thigh and I have to admit, having her here with me helps.

With a pounding heart, I fire up the computer. It takes a moment for the screen to illuminate and to click onto the internet. When my home screen pops up, my fingers hover over the keys before I force myself to type her full name into the search engine.

"Candance Radcliffe?"

"She never took my father's name," I mumble.

I stare at the name until it blurs before my eyes. My finger hovers over the Enter button. I don't realize that air has become trapped in my lungs until they begin to burn. And even then, I refuse to release it. It's only when little spot dance across my vision that it escapes, and I stab the plastic key before I talk myself out of it. A second later, a page full of information materializes on the screen.

A colorful photograph pops up.

My heart skips a painful beat.

Alyssa's fingers dig into the flesh of my leg. I don't even think she's aware that she's doing it. The pain is the only thing that grounds me in the moment. Otherwise I would float away. And that's a frightening feeling. "Is that her?"

I allow myself to time to scrutinize the picture in silence, absorbing every detail about it. The blonde hair that falls around her shoulders. The lines in her face that bracket both her eyes and mouth.

Even though sixteen years have past, it's strange for this photo to replace the image of a younger looking Candance in my mind. The one I've been carrying around with me since she walked away.

I flinch when Alyssa clicks on the photo so that it takes up almost the entirety of the screen.

"She's pretty."

There's a faraway quality filling Alyssa's voice. As if she's talking to me from beneath the water. Then again, everything around me feels murky, so maybe I'm the one under water.

I focus on Candance's profile, attempting to dissect it almost clinically.

When I was little, I remember thinking that my mother was the most beautiful woman in the world. Even when she was wearing paint splattered shirts and jeans with her hair tied up in a blue bandana, so that it would be away from her face. The few times I was allowed to watch her paint, she'd get a dreamy look in her eyes that made her seem as if she wasn't there in the room with me. Almost as if she were unreachable. Wisps of smoke.

I remember thinking that I could stare to my heart's content but never touch. I'm not sure why that memory fills me with pain, but it does.

"It says she owns a gallery where her work is exclusively displayed."

Alyssa's words are like that of a gunshot in the stillness of the room. When I remain silent, trapped int he past, she clicks on the little blurb, bringing up a full page of information.

A heaviness fills my chest as I skim over the paragraphs. A few of photographs of her paintings and the gallery are showcased. It's the last picture that has me wheezing out a painful breath.

"Oh." She shifts on the bed next to me.

It's one of a happy family.

Candance is seated alongside an older man. Each one of them holds a child in their arms. Both girls are blond with dark eyes just like Candance.

"Colton?" Alyssa squeezes my thigh again. "Are you all right?"

There's that faraway quality again.

It's kind of funny. I didn't think it was possible for this woman to hurt me any more than she already has, but I was wrong. Because this feels agonizing. Almost as if my chest is on fire.

Did she really walk away from us only to start a brand new family?

Did she really leave me behind?

"Colton?" Her voice dips, concern dripping from it. "Talk to me."

A ragged sound escapes from between my lips.

It's carefully that Alyssa pulls the computer from my hands before setting it down on the desk at the far side of the room and returning to the bed where I sit frozen in place. She maneuvers her way between my legs and threads her arms around my neck. She's so close that I have no other choice but to tilt my head in order to meet her concerned gaze.

My first instinct is to shutdown so the pain-riddled emotion rampaging through me is stopped dead in its tracks before it can infiltrate and wreck further damage. But if I did that, I'll be closing myself off from Alyssa and that would only push her away.

It doesn't escape that this situation is self-inflicted. If I had never gone looking for Candance, I wouldn't inflicted myself with all this hurt. I close my eyes and allow the grief to crash over me like a tidal wave.

Her hands grip my face, forcing me to acknowledge that I'm not alone. I take a breath and force out the words. "I'm all right."

That's a lie but it's the best I can do.

Her lips feather across mine before she whispers, "I'm so sorry, Colton."

"Yeah, me too."

"Do you want me to leave? Would you rather be alone?"

I shake my head. The thought of being left to my own devices with all this emotion crashing around inside me is a frightening one. "Stay. Please."

"Okay."

Before I can say anything more, Alyssa grabs the hem of her T-shirt and drags it up her body, pulling it over her head. My gaze skims across bare breasts as her fingers settle on the elastic band of her shorts before she shoves them down, revealing her slim form. There is nothing more beautiful in this world than the sight of Alyssa. Not allowing me time to soak in the sight before me, she grabs my hand and pulls me to my feet before hastily divesting me of my clothing until I'm just as naked as she is.

Somehow Alyssa accomplishes the impossible and I forget all about Candance and the hurt coursing through. Maybe it'll be short lived and, in an hour, the pain will once again flare back to life, but I'll take it.

With greedy fingers, I'll take it.

ALYSSA

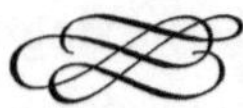

This night has swerved a direction I could have never predicted when I saw him standing outside the fine arts building this afternoon. Even though I've done everything possible to keep Colton at arm's length to avoid developing feelings for him. It's been a losing battle from the very beginning. If I hadn't realized it when we talked in his room, I do now.

There is something undeniable between us. There always has been. I'm tired of trying to fight the attraction. I'm tired of fighting the feelings that are still there. Or denying they exist in a feeble attempt to move on. I can't do it any longer. I have no idea what will happen between us or how this will ultimately end. For all I know, it could be badly. What I do know is that there is relief in finally accepting the situation.

I place my palms on his naked chest, slowly sweeping them up, needing to feel the sinewy strength that lies beneath. I rise to my tiptoes until my lips can brush across his. My hands drift from his chest to the rock-solid definition of his abdominals before dropping lower and brushing over his hard length. With gentle strokes, I slide my hand across him. He stiffens beneath my touch. With one final kiss against his lips, I sink to my knees. My head tips back so I can hold his gaze.

"You don't have to do that," he rasps, brushing the hair away from my face. "It's not why I asked you here."

"I know." My lips feather over the head of his cock. "I want to." As the comment slides from my lips, I realize how true they are. I love Colton's cock. Love the way it feels in my mouth. Love breaking him down and making him lose control. Especially now, knowing how tightly leashed he keeps his emotions. As if to prove the words, my tongue darts out to lick the crown of his cock. "I missed you the same way you missed me."

He groans as I open my mouth wide and draw him deep inside. My gaze stays trained on him as his fingers tangle in my hair, holding me loosely in place.

"Fuck, baby. I missed this," he growls as I work him with my mouth.

The feel of him turning to steel as he slides deeper down my throat is its own reward. It only proves what I've been trying to deny to myself. Sex with Colton has always been explosive. Addictive. Whether I realized it or not, Colton has been as a measuring stick I used against every guy I've ever been with. And they always come up sadly lacking.

At this very moment, with all these emotions careening around inside me, it seems foolish that I ever thought I could move on from him so easily. Or that I could will it with my mind.

His fingers tighten around the sides of my skull as I take him in deeper. It's so deep, that he nudges the back of my throat. Every line of tension filling his face eases, leaving behind pure bliss in its place.

Me. I'm the one who did that. I'm the one who wiped away all the angst plaguing him.

Instead of closing his eyes and tilting his head back, so he can enjoy the moment, his gaze stay pinned to mine.

"I love watching you suck my cock. There's nothing hotter than watching it disappear between your lips."

A punch of arousal slams into me and my panties flood with heat. No one has ever turned me on like him.

His erection grows unbearably hard. When his muscles tighten, and his fingers dig into my scalp, I know he's hovering at the edge of his release.

"I'm going to cum," he groans.

The admission only spurs on my movements. My mouth turns voracious as I draw him deeper until the crown of his cock hits the back of my throat. Until I'm able to reach the root of him. It takes everything I have inside not to gag.

"*Fuck.*"

And then he's exploding inside me. I drink down the hot spurts, milking him until his body loosens and his cock turns slack in my mouth. It's only then that I release him. I nuzzle the velvety tip with my lips. His hands loosen, sliding from my hair and beneath my arms as he drags me off my knees and to my feet. His lips descend in a hungry kiss that is both possessive and consuming.

Colton spins us around and walks us backward. Before I realize what's happening, my back hits the bed and he's falling on top of me, pinning me to the mattress.

"Do you have any idea how much I want you?" His mouth roams from my gasping lips to my chin before descending. "I always have. Even when I forced you away, I wanted you. You've always scared the fuck out of me."

His words circle through my head as I open my eyes and stare at the ceiling. Knowing everything I do now, they make sense. I admitted my feelings for him, and he pushed me away. Afraid to be hurt. He spreads my thighs wide before settling between them. He peppers soft caresses against me all the while continuing to talk. I'm not even sure he realizes the secrets he's so intent on spilling.

"I have no idea what you see in me, baby. I really don't."

When his tongue darts inside my heat, I suck in a breath.

"I never wanted you to get so close. I never wanted you to matter. I fought against it for as long as I could."

He spreads my lower lips with his thumbs. Cool air hits my core as the velvety softness of his tongue swirls around my clit. He's only begun to touch me and already I'm hovering at the brink of falling apart. This man knows exactly how to touch me. He knows exactly what will leave me in pieces.

"It doesn't make sense," he mutters. My ears prick, trying to catch the words. "How could you love me when my own mother couldn't?"

A bolt of sympathy cuts through the pleasure growing inside me, yanking me back from the precipice. It's almost as if Colton realizes that his words are counterproductive to what he's trying to achieve. With renewed efforts, he attacks my flesh. Pushing me relentlessly when I'd prefer to stop and allow me to hold him, soothing away the pain that lives deep inside him. Pain he barely acknowledges to himself and never to me. But he refuses to do that. Instead, his tongue cracks over me, spearing inside, lapping at my shuddering softness, driving me relentlessly toward orgasm until I have no other choice but to dive headfirst off the cliff.

I scream out my release, pressing a hand over my mouth and squeezing my eyelids closed as wave after wave of pleasure crashes over me. His mouth is relentless, his tongue circling my throbbing clit. When I try to writhe beneath him, squirming to get away, to lessen the intensity of the moment, his hands tighten on my thighs, not allowing me a moment of respite.

It's only when my muscles turn lax beneath him does he raise his head. My eyes crack open to meet his glowing stare. He crawls up my body and settles between my spread thighs before driving his hard deep cock inside me with one swift movement. And then he's buried to the hilt and we are locked together as one. Only then can I breathe. There is a rightness to our joining. As if this is exactly where he belongs. As if he belongs to me and I to him.

His gaze fastens onto mine and the world around us falls away.

I expect him to take me in the same manner as he just did. Instead, there's a tenderness to his movements. Almost as if he's making love to me as his body rocks gently against me. Needing to ground myself in this moment, I lift my hands until they're able to cup his cheeks. Even though I've just cum, another orgasm builds inside me.

"Please don't ever leave me, Alyssa," he whispers into the darkness. "Don't leave me the way she did."

Instead of my body splintering apart into a million jagged pieces, it's my heart.

COLTON

*J*ust as I'm adding the finishing touches to a paper, an email pops up in the corner of my computer screen. Everything inside me freezes as I stare at the name. It's as if I'm dangling at the tippy top of a sky-high rollercoaster, perched for a descent.

C. Radcliffe.

In what universe did I think reaching out to my mother was a good idea? Why did I think it would give me the closure I needed to move on with my life?

Right now, it seems like the worst thing I could have possibly done.

All of a sudden, I feel like I'm going to puke.

Instead of opening up the message and reading it, I slam the laptop closed and shove away from the table I've been working at. The more distance I put between myself and that computer, the better off I am. My chest feels heavy. It feels as if there is a thousand-pound elephant sitting on it, making it impossible to breathe.

A cold sweat breaks out across my brow as I grab my keys and wallet and head out the apartment. Less than twenty long-legged strides brings me to Alyssa's door. I rap my knuckles against the heavy wood and shift impatiently from one foot to another.

I plow a hand through my hair as the seconds pass.

Where the hell is that girl?

I'm about to raise my fist and rap my knuckles against the wood when the door swings wide and I find Alyssa standing on the other side. Her eyes widen when as she takes me in before throwing a cautious glance over her shoulder. "Hi."

My gaze shifts and I notice Mia sitting on the couch in their living room, watching us with interest.

I couldn't give a damn.

I need Alyssa. And I need her now.

When her gaze returns to mine, it only takes a moment before her expression turns to one of concerns. It's like she realizes without me telling her that something is wrong.

"Hey." My voice drops. "Can you talk?"

"Yeah. What's wrong?"

I jerk my shoulders. There's no way I can get into it here. We need to go somewhere private and talk.

Alyssa shoots another look over her shoulder before clearing her throat. "So…we're going to grab something to eat."

"Really?" Mia points to the empty food container on the coffee table. "You just inhaled an entire enchilada."

Alyssa's eyes narrow. "I have a big appetite. Are you trying to food shame me?"

Her roommate's lips twitch as her shoulders shake with silent laughter. "Not at all."

When color seeps into Alyssa's cheeks, it occurs to me that ALyssa hasn't told Mia what's going on between us. I can't exactly blame her for not telling Mia. Alyssa was more than clear about needing time. She wants to ease into this relationship slowly. After the way I treated her before, I can't blame her for that. I just need to keep proving to her that she can take a chance on me.

Not bothering with any further explanation, she mutters, "I'll see you later." Then she swipes her purse off the credenza in the tiny entryway.

"Yes, we'll definitely talk—"

Alyssa doesn't give Mia a chance to finish the sentence before she's pulling the apartment door closed behind her.

She drags a hand over her face before it settles against her mouth. The words come out sounded mumbled. "I'll have a lot to answer for when I return."

"Sorry. I'm not trying to complicate matters. It's just..." my voice trails off.

Her hand falls away from her face before finding mine. I stare at our clasped hands and focus on the connection between us. Some of the fear and anxiety that had been bubbling up inside me slowly recedes. My chest doesn't feel quite so heavy anymore.

"It's all right." She gives me a tentative smile. "I should really come clean and tell Mia what's going on between us."

For one glorious moment, I forget all about Candance as I step closer and take Alyssa into my arms. "Hmmm. Is there something going on between us?" Why does everything feel so much better when she's locked in my arms?

Her expression softens. "I really hope so."

My lips descend, sliding over hers. Just as I deepen the kiss, needing her sweetness to sooth my soul, her palms press against my chest, creating unwanted space between us.

"Tell me what happened."

That's all it takes for everything to come crashing down on me. And then I'm buried beneath an avalanche of emotion. "Let's go somewhere else and talk about it. Did you want to grab something to eat?"

Alyssa shakes her head and pats her belly. A slight smile curves her lips. "Mia was right. I just inhaled an enchilada. I'm stuffed. How about a walk?"

"Sure, that works." Maybe I can burn off some of this excess energy simmering beneath my skin. Any moment, it's going to burst free.

With our hands threaded together, I push through the stairwell door. It only takes a couple of minutes before we're walking out of the building and heading toward campus. With Alyssa's hand ensconced firmly in mine, I feel like I can breathe again. Even as everything we found on the web a few nights ago circles through my head.

She left me and started another family.

I'm so lost in thought that I don't realize we're on campus until Alyssa points to a park bench off the beaten path on a grassy knoll. "Want to sit over there and talk?"

Dread pools in my belly. As much as I don't want to have this conversation, it needs to be purged from my body before it has a chance to fester. Maybe the smartest thing to do would be to delete the email and pretend I never reached out. But what then? I live the rest of my life like this? Pushing people away so never get a chance to get close and leave like she did?

"Yeah." Not once does my hand leaves hers. I need her strength and support to get me through this.

We settle on the black iron bench. She turns her body so that it faces mine. When I remain silent, she says, "Tell me what happened."

A burst of air escapes from my lungs. "Candance wants to meet."

Alyssa's eyes widen. There's a pause before the question bursts from her lips. "You reached out to her?"

I jerk my head into a regretful nod. It was a moment of weakness in the early hours of the night when I was lying awake, questions eating away at me. I have no idea if I'm ready to come face-to-face with her. I can't image ever being ready for that. I don't even know what I'd say.

Hey, how are you?

How's the fam?

Why did you throw me away and start over?

I wince at the last thought.

"I emailed her after we found her online." I shrug. "I don't know what I was expecting."

That's not *altogether* true. I haven't heard from the women in more than a decade. I figured she wouldn't bother and then I could put to rest all these feelings inside me. Instead, she responded.

"You reached out and now she wants to meet with you." The corners of Alyssa's lips lift as if she's encouraged by this new development.

Hearing her say those words out loud makes me nauseous. I'm not ready for this. I'm not sure if I'll ever be ready for it.

When I remain silent, she asks, "This is what you wanted, right?"

I plow a hand through my hair and focus on the trees that dot the landscape surrounding us. The picturesque setting with all its greenery and red brick buildings and ivy clinging to the walls isn't enough to distract me. Already leaves are falling to the ground, creating a carpet of golds and reds. "I don't know." I hesitate before adding, "Part of me is sorry that I ever looked her up."

"You don't have to take this any further. You can change your mind." Her fingers tighten around mine. "You don't owe this woman anything."

How sad is that? The woman is my mother. Biologically speaking, anyway.

A fresh wave of grief crashes over me. It sucks that all this has done is dredge up even more emotion inside me. The hurt and pain from her abandonment still lives inside me. Only now do I realize that the memories and damage she inflicted have held me prisoner. Candance might have walked out of my life more than fifteen years ago but she's still controlling it as if she were here beside me and I'm tired of it.

Tired of her having all that power.

There has to be a way to exorcise these demons. What scares me most is that there might not be a way to put the past behind me and move forward. Maybe it's too late. Maybe these feelings are too engrained within me.

I never dealt with the havoc Candance wreaked inside me. Honestly, I thought if I stuffed it down deep enough, I would eventually forget about it. Guess the jokes on me, that never happened. And I've been paying the consequences of it ever since.

When I lived at home, Jenna would broach the subject of counseling every so often and I'd scoff at not only her, but the idea of crying on some stranger's shoulder about the bullshit in the past. I couldn't see how my mother walking out on me when I was just a kid could impact the future or my happiness.

I don't know if that would have saved me from any of the pain I've experienced but it sure as hell couldn't have hurt.

"You're right, I don't owe her anything but maybe I owe it to myself," I finally admit.

"Whatever you decide," Alyssa says, leaning against my shoulder and holding me tight, "I'll be here for you."

Little does she know that those words mean everything.

COLTON

*F*uck.

Why did I agree to this?

Why did I even reach out in the first place?

Why couldn't I have left well enough alone?

I was perfectly fine living my life.

Well...maybe perfectly fine is something of an overstatement, but it was all good.

I sit behind the wheel of my BMW in a parking space on the street in front of the coffee shop somewhere in the middle of where we both live. It's about an hour away from school. The only other person who knows I'm here is Alyssa. I couldn't bring myself to tell Dad or Jenna. They probably would have tried to talk me out of this. Maybe not Jenna. I think she would understand. But Dad?

He definitely would have. He loves Jenna but he's salty about how Candance just walked out of our lives without ever looking back.

As I stare at the cream brick and the worn wooden sign that hangs over the door, I'm kind of wishing I would have given them the chance to change my mind.

I don't want to be here. And yet, I can't bring myself to turn the key in the ignition and drive away. I'm stuck.

Frozen in place.

Instead of exiting the vehicle, I grab my phone from the seat next to me and hit the contact at the top of my list. A few seconds later, the phone rings.

Just as I'm about to hit disconnect, a breathless voice comes over the line. "Hello?"

I clear the emotion that has welled in my throat and try to keep my tone light. "Hey."

"Hi, sweetie." Her voice warms, as if she's happy that I called. "How are you?"

"Good." That's a lie but I can't bring myself to tell Jenna the truth. Even though it sits perched at the tip of my tongue, waiting to burst free.

There's a pause. I can almost hear the wheels in her head turning. That little frown she gets when she's attempting to figure out the truth. Maybe calling her was just as bad of an idea as agreeing to meet Candance.

"Are you sure?" she questions carefully. "You sound strange. Like you've got something to tell me that I'm not going to like."

That's the thing about Jenna, she's has always been perceptive. Especially where I'm concerned. I might not be her own flesh and blood, but we've always been highly attuned. Instead of coming clean, I force out a chuckle. "Nah, it's all good. I had a little time to kill between classes and thought I'd check in and see how everything's going. It's been a couple of days."

"Oh, you're so sweet. You're lucky that you caught me when the kids are at music."

Right. I forgot that she's at school.

"Oh, sorry."

She laughs. It's a soft tinkling sound that washing over me, immediately settles something deep inside. "It's not a problem. You know that I love talking to you. Even if it's just for a few minutes. Even though you're not far, it'll be nice when you move back here again and start working for your father. Then you can pop home any time you want. Or we can grab lunch."

That does sound nice. I've enjoyed my years at Wesley but it's getting old, if you can believe that. I'm ready to graduate and move on. I know some people don't feel that way. They want to cling to the party lifestyle. A few actually talked about coming back for a fifth year. Until their parents put the kibosh on that.

"So, what do you have going on for the rest of the day?"

I blink back to the present and stare at the coffee house in front of me. "Oh, you know. Class. Practice." I gulp. "Probably hit the library and study for a test."

"Sounds like college."

Yup.

When I remain silent, she says, "You sure nothing is bothering you?"

"It's all good." I feel like shit for lying to her. If there's one person I'm honest with, it's Jenna. She's never judged me for anything. Not that she didn't hold my feet to the fire when I fucked up, but she was always there, no matter what.

Can't say that about everyone.

I squeeze my eyes closed, allowing the sound of her soft melodic voice to wash over me. Two women hold importance in my life, and this is one of them. Alyssa is the other. It wasn't until she left the summer of our junior year that I realized just how spectacularly I fucked up our relationship.

It's almost as if she can sense the direction of my thoughts. "We enjoyed meeting Alyssa last week." her voice turns cagey. "Any chance we'll be seeing more of her?"

A smile tugs at the corners of my lips. "I hope so."

"Good. I'll talk to your father and we'll set something up soon."

"Sounds like a plan." I glance at the digital clock on the dash and realize that it's ten minutes past the time we're supposed to meet. "I should probably get moving."

"All right. I'm glad you called. Love you."

A thick lump settles in the middle of my throat as I parrot the sentiment back to her, meaning every single word. "Love you, too."

As soon as I disconnect, I pocket the phone, grab my keys, and force myself to exit the BMW. I grab a few coins from my pocket and add them to the parking meter before crossing the sidewalk.

One thick cement step.

Then another.

I pull open the door and step inside the small space. Air gets wedged in my throat as my gaze coasts over the tables that are crammed together. There are a few couches and chairs situated around a coffee table. Bright artwork decorates the walls. Music plays in the background. The atmosphere has a hip vibe to it. Most of the patrons look young. Early twenties or so. Definitely an artsy crowd.

It's only when my lungs begin to burn, do I realize that I've been holding my breath. It escapes from my lips in a rush as I decide what to do. No one here looks over the age of forty or what I remember Candance looking like.

So, it would seem like even though I'm late. She's later.

Or maybe she changed her mind and decided to pull another disappearing act on me.

How ironic would that be?

Instead of grabbing a drink, I head to a lone table parked in the back and settle on a chair that faces the door. Nerves skitter along my flesh as I slip the phone from my pocket and open the home screen.

She's fifteen minutes late.

I'll give it another ten minutes and then I'm out of here. I've already wasted enough time on this. If her not showing isn't closure, I don't know what is.

Alyssa had offered to make the trip with me, even to just wait in the car, but I'd turned her down.

I'm regretting that decision at the moment.

I wish she were here with me. I wish I could reach out and grab hold of her hand. She's the one person who is able to settle all the chaos inside me.

Every time the door opens and the little bell above it chimes, I have a whiplash moment and everything inside me freezes only to realize that it's not her. I glance at my phone again.

Twenty-five minutes late.

Why is this even a surprise. I should have fully expected that she would flake out on me.

You know what?

I'm done.

I'm not going to sit my ass here and continue waiting around for a woman who walked out of my life when I was five years old. If I didn't realize it before, I do now. I never should have looked her up or contacted her.

As I make my way to my feet, the door opens and in breezes a blond woman with lavender highlights and large sunglasses covering her face. She's tall and willowy.

Just like I remember.

My mouth turns cottony.

Her gaze sweeps over the space until it collides with mine. She pauses. Even though I can't see her eyes behind the dark lenses, I can almost feel the way they sweep over me. I hold my breath as my heart pounds painfully against my ribcage. She moves through the tiny establishment, skirting tables until arriving at the table. She's so close that I could reach out and touch her if I wanted to. Resisting the temptation, I squeeze my fingers into a fist, so I don't do exactly that.

She hesitates. "Colton?"

That voice.

Deep and sultry. It's akin to burrowing under a warm blanket.

My throat closes up on me, making speech impossible. I jerk my head into a tight nod. There is so much tension filling the air between us that it feels like it could shatter into a million pieces.

Uncomfortable has nothing on this.

She takes a tentative step toward me. "Would it be all right if I give you a hug?"

The question breaks the strange paralysis that has fallen over me. "Yes." The word gets blurted out before I can think about it.

Another step brings her close enough to slide her arms around my body. Even though I try to remain aloof, I find my arms banding around her slender form, pulling her closer until I'm able to bury my nose in her hair. I squeeze my eyes closed and inhale, shocked to find that she smells exactly the same as she did before. It's difficult not to tumble backward into the memories of the past.

They are like a wave crashing over me as I'm inundated with images I'd forgotten about. Time becomes irrelevant. I have no idea how long we stand embracing. Her warmth seeping into me. All I know is that it feels good. Good enough to ease some of the pain that has been apart of me since she walked away.

When we break apart, her fingers trail over my arm before tangling with my own. I stare down at the physical connection. The one she's initiating. Even as we slide onto our chairs, our hands stay connected.

She stares at me from across the small round table that separates us as if trying to catalogue every minute detail and commit them to memory. "I can't believe how handsome you've become. But then again, you always were an adorable child." She reaches out and traces her fingers over my cheek before they settle on my chin. I remain silent as she turns my face first one way and then another. It's so tempting to close my eyes and sink into the warmth of her touch but I'm afraid to do that. I'm afraid if I blink—even for a second—she'll disappear, and this will end up being nothing more than a dream.

"It's so good to see you again. I'm glad you reached out."

My head bobs as I frantically search for something to say but nothing comes to mind. I have no idea where to start. This woman is my mother. My flesh and blood. Her name is on my birth certificate. She cared for me during those first five years. And yet, she's a relative stranger. Someone I haven't seen in fifteen years. And this feels...awkward.

"I've thought about reaching out for a while. Thank you for taking that first step."

"No problem."

Her fingers tighten around my hand. "I'm really happy that we could meet up. I've thought about you so much over the years, but I was afraid to reach out. I didn't want to disturb your life."

My heart constricts. "You wouldn't have disturbed me." Maybe if she had, I wouldn't have been walking around all these years thinking that there was something wrong with me. I wouldn't have felt so abandoned. I wouldn't have pushed away the people who only wanted to love me.

She clears her throat and blinks back the tears that fill her eyes. "Tell me everything. Catch me up."

I give her the Spark Notes version of my life. From elementary school through college, along with my plans for the future. I gloss over the hurt and pain she caused. The entire time, Candance sits quietly across from me, squeezing my hand from time to time. The longer I talk, the more my muscles loosen.

"I heard your father remarried."

"Yes," I say carefully, "when I was seven." When she remains silent, I tack on, "Her name is Jenna."

"She's been good to you?"

"She has." For some reason, I'm afraid to say too much. I don't want to unwittingly say or do something that will ruin the fragility of this moment. I don't want her to shut down or push me away again. That sounds so fucking pathetic.

Instead of doing either of those things, her lips tilt into a smile. "Good. It's a relief to know that you were well cared for and loved." Her gaze drops to our clasped hands. "I didn't think you'd be able to forgive me for leaving like I did."

The words tumble out of my mouth before I can stop them. "Of course, I forgive you. I'm glad we have this opportunity to get to know each other again. Make up for lost time."

"Me, too."

She opens up and tells me all about her art and her family. I dredge my memory for every little detail of her, wanting her to know that she was never forgotten even though we weren't in contact.

I'm surprised when I glance at phone and realize that two hours have slipped by. As much as I don't want to cut this reunion short, I need to get back for practice or Coach will have my ass and I can't afford for that to happen. Not with the way I've been playing.

Without thinking, I blurt, "I'd like to meet your husband and kids." Leif and Surrey. A half brother and sister. It's so weird to think that I have siblings out there. Up until last week, I was an only kid. There were times when I was growing up that I desperately wanted siblings. Someone else who knew exactly how I felt. Hell, I would have been content if Jenna and Dad had popped out a few, but that wasn't in the cards. They tried for a couple of years and went the route of fertility drugs. Nothing worked. It would be kind of cool to pick them up and take them places. Maybe Alyssa can come with. We can go to an amusement park or the movies.

I almost shake my head.

I can't even believe I'm thinking along these lines.

"Oh." Candance pins her lower lip with her teeth before flicking her gaze away from me. "I...don't know if that's possible."

Some of the pretty façade in my head walls away as I crash back to earth with a painful thud. "Why not?"

"Well," there's an uncomfortable pause as she shifts on her chair, "my husband, Roger...he doesn't know I had another child."

I blink.

Wait...what?

Did she just—

"*You,*" it takes effort to swallow down the nausea rising in my throat, "*never told him about me?*"

"No," she whispers, I didn't."

When I retract my hand from hers, her tongue darts out to moisten her lips. "You have to understand what it was like for me."

For her?

I...have to understand what it was like for her?

You know what it feels like when you take a tumble and land on the flat of your back? The way it knocks the air from your lungs, making it impossible to breath? You gasp, can't talk, and your eyes water?

That's exactly the way I feel right now.

When I remain silent, eyes wide, full of hurt, she rushes on to fill the void of silence.

"When I left, I was in such a bad place. I didn't realize that I was in a state of depression. My therapist helped me to realize that I'd been suffering from post-partum depression since you'd been born. The creativity was no longer there and that was a frightening thing. It was like having an arm amputated. I didn't know who I was without my art. The decision was difficult, but in the end, I chose to leave." She presses a hand to her chest. "I couldn't be the mother you needed when I wasn't whole. When part of me was missing."

"So, you chose your art."

Over me.

Instead of me.

The unspoken words hang in the air between us.

Her eyes widen before she rips them away. Wetness makes them shiny. "I know that's what it sounds like, but my motives weren't that selfish."

A humorless laugh bubbles up in my throat. Or maybe it's all the emotion I've kept locked away for years.

"You might not realize it, but you were better off without me."

She might be right about that. Although, we'll never know.

"It sounds like this woman—"

"Jenna," I snap. "Her name is Jenna."

"Yes, Jenna." She swallows thickly. "It sounds like she treated you well."

For all Candance knows, Jenna could have been pure evil. Thank fuck, she wasn't. I have a couple of friends with stepparents and they hate them. I lucked out in that regard. Jenna is everything that Candance is not and could never be.

I fold my arms across my chest and press against the back of the chair, needing as much space as possible. All of a sudden, the walls of the coffee shop are pressing in on me. I suck in air through my nostrils, filling my lungs, attempting to calm everything racing around inside me. The urge to bolt hums beneath my skin, making me twitchy.

"Colton?" She leans forward, stretching her hand out on the table. "Please, talk to me."

I fight my way out of the pain pounding through me and blink down at her fingers.

I can't.

I can't touch her.

"If you had no intention of letting me into your life, why did you want to meet?"

She blinks, as if thrown off by the question. "I needed to see with my own eyes that you were all right. That I made the right decision all those years ago."

So, this was only to assuage her guilt.

Got it.

I clear my throat, unable to sit here for another moment. "As you can see for yourself, I'm good. No need to worry or think about me for another sixteen years."

"Colton," her faces goes pale, "I don't want it to end this way between us."

Yeah, well...it's a little late for that.

Sixteen years too late, to be exact.

This woman could never understand the kind of damage she inflicted. She has no idea the emotional scars I carry around with me or how they've affected every single relationship I've had. Only now am I beginning to realize it.

Silently, I rise from my chair. I think we've said everything that needed to be said.

Her dark eyes widen as she scrambles to do the same. "You're leaving?"

"Yeah." I hear my voice as if from a great distance. "I need to get back to school."

"Please, let me explain it better. I didn't do a good job."

"Actually, you did. I appreciate you telling me the truth."

She sucks in a shaky breath. "I don't want you to have hurt feelings."

I almost laugh. Is she serious? My fucking feelings are already hurt. More like they've been annihilated.

"Can we just sit and talk for a few more minutes?"

I shake my head. "No, I don't think so."

"Then let's set up another time to meet. Whatever works for you."

I drag a hand over my face before glancing at the exit. I just want to get out of here. Instead of walking away, I ask, "Do you have any intention of telling your husband or kids about me?"

Her shoulders slump.

Yeah, that's what I thought.

I jerk my head into a nod. "Take care, Candance."

On legs that feel shaky, I push my way out of the coffee house and into the crisp fall air. By the time I reach my BMW, I feel sick to my stomach. It takes a couple of times for me to jam the key into the ignition. Relief floods through me when the key slides home and I rev the engine. I pull away from the curb and glance at the rearview mirror only to find Candance standing on the sidewalk, staring after me.

With a heart that feels like it's splintering apart, I realize that's exactly where she belongs.

In the rearview mirror.

*I*t's past two and I still haven't heard from Colton.

I wish he would, at the very least, shoot me a text. Or give me a quick call. Anything at this point. I just want to know that everything is all right.

That *he's* all right.

As I push through the lobby door of the apartment building and hustle down the cement walkway, I slide my phone from my pocket and peek at it for the umpteenth time in the last thirty minutes.

I really wish he would have let me come with for moral support. He shot that idea down pretty quickly when I had offhandedly mentioned it. I could have sat in the car and waited for him.

Ugh. I sound like a needy girlfriend right about now. And you know what? We're not even going out.

It's just...

I feel like after all these years, Colton is finally allowing me a glimpse into who he truly is as a person. I'm only beginning to understand him. What I'm most afraid of is that this meeting with Candance is going to somehow close the door on that and we'll back peddle. I can't deal with him shutting down on me again and closing me out. If Colton really wants a relationship with me, then he needs to open up and let me in.

And that, unfortunately, is easier said than done.

I've got about twenty minutes to make the walk to campus for class. Just as I reach the edge of the parking lot, a glint of metallic grey catches the corner of my eye and my footsteps stutter as I turn to take a closer look.

Sure enough. Colton's metallic grey BMW is sitting in the lot.

He's back? And he didn't bother to call or text?

Hurt floods through me. It shouldn't. But that doesn't change the fact that it does. As I continue to stare, lost in my own thoughts, the driver's side door opens, and Colton unfolds himself from inside.

One glimpse of his face is all it takes for me to realize that whatever happened with Candance wasn't good. Even from this distance, there's a look of sadness filling his eyes. His mouth is a tight slash across his face and his body vibrates with restlessness. Almost as if there is something inside him trying to claw its way out.

My heart clenches. My first impulse is to go to him, to take him in my arms and comfort him, but...

I have no idea if that's what he wants.

Or needs.

Those thoughts are slammed home when his gaze flicks up and locks on mine. There's a fleeting moment of surprise before it's tucked away behind an expressionless mask.

When he stays frozen in place, I raise my hand in tentative greeting. His legs eat up the space between us before he stops a couple of feet away.

I swallow down my disappointment when he doesn't reach out and wrap his arms around me. Up close, his features look even more haunted. If he would give me a little sign that he wanted me to make the first move, I would.

Instead, I stay rooted in place. "Hi."

"Hey."

I glance at the car. "You just got back?"

"Yeah." He plows a hand through his hair before muttering, "I should go. I'm late for practice. I don't need to give Coach any more reason to bench my ass."

He takes a step and the question bursts from me before I can stop it. "Are you all right?"

"I'm fine." There's a monotone quality to his voice. One that scares me. It's like he's a million miles away and there's no way for me to reach him.

I bite down on my lower lip before asking, "I could walk with you to the field." Hesitantly, I close the space between us. "We could talk on the way." I don't care if that will make me late for class. It no longer seems important.

"I appreciate the offer, but right now, I just want to be alone."

There's really nothing more I can say to that.

"Sure, I get it." My shoulders slump under the weight of the moment. Even though it feels like we've moved been slowly inching our way into unchartered territory with this relationship, it now feels like we're taking a gigantic step back. And there's nothing I can do to change that.

Colton shifts impatiently as if he can't get away from me fast enough. "We'll talk later, okay?"

One long-legged stride puts an ocean of distance between us. If I wanted, I could leap forward and close the physical distance between us but that wouldn't change the emotional gulf that has developed in a few short hours. That, I have no idea how to breech. I don't even know if it's possible. Colton is good at closing people off. He's spent his entire life doing it. And that's exactly what he's doing now.

A shiver of unease scampers down my spine. "Yeah, sure. No problem." Pathetically, I add, "Call me."

He jerks his head toward the building. "Bye."

Before I have a chance to lift my hand, he disappears inside the glass door into the lobby without another look in my direction.

I can only stare as sadness wells inside me.

ALYSSA

$\mathcal{E}$ven though I should be plowing through this work—that is why, after all, I dragged Mia to library this evening—I'm staring off into space, lost in the tangle of my own thoughts. I can't concentrate to save my life. And that's exactly what I can't afford to be doing. I have a test on Friday and paper that needs to be outlined if I'm going to get it done on time. Between fifteen credits, getting time in the studio, and teaching a couple of classes, I've got a jam-packed schedule and more than enough to keep my busy so that I don't dwell on the Colton situation.

But guess what?

I can't stop dwelling on the Colton situation.

I give myself a good mental slap before refocusing my attention on the computer screen in front of me. Everything in me deflates as I read over the paragraph on the screen. I'm pissed that I allowed my advisor talk me into this upper-level psych course. I thought it would be a blowoff class that would allow me to focus on dance.

That hasn't turned out to be the case. The professor is actually a real hard ass.

Now I'm stuck writing a ten-page paper on the measurement of critical thinking.

The measurement of what?

Exactly.

Unfortunately, it's much too late to switch classes and pick up something else. And I can't drop it unless I want to take eighteen credits next semester. Especially when I'll be busy with my final spring showcase.

So, I'm stuck with this class for the duration.

When I huff out a breath, Mia glances up from her laptop she working at across from me. "You okay?"

That is a loaded question. One I'm not even sure how to answer.

"Yup." There's a beat of silence. "Why?"

She shrugs and sits back in her chair before stretching. We've been here for almost two hours and my back is feeling it. I glance at my screen and am even more dismayed to realize that I've done barely anything.

Ugh. I just blew two hours of prime study time.

"You just seem," her brows draw together, "preoccupied."

Oh, I sped past preoccupied doing ninety on the freeway. I'm way past that now.

I drag a hand over my face and try to shake off everything that's been weighing me down this week. Truth be told, I haven't wanted to examine the reasons for that because deep down, I know exactly what the issue is.

My teeth sink into my lower lip as I decide what to do. I have yet to come clean to Mia about Colton. Then again, is there really anything to come clean about? He's done exactly what I was afraid of and pushed me away.

It's like déjà vu all over again and it leaves a pit sitting in my belly. One that hasn't budged in days.

"So," I hedge, a little nervous about how she'll react, "I haven't exactly been honest with you."

Her brows rise as she pushes her computer to the side. "About what?"

More like who.

"Colton—"

"I knew it!" She pokers up in her chair and stabs a finger at me from across the table that separates us. "I *knew* something was going on! I could sense a disturbance in the force."

I wince at the accusatory tone filling her voice. So much for her taking this in stride. I really should have known better. "I'm sorry. I should have been straight up with you."

She folds her arms across her chest. "Why weren't you?"

I shrug and glance away. "After the way our relationship ended the first time, I felt like an idiot for getting caught up in him again."

"He really hurt you, Lys. I don't want to see that happen again. You left for a year because of him."

"That's not totally true," I mumble. All right, so maybe it's true. I wouldn't have even considered the study abroad program had Colton not unceremoniously dumped my ass. Although now I have a better understanding of why he did it.

"So what's going on now?" There's a beat of silence followed up by another question. "Are you two a thing?"

"If you'd asked me a week ago, I could have given you an answer but now?" I shrug. "I don't know."

"What happened?"

As tempted as I am to confide in Mia about Colton and his family, it's his private business. The last thing I want to do is spread around gossip. Only now has he really started opening up to me, giving me a glimpse into the demons he struggles with. As much as I hate the way he pushed me away sophomore year, I get it. Every time I think about the pain and wariness he carries around with him, it breaks my heart all over again.

The unavoidable conclusion that I've drawn from his recent behavior is that he's going to do it again. He's withing from me again. Maybe not consciously but that seems to be his modus operandi that he so easily falls back into.

"It's just something personal," I finally offer by way of explanation even though it isn't one.

She nods, eyes clouding.

In a way, Mia can understand and probably appreciate someone else not wanting to air their dirty laundry for everyone to talk about. There's been enough bullshit with her own family. Especially right now.

"What are you going to do?"

"I'm not sure. Colton has been really distant this week." And that has everything to do with his mother and what happened when they met for coffee. Even though Colton has been pretty tight-lipped about the meeting, it's obvious that it didn't go the way he'd hoped it would. The pain that had radiated from his eyes when we'd ran into him in the parking lot had been like a knife to my heart. All I had wanted to do was pull him into my arms and offer comfort, but he had refused it.

"You need to talk to him and get it figured out before it goes any further. If Colton can't be the guy you need him to, then it's time to cut your losses and move on. For real this time. I know that sounds harsh, but you deserve better."

I swallow down the thick lump that has become wedged in the middle of my throat.

She's not telling me anything that I don't already know.

As much as I've always had a thing for Colton, I'm beginning to doubt that he can be the man I need him to. And that's not a knock on him. It's just the way it is.

Decision made, I grab my phone from the table and tap on Colton's name before hastily typing out a message and hitting send before I can overthink it.

Are you busy? Can we talk?

My heart pounds a painful staccato against my ribcage as three little bubbles appear.

Can't right now.

Any hope that we could make this fledging relationship work crashes back to earth before exploding upon impact. As much as I want to make this work, as hard as I'm willing to work, I can't do it alone. That's not the way relationships work. Not real ones. The ones that survive. If Colton is unwilling to open up and let me in...

Then I guess the decision has been made for me.

COLTON

"**G**ood practice, man. Keep playing like that and you'll be back on the field in no time." Beck slaps my back as he walks past on the way to his locker.

"Thanks." I hate to jinx myself, but yeah, it kind of felt like old times out there. Everything Beck threw my way, I caught with ease. Not a fumble in sight. It was nice. Reassuring. As if one piece of the puzzle has finally fallen back into place. With each practice I've been steadily improving. it's almost like I'm getting my groove back.

All I can hope is that it continues, and that Coach is taking notice.

So far, he hasn't said anything. He's been watching from the sidelines and jotting down notes. It's enough to set my nerves on end, but I try not to let the pressure get to me.

Which hasn't been easy. Especially with everything that happened with Candance. I was afraid that it would mess with my head even more than before, but strangely enough, it hasn't. Don't get me wrong, what she said hurts like a mother fucker but...

I can't allow someone who I don't matter to, to totally fuck with my life. She's already done enough of that. It's taken me a couple of days to come to that epiphany but now that I have, there's peace to be found in the decision. Some relationship just aren't viable. And when it happens to be with your own parent, it's painful. Afterall, in a perfect world, these are the people who are supposed to love you no matter what. Who are supposed to have your back when no one else does. Who you can depend on when shit goes sideways. They aren't supposed to be the ones who bring the shit that makes life go sideways.

But that's the way it goes, right?

It just makes me realize that I'm lucky to have my dad and Jenna.

Especially Jenna.

I appreciate her now more than ever.

As soon as Coach walks into the locker room, the boisterous voices surrounding me fall silent. None of these loud mouths want to draw attention to themselves. He grinds to a halt in the middle of the space and snaps out a couple of names. "Reinholtz, Collins, and Montgomery. See me on your way out."

I give him a chin lift in acknowledgment as he stalks into his office, slamming the door behind him with a resounding thud.

Well fuck me.

I'm not sure if I'm about to get my ass chewed out or not. I'm still a little sore from the last time he lit into me. Coach isn't the kind of guy to pussy foot around a subject or hold back. If he thinks you're fucking up, you better believe he's going to give it to you straight.

In full, Technicolor detail.

And here I'd actually been feeling relaxed and good about myself after stepping foot off the turf. Instead of hanging around and shooting the shit with Beck, like I'd normally do, I strip and haul ass to the shower. I want to be the first one in Coach's office and get this over with.

Ten minutes later, with dripping wet hair, I knock on the closed office door, and peek my head inside. "Hey, Coach, you wanted to see me?"

He pauses the action playing out across the television screen and swivels around to face me before pointing a finger at the chair on the opposite side of the desk. "Park it, Montgomery."

It doesn't matter if this is my fourth and final year playing for this guy, every time I'm called in here, it makes me feel like an eight-year-old sent to the principal's office. It's ridiculous. I'm a twenty-one-year-old man.

That being said, I do what I'm told and drop my ass on the faux leather chair as the older man scrutinizes his clipboard of notes.

Paper and pencil, if I'm not mistake.

Coach is old school like that.

"Seems like whatever shit needed to get flushed out in your head has done so."

It's not a question. More of a statement.

I sit up a little straighter. "Yes, sir."

"As long as you continue to play at this level, I'm moving you to first string." He sits back in his chair and gives me a well-honed death stare. I can't help but squirm under the intensity of it. "Good. Kwiatkowski is a talented player, but he doesn't have your intuitive-ness out on the field."

"Thank you." This is the closest thing Coach has ever come to giving me a compliment.

See? It's like I secretly suspected. Beneath that crusty hard exterior lies a soft nougat filling. You just have to take the time to dig deep and find it.

"That being said, you manage to get your head stuck up your ass again, you'll be riding the pine for the season. I'm not jacking around with this. Are we clear?"

"Crystal."

"Good." He points to the door. "Now get the hell out of here."

He doesn't need to tell me twice. I practically jump from the chair and shoot through the door as a wave of relief crashes over me. Most of the guys are still is some state of getting dressed.

Collins and Reinholtz eye me with speculation, looking a little green around the gills themselves. Can't blame them for that.

As soon as I make it back to my locker, Beck raises a brow. I can't help the grin that breaks loose across my face.

"Fuck, yeah!" He punches me in the arm. "It's all about controlling the bullshit up here." He points to the side of his head before shrugging. "Or maybe it has more to do with what you're packing. All I know is that it's one head or the other."

I snort.

The guy isn't wrong.

He grabs his athletic bag and slings it over his shoulder. "You ready to get out of here?"

"Yup."

So damn ready.

I feel the need to go out and celebrate. Or maybe have a one-on-one celebration with Alyssa. I really need to fix shit with her. Unfortunately, old habits die hard, and I pushed her away, needing a little distance to figure out how I was feeling. I need to explain what happened to her so we can move forward.

Things are starting to look up.

With that thought circling through my head, I push through the locker room door before skidding to a halt when my gaze lands on Alyssa. She's leaning against the far wall with her arms crossed against her chest. For just a sliver of a moment, a feeling of déjà vu crashes over me along with a prickle of unease.

Beck bumps into me from behind. "Dude, what the—"

His gaze falls on Alyssa. "Oh, hey, Alyssa." His gaze bounces between the pair of us. A moment later, he sidesteps me and calls over his shoulder, "Bye, Alyssa." And then he's disappearing down the corridor and around the corner.

Whatever the reason she's here, waiting for me, it's not good.

"Hi." There's about ten feet separating us, but it might as well be an ocean. There's a palpable disconnect between us and deep down, I know it's my fault. I pushed her away instead of opening up and letting her in.

As if to solidify those thoughts, her lips lift into a ghost of a smile as she shoves away from the wall. "You didn't have time to talk the other day, so I thought I'd come here so we could have a conversation."

I wince.

Fuck.

This is worse than I thought.

I plow a hand through my hair. "I'm sorry about that. There's been a lot of shit going on." Shit I needed to work out on my own. "Do you want to grab something to eat and we can talk?" Maybe then we can both get on the same page.

There's a moment of hesitation. One that has the hope rising within me. But then she shakes her head, a regretful expression flickering across her features. "I can't. I'm meeting up with Zoe to work on choreography." She sucks in a deep breath before glancing away and forcing out the rest in a burst. "This isn't working out."

I can only blink as the words swirl through my head, refusing to compute. "You...*want to break up?*"

Alyssa presses her lips together before jerking her head into a tight nod. "Yeah, I'm sorry."

I open my mouth to argue before slamming it shut again. I can't believe this is happening. This is exactly what I was afraid of. Of Alyssa getting to know the real me and then walking away.

Just like Candance.

It only reinforces that I'm not good enough. That I've *never* been good enough.

I flinch at those ugly thoughts as they force their way into my brain. No matter how much you try to combat them, it only takes one little thing for them to flare to life again and take over. Kind of like a rash.

"Colton?" Alyssa's voice softens as she closes the distance between us, hesitantly placing her fingers on my forearm. "Are you all right?"

Her touch jolts me back to the present. "I'm fine." Instead of trying to explain myself, everything inside me shuts down. The one girl I've always wanted, the one I was trying to change for, doesn't want me in return.

Numbness sets in.

I'm tired of not being good enough.

Tired of people walking out of my life.

Turns out that Alyssa isn't as different as I thought she was.

I'm not sure why I thought she was.

COLTON

I pull my BMW into the circular drive and park near the front entrance before cutting the engine, grabbing my duffle bag from the front seat and exiting the vehicle. It takes only a moment before I'm up the stairs two and punching in the code on the keypad. Once unlocked, I push open the front door and step inside the two-story foyer. As soon as I do, the scent of beef stroganoff hits me full force. I inhale a big breath, doubly glad I decided to get the hell out of Dodge.

Even if it's only for the night.

Jenna pads through the hallway from the kitchen with a dish towel in her hands. Surprise lights up her eyes when she catches sight of me. "I thought I heard the front door." She closes the distance between us before rising up on her tiptoes and pressing a kiss against my cheek. I lean down, wanting to make it easier for her. Jenna tops out at five foot. Sometimes I like to tease her by asking what the weather is like down there. "Why didn't you tell me that you were coming home?"

"It was more of a spur-of-the-moment decision." When she continues to stare, scouring my face for answers, I admit, "Just needed to get away for a little."

"Well, I'm glad you decided to pop home." She waves me to the kitchen. "Dinner should be ready in about fifteen minutes, so you're just in time."

The closer we get to the kitchen, the more my mouth waters. If there's one thing I've missed while at college, it's Jenna's cooking. She's a culinary whiz in the kitchen. If you asked what my favorite dish was, I don't even think I could pick just one. There are way too many to choose from.

I beeline to the mini-fridge and grab an orange Gatorade before twisting off the cap and settling on a stool tucked beneath the massive marble island. After a quick swig, I ask, "Do you need any help?"

It looks like she's got about fifty things going on all at once. Jenna shakes her head before grabbing a strainer full of green beans and dumping them into the boiling water. The she's stirring the sauce and peeking in the oven to check the rolls. "Nope. Everything is almost done."

Like I said—total culinary whiz.

I cock my head, listening for other signs of life within the house. "Is Dad home?"

"Not yet." She shoots a glance over her shoulder. "He had a meeting that ran late but should be home soon."

I nod and pick at the label on the plastic bottle. As much as I've tried to shut out everything that happened this week, it continues to press in at the edges. If I thought I could escape it by coming home, I was wrong.

Jenna checks the noodles and green beans again. Satisfied that everything is coming along as it should, she picks up her glass of wine from the island and takes a sip as her gaze roves over my face again. "So, are you going to tell me what's going on or are you going to make me drag it from you?"

Fuck.

Did I really expect anything less? All the woman has to do is look at me sideways and she knows there's a problem. If I was trying to run away from it all, this probably wasn't the place I should have gone.

Unfortunately, it's too late.

I blow out a lengthy breath and try to decide how I'm going to handle this situation. I hate lying. *Especially to Jenna.* So I try a different tact. "I really don't want to talk about it," I mumble.

"Isn't that why you came here?"

My gaze jerks to her and I realize that she's right...

Maybe I told myself it wasn't the reason, but it turns out that I was wrong. And Jenna knows it. Just like she always does. I drag a hand over my face, unsure where to begin. My life feels like one huge overwhelming mess. One I have no idea how to untangle.

When I remain silent, her voice softens. "Does this have something to do with Alyssa?"

I shrug. "Yeah, I guess."

It's a relief when the timer on the microwave beeps and she swings away. Without her steady gaze watching me, I no longer feel like a bug under a microscope. Jenna strains both the noodles and green beans before taking the rolls from the oven and placing them on the counter to cool. Then she pulls out two plates, adds a heaping of both noodles and stroganoff along with a side of green beans and a roll before placing it in front of me. After making a plate for herself, she settles on a stool next to me at the island.

I dig in, taking a forkful of noodles, meat, and mushrooms before stuffing it in my mouth. The first bite has my eyes feather closed. Even though Jenna raised me better than to talk with my mouth full, I can't resist saying, "Mmmm, this is so good."

Her lips quirk. "Glad you like it."

"Love it," I add, shoving in another bite.

"I'm sure there'll be leftovers. I'll package some for you to take for Beck."

I straight on the stool. "Screw Beck."

She chuckles. "No, thank you."

My lips tremble at the corners before I plow my way through my dinner. What is it about a homecooked meal that helps settle everything deep inside? Or maybe it's the company.

"Feel better?"

I nod.

"Good. Want a second helping?"

I pat my belly. "If I eat another bite, I'll probably explode."

She grabs of our plates before dropping them off in the sink. Once she's settled next to me, I steel myself for what's coming next. "Tell me what's going on."

The question has everything inside me deflating.

"Come, now." Jenna reaches over and squeezes my hand. "It can't be that bad."

I force out a breath from my lungs. "It feels pretty damn bad."

"You know what I've found?" She doesn't wait for a response. "That when you keep everything bottled up inside, it always seems worse." She squeezes my hand. "Share it with me. Let's talk this out."

Unable to hold her gaze, mine drops to the white marble countertop. "I looked Candance up online." I give her a bit of side eye to catch her reaction, but her face remains impassive. As if I haven't just dropped a major bomb. I can't even remember the last time I brought her up. When she simply nods, I continue. "She's married." There's a pause as I push out the rest. "With two kids. Girls."

"I know. Your father has kept tabs on her over the years."

This information doesn't surprises me. I guess everyone knew about it but me. "Why didn't you guys tell me?"

"What would be the point? To inflict more hurt?"

My shoulders collapse at her astute assessment of the situation.

When I remain silent, lost in my own thoughts, her hand settles over mine before giving it a gentle squeeze. "Are you all right?"

I shrug. That's not even the worst part of it. I wish it were. "I reached out to her and she emailed back, wanting to know if I would be interested in meeting."

Even though Jenna's expression never falters, her hand stills over mine. "And did you?"

"Yeah."

"And how did that go?"

"Awkward at first, but then we started talking, kind of getting to know each other again and it was...nice."

"I'm glad."

It makes perfect sense that Jenna would be happy for me. She's selfless that way. If having a relationship with Candance completed me in someway or made me happy, then she would be all for it.

"She asked a lot of questions. And I guess for a little bit, it felt like me reaching out, and then agreeing to meet, was a good idea." When my voice turns bitter, Jenna's fingers tighten around mine again. "Turns out that's not the case."

"Don't say that. I'm sure she does care, Colton."

I snort out a laugh of disbelief. "Not enough."

"So what happened? Because for a little bit there, it was all good, right?"

"Yeah." I drag my other hand over my face. Heat fills my cheeks as I force out the words. "I asked if I could meet her family." I jerk my shoulders defensively. "I couldn't get over the fact that I had halfsiblings out there. Ones I had never met."

She lifts her hand to stroke my cheek. "I'm sure you like the idea."

"It doesn't really matter what I want." A fresh wave of pain crashes over me before threatening to drag me under. "Her husband isn't aware that she had another child and since it would be difficult to explain the situation after all these years, she's not really open to the idea of me being part of her or her kid's life.

"Oh, Colton." With the side of my face cupped in her palm, she closes the distance between, pressing her lips against my forehead before pulling me into a hug. My arms hang at my side as she squeezes me tight, anchoring me to her petite frame.

"Candance hasn't been a part of my life in more than fifteen. I don't understand why this hurts so much."

"I'm sorry she did this to you." I don't have to catch a glimpse of her face to know that there are tears filling her eyes. I hear the thick emotion in her voice.

Jenna squeezes me even tighter as if she is somehow able to extract the pain from my body.

"Obviously we won't be seeing each other again."

She pulls away and I realize that I'm right about the tears as her gaze locks on mine. "You realize this has *nothing* to do with you, right?"

I shrug.

How could it not have everything to do with me?

This is twice now that I've been rejected by her.

Throw in Alyssa and you have a triple whammy.

Unwilling to have her bear witness to the pathetic emotion crashing around inside me, I turn my head away.

Unfortunately, Jenna is having none of it. She grips my chin with her fingers before manually turning my face toward hers.

"Don't you dare hide from me. I've been here since you were seven years old. Bandaging scraped knees, telling you to stop playing video games and do your homework, and making sure you were home before curfew."

I can't help but smile at the last one. Dad was strict about my ass being in the house by curfew. Jenna always made sure to send me fifteen-minute warnings. She saved me on more than one occasion when it had slipped my mind.

"You've been carrying all this hurt around with you for your entire life."

"That's not true." When I attempt to shake my head and deny the accusation, her fingers dig into my chin.

"Oh sweetie," her voice softens, "yes, you have. I remember the first time your father introduced me to you. We went to a park so that you could play on the equipment."

I sift through my memories but am unable to bring that one up.

It doesn't matter because she continues, filling in the blanks for me.

"You refused to play. You wouldn't leave your father's side."

A prickle of unease blooms in the pit of my belly.

"Warren kept encouraging you to play with the other kids, but you wouldn't do it. You were so afraid that he was going to leave you."

Just like Candance.

That prickle turns into full-on nausea. "It took years before you were willing to open up and let me in. Maybe you don't remember that, but I do. And ever since, the people in your life have had to earn your trust."

I attempt to blink away the heavy emotion so that it doesn't fall down my cheeks. It occurs to me that I've spent my entire life keeping everyone around me at a firm distance. Never wanting to feel too much. And yeah, running away rather than facing it head on.

"You can't move forward if you're constantly looking back."

Maybe I didn't realize that's what I was doing, but I was. I was allowing Candance and the past to hold me back from people and experiences that could have been amazing.

"You know who I feel most sorry for?" When I shake my head, she continues. "Candance. She's the one missing out. You've grown into such an amazing man, Colton. And she missed out on that."

It takes effort to clear the emotion from my throat. "If I've turned out well, it's because you were here guiding me. *You're* the mother that she never was."

Or could be.

Fresh tears fill her dark eyes before trekking down her cheeks. "You made it easy. And I love you, Colton. I couldn't love you anymore if you were my own."

I pull her to me, this time wrapping my arms around her. "I love you, too."

When we finally pull away from one another, there's wetness on both our cheeks. Even though I feel like a big blubbery baby, I don't really care. With my hand held in hers, she settles next to me again on the stool before clearing her throat. "I know you've been adamant about not wanting to go to therapy, but it would be so helpful."

I jerk my shoulders. Normally, I've shot the idea the moment it was out of her mouth. I don't do that this time. "Maybe."

The idea of sitting in some strangers' office and pouring out my heart sounds terrible. But then again, I'm tired of dealing with it all on my own. Or maybe, the problem is that I've never dealt with it and it's been festering inside me for years.

"Have you spoken to Alyssa about this? Does she know?"

Right. Alyssa. That's another problem. One I'm unsure how to solve.

Fuck.

Maybe I do need to talk to someone.

I plow my hand through my hair. "She broke up with me the other day."

"Let me guess," Jenna says slowly, "you shut down and pushed her away after what happened with Candance."

Damn. Sometimes I think my stepmother knows me better than I know myself. Or maybe I should have done myself a favor and opened up to Jenna a long time ago. She's always been here, ready to listen and help. Whatever that might look like.

"Nailed it," I mutter, feeling defeated.

With a huff of breath, she falls silent.

We both do.

"Can I assume that Alyssa is the girl you were involved with sophomore year?"

I narrow my eyes. "Sometimes you frighten me."

She snorts out a laugh and it lightens the mood between us.

"If Alyssa is worth it—really worth it—then you need to be honest with her. I know it's scary to be vulnerable with another person. The easiest thing to do is throw up walls and keep people out, but in the end, it's a lonely place to be. I think you realize that now."

My throat closes up as the sound of my beating heart fills my ears, drowning out everything else. "I don't want to be hurt again." Barely am I able to force out the words.

"I know." Jenna's lips lift into a sympathetic smile. "But isn't this girl worth taking a chance on?"

When I remain silent, she says, "Think about it, Colton.

ALYSSA

onsieur Dupre claps his hands together and we all pause. "We will do it again until it is perfection!"

For just a moment, my shoulders sag before I lift and take my position. We've been practicing the same piece over and over. He wasn't kidding when he said that we would keep at it until the movements were perfection. The guy is a real taskmaster. Although, that's what makes Monsieur Dupre such an amazing instructor.

The music resumes and lift up onto the toes of my shoes, stretching my arms over head and holding the pose before raising one pointed foot out in front of me. The music arcs and still I hold the pose. My muscles begin to tremble.

"Bon!" he says.

Instead of dwelling on the pain, I force it from my mind and lose myself in the rhythm of the music.

Like before, the only thing that soothes the pain of this last breakup is dance. I'm able to lose myself in the precision of the movement for hours at a time. It helps me not think about—

Nope. Not going to do it.

Even when he presses in at the edges, I push my body harder so that my mind is too consumed with steps and precision to give one solitary thought to him.

As one, the class moves through the choreography like a well-oiled machine.

Or, in our case, a well-choregraphed routine.

Every so often, Monsieur Dupre will pause the music and critique our positions. Just as I spin on my toes, preparing to leap across the floor in a grand jeté, I catch a glimpse of someone in the doorway from the corner of my eye. My footwork falters and I stumble.

Colton.

What's he doing here?

Even though the question sits perched on the tip of my tongue, I can't push it out. Instead, I stare at him from across the studio. Eating him up with my eyes. Ever since I broke off our relationship, I've been avoiding him in hopes that it would make moving on a little easier.

I should have known that it wouldn't be that easy.

The music stops and the other dancers turn until everyone stares at the tall blond football player lurking at the threshold of the spacious room.

"Can I help you?" Monsieur Dupre's asks in a clipped tone, aiming a haughty look in Colton's direction.

If there's one thing our instructor detests, it's being interrupted. The world could come crashing down around us, and as long as it doesn't interfere with our performance, it would be of no concern.

Remember the band playing on deck while the Titanic sunk?

Yeah, it's like that.

Colton's gaze flickers to him before zeroing in on me again. "I'm sorry, I need to speak with Alyssa."

"As you can see," the elegant man with the dark hair waves a hand, "we are in the middle of class. This can wait, yes?"

I expect Colton to nod and slink away. Everyone is staring at him with wide, fascinated eyes. Instead of doing just that, he steps further into the sun-soaked room. It's almost like he has a death wish. "No, it can't. I need to speak with Alyssa now."

All eyes fall on me.

I gulp as my heart beats into overdrive. Like everyone around me, I can't believe this is actually happening.

"By all means," Monsieur snaps, "continue. It is not like we are here, trying to master a complicated sequence of steps."

"Thanks."

I wince. Perhaps Colton doesn't recognize the sarcasm dripping from the Frenchman's words, but I do. Even though I am one of his favored pupils, I'll pay for the untimely interruption at a later date with a punishing workout.

But...I don't care. I want to hear what Colton has to say.

No, I *need* to hear what Colton has to say.

His dark gaze stays pinned to mine as he steps further into the studio. Everyone around us falls away until it's just the two of us.

"I'm sorry, Lys. I hope you realize that I would never intentionally hurt you." When I open my mouth to tell him that's exactly what he did, he cuts me off with a nod. "I know." His voice drops but his attention remains focused on me. "I hurt you by pushing you away. What I needed was time to work everything out in my head. The meeting with Candance..." His voice trails off and my heart hitches. "It didn't go well."

From the pain swimming in his eyes, that seems like something of an understatement. It takes everything I have inside not to close the distance between us and take him in my arms. To soothe away the hurt radiating off him.

"Instead of talking to you about it, I closed down. That's the way I've always coped with the pain. It's something I need to work on. I know this and I'm willing to do it. I'll do whatever it takes to make our relationship work." He steps closer. "I love you, Lys. I always have. Even when I didn't want to, I loved you."

Emotion floods through me.

He clears his throat. "I don't deserve another chance, but I really hope you'll give me one. Let me prove that I can be the guy you not only need but deserve."

Oh God.

Almost collectively, as if this is a synchronized movement,

everyone shifts their gazes to me. Even Monsieur Dupre. A sigh escapes from a few of the girls.

"If you don't want him, Alyssa, I sure as hell do," Zoe says from across the room.

Her voice snaps me out of the fog that had descended. I don't bother to respond. Instead, I run across the floor before hurtling myself against him. With a soft grunt, his arms wrap around me, pulling me close, squeezing me tight.

"I really do love you, Lys," he whispers against ear.

I pull away just enough to meet his gaze. "I love you, too."

"So, can we get out of here?"

I glance at my instructor.

With a shake of his head, he rolls his eyes and flicks a hand at me. "Leave. You have taken up enough of my valuable time."

My cheeks heat when everyone breaks out into applause.

"You heard him," Colton says with a grin simmering around the corners of his lips, "let's get out of here."

I nod and untangle myself from him before running over to grab my bag. I shove my shoes into the small black duffle and pull on an oversized shirt that hangs off one shoulder and leggings. And then I'm ready to go.

Yes, Monsieur Dupre will make me pay for this tomorrow but I'm not going to focus on that.

Colton holds a hand out for me to take. And this time, when I slip my fingers into his, everything feels right. It feels like for the first time, maybe this really is a fresh start for us.

I have no idea what the future holds for us, but I'm excited to find out.

EPILOGUE

COLTON

*hree years later...*

I ROLL over and stretch out an arm, only to find the space next to me empty and the sheets already cooling. I crack open an eye and glance around the room. The sun is just beginning to peek over the horizon, painting the vast stretch of space with pink and purple strokes.

Where the hell did that girl disappear to?

I throw off the covers and pad over to the bathroom.

Empty.

I don't bother to put on clothes. It's just the two of us. I surprised Alyssa with a weeklong vacation at the beach. One of my father's friends owns a house on Kiawah Island in South Carolina right on the ocean. We can hear the crash of the waves from our bedroom window. It's the perfect sound to fall asleep to with Alyssa tucked in my arms.

I pad down the stairs to the first floor. The scent of fresh brewed coffee permeates the air and the door to the patio is open. I should have known that she was out here on the deck. She can't get enough of the fresh salty air.

I push open the screen door and find her sitting at the small iron table, staring out at the water in the distance. There's something hypnotic about the waves as they roll onto the sandy stretch of shore.

"Hey," I greet, "you're up early."

Her eyes flicker to mine before widening when she gets a good look at me. A chuckle escapes as her lips bow up at the corners. Her gaze skims down my naked body before settling on my cock. That's all it takes for me to stiffen right up. "Decided to forego clothing, I see."

I arch a brow. "Is that a complaint?"

I'll tell you what, there was nothing but moans coming from her when I was buried balls deep inside her heat last night.

"Nope." As if to give proof to her words, she leans forward and flicks her tongue over the tip of my erection. "Not at all."

Damn. There is nothing like the feel of her warm mouth on me.

"Good." My voice drops, turning raspy as I scoop her up into my arms and settle on the chair she'd been lounging on. "It isn't a secret that I love you naked. Speaking of which," I grab the hem of her thin tank top and pull it over her head before tossing it onto the deck, "you're wearing too much clothing." Then I hook my thumbs into her panties and pull them down her hips and thighs before dropping it.

Totally at ease with our nudity, Alyssa settles against my chest, her head resting at the crook of my neck, her legs curled up. We fit perfectly together. A sigh of contentment leaves my lips as we watch the sun rise over the water. It's almost magical.

Fuck me.

I almost shake my head.

Five years ago, I never could have imagined feeling this at ease with another person. The ghosts from my past were still fresh inside me. They had a hold on me that I never realized. All right, so maybe I realized it, but I never understood how much they were holding me back. How much I was missing out on until I made a conscious effort to face them head on.

That meant—yup, you guessed it—therapy. Spilling my guts to a dude with glasses and a beard who eventually helped me to realize that Candance's decisions have everything to do with Candance and not me. Alyssa has been there every step of the way. Holding my hand when I need it. Taking a step back and giving me space when I ask for room.

Without question, she is my person.

And to think that I almost lost her.

Thankfully, I got my shit together before that could happen.

Every day I make a conscious decision to live in the present and only look back at the past when I think reflection can help.

I'm sure that makes me sound all enlightened but I'm like everyone else, just trying to get through life the best I know how. Alyssa likes to joke that this is the Colton 2.0 version.

That girl thinks she's a real funny fucker, but you know what?

I'll take it.

A seagull cries over head as it glides on the early morning breeze and I brush a kiss against the top of her blond head. "Love you, baby."

She lifts her head until our gazes can lock. "Love you, too. Did I thank you for planning this?"

My lips hitch. "I thought that's exactly what you did last night in the shower. You mean there's more?"

Even as she rolls her eyes, a twinkling light fills them. That girl can pretend all she wants to be exasperated with me, she enjoy our sex life just as much as I do.

"You, my friend, have a one-track mind."

When it comes to Alyssa, you're damned straight I do.

Always have, always will.

Luckily, she's not going anywhere. And if she does, I'll be right there with her.

We've been going strong for three years now. I'm in my last year of business school and Alyssa is working at a dance studio in town. She also choreographs dance routines for the Wildcats dance team. We have an apartment in town that is close to campus but far enough away for us not to feel like we're still in college. If everything goes according to plan, I'll propose once I have my degree in hand and we'll move back home so I can start working with my father. I was supposed to move back after I graduated but I delved straight into business school. It was the right decision for both of us.

"You wouldn't have it any other way."

Before she can respond, I close the little bit of distance that separates us so that my mouth can capture hers. As soon as my lips make contact, she opens. Alyssa is just as needy for me as I am for her.

She tilts her chin, angling her head in order to give me better access.

There are some days that I feel as if I could devour her in one tasty gulp. Like I'll never get enough.

Her arms slip around my neck, pulling me closer. With a groan, I lift her, repositioning her on my lap so that my cock is pressed against her heat.

Fuck me that feels good.

But then again, it always feels good.

Needing to feel more of her, I thrust my hips until I'm able to slide deep inside her tight sheath. A sigh of pleasure escapes from her pussy tightens around me. For a moment, I pause, simply enjoying the heat of the sun as it strokes over our bare flesh.

"One of our neighbors could peek outside and see us." Her voice turns breathy. I can't tell if the idea bothers her or turns her on.

My guess is the latter.

"Let them look," I growl. Buried inside her like I am, there is no way I'm going to stop. This is happening. Right here, right now. If I have my way, they'll hear her before they catch sight of us.

Wanting to tease her, I move my hips and pull almost all the way out of her before surging forward again, burying myself to the hilt.

On the third thrust, her head falls back, exposing the delicate column of her neck as her eyelids feather closed. A throaty moan slides from her lips.

Stupid as it sounds, my breath catches as I watch her. I couldn't rip my eyes away from the gorgeous picture she makes riding my cock if I wanted to. Her cheeks have pinkened and her back is arched, thrusting her breasts forward.

She's so fucking beautiful.

And mine.

Five years ago, that thought would have sent a torrent of panic flooding through me. I would have pushed her away, needing to dismiss my feelings for her.

But times have changed.

And I've changed with them.

After all, this is Colton 2.0 we're talking about.

BONUS EPILOGUE

ALYSSA

Five years later...

"Hey beautiful, I was wondering if I could buy you a drink?"

I swing around at the bar only to find Colton standing next to me. A grin tips the edges of my lips as I shake my head. "Sorry, I'm afraid not. I'm waiting for my fiancé." I lift my hand to show off the glittering diamond that now sits on my second finger.

His bright blue gaze drops to my left hand before flickering up again. "Wow. He's a lucky guy."

I shrug before closing the distance between us and whispering, "Honestly, I'm the lucky one. I can't imagine my life without him."

Colton's face softens. "I'm pretty sure he feels the same way."

His hand rises to cup my cheek before he leans in and brushes his lips across mine. I tilt my face to give him better access. As soon as I open, his tongue slips inside my mouth to tangle with my own. That first touch is all it takes for the crowded restaurant to fall away and then it's just the two of us. It doesn't matter if I'm sitting at the bar in Marco's, waiting to meet friends for dinner. Colton has always had this kind of effect on me, and I don't see it changing anytime soon.

"All right, you two," a deep voice interrupts, "break it up."

We splinter apart only to find Mia and Beck. Bright smiles wreath their faces. A few people turn their heads and stare, immediately recognizing the dark-haired quarterback. He's become something of a hometown hero.

I jump off my bar stool and throw my arms around my bestie. It's been so long since we've been able to get together. She's busy in San Francisco, practicing law. Even though she works for Beck's father, Mia still puts in sixty-hour weeks. It doesn't leave time for much else.

"You look amazing!" I cry, tugging her close and squeezing tight. I've missed her so damn much.

"You, too!"

I draw away just enough for my gaze to skim down the length of her before settling on her slightly rounded belly. "I can't believe you're five months pregnant!"

Her hand flutters to the baby bump as her face lights up. "That makes two of us."

I untangle myself from Mia before stepping closer to her husband, Beck, and giving him a hug. "Congratulations, Papa."

"Thanks!" He's all smiles as I pull away. "We're excited for the munchkin to arrive."

My gaze bounces between the pair of them. It seems crazy that they're having a baby. She's the first of my friends to do so. "Have you found out what the sex is yet?"

"Yup, but we're keeping it a secret until the baby shower." Her eyes sparkle as she glances at her husband. "Beck is planning a big reveal. He's even hired a party planner to make it over-the-top."

"Hey," he chimes in, "if we're gonna do this, we're doing it up right."

There was a time when Beck used to plan massive pool parties. And now he's organizing baby reveals? It's enough to make me laugh.

"Oh, come on!" I narrow my eyes. "You won't even tell your bestie? How about a clue? Just one."

She presses her lips together and shakes her head. "Sorry. I've been sworn to secrecy for the time being."

"Damn," I say with a mock pout. "And I can't even get you drunk to pry the information out of you." Honestly, I don't care what the gender is. I'm thrilled for both of them. And me, of course. I get to be an aunt.

Laughter falls from her lips. "You only have to wait a couple of months and then the cat will be out of the bag."

Colton wraps his arms around me from behind as Mia's gaze falls to my left hand before zeroing in on the ring.

Her brows rise. "Looks like I'm not the only one with exciting news!" She grabs my hand to get a better look at the sparkler now adorning it. "When did this happen?"

"Last weekend." I twist in Colton's arms to meet his stare. "He surprised me with a four-day trip to the Bahamas and that's when he proposed."

"That's so romantic," Mia says with a sigh.

It really was. Colton spoke with the owner of my dance studio and asked her to give me a couple of days off. Then he secretly packed our bags and had them waiting in the car. When I woke up Thursday morning, he asked if I wanted to run a few errands. It's only when we ended up at the airport that he told me he'd planned a trip for us.

I mean, come on—how can you not totally love a man like that?

Colton asking me to be his wife was the cherry on top of an already amazing sundae. And I've been floating on cloud nine ever since. There are times when I think back to college and how we broke up sophomore year. As much as I tried to move on from the blond heartbreaker, I couldn't do it.

"Maybe we can plan a trip for the four of us before the baby is born," Beck adds.

"That would be amazing." I love the idea of spending some quality time with my bestie.

"Yeah!" Mia adds. "That would be so much fun. One final hoorah before sleeping through the night becomes a thing of the past."

The guys grab drinks from the bar as Colton peppers Beck with questions regarding the NFL. It's been four years, and his career is still going strong. His agent just renegotiated a lucrative deal with San Francisco.

I pull Mia to the side and give her another hug. "I'm so happy for you, girl."

"Right back at you!"

I glance at our significant others and shake my head. "When we were in high school, could you have imagined our lives turning out like this?"

"Nope." She snorts. "Not in a million years did I ever think I'd be married and expecting a baby with Beckett Hollingsworth."

I can't help the laughter that escapes from my lips. No, I'm sure she didn't. There was a time when Mia could barely tolerate being in the same room with Beck. "I think everything turned out the way it was supposed to."

"It did." Her dark eyes turn dreamy. "Work is good, married life is even better, and this baby," she places both palms on her belly, "will be everything to us."

My heart melts. They're going to make the best parents.

"How about you?" She tilts her head. "Are you doing well?"

My gaze settles on Colton. The man who will one day be my husband. A little thrill slides through me at the thought. "Yeah, I am. Somehow, I managed to get everything I ever wanted."

"I think we both did."

"Hey," Beck says, cutting into our conversation, "what are you two talking about over there?"

"Nothing," we say in unison before offering up matching grins.

Colton shakes his head. "Somehow, I doubt that."

My fiancé closes the distance between us before encircling me in his arms. "Love you, babe," he whispers in my ear.

"I love you, too." More than I ever dreamed possible.

"I can't wait to be your husband."

"I can't wait to be your wife." The thought gives me butterflies. I'm so excited to plan our wedding.

My gaze lands on the couple standing next to us. Beck has Mia wrapped up in his arms as one hand protectively cradles her belly. The love they have for each other is obvious.

Next to our families, these are the two people who matter most. Make that three—who could forget about baby Hollingsworth?

I'm so excited to discover what the future has in store for all of us. If it's anything like the past couple of years, it'll be amazing. How could it not be, when I get to marry the love of my life?

The End

CAMPUS PLAYER

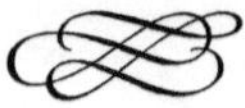

DEMI

"Morning, Demi!" Gary, one of the stadium custodians, calls out with an easy smile and wave as he saunters toward me. "Up and at 'em bright and early this morning, I see."

My heart jackhammers beneath my ribcage from the twenty-minute run as I flash him a grin. "Always!"

"You have a good one! I'll see you tomorrow!"

Since I've already moved past him, I holler over my shoulder, "Same place, same time!"

Even with *The Killers* pumping through my earbuds, I almost hear the deep chuckle that slides from his lips. Our morning greetings are a ritual three years in the making. I've been running through the wide corridor that leads to the stadium football field since I stepped foot on campus freshman year. This will be something I miss when I graduate in the spring. Five days a week, I'm up at six, logging in a four-mile run before returning home, jumping in the shower, and heading off to class.

At this time of the day, the stadium is still relatively quiet, with only a few people wandering the hallways. There's something both serene and eerie about it. I've been here on game days when there are thirty thousand fans packed shoulder to shoulder, rooting on the

Western Wildcats football team. Three-fourths of the stadium filled with black and orange is an amazing sight to behold. Football is a religion at Western. Unfortunately, the same can't be said for the women's soccer team. We're lucky if there are a couple of hundred spectators in the stands.

I've come to terms with it.

Sort of.

I keep my gaze trained on the light at the end of the tunnel and push myself faster. As soon as I burst out of the darkness, bright sunlight pours down on me, stroking over the bare skin of my arms and shoulders. It's late August, and summer is still in full swing. A whistle cuts through the silence of the stadium, and my gaze slices to the field. Nick Richards has been head coach of the Wildcats for the last decade. He also happens to be my father.

Two days a week, the guys are up at six in the morning for yoga. Dad is a big believer in flexibility. Even though I'm winded, a smirk lifts the corners of my lips. Watching two-hundred-and-eighty-pound linebackers contort their bodies into Downward-Facing Dog, the Warrior II Pose, and the Cobra is enough to bring a chuckle to my lips. Some of the guys actually like it, but most grumble when they think Dad isn't paying attention. Little do they know that he sees and hears everything.

My father catches sight of me and flashes a quick smile along with a wave in my direction. He has a black ball cap pulled low and aviators covering his eyes. There's a clipboard in one hand as he paces behind the instructor.

When I point to the field, he shakes his head. He might make the guys do yoga, but he refuses to participate. Something about old dogs and new tricks. Every once in a while, I'll tell him that he needs to get out there and set a good example for the team. He usually shoots me a glare in return.

Every Wednesday night, Dad and I get together. Our weekly dinners became a thing when I moved out of the house and into the dorms freshman year. He's busy coaching football, and my schedule is packed tight with school and soccer. Getting together once a week is the best way for us to stay connected. It doesn't matter if we're in the middle of our seasons; we always make time for each other. Especially since Mom lives in sunny California. After eighteen years of marriage, she got fed up with being a distant second to the Western University football program. She packed up her bags and walked out. I hate to say it, but Dad didn't notice her absence for a couple of days. Which only proved her point. Now she's remarried, learning to surf, and is a vegan. I visit for a couple of weeks during the summer before soccer training camp starts up at the end of June.

Even though it's only the two of us, our weekly dinners are set for three people.

I tell myself to stare straight ahead and not glance in his direction.

Don't do it!

Don't you dare do it!

Damn.

My gaze reluctantly zeros in on him like a heat-seeking missile. Long blond hair, bright blue eyes, sun-kissed skin, and muscles for miles. And he's tall, somewhere around six foot three.

I'm describing none other than Rowan Michaels.

Otherwise known as the bane of my existence.

My dad discovered the talented quarterback the summer before we entered high school and took him under his wing. Which has been...aggravating. In the seven years since, Rowan has become an irritatingly permanent fixture in my life. He's the brother I never wanted or asked for. He's the gift I wish I could give back. He's the son my father never had but secretly longed for.

On a campus with over thirty thousand students, one would think that avoidance would be easy to accomplish. That hasn't turned out to be the case. Somehow, we ended up in the same major—Exercise Science. I get stuck in at least one class with the guy each semester. This time it's statistics, which is a requirement. Three times a week, I'm forced to see him. And then there are the weekly dinners at Dad's house.

Every Wednesday, Rowan shows up without fail.

It's so annoying.

No, *he's* annoying!

Our gazes collide, and electricity sizzles through my veins before I immediately snuff it out and pretend it never happened.

I am not attracted to Rowan Michaels.

I am not attracted to Rowan Michaels.

I am not attracted to Rowan Michaels.

Maybe if I repeat the mantra enough times, it'll be true. That's the hope I cling to. I've made it through the last seven years trying to convince myself of this. I only have to get through our final year together, and then we'll go our separate ways—me to graduate school or maybe to the Women's National Soccer League, and Rowan to the NFL. He's one of the most talented quarterbacks in the conference. Hell, probably the country. There is little doubt in my mind that he'll be a first-round draft pick come next spring.

Trust me when I say that Rowan Michaels fever is alive and well at Western University. His fanbase is legendary. The guy is a major player.

Both on and off the field.

Girls fall all over themselves to be with him. They fill the stands at football practice, show up at parties he's rumored to be at, and basically stalk him around campus.

It's a little nauseating. Don't these girls have any self-respect when it comes to a hot guy?

I wince at that unchecked thought.

Fine...I'll begrudgingly admit it; he's good-looking.

I shake my head as if that will banish the insidious thoughts currently invading my brain. Enough about Rowan. It's time to focus on the reason I'm at the stadium at this ungodly hour. I rip my gaze from him as I hit the cement staircase. After half a flight, all thoughts of the blond quarterback vanish from my mind. How could they not when my quads, glutes, and calves are on fire, screaming for mercy as I force myself to the nosebleed section. By the time I finish, my legs are Jell-O, and I still have a two-mile run back to the apartment I share with my best friend off-campus.

I give Dad a half-hearted wave before leaving. It's the most I can muster. His lips quirk at the corners as he shakes his head. He thinks I'm crazy. At the moment, I can't argue with his assessment of the situation. Although, it's the extra training I put in that helps me run circles around the other team in the second half of the game.

The jog home feels like it will last forever. By the time I unlock the apartment door, I'm ready to collapse. I beeline for the shower and jump in before it's fully warm. My skin prickles with goose flesh, but it feels so damn good. Twenty minutes later, I'm dressed and ready to take on the day. My hair has been thrown up in a messy bun, and I'm making a protein smoothie that will fuel me for my morning classes.

Just before taking off, I poke my head into Sydney's room. I know exactly how I'll find her, and that's buried beneath a small mountain of blankets. She doesn't disappoint. We met the summer before freshman year in training camp and have been besties ever since. She's the yin to my yang. The peanut butter to my jelly. The Thelma to my Louise. Where I'm more introverted and cautious, she's loud and boisterous. She's been known to leap without necessarily looking at what she's jumping into. Every so often, it gets us into trouble. Sydney and I have lived together since sophomore year. I gave up trying to cajole her ass out of bed for a six o'clock run after the first week of us cohabitating when she nearly took my head off with an alarm clock.

"It's that time again," I sing-song obnoxiously, "rise and shine."

There's a grunt and then some shifting from under the blankets that tells me she's alive.

When I chant her name repeatedly, each time escalating in volume, she growls, "Get the fuck out!"

"Awww," I mock, "that's so sweet. I love you, too."

Sydney snorts before a hand snakes out from beneath the blankets to give me a one-fingered salute. Then she grabs a pillow and tosses it in my general vicinity. It falls about five feet short of its mark.

I stare at the dismal attempt. "If you're trying to cause bodily harm, you'll have to do better than that."

"Piss off."

"All right then." I shrug. "See you after class." With that, I close the door behind me.

My farewell is met with another indecipherable mouthful. If this weren't something we went through on the daily, I'd worry she was in the midst of a stroke. Sydney is definitely not a morning person. She's more of an early afternoon person. Another thing I've learned over the years? The action of waking up to a brand-new day is a gradual process. She's like a bear rousing prematurely from hibernation. It's not a pretty sight. She's lucky I don't take her insults personally.

I grab my backpack from the small table crammed into the breakfast nook area along with a coffee before heading out the door. The apartment I share with Sydney is located three blocks from campus, which is highly sought out real estate. We're fortunate Dad is friends with the guy who manages the building. It's probably one of the only perks of having a father who is a head coach of a college football team.

You'd think there would be more, but you'd be wrong. Honestly, being Nick Richard's daughter is more of a hindrance than anything else. People assume you receive special treatment on campus, from professors, or that you have an in with all the football players.

Or worse...

Much worse.

After a bunch of ugly—not to mention untrue—rumors circulated freshman year, I've done my best to distance myself from the Wildcats football team. They're a great bunch of guys, but I don't need all the ugly gossip and speculation that comes along with being friends with them.

As I reach Corbin Hall, the mathematics building for my stats class, my gaze is drawn to a clump of students standing around outside the three-story, red-brick building. In the center of that crowd is Rowan. I don't have to see him physically to know that he's close. The muscles in my belly contract with awareness. It's like a sixth sense. One I wish would go away. He's the last person I want to be cognizant of.

As I jog up the wide stone stairs to the entrance, my gaze fastens on him. A smirk twists the edges of his lips, and my eyes narrow before I drag them away and yank open the door to the building.

Relief rushes through me as I step inside the air conditioning and disappear from sight.

"Hey, Demi, wait up!"

I turn at the sound of my name before slowing my step. The dark-haired guy jogging to catch up smiles before falling in line with me.

Justin Fischer.

He's a baseball player and teammates with Sydney's boyfriend, Ethan. We've been seeing each other for about a month. It's still casual at this point. With school and soccer, I don't have a ton of time to invest in a relationship. He seems to understand that and isn't pushing to be more serious.

When he leans in for a kiss, I angle my head. At the last moment, he tilts in the opposite direction, and we end up bumping teeth instead of locking lips. With a grunt, I pull away and chuckle. My fingers fly to my mouth to make sure I haven't chipped a tooth.

Maybe I've been reluctant to admit it to myself, but that kiss sums up our relationship perfectly.

Awkward and a step out of sync with each other.

"Sorry," he murmurs with a slight smile. I search his face and wait for any telltale sign of sexual chemistry to ping inside me. Unfortunately, my insides remain completely unfazed, which is disappointing but not altogether unexpected. I had a sneaking suspicion when we first got together that it might turn out this way.

"No problem," I say, hoisting my smile and brushing aside those thoughts.

"I haven't seen you for a couple of days," he remarks as we turn a corner and continue walking.

"It's been busy." Which isn't a lie. School might have recently started, but the academics at Western are rigorous. And being a Division I athlete is more like a job. If you're not ready to put in the work, don't bother showing up. There's no half-assing it around this place.

"When's your next game?" he asks.

"Tomorrow at six." My gaze flickers in his direction. Not that I expect him to come, but...

Fine, so maybe I do. If he wants to be my boyfriend, then he needs to show a little support.

His dark brows draw together. "That sucks. I've got a mandatory study hour I have to attend."

I shrug off the disappointment. It's another nail in the coffin of this relationship as far as I'm concerned. "That's cool. It's not a big deal."

"But I'll see you tonight?"

Oh. Right.

Tonight.

Well, damn. In a moment of weakness, I threw out an invitation to join our Wednesday evening dinner. It's one I now regret. If only there were a gracious way to rescind the offer.

"If you're busy, I totally understand—"

"Are you kidding? No way." With a grin, he shakes his head. "I wouldn't miss it for the world. I'm looking forward to meeting Coach Richards."

Great. So this is more about my father than me? Exactly what every girl wants to hear.

I force a brittle smile. "Awesome. He's excited, too."

That might be something of an overstatement.

Justin nods toward the end of the corridor. "I better get moving. Professor Andrews is a real stickler for punctuality."

"Yup. See you later."

This time, when he leans in, our lips align perfectly. The kiss is nothing more than a fleeting caress. There and gone before I can sink into it.

And I'm left feeling...absolutely nothing.

I bury the disappointment where I can't inspect it too closely before giving him a wave as he takes off. For a moment, I stand rooted in the hallway and watch as he disappears through the crowd. There's nothing to distinguish Justin from the thousands of guys who look exactly like him on campus. He's of average height and build with dark hair and espresso-colored eyes. He's nice enough. Although, if I'm completely honest, he's a little self-absorbed. He talks about baseball all the time. If Ethan hadn't introduced us, he's not someone I would have looked twice at. We don't have a ton in common.

As much as I hate to admit it, this relationship has probably reached its expiration date.

Now it's a matter of pulling the plug.

Ugh. I hate breakups. Although, it's doubtful this will end up destroying him. I'll have to make it through tonight and figure out the rest.

With a sigh of resignation, I head to the classroom and find a seat tucked away in the far corner of the small lecture hall. A lanky guy I recognize from a few of my other classes settles beside me. He flashes a dimpled smile as we empty our backpacks.

The tiny hair at the nape of my neck rises seconds before Rowan enters the room. It's like my body knows when he's within a thirty-foot radius. I glance at him from beneath the thick fringe of my lashes before shifting away. Air becomes wedged in my lungs as I wait for him to take a seat. And it won't be next to me because I'm—

"Hey man, would you mind moving?"

Surrounded on both sides.

Damnit. I'm hoping the cutie next to me will tell Rowan to go take a flying leap.

What? It could happen. Not everyone at this university is enamored of the football-playing god. Although I realize the odds aren't stacked in my favor. Rowan is the most recognized athlete on campus. People fall all over themselves to accommodate him.

It's a little sickening.

Okay, maybe more than a little.

"Sure, no problem, Michaels." The guy next to me hastily packs up his books before vacating the desk. Unable to ignore him any longer, I glare as Rowan slides onto the seat next to me.

"Did you really think you could evade me that easily?" Laughter brims in his deep voice. A voice, I might add, that does funny things to my insides.

"One can always hope, right?"

"Oh, answering a question with a question." He leans closer, eating up some of the much-needed distance between us. "I like it."

I roll my eyes as his lips stretch into a satisfied grin. Irritation bubbles up inside me when sexual tension blooms at the bottom of my belly. Or maybe that tension has settled a little lower.

It's definitely lower.

I'm tempted to swear like a sailor. How is it possible that I feel nothing for the guy I'm actually dating, and yet my pulse skitters out of control for someone I don't even like? It's so freaking ironic. It's been this way since we met, and nothing I do stomps it out. I can try to fool myself into believing it's not there, but that doesn't make it any less true.

It's a relief when Professor Peters takes his place at the podium and clears his throat. Once he's captured everyone's attention, he delves headfirst into the probability of dependent and independent events.

Grateful for the excuse to ignore Rowan for the next fifty minutes, I open my textbook and concentrate on the lesson. Just as the blond boy fades into the background, his bare knee bumps into mine. Electricity ricochets through my entire being. I glance at him to see if he's noticed the strange energy we always seem to generate and find his ocean-colored gaze fastened to mine.

My guess is that he does.

Damnation.

Want to read more of Demi and Rowan's story? You can buy the book here -) https://books2read.com/u/mYAxqV

Want to read Campus Flirt for free?
Get it here -)
https://dl.bookfunnel.com/8nymppvbxk

KING OF CAMPUS

Ladies, and a few guys as well, ;) keep those Roan King sightings pouring in. Especially the ones of him at football practice. Hot, sweaty, with an extra shot of gorgeous is exactly how I take my Roan King. Don't mind me while I type away with one hand... KingOfCampus.com

"**H**oney," I holler at the top of my lungs before kicking the door shut, "*I'mmmm home!*"

Those words are met with a loud shriek as Lexie flies around the corner before hurtling her small curvy body at me. I'm given roughly two seconds to drop my bags in anticipation of impact. She's lucky I have fairly decent—

The breath gets knocked out of me as we both go crashing to the floor.

Apparently, reflexes are no match when that much force and weight are careening toward you at the speed of light. Physics, I'm guessing, is exactly how I end up sprawled on my back with my best friend and roommate spread out on top of me in our brand-spanking-new apartment. There's a completely manic light filling her big brown eyes. Matching the look, I can't help but beam up at her because it is so freaking good to see her gorgeous face.

It's been precisely fifteen months since we've been in the same room together. Actually, it's been fifteen months since we've been on the same continent. I spent my sophomore year of college studying abroad in Paris.

Needless to say, it was as amazing and spectacular as you'd imagine it would be. Even thinking about it leaves me with a tiny pang of nostalgia for the life I'd left behind.

"Damn, now that's hot! Can I snap a shot for my wallpaper?"

We turn to stare at the tall, good looking male grinning...or maybe the correct term would be—*leering* down at us. His eyes slide oh-so-slowly over our entwined bodies as if he's trying to singe this moment into his memory for all eternity. But it's not in a pervy way...what the heck am I saying? Of course, it's in a pervy way. Which is precisely when I realize that my dear friend, Lexie, seems to be missing the lower half of her outfit.

Yep...she's only wearing panties.

She smothers a giggle before clearing her throat. Rather impressively, her voice whips out in a perfect imitation of a mother scolding her three-year-old toddler. "You damn well better not snap a picture or you won't be seeing this ass for a very long time." To emphasize this point, she gives it a little shake and her boyfriend groans in response.

"Please?" There's a whole lot of whine filling his deep masculine voice. Which is kind of hilarious because he's well over six feet tall and is seriously broad in the chest and shoulders. This one is definitely all man. Lexie, of course, filled me in via Facetime on the football playing boyfriend she acquired about seven months ago. Needless to say, she wasn't exaggerating.

He's pretty damn hot.

If you're into big and muscly.

Which I'm not going to lie... I am.

"The mental snapshot you're burning into your brain will have to suffice."

Folding his muscular arms in front of an equally solid looking chest, he grumbles under his breath, "You always have to be such a hard ass."

Lexie gives me a little wink. "You wouldn't have it any other way, babe."

"True," he sighs in agreement, "very true."

Since Lexie isn't showing any indication of removing herself from my person anytime soon, I'm forced to point out the obvious. "You might want to get off me before your boyfriend has an embarrassing moment in his shorts."

I'm joking, of course.

Sort of.

"You don't have to get off on my account," he quickly chimes in as he continues to ogle us.

Lexie rolls her eyes at me.

"Have I mentioned just how hot you look in that thong?" His voice sounds all heated up and I'm seriously considering shoving Lexie off me before something unfortunate, not to mention awkward, happens and I'm no longer able to look this dude in the eyes again.

"Jeez, Lex, did you have to molest me while only wearing a thong?" No wonder her boyfriend is all but sporting a woody over there.

"Be happy you didn't arrive ten minutes later, I wouldn't be wearing anything at all."

I shake my head to loosen that mental image from my brain. "That wasn't something I needed to know."

Continuing to grin, Lexie smacks my lips with a big wet sloppy kiss. "Goddamn but I missed you, Ivy." Then she does her damnedest to squeeze the very life out of me before rolling gracefully to her side.

"I'm glad to be back, too." As the words automatically spill from my mouth, I realize that I don't necessarily mean them. There's a large part of me that wishes I were still living my life in Paris. With an ocean between me and my dad, I didn't have to dwell on him and the new family he created for himself so quickly after Mom died.

Dad's life carried on while mine fell apart. Even though it's been five years since she died, the ache still feels painfully tender.

Returning to Barnett means that I no longer have an excuse not to visit them.

Shaking those thoughts away, I realize I'm still sprawled on the carpeted floor. I blink my eyes a few times as a handsome face peers down at me before crinkling into a large friendly smile. I don't bother hoisting myself up just yet. Instead, I say in my most formal tone, "Mr. Sullivan, I presume."

His grin intensifies, making him appear even more striking than I'd originally thought. Lexie had gushed about how gorgeous her new guy was. And it's not like I didn't believe her, but it's obvious she wasn't exaggerating.

Like at all.

Because Dylan Sullivan is seriously hot.

Golden blond hair, deep brown eyes, sculpted jaw, and athletic body.

According to Lexie, he treats her like a total princess. Which is exactly how it should be. Lexie deserves someone who appreciates how smart, loyal, and gorgeous she is. She's a damn good friend and I'm lucky to have her in my life.

"The one and only," he beams in response, throwing a flirty wink in for good measure.

Oh, this guy is totally dangerous.

Could they be more perfectly suited to one another?

I absolutely love it.

"Umm, isn't your father Dylan Sullivan the first?"

He shrugs his broad shoulders. Self admittedly, I'm kind of a shoulder and arm girl myself. And Dylan Sullivan certainly has nicely chiseled ones.

"Shhh, you're ruining the moment, babe."

That being said, Dylan offers me a hand, which I grab hold of, before being hauled off the floor and set back onto my sandaled feet. I dust my backside off before my gaze slides to Lexie. The unexpected glassy sheen of tears shining in her big brown eyes has my own widening in confusion.

"Lex, why are you—"

I don't get a chance to wrap my lips around the last word before she's hurtling herself in my direction. Her arms slip around my body before tugging me close.

"I missed you, Ivy-girl," she whispers fiercely against my ear, "so damn much! Fifteen months is a long time to stay away. Don't ever leave me like that again."

I'm not normally an emotional person, but her heartfelt words have me choking up and I squeeze her to me.

She pulls back to search my eyes before admitting quietly, "I was afraid you might decide to stay over there."

That just goes to show you how well Lexie knows me. What I don't mention is that I tried my damnedest to make that happen. To finish out college, find a permanent place to live, a dance gig, all so I could postpone coming home indefinitely. Being back here, even though this is a new apartment, still reminds me that my mom is dead, and my dad has moved on and I no longer have a home to return to.

Not one that feels like home used to feel.

"I'm just so glad you're finally back."

"Me, too," I whisper as hot licks of emotion prick the back of my eyes. I hug her tightly one last time before releasing her.

Lexie and I have been best friends since fourth grade when her family moved in down the block from mine. We made it through middle and high school with our friendship intact and decided to apply at some of the same colleges so we could room together. Luckily, Barnett was on both of our short lists. It has a highly regarded fashion design program for Lexie and a kickass dance program for me.

There's absolutely no one in this world I can count on like Lexie Abbott. I'm actually a little ashamed of myself for failing to remember that. In trying to escape all the painful memories, I forgot about the good stuff, too.

Lexie backs up until she's standing directly in front of Dylan. As soon as she's close enough, he wraps those huge arms around her before pulling her flush against the front of his body. Looking ridiculously contented, he settles his chin on top of her head like he's done it a hundred times before.

Like it's the most natural thing in the world.

I can't help but feel thrilled that Lexie has found someone who appreciates the amazing woman she's grown into.

Unwilling to get anymore sappy than I already have, I shake my head. "Do you two come with barf bags? I've only been here for ten minutes and you're already making me sick to my stomach."

They both flash big cheesy grins at me. I want to roll my eyes before sticking my finger down my throat like I'm going to puke. "I suppose you're going to be practically living here with us?" Yep, I can already see how this will go. Dylan will be our unofficial apartment mascot.

With big innocent eyes, she says, "Didn't I mention that Dylan lives in the apartment next to us with two guys from the football team?"

"Nope," I shake my head, "you definitely did not mention that. I guess that makes things convenient."

"Totally convenient," Dylan adds with a sly grin aimed in my direction.

This time, I actually roll my eyes. "So which room is mine?"

In her exuberance, Lexie all but jumps out of Dylan's arms before leading me down a short hallway. As I trail after her, I'm reminded that she's only wearing a thong.

I mean, sure, she has a great ass but still…

"Er, maybe you should put your shorts back on before you give me the grand tour." Out of the corner of my eye, I see Dylan open his mouth. My narrowed gaze slices to his. "Don't even say it," I warn.

Biting her lip, Lexie stifles another laugh before dashing into her bedroom. In twenty seconds flat she rejoins us sporting tiny white shorts. Then she leads the way into a sunny little room before doing her best auto show model imitation as she gestures with wide sweeping movements to all the wonderful amenities my room has to offer.

She points toward the two large windows lining the wall. "Look at all the gorgeous sunlight that pours in!" Then she throws open the bifold closet doors. "And a humongous closet for all the clothes you brought back from Paris." Her arms drop to her sides as she swivels toward me. Her auto show model imitation is forgotten in lieu of possible new stylish European clothing. "You *did* bring me back some clothes, right?"

For a moment, my eyes travel around the room, taking everything in. It's not huge by any means but after living in Paris, it sure feels like it is. I'm used to about a third of the space. So this feels pretty damn luxurious. I can't imagine what I'm going to do with all this space to myself. Then my eyes fall to the double sized mattress shoved up against the far wall and my heart actually swells with unfettered joy.

Oh my god, it's so big! I've been sleeping on a twin bed for the last fifteen months. I literally can't wait to spread out on that huge mattress. Maybe roll around a bit. Make some snow angels...minus the snow. Already I'm looking forward to hitting the sheets tonight.

I spent a little more than eight hours on a plane with a two-hour layover in Amsterdam. And France is six hours ahead of us. So, I'd like nothing more than to fall into bed for a nice long nap.

When I don't respond, a thread of worry weaves its way through her voice. "Ivy?" Her concerned tone snaps me right out of my thoughts.

"Of course I did," I say. "There's a short, thigh length pleated skirt, two hand woven scarves, one cashmere sweater, a gorgeous black knit top and these creamy trouser pants that your ass will thank me for."

If watching Lexie sprawled out on top of me, wearing nothing more than a lacy little thong and a tank top is Dylan's idea of a wet dream, hearing about all the beautiful clothes I brought back from Paris is hers. We're talking flushed cheeks and dilated eyes.

And yes, it's entirely possible Lexie could have an embarrassing moment in her shorts. Although I hope not.

"Oh, I can't wait to see them," she squeals in delight, practically jumping up and down with unbridled enthusiasm.

Fashion design is Lexie's life. She was a budding fashionista way back in middle school before I ever cared about what top went with what bottoms. Thank goodness for Lexie or I probably would have been much more of a walking fashion disaster than I was.

I scraped together enough money and perused a few vintage boutiques to find unique pieces I knew she wouldn't be able to get here in the States. I hope she loves them half as much as I think she will.

"What about some hot French lingerie?" her boyfriend asks.

Since Dylan is standing directly behind Lexie, she doesn't bother turning around to admonish him. Instead, she rams her elbow into his gut. He grunts in response. If she hadn't done it, I probably would have.

"Just stand there and look pretty," she mutters under her breath.

My lips twitch because he is definitely pretty.

Lexie gives me a little wink as if she can read my mind. "Don't let his good looks fool you, he's smart, too."

Of course he is.

Because gorgeous and smart are exactly the kind of guys Lexie attracts. While I, on the other hand, had the sad misfortune to fall for a hot athletic jerk who assured me he was going to remain faithful to his study-abroad-girlfriend when in actuality, he started hooking up with other girls as soon as above-mentioned-girlfriend was out of the country.

I've had the last fourteen and a half months to get over Finn McKenzie. And I have. I am totally over him. Unfortunately, he's been calling and texting almost relentlessly for the last week, which means he's been occupying my thoughts way more than I'd like.

Perhaps I should say he's been *trying* to call and text. I haven't bothered to pick up his calls or respond to his rather lengthy and apologetic text messages. I mean, can you seriously believe that? The guy has some nerve reaching out to me after what he did. Is he so delusional as to think we're going to pick up where we left off now that I'm back at Barnett?

Apparently, he is.

We'd been together for about six months before I left for Europe. And yes, I knew having a long-distance relationship would be difficult, but I was willing to give it a shot. I'd grown to like Finn. I hadn't been gone more than two weeks when Lexie Facetimed me about what Finn had been busy doing...which had been, in case you're wondering, other girls.

And that, my friends, had been the end of that.

Lexie's advice was to forget about my cheating asshole of an ex by hooking up with a bunch of hot French guys.

I hooked up with two semi-hot French dudes and buried myself in dance which was the reason I'd been accepted to study at the Conservatoire de Paris in the first place. After a few months, my heartache lessened. I stopped thinking about Finn, my dad, his new wife, their kids, and I concentrated on soaking up everything I possibly could.

It took some time to adjust but after two months, I found myself with an amazing new life in a city renowned for its art and culture. There was no way I was going to allow anything to ruin this once in a lifetime opportunity. Right around the year mark, I stopped thinking about Lexie and returning to Barnett University and started wondering if maybe I could live here for the rest of my life.

Or, at the very least, the next few years.

When I mentioned this possibility to my dad, he made it perfectly clear that he would not be footing the bill for a life in Paris and said, in no uncertain terms, he wanted me back at Barnett come August. Undeterred by his directive, or perhaps because of it, I'd searched for enough scholarship and grant money to pay for me to continue studying in Paris. Needless to say, I hadn't been able to pull it off which is exactly why I was back at Barnett for my junior year.

"So, do you like it?"

My eyes swing back to Lexie who is standing there with all this hopeful expectation lighting up her face. A tiny smile tugs at the corners of my lips because it really is good to see her after all this time apart. "It's absolutely perfect."

Looking very much like the best friend I left behind fifteen months ago, a huge grin spills across her beautiful face before she hurtles herself at me for a third time.

Want to read more?
You can check out King of Campus here -)
https://books2read.com/u/bPX7WY

ABOUT THE AUTHOR

Jennifer Sucevic is a USA Today bestselling author who has published twenty-five New Adult novels. Her work has been translated into German, Dutch, Italian, French, Portuguese, and Hebrew. Jen has a bachelor's degree in History and a master's degree in Educational Psychology. Both are from the University of Wisconsin-Milwaukee. She started her career as a high school counselor, which she loved. She lives in the Midwest with her family. If you would like to receive regular updates regarding new releases, please subscribe to her newsletter here- Jennifer Sucevic Newsletter (subscribepage.com) Or contact Jen through email, at her website, or on Facebook.

sucevicjennifer@gmail.com

Want to join her reader group? Do it here -)

J Sucevic's Book Boyfriends | Facebook

Social media links-

https://www.tiktok.com/@jennifersucevicauthor

www.jennifersucevic.com

https://www.instagram.com/jennifersucevicauthor

https://www.facebook.com/jennifer.sucevic

Amazon.com: Jennifer Sucevic: Books, Biography, Blog, Audiobooks, Kindle

Jennifer Sucevic Books - BookBub